DON'T LET ME DOWN

A DON'T LET ME NOVEL

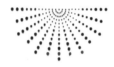

KELSIE RAE

TWISTY PINES PUBLISHING, LLC

Don't Let Me Down
Cover Art by Cover My Wagon Dragon Art
Editing by Wickedcoolflight Editing Services
Proofreading by Marjorie Lord
Published by Twisty Pines Publishing, LLC
June 2023 Edition
Published in the United States of America

To Dory from Finding Nemo.
Thanks for reminding me to, "Just Keep Swimming!"

PROLOGUE

A few years ago...

Two Men Arrested in Connection With Body Found Near Lockwood Heights Train Station

Two men were arrested for the murder of Buddy Rutherford yesterday evening. Martin Hayes and Troy McAdams were taken into custody on Friday after new evidence came to light,

connecting the men to Mr. Rutherford's disappearance.

The Lockwood Heights coroner ruled Rutherford's death a homicide after his body was discovered near Lockwood Train Station.

Hayes is a known drug dealer and loan shark in the area. Police suspect he loaned Rutherford a large sum of money. When the victim was unable to repay the loan, he was brutally tortured. It is believed that Hayes called McAdams, the son of businessman Dick McAdams, to assist in disposing of the body after the torture went too far.

The McAdams family is closely tied with gubernatorial

candidate Christopher Buchanan, and some have questioned his involvement in the case. Troy McAdams is a long-time friend of Henry Buchanan, the candidate's son, and the elder Buchanan and McAdams men are joint partners in B-Tech Enterprises.

The police are adamant there is absolutely no evidence indicating the Buchanans were involved in Rutherford's disappearance and slaying. They are pleading with the public to please give the family space to mourn the loss of their friendship and business relationship with the McAdams family.

Rutherford is survived by his sister, Hadley Rutherford, his ex-wife, Isabelle Hill, and their daughter, Mia Rutherford. They have yet to respond to our requests for an interview. Everyone at the Lockwood Post sends them our deepest condolences.

1

MIA

The band is killing it on the stage. They're not Broken Vows, my uncle's band, but they're pretty good. Alternative rock with a dash of blues. From behind the bar, my head bobs up and down with the music's beat as I wipe out a freshly-washed glass with a clean towel.

Over the past couple of years, since I started working at SeaBird, it's slowly become my home away from home. I love the atmosphere. The smell of coconut and salt lingering in the air. How the lights can go from dim to flashing in an instant. The customers. Well, most of them, anyway. Some are assholes, but I've had a habit of attracting them since I was a kid, so I'm not sure if the problem is SeaBird or if it's me. Regardless, if being a bartender paid better, I'd almost consider sticking around and working here for the rest of my life since my initial plan to work as a nurse hasn't exactly panned out the way I hoped.

Not yet, anyway.

I shove the familiar little black thought aside and set the clean glass next to the others when someone approaches me.

Well, well, well. If it isn't the devil himself.

Henry Buchanan.

The suave billionaire from new money is not only the son of a former governor, now a US senator, he's also a recently-retired LAU professor and the new owner of the NHL Lions.

I took a couple of his classes when I was a student, but even if I hadn't, I'd still know him. Everyone knows Henry Buchanan. Or at least, they know *of* him. He has this air about him. The way he demands attention without uttering a single word. Hell, he enters a room, and people *feel* his presence. At this point, I'm not even sure if it's because of his family name and the weight it holds or if it's simply...Henry.

I force myself to ignore his strong jawline and pick up the same freshly-cleaned glass instead, hoping it'll distract me enough to keep me from checking the guy out as he strides into SeaBird. He was here earlier this week. Probably because he wanted to talk to his new center and left wing for the Lions, who happen to be dating my friends, Ashlyn and Blakely. Yeah, Colt Thorne and Theodore Taylor are hockey gods, and they definitely know it. Thankfully, they're good dudes and treat my friends like gold. If they didn't, I'd neuter them, and they both know it.

However, they aren't here tonight. Which begs the question, *why* is Buchanan?

"You know, if you lost the suit, you might not stick out like a sore thumb around here," I add as he takes a seat on the barstool in front of me.

"Yeah." He looks down at his dark, fitted suit as if he's only now realizing how little he blends in while wearing it. Not going to lie. It makes him look like a *GQ* model surrounded by peasants. As he smooths down the rich fabric, light reflects off the Rolex wrapped around his sexy wrist, catching my attention. I didn't know wrists could be sexy, but with the dapple of dark hair and veins popping along the top of his hand, I stand corrected. I'm not surprised. The man was voted the sexiest bachelor alive before his girlfriend took him off the market. If that isn't an accomplishment, I don't know what is.

"Guess I forget I don't look like a student anymore," he adds dryly, assessing his odd choice of clothing compared to everyone else around him.

Yeah, no. Not even close. The guy's at least thirty-three and has aged like a fine fucking wine. I started paying attention to the Buchanan name when I found out Evelyn Buchanan, Henry's little sister, was dating my father's killer. Well, technically, two men were arrested for my dad's murder, but still.

Man, it feels like a lifetime ago.

Thankfully, the Buchanans weren't involved in my father's disappearance. However, their names were still dragged through the mud thanks to Buchanan's dad running for governor at the time.

After the police made the connection, the Buchanan name hit the newspapers for weeks. Eventually, Henry's dad squashed the rumors and distracted the media with a new story.

Henry was best friends with one of the guys too. Troy McAdams. The asshole frat boy who became friends with a lowlife loan shark named Marty. After loaning my dad a bunch of money and realizing my father would never be able to pay him back, Marty killed my dad and asked Troy to help him cover his tracks. Apparently, Buchanan's had a hard time allowing anyone to get close to him ever since.

I don't blame him.

I don't let people get very close to me, either.

But what would you know? My path crossed with the infamous Henry Buchanan a few years later, and I ended up having him as a professor at LAU.

It's eerie how small the world feels sometimes.

And how much fate likes to screw with me.

Then again, I could've moved across the country to escape it all. I could *still* move across the country to get away from it all.

But I won't.

Because my mom and my friends, who have become my family, are here in this small town, and I doubt they're going anywhere anytime soon.

"Missing the good ol' days, Professor?" I quip. "When you'd blend in with the rest of the students at SeaBird instead of sticking out like a sore thumb?"

Apparently, Henry Buchanan went to LAU, too. Rumor has it this is the same bar where his little sister met her husband, Jake Jensen. And it's a good thing she found such a perfect fit for her snooty-tooty family because the guy's a software nerd who took over B-Tech Enterprises after Buchanan passed along the responsibilities and decided to become a professor.

He presses his full lips together as he scans the bar, barely casting me a glance. "You've graduated," he reminds me. "You don't need to call me professor anymore."

"And what would you prefer I call you, Professor? Daddy? *Doctor* Buchanan?" My sultry voice hangs in the air as my mouth pulls into a shameless grin. But I can't help it. The guy's grumpier and more guarded than a rhinoceros. He's always had his guard up high around me. Which is fine. My guard's high around *everyone*. But it does make me want to poke at him for it.

"Henry's fine," he grunts, refusing to give in to my teasing.

"Okay, *Henry*," I purr. "What can I get ya?"

The guy scans the bar again, still not bothering to look at me. "Whiskey. Top shelf."

I turn around, stand on my tiptoes, and reach for the

most expensive bottle SeaBird owns, pouring two fingers of the caramel-colored liquid into a glass tumbler.

"So, what brings you in this time? Looking to have another chat with Theo and Colt?" I ask, setting the drink in front of him.

He doesn't answer me as he shoots the liquid back and sets the glass on the counter again. With a dark look, he waits for me to refill it, so I do.

"Or maybe you're looking for your girlfriend?" I add.

His gaze narrows. "Has she been in here?"

"Yup."

"Was she with a guy?" he grits out.

And damn. I can see why he's such a shark in the business world. The hair along the back of my neck raises as if he's daring me to lie. To withhold what he wants. To push him when he's clearly not in the mood to be *pushed.*

I know this look, though. This look tells me he already knows the truth without needing to witness it firsthand. This look shows me he's already seen the red flags but wants proof. *More* proof.

He won't get it here. Not when I have less faith in the opposite sex than I do in aliens or God.

"She was out with her friends," I lie. I shouldn't. He deserves the truth. But it isn't my place, and I don't know the full story. Hell, maybe Buchanan's had someone on the side for months now, and his girlfriend recently found out and is looking for revenge. Maybe they already broke up, and he's stalking her. I don't think he would, but... I cock my head, examining his tight jaw and the vein throbbing in his neck. Actually, scratch that. Professor Buchanan definitely looks like someone who isn't afraid to get his hands dirty if it gets him what he wants.

"So she left?" he demands.

"Yup."

His ever-perfect posture slumps slightly, and he turns to me fully, giving up on his search as he takes another sip of whiskey from his glass. "How's your mother?"

My expression sours. Not because I hate my mother, but because Buchanan's the one asking about her.

"She's fine."

"And your uncle?"

"Fine," I repeat.

Henry Buchanan knows me too. Mia Rutherford. The girl with the murdered daddy. To be fair, most of Lockwood Heights knows me. My face was splashed all over the news for weeks after my dad's body was found, the same way the Buchanan name was. I should've moved away, but I didn't want to give the assholes who took my father from me the pleasure.

"You find a job yet?" he questions.

I straighten my spine.

Sometimes I hate the way he keeps tabs on me. Hell, he's worse than Uncle Fender. Part of me wonders if it's because he feels guilty. For knowing Troy McAdams. For being friends with him. For not spotting the red flags or how dangerous his friend really was. I don't blame him. I've fallen for a wolf in sheep's clothing on more than one occasion.

"No," I answer.

"Why not?"

Resting my elbows on the counter separating us, I steeple my fingers in front of me and hold his dark gaze. "Because I started selling pictures of my body on the internet to make ends meet, and now every doctor's office and hospital within a hundred-mile radius knows about it and wants nothing to do with me."

I don't know why I say it. I shouldn't. It's none of his business, anyway. Shining a light on the mess of my life probably isn't the brightest thing I've ever done, but I can't help it.

Wanting to shock the impenetrable bastard in front of me. To see him flinch. To see him *feel*. Something. Anything. Even if it's only disgust.

His dark, flinty eyes dip to my low-cut black tank top, traveling south along my waist and hips, leaving me squirming.

I'm used to being checked out.

Call it a blessing or a curse, but it is what it is. I'm pretty in an emo, untouchable, this-girl's-got-daddy-issues kind of way. Add it to the fact I'm a bartender who looks like she enjoys getting freaky in the sheets, and I've been hit on more times than I can count.

But being checked out by Henry Buchanan? This is new. The man's a stone-cold statue, and I'm not sure how I feel about it.

"Eyes up here, *Professor*," I warn.

His nostrils flare as his eyes meet mine again, and he tips the rest of his drink back. The glass clinks against the bartop once he's finished while his gaze continues holding mine hostage. "Selling pictures of your body on the internet was a poor decision."

"One of many," I point out.

Without a word, he pulls a small stack of bills from his wallet and sets them on the counter. "Keep the change."

He walks out of the bar without a backward glance. When the door closes behind him, I pick up the bills, my jaw dropping.

Five hundred bucks.

His tab was maybe a hundred.

Sometimes, I hate his pity.

Always, I hate his charity.

And lately? I've hated how he gets under my skin whenever he's around.

2

HENRY

My jaw is tight as I press my phone to my ear outside SeaBird. Even though it's past midnight, the air is still warm from the summer sun, leaving me hot in my suit. Irritated, I tug at the top button as if it's strangling me and wait for the head of my IT department to answer the phone. The call rings twice before Gordy's voice cuts off the rhythmic ringing.

"H-hello?" His voice is rusty from sleep, but I don't apologize for waking him. I pay him enough to be on call at all times. He knows it as well as I do. Tonight isn't any different.

"There's a girl named Mia Rutherford," I tell him. "She has indecent photos online. There may be some videos as well, I'm not sure. Regardless, I need them wiped from the internet."

"Mia...what was the last name?" His yawn echoes into my ear, followed by the familiar ding of Gordy's computer turning on.

"Rutherford," I grit out. A headache slowly builds behind my eyes as I shift my phone to my other ear. I attempt to rein in my annoyance after my conversation with Mia, but it's proving to be difficult. The girl is so damn frustrating, part of me wants to strangle her, and the other part wants to wash my hands of her altogether.

"Rutherford," Gordy repeats. The *click-click-click* from his fingers tapping against the keyboard picks up speed. "Uh, yeah. I'll take care of it right now."

"Good."

I hang up the phone and head back to my apartment. It's on the south side of town in the tallest building outside of LAU's college campus. I purchased the building as an investment and moved into the penthouse when I began teaching. After taking a hiatus from the classroom to focus on the Lions organization, I debated whether or not I should move out so I could stay closer to my office at B-Tech Enterprises but decided against it. After all, it's my home, and my girlfriend would pitch a fit if she found out I wanted us to move.

B-Tech Enterprises is my father's business. After graduating from LAU for the first time, I became the president of the corporation until my sister, Evie, met Jake. Jake was a much better fit for the role, and I had no problem passing along the responsibilities so I could focus on receiving my doctorate.

My father would never have signed off on the idea if Jake was anyone else. But since my brother-in-law has the same passion for technology my father does, it didn't take long for Jake to be welcomed into the role with open arms.

My career change, however, was a much more difficult pill for my father to swallow. And ever since I paid nearly eight hundred million dollars to create the Lions, he's even less impressed.

Too bad I don't give a shit.

I have multiplied my trust fund hand over fist since I turned twenty-one and gained access to the money. If I learned anything from my endeavors, it's to trust my instinct.

And for the past year, it has been screaming at me. LAU's hockey organization has earned a lot of support over the past decade. Despite my father's lack of faith, the town is ready for a professional team. I know it.

I should have driven to SeaBird, but I walked, too frustrated with Scarlett's text to get behind the wheel. Good thing it only took me ten minutes. Besides, I needed the time to think. To figure out my next move. Scarlett and I have been dating for a year and a half. We met when I was in Milan for a business meeting. Scarlett was modeling for a designer who was dating one of my business associates and joined us for dinner. Almost as soon as I laid eyes on her, I took her back to my hotel and fucked her. We've been together ever since.

She told me she was with Gianna tonight, but Gianna's at an event with my sister and brother-in-law. Which means Scarlett lied. *Again.*

It's growing more difficult to push them aside. The lies. The impromptu trips with friends. The canceled dinners.

My hands clench at my sides as I reach my building and dip my chin at the doorman.

"Good evening, Dr. Buchanan," David murmurs, opening the door.

"Goodnight, David." I slip past him and head inside. When I enter the elevator, I press my keycard against the lock pad and push the button for the top floor as the doors slide closed. They open a few moments later, revealing my penthouse.

The blinds are drawn, and the kitchen light is on, casting shadows along the slate-colored walls and chrome finishes. Not a thing is out of place. It's cold. Lifeless. Just like me. Slipping off my suit jacket, I lay it on the back of the black leather couch when my phone rings.

"Hello?" I answer.

"Hey, it's me," Gordy replies. "I sent you all the photos and wiped them from the internet. Ms. Rutherford made her OF account inactive a few months ago, but I went ahead and deleted it permanently."

"Thank you."

"Sure thing," he replies. "What do you want me to do with her other accounts?"

"What accounts?" I growl.

"TikTok, Instagram, BeReal…" He continues rattling off the social media platforms as I pinch the bridge of my nose. "She has quite the following, sir."

"What kind of following?" I flip the call to speaker and pull up the photos Gordy forwarded to my email account.

"Depends on the platform, but across the board? A little more than three million. I can only imagine how much she made on OF because the subscribers alone had to bring in at least a hundred grand a month."

My eyes zero in on the toned body in a white, lacy thong in the photograph. The picture is cut off at the girl's throat, but I would recognize her tattoo sleeve anywhere. The intricate swirls. The flowers on her shoulder. The word "Pixie" inked along the inside of her delicate wrist. Her back is angled toward the camera, showcasing her long spine, thin waist, and round ass usually hidden beneath her clothes.

My dick jerks at the sight.

"Sir?" Gordy's voice cuts through the haze of lust like a hot knife through butter.

"What content does she post on the other platforms? Is it like the photos you sent?" I demand, unable to tear my attention from the image despite the shot of disgust pulsing through me.

She's on *more* platforms?

My blood boils at the thought.

Stupid. Fucking. Girl.

13

She really thought this was a good idea? Posting naked photos on the internet? It doesn't matter if Gordy took them down. He can't hack into every single person's server to delete any downloaded pictures from their computers.

What the hell was she thinking?

If she needed money, I would have given it to her.

"Nah, she doesn't post stuff like this on her other platforms," Gordy answers. "More like makeup tutorials. Life as a bartender. Exercise hacks. Those kinds of things. Honestly, they're pretty good. I can see how she's built such a big following. The girl has a knack for marketing."

I stare at the photo for another second, then close the email app on my phone.

"So, what do you want me to do with the other accounts?" Gordy prods. "Keep or delete?"

"Keep them," I decide.

"All right. Do you need anything else, sir?"

"That will be all. Thanks, Gordy."

"Sure thing."

3

MIA

My lungs are on fire as I sprint down the sidewalk, finishing the last stretch with all my strength. I've always loved running. The way it turns my brain off. The way it distracts me from all of life's lovely gifts. The way it feeds me endorphins and man, I've been needing them more and more lately.

When I reach the fire hydrant at the end of the street, I slow my pace and attempt to catch my breath, my mind finally receiving the hit of dopamine I've been craving. Wiping my forehead with the back of my hand, I bend down and touch my toes before realizing I'm most definitely not alone.

What the hell is my landlord doing here?

"Mia," Gertie greets me. Her hair is still in curlers despite it being almost two in the afternoon. A fluffy floral robe is wrapped around her pudgy body as she shuffles closer to me, clutching a newspaper to her chest.

"Oh, hey, Gertie." I look at the house we're in front of, and my brows knit together. "Did you move?"

I've run past this house a hundred times since living in

this neighborhood and never run into Gertie. *Ever.* I would've found a new running route as soon as possible if I had.

Gertie glances at the tan stucco townhouse with daisy-filled planter boxes and freshly trimmed grass, looks back at me, and nods. "My son finished remodeling this one a few weeks ago, so I decided to move in for the time being. You know how it is, dear. Sometimes it's best to stay close to your investment properties."

"Good point." I motion to the adorable house. "Tell your son he did a great job."

"He did, didn't he?" She steps closer to me. "Unfortunately, this property will have the same requirements as the one you're being evicted from. I'm sure you understand since you've graduated and all. I think it's best to leave the housing available for students currently enrolled in college. No hard feelings, of course."

I shake my head. "Oh, I wasn't asking to move in or anything--"

"You know how it is. Properties like this are hard to come by. Speaking of which, any luck finding yourself a new place? Because the clock's ticking."

"Yes, I understand," I mutter. "And don't worry. I haven't forgotten our agreement." The words taste bitter on my tongue, but I swallow my resentment. It isn't Gertie's fault she wants to help students instead of extending one of her leases to a very pathetic, very poor college graduate who can't find a job for the life of her.

"Good," Gertie replies. "Because I think I've been quite generous by allowing you to stay until the end of summer."

"Yes, very generous," I say through clenched teeth while attempting to maintain my smile. "And like I said, you don't have to worry. I'll be out of the house in a few weeks."

"You sure about that?" Her dark, drawn-on eyebrow

arches as she steps closer to me, dropping her voice low as if gifting me with the latest gossip. " I have a friend who works at the doctor's office down the street. She said you were still looking for a nursing position, and--"

"Yes, I'm aware of my situation," I snap but force another smile in hopes of softening my comment. "Thank you for keeping tabs on me, though. You're really thoughtful."

"Of course, Mia. You know I look at all of you girls like you're my own daughters." She wags her newspaper around, then brings it back to her chest, using it to shield her floral pajamas hidden beneath her floral bathrobe.

Seriously, does the woman not believe in any other print? Hell, even leopard spots would do.

Mix it up, Gertie. You can do it.

"Although, I will say the rest of those girls have found quite the strapping young men, haven't they?" she continues, her tone dropping another octave.

Colt, Theo, Macklin. Yeah, my friends are all a bunch of peaches and are lucky to have found their soulmates. But discussing my friends' successful relationships and my nonexistent one with Gertie is the last thing on my to-do list.

I take a step toward the sidewalk, anxious to get the hell out of this conversation as I answer, "Yes, all the guys are really awesome."

"But you're not dating anyone?"

My steps falter. "Uh, not really, no."

"Ya know, I'd offer to set you up with my son,"—she glances over her shoulder at his handiwork—"but he likes strong Christian women and isn't much of a fan of piercings and tattoos and such, so…"

Her nose scrunches as she takes in my sports bra and spandex shorts. My sleeve of tattoos is on full display, along with a sliver of the thigh piece I had done last year.

Wow.

"I should probably get going, Gertie."

"Of course, of course," she replies. "One more thing."

I pause. "Yes?"

"Rent is due in four days."

Did she seriously just say this to me? Duh.

It's not like the due date has changed in the four years I've lived here. Sure, I was late on a payment or two, but I've always reached out to her with a day she could expect the payment, along with an extra fifty dollars for her patience. But I haven't been late with my rent payment in almost a year.

"Is that a problem?" she prods.

"Not at all," I tell her, the last of my restraint slowly slipping. "I'll be sure to give it to you in four days...when it's due."

"Of course, of course." She waves me off. "Have a good run, dear."

My hands clench at my sides, and I give her another fake-ass smile. "Thanks."

I turn on my heel and take another lap around the block, hoping another wave of endorphins will hit since Gertie ruined my last one.

4

MIA

I flip the tequila bottle into the air and catch it behind my back while the Kappa Pi girls cheer in front of me. The clear liquid pours in a steady stream into the little glasses lined up along the bar as I fill up ten shots. Each of them is grabbed in an instant, the girls shooting the liquid while the spotlights hanging from SeaBird's ceiling flash around them.

The energy's more charged tonight. Probably because the band on stage is rocking out like their lives depend on it. Just a hunch, but I'd bet twenty bucks someone tipped off their manager that Sammie, my boss, invited her husband to SeaBird tonight. And who is Sammie married to, you might ask? Why, she's married to Hawthorne, a highly-coveted music executive who happened to sign my uncle and his band to the big leagues nearly a decade ago.

Yeah. Everyone wants the golden ticket Hawthorne can give, but not everyone has the gift. Not everyone has the luck and the talent and the drive to grab hold of their future and make it into what they want.

I get it.

I'm not exactly one to talk.

My future's been hanging over my head like a bad omen for years, and there's nothing I can do to stop it.

I received another rejection yesterday. Not surprising. After a sweet admin assistant from Lockwood Medical informed me most Human Resources departments have a habit of Googling potential hires, I realized how unlikely it is I'll ever land a job in the nursing field.

Stupid Google.

I need money if I want to have a roof over my head. If only I didn't have such an aversion to a savings account, I might not be in this position.

Stupid, stupid Mia.

I make a mental note to ask Sammie for a few more hours when I catch a glimpse of Henry Buchanan walking through SeaBird's entrance.

What's he doing here?

My friends are all attending the Lions' banquet tonight, and since Buchanan's the team's owner, shouldn't he be there too? Then again, I don't think it's supposed to start for another hour or so.

Maybe he's meeting Scarlett here for drinks?

I shouldn't care. I shouldn't even know his schedule.

It's been a week since he was here last, but the bastard's still wearing a suit. Pretty sure he lives in those things. Even when he taught at LAU, he always dressed nicely. Part of me wonders if he even owns a T-shirt. But why would he when the guy looks damn near lickable in his suit?

Tearing my attention from the sex on a stick who just walked in, I bite the inside of my cheek and pour another round of shots for the sorority girls littered on the opposite side of the counter.

I really need to get laid soon. Because this? This attraction to a guy I have no desire to actually hook up with is weird. And inappropriate on so many levels. My taste in men has never exactly been healthy, so I shouldn't be surprised I'm attracted to the cold, calculating business shark already in a relationship.

Good one, Mia. Super classy.

Ignoring the Adonis dressed to the nines, I remind myself I'm very much at work and find another familiar face on the other side of the bartop waiting for me to take his order.

When I recognize him, I grin. "Well, if it isn't the Tukani Tsunami. Long time no see."

"Hey, Mia," Tukani returns. "Yeah, I went home for a few weeks to see some family. You miss me?"

"Of course!" I lean across the bar and give LAU's starting goalie an awkward half-hug. The guy's adorable. Seriously. He's like a big, sarcastic teddy bear. We've known each other for a few years but were especially close when I was dating his friend and hockey teammate, Shorty, aka Bradley Ackerman.

It's too bad Shorty wound up being an abusive asshole who still enjoys making my life a living hell despite having graduated from LAU and signing with an NHL team a few states away.

If only I'd dated Tukani instead. If I had, I might've actually had a chance at getting a nursing job. After breaking up with Shorty, I created an OnlyFans account in hopes of earning some extra cash. It would've been fine if my ex hadn't stumbled upon my indecent photos. When he realized it was me, he tweeted my true identity, putting a massive target on my back for creepers. Afterward, he went on his merry little way to play for the Tumblers with zero consequences for his actions. Meanwhile, I'm still dealing with shady men who want to see my boobs in person.

Asshole.

"How've you been?" Tukani asks, bringing me back to the present. He squeezes me tightly but quickly lets me go.

Once my feet are back on solid ground, I answer, "Good, you?"

"Not bad. Trying to find a new place to live since Mama and Papa Taylor are selling the Taylor House," Tukani informs me.

The Taylor House is basically a bachelor pad where most of LAU's hockey team lives. Or lived, considering it's being sold, and they're all looking for new places now.

"Well, you're not the only one who's gonna be homeless if they can't find a new place," I tell him.

"Ah, you're moving too?" he asks.

"Yup. My lease is up, and my landlord is kicking me out in a few weeks."

"That's a shame. Maybe we can find a place together, yeah?" His eyebrows bounce up and down as his gaze shamelessly slides down my body.

With a laugh, I shake my head. "Pretty sure all of your one-night stands would hate me if we lived together."

"Come on, living with a bartender would be dope."

"For you, maybe." I grab his usual order of the cheapest beer SeaBird offers, popping the cap off and setting the opened beverage onto the lacquered counter in front of him. "Bottom's up."

"That's my girl." He lifts the bottle in a silent *cheers* motion. "You should let me buy you a drink tonight so I can convince you to move in with me."

The idea alone is laughable. Tukani might be a sweetheart, but he's also a total player and loves the bachelor life more than almost anything.

"I'm working," I remind him.

With a wry grin, he offers, "Okay. How 'bout after?"

My mouth opens to answer him, but I hesitate at the last

second, distracted by the same familiar but annoying presence to my left.

I swear I can feel him. Henry Buchanan. Despite already knowing he was here, a small part of me hoped he'd found whatever he was looking for and decided to book it home. Too bad I've never been a lucky kind of girl.

The guy has serious *don't fuck with me* vibes on a good day, and right now? He looks ready to strangle someone as he approaches the bar, causing the sorority girls to scatter and head to the dance floor.

"So, what do you say?" Tukani prods. "You'll let me take you out?"

"Maybe some other time," I tell Tukani, tapping my knuckles against the counter separating us. "Enjoy your drink. This one's on me."

He clutches at his chest. "Stealin' my heart, Mia. Stealin' my heart." He grins shamelessly, turns, and ambles toward a table in the back, slipping into the booth beside Gwyn, his on-again, off-again fuck buddy.

Wanted to take me out, my ass.

Suppressing my laugh, I turn to Buchanan, doing my best to appear unaffected by his presence. "Hello again, Professor. Don't you have a dinner to attend tonight?"

"Do you always flirt with the customers?"

With a frown, I glance at Tukani and back to Buchanan. "Who? Tukani?"

"Can I get a drink, please?" he grits out.

"Someone's testy today."

He unclasps the buttons on his navy suit jacket and sits on the barstool across from me. "I said *please*," he points out.

Without waiting for his order, I reach for the top shelf, ignoring the hit of deja vu as I fill a glass tumbler with Pappy Van Winkle and set it in front of him.

He doesn't notice the glass. He's too busy looking at the

23

KELSIE RAE

tattoo along the inside of my wrist. The word, Pixie, is etched in a soft feminine but blocky font. It's mine. My handwriting. In honor of my dog, Pixie.

He wants to ask me about it. Everyone does. Whether it's my Pixie tattoo or one of my others, everyone always asks, and I always tell them to fuck off. Okay, not always. I actually don't mind talking about my tattoos. But when guys bring them up in hopes of acting like they're genuinely interested in me as a person instead of only wanting to get in my pants? Yeah, not so much.

Thankfully, I doubt it's an issue with Buchanan. I've seen the women he dates. To say I'm not exactly his type would be a massive understatement. He's used to primped and polished women who have their shit together. Me? Well, I'm lucky to even take my makeup off before I climb into bed at three o'clock in the morning.

"You gonna leave me another four hundred dollar tip this time?" I ask.

His gaze flicks to mine. "Do I need to?"

I snort. "No, but my credit card bill would thank you for it."

"You carry a balance on your credit card?" he demands as if the idea alone is ludicrous.

"You don't?" I challenge. I wipe down the counter with a white dishrag but hesitate when I catch one of the sorority girls stumbling near the exit with her nose in her purse.

"Mia?" Buchanan questions.

I lift my forefinger. "Give me a second."

Despite the other customers yelling their orders at me, I round the edge of the bar and head toward the girl. Her dress is silver and shimmery and leaves little to the imagination. When I reach her, I fix the fallen strap back into place on her shoulder and ask, "Hey, can I help you find something?"

24

"Looking for my keys." Her words are slurred and messy, like her makeup.

Yeah, this girl has had way too much to drink.

"Let me find you an Uber."

"It's fine," she slurs, nearly stumbling into me as she looks up from her clutch. "I can't afford an Uber anyway."

"It's SeaBird's treat," I lie. I pull my phone out and confirm her address, telling our bouncer, Rhodes, to keep an eye out for a black sedan along with the correct license plate number. Satisfied the big, burly dude can take care of the girl until her Uber arrives, I head back to the bar while ignoring Buchanan altogether. I shouldn't. It's rude. But I'm pretty sure the stick up his toned ass can keep him company until he needs another drink. I can feel him watching me. His judgmental eyes follow my every move as I pour a few more drinks for a couple of customers.

Then, I get to work tapping a keg and filling two mugs, setting them on top of the waitress's tray so she can deliver them to table three.

Once I'm finished pouring some drinks for a couple who are clearly on their first date, I head back to Buchanan and say, "Okay, spit it out."

"Spit *what* out?" he questions. His tone is slow and controlled, as if the words alone are foreign to him. He's probably not used to someone using slang, even if *spit it out* is about as integrated into our society as *Hey, how you doin'?* I guess it makes sense considering the private tutors he was likely raised with.

I fold my arms, refusing to let his snooty upbringing deter me from pulling an answer out of him. Besides, I'm curious. Why he's sitting here. Why he's been watching me. Why I even care.

"Tell me what you're thinking and why you've been staring at me for the past ten minutes," I demand.

His gaze pinches for the briefest of seconds. It makes him look as annoyed as when he first saw me talking with Tukani.

"Did you hire an Uber for the girl?" he finally asks.

"Yeah." I glance at the exit, confirming she isn't standing there anymore. "So?"

"With your own money?" he prods, scoffing into his drink. "Oh, wait. What was I thinking? Apparently, you don't have any money."

My jaw drops. "Excuse me?"

"Is your landlord really kicking you out?"

"You overheard, huh?" I lean forward, giving him a glimpse of my cleavage as I rest my elbows on the bartop, but he doesn't take the bait. "Were you eavesdropping on my conversation with Tukani?"

He brings the beverage to his lips again and takes a sip. "Have you found a job yet?"

"I think we both already know the answer to that one," I counter.

"Hmm," he hums, swirling the amber liquid in his glass, staring at it as if lost in thought as he comes to some kind of conclusion, though I have no idea what it is. "I own a building over by LAU's campus. You can stay there."

Uh, what?

"Did you just offer me a place to stay?"

"Did I stutter?"

Hiding my surprise, I quirk my brow instead and say, "While I appreciate your concern for my well-being, I don't need a handout, Professor."

"I'm not your professor anymore."

"Of course not." I give him a cheeky grin. "Now, do you need anything else, or can I help a few more customers?"

"Depends."

"On what, exactly?"

"Are you going to pay for any more Ubers you supposedly can't afford?" he asks.

Money I *apparently* don't have. Ubers I *supposedly* can't afford.

What? Does he think my lack of riches is an act or something? Or is he still trying to turn the stick up his ass into a diamond rod?

Propping my hand on my hip, I glower at him. "Not that it's any of your business, but if I didn't pay for her Uber, she would've gotten behind the wheel and possibly killed herself or someone else. Thirty dollars out of my paycheck seems like a pretty small price for keeping someone safe, don't you think?"

"Depends on how much credit card debt you are accumulating," he mutters into his glass.

"Wow." I laugh, though there isn't humor in it. "Good to know where your priorities lie."

"What happened to the money, Mia?" he asks.

Surprised by the out-of-left-field comment, I shy away from him. "What money?"

"From your OF account."

My OF account?

Screw. Him.

I knew I would regret telling him I'd sold photos of myself online, but it *had* to be at this moment when he decided to bring it up, didn't it?

"You're a pretty girl," he continues, "I bet you had a lot of fans. Made a lot of money." He tilts his head. "Where did it go?"

"Pretty sure it's none of your business," I counter.

"But it's gone?" he pushes.

"Again, I'm pretty sure it's none of your business," I repeat.

He studies me carefully as the bastard digs into his pocket

27

and sets several hundred dollar bills on the counter separating us, like the last time he visited.

It only pisses me off more, especially after tonight's conversation.

"I don't want your money," I tell him.

"And I don't give a shit."

My blood runs hot and thick as I glare at him, refusing to even glance at the small stack of bills in front of me. "No offense, but if I wanted a sugar daddy, I'd choose someone who's a little less surly."

"You think I need another brat to take care of?" he challenges.

"Yet here you are. Handing a random woman a stack of cash. Careful, or your current *brat* might think you're looking for a new girlfriend to annoy."

"Trust me. You're not my type." He adds a black business card to the small stack of cash, confirming my earlier assumption.

Yup. I'm definitely not this guy's type.

Ignoring the slight sting to my ego, my eyes pinch as I take in the bold font typed across the black business card. "What's this for?"

"It's for when you realize you don't want to be homeless and are smart enough to take me up on my offer." He taps his index finger against the card. "This is my personal number. Don't make me regret giving it to you."

"Who said I'm gonna call you?"

The bastard doesn't even bother answering me. He simply slips off the barstool, rebuttons his suit jacket, and walks outside.

It irks me.

A lot, actually.

His assumptions.

The way he feels like he can boss me--and everyone else--around without any repercussions.

Clearly, he doesn't know who he's dealing with, and after the shitty day I've had, I'm not afraid to show him.

5
HENRY

I should have stayed away from SeaBird. Scarlett told me she would drive separately to tonight's event, and I was curious if she thought she could slip in a quick fuck before the banquet. Instead, all I did was expose myself to another annoying dose of Mia Rutherford.

The way she flirted with Tukani and gave money away so recklessly when she is already in a precarious financial situation only frustrates me more.

Unless she isn't in a precarious financial situation...

What did she do with the OF money?

I don't think she was lying.

She doesn't have it.

So, where did it go?

And why do I care?

Not the time, I remind myself as I step into the banquet hall my assistant, Erika, reserved for this evening. After the NHL draft last week, I decided to invite a few reporters, along with everyone in the organization and their significant others, to a team dinner. It was the least I could do if I wanted to encourage a sense of camaraderie with the team. My dad might not be perfect, but he knew the importance of creating cohesive relationships in the workplace. I plan to run my organization the same way.

The players mingle with other personnel throughout the large banquet hall. Chandeliers glitter from the ceiling, and hors d'oeuvres are passed on trays carried by caterers in black suits. I'm not usually a fan of these events, but everyone looks like they are enjoying themselves. Erika helped fine-tune all the details, and I make a mental note to thank her for her diligence.

Round tables covered in cream-colored tablecloths are scattered throughout the main space. Most guests have already found their seats, while some still linger at the open bar along the back wall. I don't blame them. I could also use another stiff drink, especially when my attention catches on my father at the edge of the room.

He is beside my mother, sipping a drink and appearing bored. Sports have never quite held him captive as they do with most men. Unless it involves golf.

But hockey?

The sport is far beneath him. It was beneath me until I began teaching at LAU and saw the potential. If only I could convince my father to see it too.

Approaching the bar, I order a stiff drink and throw it back. The familiar burn slides down my throat, and I savor it while striding toward my parents.

"Henry!" my mother gushes when she sees me. She grabs my cheek and kisses it.

"Hello, Mom," I return as she lets me go. "Dad," I acknowledge my father beside her.

"Henry," he grunts.

"Glad you could make it."

"Your sister insisted we come and celebrate your latest

venture," my mom replies. "Where is Scarlett? I've yet to see her."

"She's running late," I lie, checking my watch.

"Oh, of course," my mother replies. "It's a lot of hard work getting all dolled up for our men and coming to these events." She winks at my father. "How is everything going? Are you ready for the season?"

"Not yet, but we will be," I tell her. "Coach Dawson is confident we filled our roster with the best players, and I think he's right."

"Doesn't matter who you choose," my dad interrupts. "What matters is whether or not you can fill the seats. We stopped by the new arena--"

"Which is lovely, by the way," my mom adds, threading her arm around my father's bicep.

"It's big," my father notes. "How are ticket sales?"

It's an excellent question. One I've been keeping a close eye on for weeks. Unfortunately, they are a little lower than we initially calculated due to some recent bad publicity. However, my sales team assures me they will pick up soon.

But explaining this to my father sounds about as pleasant as receiving a root canal. Instead, I say, "They're fine."

"Fine won't replenish your trust," he counters.

"Money is meant to be invested," I reply. "You taught me that."

"Only on ideas worth investing."

My eyes thin, and I scan the banquet hall filled to the brim with Lions personnel, knowing each and every one of them depends on me. My gut. My decisions. My experience.

"And hockey?" A mocking laugh slips out of my father, and he takes a sip of his drink. "I'm yet to be convinced."

"Then, I guess it's a good thing it's not your money tied to the Lions' success."

"But yours is." His hand is heavy as he grabs my shoulder

and squeezes. It isn't rough. But the weight is considerable, reminding me how quickly things can turn sour if this season doesn't go according to plan.

With a slight shake of his head, he lets me go. "What is going on inside your head, son? When you stepped back from B-Tech Enterprises, I supported your decision because you earned your Ph.D. and became a professor. But this? Hockey? It's hardly a reputable investment. Ever since Troy's arrest, you––"'

"Christopher," my mother warns. "Now is not the time––"

"Your success is important to me, Henry," my father continues. "But I can't believe you drained your trust and sold most of your stock at B-Tech Enterprises for..."––he looks around the crowded room––"*this.*"

Unfortunately, this conversation is not new. It's one we have repeated more times than I can count, not only regarding the Lions but also most of my life choices. After my best friend's arrest, I took a step back from everything. I questioned every decision I had ever made. How couldn't I, when I had spent the majority of my time with a person I judged so poorly? My best friend––my brother––helped cover up a murder, and I had no idea.

It doesn't matter how many years have passed or how much time I spent learning to trust my gut again. Hearing my father's lack of respect regarding my decisions never gets easier.

But Buchanan men aren't weak. And they sure as shit are *not* impatient.

I am a Buchanan, even when it means it's necessary to double down on a situation until it pays off.

The Lions will pay off.

I know it.

"If you care about my success," I reply, "I suggest you buy

33

season tickets while they are still available." My phone buzzes in my pocket, and I pull it out, scanning the screen. I don't give my personal number to many people. Only a handful have it. The caller is unknown. My mouth lifts, realizing it must be Mia. She wasn't very patient. I only gave it to her an hour ago. Two, tops. She must be having a tough shift.

Against my better judgment, I glance at my parents and murmur, "One minute." I answer the call and bring the device to my ear. "Surprised you gave in so easily."

"Wait, who's this?" a low voice asks.

I cock my head but stay quiet.

"Mia?" the voice prods. "Mia, are you there?"

Avoiding my father's astute gaze, I shift my phone to my other ear and growl, "Who is this?"

"This is Joey. You said you was lookin' for a sugar daddy and gave me your number when you was closin' out my tab."

"You have the wrong number, *Joey*," I tell him through gritted teeth.

"But you was——"

"Mia was playing with you," I inform him. "Have a good night." I hang up and block the number, but another follows a second later.

Well aware it's a mistake, I answer. "Hello?"

"Hey, Mia. What's up, sugar baby?"

"Wrong number." I hang up again, blocking the number the same way I did the last one.

"Who's Mia?" my father asks. The man might be old, but his mind is still as sharp as a tack.

"No one." I reach for a flute of champagne on an errant serving tray and finish it. I don't know why. I hate champagne. But I need the buzz it provides to drown out my annoyance.

She gave my number away when I specifically told her not to. The brat needs a spanking. If only she could refrain

34

from pissing someone off long enough to allow them to slip into her bed and discipline her firsthand.

"Mia *Rutherford?*" my father prods.

The image of Mia's round ass propped in the air with a handprint evaporates as I register his words.

Of course, he remembers her.

The entire family does.

It's what happens when the Buchanan name is tied to a stranger's in an irrevocable way. After Troy was arrested, my father hired a bodyguard to sit outside Mia's house for a few weeks until things calmed down, though I doubt she noticed. It still doesn't erase what happened or how quickly an innocent girl's life unraveled in front of everyone, leaving a shell of the girl she used to be.

A broken *anything* is frowned upon from my father's perspective.

I set the empty champagne flute on the bar, refusing to confirm his assumption as I scan the crowded room once more and check the time on my watch. "If you'll excuse me, I have a speech to make."

"Henry," my father warns, "I told you to keep your distance."

I head toward the stage on the back wall without allowing him to finish his lecture. I know my father means well when it comes to Mia as well as my own financial decisions. I know he only wants what is best for his family. It doesn't matter how he started his own company and built it from the ground up. He knows all it would have taken was for a single detail to be out of place, and his future would have crumbled, leaving him and his family destitute. The idea of it happening to me is almost more than he can bear.

A small part of me feels guilty for causing him stress by investing in the Lions. The other part doesn't give a shit. I toed the line for years. Kissing his ass. Bending over backwards to do whatever was asked of me. I joined his fraternity. I mingled with the people he deemed worthy of my time. Of *our* time. Until one of them wound up being an accomplice to murder. Which is when I learned I had been trusting my father's instinct instead of my own. It might have delivered him to where he needed to be, but it only fucked with my future. After Troy was arrested, I refused to allow my father's unrequested guidance to influence my decisions any longer.

I take the stairs onto the platform and step behind the small podium, reaching for the microphone. When I announced the Lions organization would hold a banquet after the draft, Theodore Taylor approached me, asking if I would permit him to steal the spotlight for the evening so he could propose to his longtime girlfriend in front of everyone. I hesitated at first. But Jeffry, the head of public relations for the Lions, made a valid point.

Everyone loves *love*. An engagement announcement involving our starting left wing would create some positive buzz for the Lions. The kind of buzz we desperately need. I agreed, and now, I need to get the ball rolling.

I scan the crowded tables beneath me, noticing Scarlett has yet to make an appearance. My grip on the microphone tightens as I clear my throat. "Ladies and gentlemen, I would like to thank you for joining us today. As you all know, we are excited to hit the ground running this season. I want to thank our players and their spouses or significant others for their support. We all know who keeps these men in check, and without you, most of them would still have their heads up their asses." The crowd laughs, and I wait for everyone to settle. "Since one of them insisted he needed to prove it in front of everyone, let me turn it over to our new starting left wing."

Theo smirks and pushes his chair away from the table in

front of the stage as his girlfriend's jaw drops. Joining me behind the podium, I hand Theo the microphone and step aside, giving him the spotlight.

"I want to thank everyone for being here," Theo announces as I stride off the platform. "But especially, I want to thank the Thorne in my side, and no, I'm not talking to you, Colt."

The crowd laughs.

A splash of red at the back of the room near the open bar catches my attention, causing my hands to fist at my sides. Scarlett's dress hugs her slim figure as she brings a glass of champagne to her full red lips, waiting for me to approach her. I glance at my Rolex, noting the time. She's an hour late. To her boyfriend's event.

Annoyance simmers beneath my skin, but I'm well aware of the cameras scattered throughout the vicinity. I stride toward her as Theo continues his proposal.

"Hey, sorry I'm late," Scarlett whispers when I reach her. She kisses my cheek and grins over my shoulder, posing for the camera I have no doubt is pointed our way. Smoothing down the lapel of my suit, she keeps her voice quiet. "You're mad at me."

"Where have you been?" I ask as cheering erupts around us. I don't bother to look at the stage. I can already guess what is happening. Blake probably rushed the platform, or Theo jumped off it, and they are embracing each other, kissing and crying and making the perfect scene for photos. I might be happy for them if I wasn't so frustrated with the woman in front of me.

"There was an issue with the dress," she explains.

"I don't want to hear it."

She leans in and kisses me softly, pressing her breasts against my chest. The cameras continue snapping photographs around us.

37

"I promise to make it up to you tonight," she whispers, her teeth nibbling my ear lobe.

My phone vibrates with another call. I look down at the unknown number.

"Who is it?" she asks.

"No one."

"You sure?"

I send the call to voicemail and tuck my phone back into my left jacket pocket. "Yes."

"You don't normally hand out your personal number." Her lips purse as she pulls away from me slightly. "Is it a woman?"

"Not sure why it matters."

"I think it does."

"Are you jealous, Scarlett?" I ask.

"Of course not." She flips her long, dark hair over one shoulder and chews on her bottom lip. "But I *do* think we should leave this party so I can show you how sorry I am for being late." Her hand slides down my front and brushes along the edge of my cock. She looks up at me through thick fake lashes.

She *is* jealous.

Good.

Maybe this will serve as a reminder of what she will lose if she isn't careful.

I grab her wrist, squeezing until a gasp slips past her parted lips, and her dark eyes heat.

"Or maybe we can find a private bathroom," she suggests. "Whatever you need."

Whatever *I* need.

I chuckle darkly and lean forward, anxious to work off my frustration. At Scarlett and her tardiness. At my father and his lack of trust. At Mia and her stubbornness.

"Follow me," I growl.

6

HENRY

Rubbing my temple, I scan the article for the hundredth time. My blood boils. After Theo's proposal last night, he invited the team to SeaBird to celebrate. Things got out of hand. I was busy working off some steam with Scarlett, so I'm not entirely sure what transpired inside SeaBird's four walls, but according to the article and photographs, Colt Thorne and Theodore Taylor are posted front and center.

Some people say bad publicity is still publicity and is, therefore, *good* publicity.

Clearly, those people have never had to deal with articles like this one.

"We need to get a handle on this. *Now,*" I spit, tearing my focus from the article and turning to the head of public relations sitting across from me. Jeffry has bags under his eyes, and his brown hair is sticking up in every direction as if he's been put through hell since waking up this morning.

Good. So have I.

After the shitshow hit the papers, I called Erika and

Jeffry--who should have fucking seen this before I did--insisting they meet me at my office at B-Tech Enterprises.

They arrived twenty-seven minutes later, appearing as frustrated as I am.

"The reporters were supposed to be highlighting the engagement," I snarl, snapping my laptop closed.

"Yes, well, it looks like when Colt pushed the girl, the reporters decided to take a different angle with the story," Erika murmurs. She scans her own copy of the article, her lips tilting down.

"I can see that," I reply. "Did you know Blakely was under twenty-one, Jeffry?"

"Unfortunately, not until this morning," he returns.

Lips pursed, Erika shifts in her chair across from me. Apparently, she doesn't like Jeffry's answer any more than I do.

"So what do we do?" I demand.

"Honestly, I'm not sure." Jeffry's frown deepens. "Colt's history with the paparazzi is problematic at best, and how the article spins Blakely into a faceless, underage puck bunny is--"

"What is the damage?" I seethe.

Jeffry looks down at his iPad again and runs his hand over his head, deep in thought. "It's a little too early to tell, but as of right now, preseason ticket sales have dropped by forty percent."

"*Forty percent?*" I nearly choke.

He gulps and looks up at me again. "If we can't start spinning these stories into something positive, I'm afraid this will only continue to hurt ticket sales in the long run."

"So, no more stunts like this," I say, stating the obvious. I lean back in my chair and stare out the floor-to-ceiling windows behind me. This is a problem. A *big* problem. I need to find a solution. Soon. With a deep breath, I order, "Erika, have the legal department create a contract stating if Colt or Theo become involved in anything like this again, they will be terminated from the team."

Erika gasps. "But they're two of our best players."

"And now, they will know I mean business," I tell her. "Perception is everything. This organization needs players who don't look like they beat women, cheat on their girl-friends, or promote underage drinking, don't you think?"

"Well, yes, but--"

"Get it done. I have them coming to the office in an hour."

Erika scribbles something on her iPad, and Jeffry does the same as his head bobs up and down in agreement.

Once they finish, they look up at me again, waiting for my next order.

"Tell me your ideas for pushing more positive content?" I demand.

Jeffry pauses, scratches his temple, and tugs at the collar of his not-so-crisp plaid button-up shirt. "I'm not exactly sure *how*, but we need to counteract all of this...less than desirable publicity as soon as possible."

Duh.

I don't bother to hide my annoyance as I stare back at him blandly. "As the head of public relations, I would like to think we pay you enough money to bring a few ideas to the table."

"What if we invite a few influencers to the first game next month?" Erika interrupts.

"Most influencers aren't interested in hockey," Jeffry argues. "Besides, I can handle the team's PR. We don't need--"

"Erika might be onto something," I announce, scratching my jaw as the thought takes hold.

Yes. This could work.

It might be the death of me, but it *could* work.

"I'll take care of it," I add.

Confused, they turn to me. "You will?"

"Yes. Put out as many fires as you can. *Both* of you." I give Jeffry a hard stare. "I will be hiring a social media manager with experience in positive branding."

Surprised, Erika preens and leans back in her chair, crossing one plaid-covered leg over the other. "I think it's a brilliant idea. Do you already have someone in mind?"

"I'd be happy to find someone, sir," Jeffry offers. "Why don't we take a day or two and––"

"I said I will be the one to take care of it," I snap.

With his tail tucked between his legs, Jeffry stands and dips his chin. He beelines it to the exit like his ass is on fire.

Good.

He should be ashamed he didn't know Theo's fiancée's age when Theo suggested the entire organization celebrate their engagement in a twenty-one and older bar. He should have also been the one to see the article this morning and called me instead of the other way around. A tiny voice in the back of my mind, sounding a hell of a lot like my mother's, reminds me everyone makes mistakes, and I force myself to reel in my temper. For now.

Jeffry better hope his mistakes are few and far between for the foreseeable future, or I will be forced to make some changes. Er, *more* changes. And he won't like those any more than he likes the idea of me hiring someone to handle our social media presence.

"Okay. I guess that's it then," Erika says. Balancing her iPad in one hand, she runs her opposite one along the chain of her gold necklace, toying with the crescent moon encrusted with diamonds as she stands and smoothes down her black blouse tucked into plaid slacks.

"Good day, Dr. Buchanan." She clears her throat, turns on her black Jimmy Choo heels, and gets the hell out of my office.

It's just as well.

She might be relatively young, but we have worked with each other long enough for her to know when I'm close to snapping, and she does *not* want to be around when it happens.

Smart lady.

My phone buzzes for the tenth time, but I send the call to voicemail, knowing it's either someone from the team's board of directors or another horny asshat hoping to score with Mia.

If she wanted to prove her point, she succeeded.

Satisfied by my phone's silence, I dial Gordy's number.

He picks up on the first ring. "Hello, sir."

"I need you to find me Mia Rutherford's contact information," I order.

"Sure thing." The familiar *tap-tap* of the keyboard grates on me before Gordy adds, "555.346.4459."

"Thank you." I hang up and jab Mia's number into my cell.

But I don't call it.

Not yet.

Not when I'm already wound this tight.

Instead, I save the contact information, promising to call her as soon as I finish my meeting with Colt and Theo.

7

MIA

A familiar buzzing wakes me, and I roll onto my side. "Noooo," I groan. "It's too early."

Shoving my hot pink sleep mask on top of my head, I check the number. I don't recognize it. Too curious for my own good, despite my lack of sleep, I slide my thumb across the screen and answer the call.

"Hello?" I croak.

"I told you it was a private number," a low voice growls.

My eyes pop as I place the voice, and a laugh bubbles out of me. Rolling onto my back, I stare at the ceiling, not even bothering to hide my triumphant grin. "Dude, we both know you deserved it."

"Oh, we do?"

"Yup. You were being a condescending ass, remember?"

"I had a shit day, am *still* having a shit day," he clarifies, "and my phone hasn't stopped ringing since I handed you my card, but *I'm* the ass?"

"If the potential sugar daddies bother you so much, I'm sure your assistant can change your precious private number for you," I suggest.

44

"Brat."

"Ass," I volley back at him. "And you're the one who woke me up, so you'll have to forgive me for not being very sympathetic to your situation."

"It's noon."

"Dude, I work at a bar," I remind him. "I didn't get home until after three." With another yawn, I arch my back and stretch like a cat on the lumpy mattress beneath me.

Man, it feels good.

Not the mattress. The stretch.

I'm gonna miss this room. Sure, I get to take my bed with me, but these four walls have been a constant in my life since freshman year. The reminder I'm leaving it and will be homeless in the next few weeks is depressing at best. I applied to two more doctor's offices this week. Neither even bothered to interview me. I'm seriously screwed.

Shaking off the morose thought, I ask, "How did you get my number anyway?"

"I have my ways."

"Of course you do. You're Henry Buchanan," I chirp, letting out another yawn. "Suave businessman with a side of sugar daddy. You *always* get what you want, don't you?"

Silence fills the speaker, and I pull the phone away from my ear.

"Professor?" I pause, curious if I crossed a line or something. "You still there?"

"How many boys did you give my number to?" he asks.

"I dunno? At one point, I was basically handing it out like candy. Now, is there a reason you're calling me this early?"

"I would hardly call noon early," he counters. "But yes. I have a proposition for you."

"What kind of proposition?"

"You will be coming to work for me."

With a huff of amusement, I shift onto my stomach,

kicking my feet into the air and crossing my ankles as I register his words. "Well, for starters, that didn't exactly sound like a proposition. It sounded more like an order. And second, did your short attention span already shift from the hockey industry to the medical field, or are you smoking something?"

"Despite my IT department wiping your naked photos from the internet, I'm afraid you already fucked over that particular career path if you plan to stay in Lockwood Heights," he informs me.

My head pulls back. "Ouch."

"But," he continues, "I found an alternate opportunity you show promise with."

"Wait. Back up. You *wiped* the photos from the internet?" I ask, convinced I need to clean out my ears or pinch myself because I'm either going deaf or must still be sleeping.

"Someone had to," he mutters.

My jaw drops, and I sit up fully in bed, letting the hot pink sheets fall around my waist. Because there's something about this conversation. About him. The way I can feel him judging me through the freaking speakers. Like he did me a favor despite the fact I never asked for his help, and it pisses me off.

"Did you see them?" I demand. "The photos?"

His silence is the only proof I need to know I'm right. He's seen them. He knows what I look like naked or at least almost naked. I wonder if he's seen the videos too. Probably. I wonder if he liked them. If they turned him on the same way they've turned on countless other men.

Gross.

Not Henry. The other men.

The ones who don't leave me alone. Who think they have a right to my body simply because they've purchased a few photos of me from a website.

The reminder makes me feel dirty, and I pray Buchanan can't tell. Because I'm not an idiot. I know it was a dumb idea. I know I should've caved and asked my uncle for money instead of uploading inappropriate videos online. But I'm stubborn. And impulsive. And I hate handouts more than almost anything. I hate them even more than the judgment Buchanan manages to hand out in spades, especially whenever I'm around.

"Look, it doesn't matter if you saw the photos," I mutter. "I already told you I don't like handouts."

"I'm not *handing* you anything."

"Last night, you handed me your business card with your personal number on it along with five hundred dollars," I remind him. "If that isn't a handout, I don't know what is."

"Are you saying you don't need the money?" he challenges, and dammit, I can almost see the smug look on his face. He already knows the answer. He probably even snooped into my finances and knows exactly how much money I owe on my credit card and student loans, despite what I earned from selling pictures of myself before giving it all to charity. My dad literally died because he borrowed money from a loan shark for my schooling, but the cash barely covered my first semester at LAU. And it's not like I could drop out. Not when my dad sacrificed his life so I could attend my dream school.

Fuck.

My head falls, and I close my eyes, melting into the hot pink sheets. "I can figure this out on my own," I tell him, feeling like a broken record. But it doesn't erase my unease. My problems. My impending eviction.

I'm so screwed.

"You have been figuring this out on your own for years," he counters. "How far has it gotten you, Mia?"

Wow.

47

His words hit like water splashing into a hot pan. They sear me, but I don't acknowledge the burn as I push myself up again and bring my knees to my chest. "It's gotten me far enough."

"Put in your two weeks' notice at SeaBird."

"I'm not quitting SeaBird."

"Why not?"

"Because I like my job."

"They don't give you enough hours. They don't offer health insurance. They don't——"

"Have a good day, Professor."

"I'm not your——"

The call cuts off as I hang up on him, but the phone rings a second later.

I ignore the first call, but when it rings again, I give in.

"What do you want?" I ask, cradling my phone between my ear and shoulder as I pick at my cuticles. I should probably paint my nails again. The black polish is chipped and dull.

"Fine, you can keep your job at SeaBird as long as they will allow you to travel," Buchanan concedes.

"Travel?" My eyes nearly bug out of my head, and I drop my hand to my lap. "Where am I going to travel? I can't afford——"

"Your job will require you to travel, which means your employer will cover your expenses."

"What job?" I demand, my exhaustion swallowing me whole.

As if he's talking to a toddler, Buchanan lets out a slow, controlled breath and explains. "The job I'm trying to offer you if you would listen for one minute—"

"What job are you offering a girl with a nursing degree and *no* background in sports medicine?" I interrupt.

"I never mentioned sports medicine. You did."

My brows knit. "So you don't want to hire me as a nurse?"

"The Lions don't need a nurse."

"Exactly what I've been telling you!"

"Will you close those pouty lips for two seconds, Mia?" he snips.

My mouth snaps shut.

When he's satisfied with my silence, he announces, "I want you to be the social media manager for the Lions."

I blink slowly, attempting to keep up, though my brain feels like it's been smeared with peanut butter and handed to a bunch of ants.

Did he say he wants me to be the Lions' social media manager?

Yup. I most definitely need to have my ears checked.

"Is that a problem?" he prods.

Shoving my hair over one shoulder, I admit, "I guess I'm a little lost. You want to hire me as a social media manager?"

"Yes."

I shake my head. *"Why?"*

"You're talented. Experienced. You have a way of attracting people. And we both know the Lions could use some good publicity after all the messes with Thorne and Taylor."

The man has a point.

The Lions could definitely use some good publicity after all the chaos surrounding Colt and Theodore. For some reason I still don't fully understand, their names have been splashed in the media left and right. And as the articles are published, each one slowly shifts from good publicity to... not-so-good publicity. Especially after the shitshow last night when Colt was alleged to be an abusive cheater, and Theo was accused of serving alcohol to someone who's underage and happens to be his fiancée.

Yikes.

When I've stayed silent for too long, Buchanan continues.

49

"Your salary will start at one hundred thousand dollars a year with benefits and all expenses paid during travel."

"A hundred thousand a year?" I nearly choke out. "Are you kidding me?"

"Are you saying it isn't enough?"

"I'm saying I don't like handouts," I remind him for the hundredth time, "and it's a *lot* of money. I have no experience, I—"

"You have over three million followers across your personal social media platforms and have taken zero contracts from companies who would happily compensate you for your time. Instead, you choose to pay for everything you review out of your own pocket, which has garnered more trust from your followers than the majority of influencers on any platform. Your videos and posts have a seventy percent interaction rate, and—"

"You've done your research," I note. "Still doesn't mean I like handouts."

"This is *not* a handout."

"It's definitely a handout, and we both know it. I don't need your help."

"I appreciate your grit, Mia," he murmurs. "I do. It's rare to find these days. While I appreciate your determination, I won't sugarcoat the corner you have backed yourself into. Lockwood Heights is a relatively small town. If you plan to stay here, you *do* need my help. And there is absolutely nothing wrong with taking it."

"There's everything wrong with it," I argue.

"What is so wrong with needing my help, Mia?"

"Because I don't want it," I blurt out. "Whatever...obligation you feel toward me isn't necessary. Being a former friend of Troy's doesn't mean you're required to clean up his mess. And to be honest, we both know who my father was, and the likelihood of me following in his footsteps and being a fuck-up like him isn't exactly a stretch, so just...stop."

I suck in a deep breath, surprised by the word vomit I've spewed all over this conversation. But what's worse? The quiet following it.

I should be used to it by now.

Anytime someone finds out about my dad's death, an awkward silence woven with pity falls over the conversation, and there's nothing I can do about it. I shouldn't be surprised Buchanan's acting the same way. After all, we've been tiptoeing around our tangled pasts and how they've been snarled together into some fucked-up knot for years. But it would be nice if we could have an actual conversation about it. Instead, we're going to keep pretending the only reason he's helping me is because I'm qualified for the job when I have no real experience. At all.

Hello, Land of Delusion.

Chewing on my thumbnail, I play devil's advocate and consider the idea.

Okay, yes. I'm good at social media. And, yes. I have a lot of followers. It's an escape. A way for me to disconnect from the real world and focus on random shit I enjoy without worrying about repercussions or opinions from the people around me. But it doesn't mean I'm qualified to do it for an actual corporation or anything.

He's crazy.

He has to be.

As if he can feel me actually losing my marbles and considering his offer, Buchanan orders, "Take the job, Mia."

"No."

"Take the job," he repeats.

"Not unless you admit you're only offering it to me because you feel guilty for my dad's death."

I don't know why I need to hear it. Why I need to have

my nose rubbed in the fact I can't do this on my own. Maybe it's my own warped self-deprecation taking the wheel, but I can't help it. I wanna know. I wanna know the truth in all its dirty glory.

"Fine," Buchanan growls. "I feel guilty. I should have seen the signs with Troy. He was my best friend. I should have seen him spiraling. Should have recognized how far gone he was. He was dating my little sister at the time. He could have hurt her the same way he hurt your father. He fucked up your mom's life and yours. So, yeah. I feel guilty. But I'm also a selfish man, Mia. A selfish businessman. Have you seen the articles posted after last night regarding Colt and Theo? The publicity is making the Lions look like a train wreck, and I need your help to rectify it. To put the team in a better light. If I didn't think you could handle the position, I wouldn't offer it. I watched your work. Studied your posts. You have a way of making people...*feel*. Of making people want to root for you. I need people to root for the Lions, and I think *you* can make them."

Well, damn.

I have a feeling a compliment from Henry Buchanan is a rare treat, and he just gifted me with one.

Biting my thumbnail again, I consider his offer, letting it marinate for a few long seconds.

Dropping my hand back to my lap, I ask, "And I can still work at SeaBird?"

"You can do whatever the fuck you want, Mia. You always have. Why do you think this would be any different?"

My mouth flickers with amusement, but I hold it back. "The salary's too much."

I swear I can hear the mirth in his voice as he says, "I'm not going to cut your salary simply because you're too stubborn to see your own worth."

He thinks I'm worth 100k per year?

I'd laugh if I wasn't so desperate for financial freedom. And I am desperate. Despite my pride and my need to handle everything on my own, the prospect of a new apartment and a job allowing me to travel *and* excellent pay is almost more than I can bear. And this time, I won't let my aversion to money ruin my future like it did the last time. This time, I'll be smart. I'll save. I'll still give to charity, but I won't do it to my detriment. I'll actually think things through instead of being impulsive.

I will.

Don't be stupid, Mia. Don't let your pride get in the way of your future.

"Do we have a deal?" Buchanan prods.

"Fine," I concede, even though it kills me.

"Good. As I mentioned, I expect you to travel with the team. Be present at the press conferences and games. You will shadow the players inside the locker room and outside of it and compile photos, videos, and every other thing you need to convince people to care about the Lions. To root for the team. To purchase tickets."

"Okay." I calculate the timeline of when I need to be out of Gertie's hair and if I'll have enough pay stubs showing my new salary by the time I sign a new lease somewhere, realizing it'll be close. Really close. And I don't want to ask Kate or Ash if I can crash on their couch for a few days.

I'll figure something out.

"Have you found a place to live yet?" he questions as if the bastard can read my mind.

"Not sure it's any of your business."

"If you lease in my building, I can save you fifty percent on rent."

Fifty percent?

Has the man lost his mind?

"Do we have a deal?" he prods.

53

"Is this a Mia-exclusive offer, or are you giving fifty percent off to all of your employees?" I ask.

"If I say it's Mia-exclusive, will you take the offer?"

I bite the inside of my cheek to hide my smile despite Buchanan not being here to witness it. "I think we both know the answer to that."

A low rumble vibrates through the phone. He mutters, "Fine. It's for any new employee."

"Fine," I mimic him. "I'm in."

"Good. Now, you can buy Uber rides for irresponsible people to your heart's content."

"Good," I repeat. "And Buchanan?"

"What?"

Regret floods my veins, but I don't let it stop me from telling him the truth. Even if it's stupid. Even if I'll regret it in the long run. Even if it'll piss him off.

"It isn't your fault, you know," I murmur. "Troy fooled--"

"Goodbye, Mia."

The call ends.

8

MIA

My keys clatter to the floor, and the box in my arms finally slips, crashing into a mess of underwear and tank tops at my feet.

"Shit," I mutter under my breath and bend down to shove the clothes back into the cardboard box.

I knew I should've caved and asked the guys for help, but since the only pieces of furniture I own are a mattress and an ugly-ass floral armchair, I figured I could handle it myself.

Okay, maybe not the mattress part, but I'll figure it out. Besides, Colt, Theo, and Macklin are helping Blakely move her things into her and Theo's new house. And after Tukani offered to let me borrow his truck, I figured, why ask everyone to double their load?

Sometimes, it still blows my mind. To think that Blakely's engaged, Kate's pregnant and engaged, and Ashlyn's basically a step-mom who I have no doubt will *also* be engaged by the end of the year. I knew it'd be weird. Seeing everyone moving on after graduation. Seeing everyone finding their happily-ever-afters. Seeing everyone finding new places to live and new lives to build. But it's only been a few months, and everything has changed. *Everything.* I know it's okay. I know it's inevitable. But sometimes, I feel like it's moving so quickly I can't keep up. Like I'm running as fast as I possibly can, but the finish line keeps moving, rendering my efforts useless and my energy exhausted.

Even the career path I planned out has been tilted on its axis.

I'm not going to be working as a nurse.

I'm going to be a social media manager.

For now.

Strange.

But after my phone call with Buchanan, I think he's onto something. I might as well lean into my natural talents while I can until the next curveball is thrown my way, and I have to pivot.

Like right now. In my new...*home.* The word feels foreign. Like a cheese grater rubbing against my skin. If I was smart, I would've toured the place before bringing up my first box because this? It's the last thing I expected. Pushing myself up, I leave my things scattered on the floor and brush my hands against my bare thighs, tugging at the hem of my shorts to keep them from riding up my crotch. The hardwood floor is a warm, light color. The walls are pale, too, almost white, with a soft undertone of gray. Navy cabinets line the kitchen, and white granite countertops with flecks of gray tie in the walls, making the place look straight out of *Southern Living* magazine. It's gorgeous. Homey. Warm.

There's a fireplace too.

A freaking fireplace in an apartment.

Like, what world do I live in?

Ants crawl beneath my skin, leaving me itchy as I give the cozy family room my back and head down the hallway to my left. The same hardwoods cover the floor leading to a large bathroom with a glass shower, white cabinets, and a clawfoot bathtub tucked into the corner. Sucking my teeth between my lips, I flip the light off and head to the bedroom. It's as large and as extravagant as the rest of the house. A laugh slips out of me as I imagine my used mattress sitting in the center of the room since I don't own a bed frame or anything. This is ridiculous. I don't belong here. A closed door taunts me at the back of the bedroom, but I don't bother to open it, knowing it'll only depress me more. It's probably a walk-in closet bigger than my entire room back at the townhouse I shared with the girls.

The girls who have all moved on with their lives.

Which means I need to, as well.

Even when it's uncomfortable.

But this place?

It's too much.

Too nice.

Too foreign.

Pulling out my phone, I dial Buchanan's private number, hating myself more and more with every passing second.

"Hello?"

"You never told me the apartment has a fireplace."

"Is the fireplace a problem?" he asks.

"Maybe."

"Do you have a thing against fireplaces?"

"I have a thing against living outside of my means," I argue.

A beat of silence passes, and Buchanan murmurs, "I know your salary, Mia. You are *not* living outside of your means."

I glance around the massive space, taking in the tall windows and the view of rolling hills and green grass.

"Yeah, well, it sure feels like it," I whisper. "This place is too much."

"Do you need me to come down on the price?"

"No." I look down at my scuffed-up sneakers against the

freshly-mopped maple floors. "I need you to make it...shittier."

His laugh borders between annoyance and amusement as it echoes through my cell. "Are you calling me because you're disappointed the apartment isn't in worse shape?"

It's ridiculous. I know it is. But hearing him state the obvious out loud? It hits on a whole new level and leaves me feeling stupid.

"Give me a call if you have a real complaint," he tells me. The line goes dead, and I puff out my cheeks.

I could always back out. I could always tell Buchanan I found a new place. Considering the salary he offered, he's right. I can afford to live anywhere I want at this point. But if I stay here, I'll save more money thanks to the discount he's offering. And if I save more money, I can give it to people who need it. People who need it more than me. More than I've ever needed it.

Gnawing on my thumbnail, I take in the massive, extravagant bedroom for another second, then close the door and head back to the cardboard box in the foyer as the familiar weight of loneliness falls over me.

I should be used to it by now.

The loneliness.

But it only makes me feel worse.

Giving into the weakness, I pull out my phone and call Ashlyn.

"Hello?" she answers.

"Hey," I reply. "How's moving going?"

"Meh. Not too bad," Ashlyn replies. "Colt and Theo are dealing with all the heavy stuff. How 'bout you?"

I look around the empty apartment. "It's fine."

"You sure you don't need help?"

"Yeah. The doorman offered to bring my things up with the superintendent later," I lie.

"You have a doorman?"

I groan. "Don't ask."

"Damn, girl. I'm impressed."

"Don't be," I mutter. "Seriously."

"Ya know, normally I'd tell you Colt and I are coming over even though you're being a butt and won't accept our help willingly, but we're actually picking up Jaxon after Colt finishes with Blakely's dresser, so..."

"Oh."

Jaxon is Colt's baby from a previous relationship, although you'd never know Ashlyn isn't his mom. She's taken to mama duty like a natural and loves the little guy more than almost anything, including her friends. Which I completely understand and support, even when it does knock me down a peg or two. Like today. When I could really use my best friend.

Sensing my disappointment, Ashlyn rushes out, "I thought you said the doorman and superintendent are helping?"

"They are," I reply. "I was just curious if you guys were going to hang out together after Blakely settles in or something."

"Not really, but I can always ask Colt if he's okay with you coming––"

"Don't worry about it," I interrupt. The idea of a pity hang-out with Ash, Colt, and his one-year-old kid sounds even worse than hanging out alone in a massive apartment that feels about as homey as a museum. "I should probably unpack anyway since the first away games are right around the corner," I add. "Thanks, though."

"For sure. Theo and Blakely will be doing the same thing tonight, too, so you aren't missing much."

"And Kate?" I ask. "Do you know what she and Mack are doing?"

"I think they're gonna stick around to help Blake unload a few more things and grab some pizza. One sec. Let me see if it's still the plan."

"No, don't worry about it," I blurt out.

She pauses. "Are you positive? I'm sure they wouldn't mind if you came over."

"It's okay. Really."

"Mia," Ash starts, but I cut her off.

"Seriously, I'm fine. I'm a big girl and can handle this on my own."

"You sure?"

"Yup. Positive," I repeat. "Besides, I'm kind of craving a girls' night."

"Me too. A girls' night sounds perfect. Maybe we can plan one after things calm down a little bit."

"Good idea," I reply.

"Is there a time we can come see the new place? Maybe next week or something?"

Again, my eyes fall on the gorgeous family room and huge windows nearly identical to the ones in the master bedroom overlooking LAU's campus. "We'll see."

"Mia——"

"I'll talk to you later, okay?"

"Love you," she reminds me.

"Love you too."

I hang up the call and drop the phone in my lap, leaning back on my hands.

"Welp. I guess it's me, myself, and I tonight," I mutter to no one in particular. "Lovely."

9

MIA

Fun fact: locker rooms stink. They're also loud. Like, everyone can hear each other's conversations kind of loud. Part of me wonders if I should've asked Blakely for any advice she could give me since she interned with the LAU hockey team last year until she was hired as an events coordinator for my uncle's charity. But I figured if she could deal with being surrounded by hockey players, so could I.

If only I'd taken into account the whole sexy alpha men vibe.

Hot damn.

Everyone's in their practice gear. I don't miss the curious glances cast my way as I hang out by the tunnel leading to the rink with my new DSLR camera hanging at my side. Before I was hired, I used the camera on my iPhone to take pictures and record videos for social media. But after my conversation with Buchanan, I decided I could splurge a little. And now that I'm here, I have a feeling buying this bad boy is the best decision I've ever made.

I feel...professional. Legitimate. Like I'm *not* an imposter.

No one has introduced me to anyone yet. No one has even greeted me. I feel like a fish out of water or a fresh piece of meat being thrown to the wolves. Other than a text message with a time and address delivered to my phone, I have no idea what to expect.

It's the first practice for everyone in the Lions organization, and part of me wonders if the players feel the same way I do. Lost. Anxious. But excited too. And ready to work their asses off.

I kind of want to start filming right now in hopes of capturing the anticipation buzzing through the locker room, but I stop myself, unsure if I should wait for approval first.

It'd be great if I could find someone who knows what I'm supposed to be doing right now.

Rocking back on my heels, I side-eye the guy in a full Lion costume beside me. He hasn't introduced himself to me yet. Nope. He's been bouncing on his feet and rolling his shoulders like he's preparing for battle, though I have no idea why. He's a mascot, and this is only practice, so...

Clearing my throat, I announce, "Hey, I'm Mia."

The lion's head snaps in my direction, and he waves his big paw at me.

"I assume you're the team mascot?"

The giant lion's head nods.

I stare at the sewn-on eyes, unsure where else to look for another beat. "What's your name?"

He points to a name stitched into his jersey.

"Leo," I note. "Cool." Apparently, he isn't very chatty. "I assume this is your first day too?" I prod.

He makes a lip-zipping motion and moonwalks to the opposite side of the tunnel, effectively ending our conversation. I bite the inside of my cheek to keep from laughing out loud as I watch him and turn back to the bustling locker room.

Okay, then.

When Colt sees me hanging out near the tunnel, he waves, then rummages in his locker for his gloves. At least there's one familiar face. Two, if I count Theo, but I haven't seen him yet. Macklin should also be here, although he's not in the locker room. Maybe the medical guys aren't required to be here for practice? Honestly, I have no idea.

An attractive gentleman in an orange polo with a whistle draped around his neck appears from the back office, along with two more men in white polos and matching tan pants. A thin sourpuss follows behind them with an iPad clutched to his chest. When the man in the orange polo spots me, he walks over and lifts his chin.

"Are you Mia?" he asks.

"Hi." I offer my hand for him to shake, and he takes it. "Yes, I'm Mia. Nice to meet you."

"You, too," the stranger returns, tilting his head toward the thin sourpuss. "This is Jeffry, your boss."

I smile at him, surprised he didn't make the introduction himself. "Oh. Hi."

"Hello," he snips coldly.

"Buchanan said he'd give you an introduction after practice since he has a meeting this morning," the man in the orange polo continues. "For now, record whatever you want. Everyone's already signed a waiver, so you should be good to go. I'm Dawson, by the way," he adds as if only now realizing he hadn't properly introduced himself. "I'm the head coach for the Lions."

Ah, so that's who he is.

Subtly, I check him out, having heard a lot about him. He's a little older than me, maybe thirty? Thirty-five? With blonde hair and kind eyes. When I told my friends I'd been hired, Colt and Theo gave me a rundown of what to anticipate. They also mentioned the head coach played hockey professionally for a few years but shattered his knee. Theo thinks Dawson has a good eye for plays, which is probably why Buchanan hired him.

Apparently, he cherry-picked his coaching staff along with the rest of the players and medical team. He's bold, considering the fact none of us have any actual hands-on experience. But if it pays off, it'll pay off big time, and I'm not the only one curious to see how this season plays out for the Lions.

"Nice to meet you," I tell him.

"Nice to meet you too," Dawson returns. "Let's get to work." He claps his hands loudly and addresses the rest of the players. "All right, guys, listen up."

The locker room quiets as everyone turns to Dawson and waits.

"Most of you have already met at the banquet, but as a quick refresher, I'm Dawson, the head coach for the Lions. You can call me Coach, Coach Dawson, or Dawson. Honestly, I don't give a shit what you call me, but I do expect you to show up, be on time, and be ready to do what I tell you. Unless the medical team says for you to take it easy, I expect you to give me a hundred and ten percent every single day. Yes, including practices. The first game is in a month, which means we have some conditioning to do. It will be brutal, and I will piss you off. But unless you're puking or passed out on the ice, I expect you to keep pushing yourself. Any questions?"

Silence.

"Good," Dawson decides. "Oh, and this is McCarthy and Bowers, two more coaches on staff. This is our mascot and my little brother, Mitchell." He points to the mascot. The lion's head twists, and he folds his arms, appearing unimpressed. Dawson clears his throat. "But he's superstitious and considers it bad luck to show his face or step out of character whenever he's in the arena, so please call him Leo the Lion if you ever need to address him." The mascot instantly relaxes and gives a thumbs-up as I bite back my amusement.

Is he for real?

"And this is Mia," Dawson continues. He hooks his thumb at me. "She's our head of social media and works under Jeffry for now. Do what she says, or you'll piss Buchanan off. Let's go."

The team heads down the tunnel toward the rink as I turn to Jeffry, waiting for instruction. Once we're alone, he slides his tongue between his teeth and upper lip, finally gracing me with eye contact.

"I assume you've done this before?" he asks curtly.

I shrug one shoulder. "I've built a few brands independently in the past, but this is my first official experience as a social media manager for a corporation."

"I'm the head of public relations," he informs me.

"Awesome. I assume we'll be working closely together?"

"Like Dawson said, I'm your boss. Don't fuck this up." He turns on his heel, heading in the opposite direction of the rink.

"Am I supposed to follow you?" I call.

He faces me again. His annoyance permeates the air around him as he lifts his pointy nose toward the ceiling. "Aren't you supposed to be filming for social media?"

"Well, yeah, but--"

"I suggest you make your way to the ice."

Without another word, he leaves.

Okay, then.

～

I never expected everyone to be so...friendly. Well, other than Jeffry, anyway. Thankfully, I haven't seen him since the locker room.

Buchanan has yet to make an appearance, but Colt and Theo have officially taken me under their wings. At least as much as they can while still paying attention to the new coach's instructions. It's been two hours, and the players are all huffing and puffing from conditioning. They've clearly taken Dawson's instructions to heart and are pushing themselves to their limits, giving him a hundred and ten percent. But if I had to guess, it's par for the course. This is their job. Of course, they want to push themselves. To show up and try their hardest. This is what they've been working for, and they aren't about to let it go, not with their NHL dreams finally in their grasp. Gotta give them credit. It's kind of hot.

"Come on, Beck," Coach Dawson bellows from the bench at the new goalie lagging behind the rest of the team. "Pick up the pace! These are called sprints for a reason. Now, *sprint!*"

The goalie grumbles but pushes himself a little harder, pumping his arms back and forth and catching up to the rest of the players. The team is drenched in sweat as they rush from one end of the rink to the other. Flurries of ice crystals float in the air while the players' skates cut into the ice at a furious rate. I want to capture it. This moment. The adrenaline. The determination. The anticipation. Everyone's feeling it. The players. The coaches. Even me.

Laying on the small patch of concrete separating the benches from the rink in hopes of achieving the perfect angle, I record the players sprinting from one goal to the other. Their skates. The spray of slush. The arena lights shining from above. The damp hair clinging to their foreheads. It'll be an excellent addition to the earlier shots I've taken.

Seriously, this is gonna look awesome.

"Good job," Dawson yells when the players reach the opposite side for what feels like the hundredth time. "Let's call it a day."

Pushing to my feet, I search the stands for Buchanan but come up empty. Dawson said he'd be here to make an official introduction or something, so where is he? When I don't find him, I hustle to Dawson's side and take control of the situation. "Do you mind if I ask the team to stay for a few minutes? I want to record a couple more shots if possible."

As if only now remembering I'm here, Dawson searches the stands for Buchanan, too, but when he doesn't find the guy, he nods at me and raises his voice again. "Mia wants to grab a few more shots before you pack it in. Do what she asks. When she says you're done, you can shower. Good practice today. We'll see you tomorrow."

He turns on his heel and walks away as the rest of the team lines up in front of the bench, waiting for further instruction.

Well, alrighty then.

I clear my throat and rest the brand-new DSLR on my shoulder, debating where I should begin. This is so surreal. Having nearly two dozen brooding hockey players staring at me, waiting for me to tell them what to do.

"So?" Colt prods. His helmet hangs at his side, and his chest heaves from exertion. "What do you need from us?"

Right.

"Okay, gentlemen," I start. "I'm not sure how familiar you are with social media, but there are trending videos and sounds that push content. When utilized properly, they can really help build the Lions' brand and, therefore, sell a lot of tickets which is our goal, right?"

Their heads bob up and down slightly, but none of them comment.

Wiping my free hand against my jeans, I continue. "Today, we'll keep things simple and capture a few slow-motion videos and similar things. In the long run, I'd also like to have some volunteers who would be willing to learn some trending dances and possibly lip sync a few songs."

Silence.

"I know it sounds dumb, but it isn't too hard, and I want us to go viral as often as possible, meaning we need to put out a lot of content, especially in the beginning. Do I have any volunteers?"

Silence.

"Come on, boys," I push, giving them my signature smirk. "Girls are suckers for guys who aren't afraid to make fools out of themselves. Trust me."

Another beat of silence passes, and Theo steps forward. "Fine." He nudges his best friend's shoulder. "Colt and I will help you out."

I grin back at them. "Thank you. Any other takers? I promise I'll make it as painless as possible."

The new goalie, Beck, grumbles under his breath but lifts his hand into the air. "Yeah, I'll do it too."

"Yay, thank you. Okay, let's start with something simple so we can introduce the whole team to your fans. Everyone line up on the opposite side of the rink and skate toward me one at a time but stop short so I can have a nice spray of ice. I think it will look really cool. Make sense?" I wait, then add, "Oh, and make sure you smile at the camera like you want to melt my panties off."

"But we're all sweaty," Beck tells me. With his helmet resting at his side, he skates closer and bends his head as if to prove his point. Sure enough, sweat clings to his forehead and drips down his temple, making his chiseled jaw even more lickable. The guy's a catch and will be perfect for hooking the audience. My grin spreads, and my heart flutters with excitement. Seriously. This is going to be so good.

"Girls love sweat. *Good* sweat," I clarify. "And this?" I rub my hand against his messy, damp blond hair. "*This* is good sweat. Trust me." My hand drops back to my side, and I wipe it on my jeans.

I raise my camera. "Let's get started."

The players follow my instructions, and before I know it, I'm laughing at their antics, and my hoodie is covered in white slush, leaving it cool against my skin. Some of the players are loosey-goosey. Others are more rigid than a two-by-four. But the variety only adds to the appeal. There's someone here for everyone. Yup. I can definitely spin these videos into something engaging. They're going to work out just fine. And by some miracle, the guys are taking it all in stride, being more helpful than I'd ever anticipated.

When Beck lifts his practice jersey and wipes his forehead with it, I'm given a glimpse of his washboard abs. The view sparks an idea, and my mouth spreads into a grin.

"Beck, come here." Beck skates closer to me. "Are you okay if I create some thirst traps of you? Nothing too crazy, and I promise I'll get your approval on every video, but I think we could get a lot of views with some videos of your abs. What do you think?"

"Yeah, sure. I'm in."

"Perfect." I reach for his practice jersey, lifting it at an angle, and giving the motion a more peekaboo effect. "Do it like this."

"Like this?"

He follows my instructions, and I nod. "Exactly."

Lifting the camera, I click record, zeroing in on the tan skin and sexy V slipping beneath his pads when a cold voice barks behind me.

"Enough!"

Flinching at the sharp words, I turn around and search for the culprit. Buchanan's in the stands. He's glaring at me. *Hard.* Like I shit in his coffee or something when I've been on nothing but my best behavior.

"Is there a problem?" I call.

Seriously. The guy's pissed, and I have no idea why.

"We are *not* selling sex."

"Uh, sex is exactly what we're selling," I interrupt with a laugh, but the rest of the players stay quiet.

With heavy footsteps, Buchanan strides down the stairs from the top of the arena, his body practically vibrating with dominance and testosterone until I can almost taste it from here.

Yup. I was right.

He's pissed.

At me.

Why am I not surprised?

But if he thinks he can push me around with all this sexy alpha mumbo-jumbo, he's sorely mistaken. I lift my chin and hold his frigid gaze as his foot hits the last step, leaving him more than a foot taller than me while the rest of the team stares at us from the ice.

"I did not hire you to sell sex," he growls.

"Do you want to sell tickets, Buchanan?"

The muscle in his jaw ticks.

"*This* is gonna sell tickets," I tell him.

And I'm not wrong. I know I'm not. People might like living in la-la-land, where rainbows and butterflies mingle with cotton candy, but the truth is, sex sells everything. Even this. Hockey tickets and jerseys and lanyards and mugs. The list goes on and on and on. It doesn't mean I can't do it tastefully. And when paired with the right music, Beck's abs will easily accumulate a hundred-thousand views.

Buchanan doesn't budge. He towers over me, a dare in his

dark eyes, curious to see if I'll back down since he's pulled out the big guns. Yup. Here's the business shark. The one used to getting what he wants. Too bad he doesn't know everything. He's waiting for me to backpedal. To say he's right and delete the video of Beck's abs. I won't. For one, I'm stubborn. And two, I won't let him push me around, even if he is my boss. The man hired me for a reason, dammit. If he would simply trust me, this would go a lot more smoothly, and I'd deliver exactly what he wants.

Sales.

Realizing I'm not going to give in or cower from his scrutiny, Buchanan orders, "Everyone. Out." But he doesn't break his stare. He glares at me. Waiting to see me crumble.

Clearly, he doesn't know me very well if he honestly thinks a solid death glare will have me shaking in my boots. But if he needs time to cool down, I'm happy to give it.

"Great idea." I start toward the locker room. He grabs my bicep and holds me in place. "Not you."

Sensing the tension crackling between us, the rest of the team slips past me except for Colt and Theo. They hesitate in my periphery, sending me concerned looks.

I cast them a quick glance and murmur, "It's fine."

Relatively satisfied, they follow the rest of the team, disappearing down the tunnel and leaving me alone with the one and only Henry Buchanan. I tilt my head to one side, waiting for him to, I dunno, say *something*. Instead, those dark eyes pin me in place. Waiting.

Peeking at the hand wrapped around my bicep, I roll my shoulder back, slipping out of his firm hold and crossing my arms. "Is there a problem, *Professor*?"

His molars grind at the pet name, but he doesn't correct me. "What are you doing?"

"I'm doing what you hired me to do."

"I do *not* want to recreate your OnlyFans account."

"You know, you're an asshole," I seethe. "And I'm not recreating my OF account."

"You have my players stripping––"

"I have your players showing they're funny and sexy and entertaining and down for a good time. *That?*"—I motion to the now-empty ice—"was gold. And when it's paired with the right music, it's gonna show how fun and entertaining the players are. Women want fun and entertaining."

"We aren't advertising to women—"

My laugh cuts him off. "Ya know, for a guy who's supposedly good at business, you're missing a huge demographic if you honestly don't think we're advertising to women as well as men. What happens when a married guy comes home and says he wants to buy tickets to a Lions game? Huh? The wife usually says, *Okay, have fun.* But with videos like the ones I want to create flooding their social media, it'll be a different story. Because when that woman registers what team her husband's talking about, she'll remember the video her friend sent her. The one where a bunch of attractive hockey players danced to Taylor Swift or did something else stupid but hilarious at the same time. And guess what the wife will say to her husband once she realizes he wants to go to a Lions game, Buchanan?" I step closer and jab my forefinger against his chest. "She'll say, *Oh, the Lions? I've heard of them. It sounds like a fun date night. Can I come too?* Bam. Two tickets instead of one."

His eyes fall to my finger outstretched between us. I pull it into a fist but don't step away.

His gaze flicks to mine. "I don't want my players stripping for you, Brat."

"Why?" I demand, caught between exasperation, anticipation, and my freaking libido, who's decided this would be the perfect time to mess with me.

"I hired you to work and to sell tickets," he seethes. "Not to hook up with my players."

"So that's what this is about?" I let out a dry laugh and shake my head. "You don't want them stripping for me because you think I'll like it?"

The guy looks like he's about to blow a gasket but doesn't confirm my suspicion, so I continue. "Don't get me wrong. Beck's body is fine as shit, but I dated a hockey player once. I will *not* be doing it again." My expression sours at the thought, along with my libido. "And they aren't stripping for me. They're flirting with the camera, which is exactly what they should be doing. I'm not gonna make the Lions look like a bunch of sex fiends. I'm gonna make them look entertaining. And fun. Two things of which you clearly have no understanding."

"You think I'm not entertaining or fun?"

"Says the guy in the stuffy suit?" I run my gaze along his sexy outfit. The jacket fits him like a damn glove and hugs his biceps, all while giving me the perfect view of his long, thick throat. Refusing to let him see how much it affects me, I force a scoff and meet his gaze again. "Yeah, no. But I think the real problem here is whether or not you trust me. You hired me to build a brand and to help sell tickets. That's what I'm trying to do. So tell me, Professor. Do you trust me?"

"Not your professor anymore," he murmurs. His eyes fall to my mouth for the barest of seconds, but I swear I can feel them. Like a caress or some shit, and it leaves me off balance. Unfocused. And a little more turned on than I'd like to be, considering the circumstances.

I drag my tongue along my bottom lip and suck it into my mouth, hoping the sharp bite of pain will help me focus on our actual conversation instead of what Buchanan tastes like.

I *seriously* need to get laid.

Clearing my throat, I ask, "Do you trust me, Henry?"

I've never called him by his first name before. It's always felt too intimate. Too personal. And right now? When our chests are practically smashed together, and his cologne tickles my nostrils, I realize exactly how bad of an idea it really was. To say his name. To feel it roll off my tongue.

Whoa, girl. Breathe.

My cheeks feel hot as a low vibration travels up his throat, and he cocks his head. "You will show me the videos before you post them," he demands.

Videos. Work. *Right.*

I tuck my hair behind my ear and tilt my chin up at him. "I'm going to be posting videos three to four times a day."

"Then you will send me three to four videos a day."

"Are you serious? Even Jeffry isn't making me send any to him for approval."

"I don't give a fuck what Jeffry is or isn't making you do," he tells me. "You will show me every video before you post them."

"Fine," I snap.

His mouth lifts but quickly disappears into his usual look of calculated indifference. "Fine."

10

HENRY

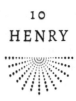

They are good. The videos. Tasteful. Entertaining. Fun.

I'm still not entirely sure why I was triggered in the first place, and I refuse to analyze my reasoning. Besides, all I care about are sales and traction. As long as Mia is delivering on both, I'm happy.

My phone buzzes with another incoming text. I watch the video of the entire team lip-syncing a song I've never heard and send Mia a single word in response.

ME

Approved.

MIA

Thanks, Boss.

My eyes threaten to roll, but I keep them in check and set my phone back on my desk as Erika continues running me through our itinerary for the upcoming week.

"Everything looks really great," she notes. "There was a little hiccup with the hotel for our first away series, but I think I ironed everything out, and we should be good to go on all fronts."

"Sales?" I question.

"Excellent." She looks down at her iPad, scanning the numbers our accounting department sent earlier today. "Season pass tickets are selling forty percent better than we'd initially anticipated, and our online merchandise store is doing really well." Her eyes widen as she takes a closer look at specifics. "Like, incredibly well."

"Good."

"Yeah, I'm not gonna lie. Jeffry was a little concerned when you said you'd handle finding someone to take over social media, but Mia's killing it."

"Good," I repeat, surprised by the jump in my pulse at the mention of Mia. The woman is good at getting on my nerves. Very good.

"Seriously. Excellent choice," Erika compliments. "Where did you meet her? I looked for her resume, but it wasn't in Mia's file."

"She was one of my students at LAU," I reply.

Erika clicks her tongue against the roof of her mouth and nods. "Ah, I see. Well, the players love her, and so does Coach Dawson, so no issues there with travel and everything. Although, I did have a couple players ask if we have a no fraternization policy." She looks up from her iPad and waits expectantly.

My eye spasms, but I shove the unwarranted frustration aside. "No policy."

"All right." She scribbles something on her iPad. "I'll let everyone know."

"Everyone?" My composure slips, but I force it back into place. "Who asked?"

"Brantley Beck, Carlos Greer, and…" She nibbles on the back of her iPad's pen, lost in thought. "Coach Dawson."

"Dawson is too old for Mia."

Erika's brow quirks behind her black-framed glasses. "Dawson's your age."

"I'm too old for Mia."

"Good thing you're not interested in dating her, then." She looks back at her lap and turns her iPad off. "But I'll make a note. Would you like me to pass your opinion along to Dawson, or...?"

I swear the woman is too snarky for her own good. Clearly, we have worked together far too long if she doesn't fear me the way most do. It might bother me if I didn't rely on her so much. She is practically family at this point. Annoying but indispensable, and she knows the truth as well as I do.

Leaning back in the leather office chair, I stare out at the skyline and mutter, "Keep it to yourself, Erika."

"Got it." With a smirk, she stands and heads to my office door but hesitates and turns back toward me. "How's Scarlett doing, anyway?"

I swivel my chair toward her, my gaze narrowing. Erika never asks about Scarlett. She doesn't like her. I'm not entirely sure why, but my girlfriend has always rubbed Erika the wrong way. Even though my assistant is always professional, the subtle huffs and eye rolls whenever Scarlett is around have not escaped my notice. Why would she ask about Scarlett now?

"Scarlett is fine," I answer carefully.

"Still traveling?"

"She came home last night. Why?"

She taps the iPad stylus against her chin and asks, "Isn't she the same age as Mia?" Not giving me a chance to answer, she shrugs one shoulder and adds, "It doesn't matter, of course."

Suspicion swells in my gut. The woman is speaking in

77

riddles, and I have enough on my plate without having to deal with her meddling.

Leaning forward in my chair, I warn, "Get to the point, Erika."

"I'm curious if Scarlett plans to attend this week's away game with you?" Erika returns. "I want to ensure I've booked the correct number of rooms."

"If she's staying with me, I'm not sure it matters how many rooms you book," I point out.

"No offense, but we both know she can be a bit...*particular* when it comes to amenities and such."

"Yes, I'm aware." My annoyance flares, and I rub small circles in my temple. "Don't worry about making any arrangements for her."

"Oh?"

"I have a theory that Scarlett is cheating on me."

"A theory?" Erika prods, yet she doesn't look surprised.

My phone signals another incoming text, but I don't check it as I hold Erika's unreadable stare. "That will be all."

"Of course."

As she leaves, I pick the phone up, scanning the message.

MIA

Here's another one so you don't get your panties in a twist.

I watch the short ten-second clip showcasing Thorne and Taylor passing drinks to each other and grinning while "When You're The Best of Friends" from *The Fox and the Hound* plays in the background. It's ridiculous. And cringeworthy. Yet I find my amusement sparking and end the video early so I can type my response.

ME

Approved.

MIA

Thanks again, Professor.

Professor.

Makes me want to pull a ruler out and smack her ass, but I refrain from playing the scenario in my mind and set my phone back on the desk--again--despite the itch in my fingers to write her back.

Yeah. Pretty sure the girl will be the death of me if I'm not careful.

She may wind up being the death of Dawson too.

And Greer. And Beck.

Part of me wonders if it was a good idea to pass on implementing a no-fraternization policy, but I have never had one, and I refuse to allow Mia to crawl under my skin long enough for it to affect how I run the team.

I have more willpower than that.

Don't I?

Besides, I have enough problems with the opposite sex, and it's past time I rectify the situation.

11

HENRY

Scarlett's red dress hugs her slim figure as she sways toward me. This one is different from the dress she wore to the banquet a few weeks ago. The one I ruined in the bathroom when I ripped the flimsy fabric up to her waist and shoved myself deep inside her.

Her dresses are almost always red.

It's Scarlett's favorite color.

I had booked our dinner reservation for 9 pm. I glance down at my Rolex. It's nine-thirty.

"Hey, sorry I'm late," Scarlett apologizes. She kisses my cheek and sits across from me.

A waiter strides toward us almost instantly, balancing two empty goblets. He sets them down in front of us and pours the Petrus 2016 red wine into the glasses. He opened it when I arrived, allowing the oxidation process to begin. Now, it's time I enjoy it. Or at least, I would if I was sitting across from anyone but Scarlett. After my conversation with Erika, I concluded my patience with this woman is nearly nonexistent. Even the feel of her lips on my cheeks seems lacking.

Insignificant.

This needs to be done. Quickly.

After Scarlett asks for a salad with the dressing on the side, I wave the waiter off without bothering to add my order. I won't be here long enough to enjoy it.

"You aren't ordering anything?" Scarlett asks.

"Afraid not." My phone buzzes in my pocket, interrupting Scarlett's response.

Her red-painted lips pucker with distaste as she watches me pull it out of my slacks.

The message is from Mia, requesting my approval for another video. Without watching it, I type my response.

> ME
>
> Looks fine.

> MIA
>
> Gee, thanks. Did you even watch it, Professor?

> ME
>
> Do I need to?

> MIA
>
> Technically, no, but since you're the pain in the ass who insisted I send them to you for approval, I assumed you'd take the time to actually APPROVE the content before allowing me to post. But hey. You do you, Boss.

"Who is it?" Scarlett questions.

I set my phone screen side down on the tablecloth. "No one."

"You were smiling," she notes.

I was?

I school my features and scratch the five-o'clock shadow along my jaw. "Am I not allowed to smile?"

"Is it a woman?" She reaches for her glass of wine and sips it.

"It's an employee."

"A *woman* employee?" she pushes.

I smooth a small wrinkle in the linen tablecloth. "I'm not sure why it matters, but yes."

"Is she pretty?"

"This is starting to feel like deja vu from the Lions' banquet," I note. My eyes fall on the low 'V' showcasing her cleavage. "You're even wearing a red dress and acting jealous."

"Well, if you play your cards right and stop texting a random woman, I might even let you ruin this one." Her botox-injected forehead doesn't move an inch, but her lips purse as she takes another sip of her wine.

She's upset.

The irony isn't lost on me.

"Or maybe not," she adds.

Irritated she even has the audacity to act jealous, I demand, "Who were you with last week?"

Her lips part, hinting at her surprise, but she recovers quickly. "What do you mean? I told you I was in New York with Gianna."

"Just like you had dinner with her last weekend?" I growl. "And the previous weekend?"

Her lips pull down, and she places her hand on top of mine resting on the table. "I told you Gianna bailed last weekend, and I ended up hanging out with Camila and––"

"Do you think I'm stupid, Scarlett?" I ask.

She jerks back as if I've slapped her, and her hand leaves mine. "What? Of course, I don't think––"

"I think you do." I lean back in my chair and spread my legs wide. "Because I would have to be stupid to *not* piece together what you are doing behind my back."

Again, she reaches for my hand across the table, but I pull it out of her reach.

"I haven't been doing anything behind your back, Henry," she whispers, wringing her fingers in her lap. "I love you. You mean the world—"

"I want all your shit packed and out of my house by the time I return from Creekside."

The blood drains from her face, and she looks around, searching for someone who might snap a photo and document her embarrassment. She doesn't need to worry. I'm embarrassed enough for both of us and made it a point to have security keep all potential reporters and paparazzi from capturing this moment and posting it online.

Still, Scarlett cheated on me. I previously assumed, but now I know with certainty.

Then again, I guess I always knew. I felt it in my gut. It doesn't matter that we never loved each other. It doesn't matter how I'm happier alone than when I'm with her. She still cheated. Still tried to hide it from me. Still attempted to manipulate me.

It's unacceptable.

"No," I decide. "I want your shit packed and out of my house by tomorrow morning."

"You don't mean that, Henry," she whispers. "Give me a chance to explain—"

"We're through, Scarlett." I push the chair away from the table and head to my car parked outside. I had already paid the waiter for the bottle of wine. As for her salad? Well, I think she can handle paying for one meal after charging her fuck-cation to the credit card I gave her.

I need to ask Erika to cancel it tomorrow morning.

But at least it's over. We're over.

At least our sham of a relationship can be laid to rest.

At least I never loved her.

1 2

MIA

Welp. My bags were packed, and the flight was pretty uneventful. I played cards with Beck, then watched part of *The Lord of The Rings* with Colt and Theo. And when we landed, we took a big, fancy bus to the hotel.

It's nice.

Like, super nice.

With gold chandeliers and marble pillars. The most expensive hotel I've ever stayed in was a Fairfield Inn. Still clean. Nice. Comfortable. But compared to this? It might as well have been a trailer park. My lips part as I step past the doorman, taking a seat on one of the sofas across from the in-house bar while Erika checks everyone in.

One by one, the players find their rooms, leaving the hotel lobby more and more empty until only a handful of us remains.

Erika's face turns red as she pulls her iPad from her large Coach purse decorated with little bees and searches for something, but I don't know what she's looking for. A minute later, the hotel manager approaches and stands

84

beside the poor man trying to help Erika. He's apologizing to her. Or at least, I think it's what he's doing. I'm not exactly a lip reader.

The tension, though? The way Erika keeps scanning the lobby and furiously searching her iPad? Yeah. Something is going on, and I have no idea what the problem is.

Another minute goes by, and my curiosity gets the best of me. Standing, I head toward the quiet chaos at the check-in area, but they're too distracted to notice my presence.

"I'm sorry. We're completely booked," the hotel manager says from behind the desk. His fingers tap furiously against the keyboard. He shakes his head as the initial worker manning the desk stands idly beside him. "My associate is right. There's nothing."

"I need four more rooms," Erika states.

"What's the problem?" a low voice barks.

I flinch at the sharpness in Buchanan's voice as he strides toward the check-in area with sure, confident steps.

Erika gulps but explains, "They don't have the last four reservations. I called--"

"I'm sorry, sir," the manager interrupts. "There's a marathon this weekend, and the majority of rooms have been booked for over six months. I understand Miss Brewer,"--the hotel manager motions to Erika--"initially called and made a change to her reservation, but we believe there was a miscommunication on our part, and we don't have enough rooms available for a party your size."

Buchanan's jaw tightens, but he hides his frustration well as he turns to Erika. "How many people still need rooms?"

She scans her iPad for the hundredth time and scoots her wire-rimmed glasses further up the bridge of her nose. "You, Beck, Greer, and Ms. Rutherford. I have family in town, so I wasn't planning to stay at the hotel, or else I'd be more than happy to give up my own room, but--"

"Let me check something," the manager interrupts. The familiar *tap-tap* from his keyboard echoes throughout the nearly silent reception area. He sighs and looks at Buchanan. "We have a two-room suite available, as well as a standard king-sized bed. I'm sorry, but it's the absolute best we can do."

"Don't get me wrong," Greer chirps behind me. His shoulder is pressed against one of the marble pillars in the lobby, and his eyes are glued to his phone. "I love Beck and all, but I'm not sharing a bed with anyone unless it's Mia."

"Dude, if anyone's sharing a bed with Mia, it's me," Beck argues from the couch. I hadn't noticed they'd been eaves-dropping, but apparently, they deserve more credit. Ever the gentlemen, wanting to share a room with a single woman.

Subtle, boys. Really subtle.

I start to tell them off when Buchanan interrupts, "You two will share the suite. Mia will take the standard room for herself."

"And you?" Erika asks him.

He lets out a slow breath but announces, "I'll stay at a different hotel."

"Everywhere is booked," the manager states. "Like I said, because of the marathon this weekend, along with the first game for the Stinging Nettles against the Lions—"

"I'm aware the Lions are playing," Buchanan mutters.

The manager grimaces. "Of course. Well, then you can see why everywhere is at full capacity and no one has any vacancies. Obviously, I'll be happy to call around and see if I can find anything, but I don't want you to have any unrealistic expectations."

"My expectations involved each of us having our own rooms as we initially reserved," Henry growls.

Erika turns to her boss and whispers, "Henry, I swear I didn't do this—"

"It's fine," I interrupt. Silence follows as everyone's attention falls on me. It's like they're surprised I'm here and can speak for myself despite the fact I've been standing in the same spot near the reception desk for the last five minutes. Ignoring their pointed stares, I clear my throat and offer, "Buchanan and I can stay in the same room."

His cold gaze pins me in place, practically burning a hole in the side of my head, but I don't look at him. I simply squeeze Erika's hand instead. "Thanks for helping to figure everything out. Seriously. I can't imagine how stressful this must be."

Erika's frown deepens. "I can't expect you to stay with--"

"Buchanan and I are both adults. We'll be fine." I look up at him. "Right, Boss?"

His nostrils flare. "Apparently."

"Perfect," I announce.

"Perfect," Erika chirps.

"Fucking perfect," Buchanan grunts under his breath.

13

MIA

The elevator ride to our floor is suffocating. Pretty sure smoke will start pouring out of Buchanan's ears at any second. I study him from my periphery, waiting for the angry red and yellow flames to appear from his ears in case I need to duck and cover, but he stays quiet, ignoring me. I can't decide if he's pissed at me or Erika. To be fair, I probably shouldn't have stuck my nose where it didn't belong, but so help me, if Buchanan yelled at one of the nicest people I've ever met in the middle of the hotel lobby all because of a simple misunderstanding, I was gonna lose my shit.

"Ya know, it's not Erika's fault," I defend. "It was an honest mista--"

The ding of the elevator cuts me off, and he motions for me to leave.

"Okay, then," I mutter under my breath.

The wheel on my suitcase squeaks softly as we walk to our room. It cuts through the silence like nails on a chalkboard while Buchanan follows me down the long hallway lined with doors. When we reach ours, I pull the room key out and slide it into the lock, my muscles coiled with tension. Seriously. What's this guy thinking? He's always the definition of detached and controlled, but right now, I swear I can hear the quiet *tick-tick-tick* of a time bomb ready to explode any second now. As I pull the keycard from the lock, a soft *click* sounds, making me flinch, and a little green light appears above the door handle. I push it open.

Yup. It's a standard room like the rest. One king-sized bed sits in the center. It's covered with a white comforter, white sheets, and four pillows. I'll definitely be stealing those. There's also a television sitting on a long, black credenza and a small table and chair tucked in the corner where I'll probably set my laptop for edits after the game.

I slip the strap of my laptop case from my shoulder and set it carefully on the table, finding my disgruntled boss standing near the room's entrance.

"Ya know, if you're gonna throw a fit, I'm pretty sure Greer or Beck would trade you," I tell him.

He glares back at me. "You'd like that, wouldn't you?"

"I don't care who I sleep with––next to," I correct myself. "Actually, scratch that. Greer can be kind of smelly after practice, even after he's showered, so I think I'll pass on him, but Beck's not too bad."

"You're saying you'd prefer to stay with him over me?"

"I'm saying if you're gonna pout because they didn't have your precious reservation, I'm sure Beck would be fine taking your place. But I suggest you make a decision before I unpack and get comfortable."

His annoyance taints the air as he steps inside and slams the door behind him. The sharp sound makes my body jerk, causing a spike of adrenaline and fear to pulse through me while digging up memories I'd prefer to stay in the past. Memories of another surly asshole with a short fuse. I shove them away and square my shoulders.

Yeah, no.

I'm not gonna do this. I'm not gonna play this game or stay in the same room as someone who's clearly pissed off and won't let something so inconsequential go.

Nope. Not happening.

"Forget it," I announce. I hoist my laptop case back onto my shoulder and head toward the door. "I'm going to ask Beck if I can stay in his room, so you can have this one all to yourself."

I start to step past him, but he blocks my way, his firm grasp wrapping around my bicep as he towers over me. We've been here before—at the rink. The testosterone wafting off him in this moment is potent, leaving me speechless.

"Don't," he growls.

I tilt my head up, meeting his tumultuous gaze. "You're the one throwing a tantrum, not me."

"I am not throwing a tantrum."

"Then what would you call it?" I challenge.

"Do you like Beck?"

I blink slowly, convinced I've heard him wrong. "What?"

"Do. You. Like. Beck?"

"I don't like *anyone*," I clarify.

"So, you aren't interested in anyone on the team?"

"One, no. Like I've already said, I dated a hockey player once, and it blew up in my face. I will *not* let it happen again. And, two, why do you even care?"

"I don't." His firm grasp on my arm disappears, but he doesn't back away. "I simply prefer when my businesses run smoothly. I don't like when unanticipated events throw a wrench in them."

"Such as this?" I glance at the freshly-made bed to my right.

His chin dips. "Exactly."

"Okay. I'll go sleep with Be--"

"You're not sleeping with Beck."

"Oh, I'm not?"

"No. You're not."

"Then, who am I sleeping with, Boss?"

The man grinds his teeth, glancing at the bathroom behind me and down at his suit.

"Is there a problem?" I question.

"I need to shower before the game."

My brows pinch. "Okay?"

"I don't usually share a room with other people."

"Neither do I, but it's not a big deal."

His left eye spasms, hinting it most definitely *is* a big deal, though he stays quiet. I shouldn't be offended, but I kind of am. Like seriously. What's his problem? Most guys would jump at the opportunity to stay in the same room with me. I take showers. I smell nice. Sure, I can be a little messy sometimes, but I've never had a guy complain. And it's not like I'm gonna jump his bones or anything.

When I feel like I'm drowning in his silence, I huff, "Look, if it's a problem, I'll stay with Beck."

"You're staying here."

He jerks at the belt around his waist, giving me whiplash. The sound of leather slapping does weird things to me as he tosses it onto the bed, yet I'm too stunned to do anything but stand here.

"What are you doing?" I ask.

"I need to shower off the airplane." He slips his suit jacket off and lays it carefully on the mattress. Even his direct movements do nothing to hide the frustrated beast barely restrained beneath his indifferent facade.

I stand there motionless, my brain attempting to catch up with what's happening in front of me, but I'm as lost as before.

He releases the buttons on his cuffs, and his expert fingers begin undoing the ones down his front. Inch by inch, his tan skin is exposed, and my lips part on their own volition.

"What are you doing?" I whisper.

"I already told you."

"Bathroom's over there," I remind him, but my eyes don't leave the smooth tan skin dusted with hair.

"I'm aware."

"Then what are you doing?" I repeat, my voice even more breathless. More embarrassed.

Is it hot in here?

"Changing."

"In front of me," I point out.

"Are you telling me you haven't been in the locker rooms?" he challenges.

"I've been in the locker rooms."

"Then you've seen a naked chest."

"Well, yeah. But…" My voice trails off as I find the happy trail leading to the waist of his slacks and the package not so well hidden beneath.

Holy shit is that his––

"Is there a problem, Ms. Rutherford?"

My gaze snaps back to his. "I'm curious if your girlfriend would approve of you stripping in front of me while having a hard-on."

"I don't have a hard-on."

I stare at the bulge in his pants as if to say, *exhibit A* and bring my attention back to Buchanan's stupidly arrogant yet indecipherable gaze.

"Maybe I'm just big," he offers.

"Then I'd say your girlfriend's lucky," I quip, "*if* you weren't currently talking about the size of your package while undressing in front of an employee."

"I don't have a girlfriend."

I pull back, surprised. "What about Scarlett?"

Slipping his shirt off, he adds it to the carefully placed suit jacket on the bed. The guy's half-naked, the heat from his skin warming my own. He's so close I can touch him. I won't. But I could. Hell, I'm pretty sure if I leaned forward another inch, my nose would drag along his chest, and I'd be given front-row tickets to his rich, earthy scent.

"Why didn't you tell me she was cheating on me?" he demands.

I blink and lift my eyes to his. "Why would I have known your girlfriend was cheating on you?"

"Don't play stupid, Brat." He undoes the top button on his slacks but hesitates. "She used my card at SeaBird more times than I can count. Why didn't you tell me?"

He's right. I did know. I've known for months. The way she'd bring her boy toys to SeaBird. Dancing with them. Touching their chests or biceps. Hell, it was like foreplay. There's a difference between innocent flirting and full-blown, I'm-sleeping-with-the-person touching. And Scarlett? She was clearly sleeping with them. Each and every one of them.

"Answer the question," Buchanan growls.

"You really wanna know why I didn't tell you about your girlfriend cheating on you?"

"Yes."

"Because guys are assholes, and what Scarlett was doing was none of my business." Even I can hear the animosity in my voice. The resentment buried deep in my bones, thanks to Shorty. But I never claimed to be unbiased when it comes to the opposite sex, and guys? Yeah. They're assholes. Even the one in front of me.

"Am I an asshole?" he asks.

93

My gaze slides down his half-naked body. "You tell me," I challenge.

Glancing at his neatly folded pile of clothes on the bed, he mutters, "I have a thing about germs…"

"A *thing*?" I question.

"I don't like having my clothes in the bathroom." He almost shivers at the prospect alone. I bite the inside of my cheek to keep from showing my amusement. Who knew the guy's kryptonite involved something so…random?

"Oh," I murmur, unsure what else I'm supposed to say.

He scratches his jaw. "Yeah."

"And you couldn't have told me *before* I caught a glimpse of your…?" I motion to his crotch area.

"Didn't think you would look."

"Of course you didn't," I say, my tone laced with amusement. "And I wasn't, by the way. You just threw me off a little when you started undressing."

"I'm not used to sharing a room with other people," he repeats.

"Not even Scarlett?"

"We understood each other's boundaries." He says it like I should understand them too.

I gnash my lips together before offering, "To be fair, if I knew them in the first place, I might be a little more accommodating."

"Like right now?" He reaches for the button on top of his slacks again and waits.

"Oh." I turn around and face the wall as the familiar sound of a zipper lowering causes my heart rate to pitch a fit. He has no idea what I'd give to turn around and see if he's lying about his girth, but I stay strong and stare at the closed blinds across the room. A few seconds later, a quiet click greets me, and I glance over my shoulder.

He's gone.

94

Into the bathroom.

And me? Well, I'm left weirdly sexually aroused and more confused than I have any right to be, considering the circumstances. Unsure what to do when I hear the shower turn on, I rock back on my heels and rub my hands up and down my arms.

That was weird, wasn't it?

I shouldn't read into anything. Even the fact he broke up with Scarlett has nothing to do with me and everything to do with her side pieces. So I shouldn't care, and it definitely shouldn't matter.

And neither should our sleeping arrangement tonight.

The bed taunts me as I stare at the crisp sheets, well aware I'll be sharing them with a guy who's newly single, sexy as hell, and has a weird way of getting under my skin and annoying me like no one else on the planet.

Yeah. This will be a walk in the park.

I almost roll my eyes as I head back to the desk and pull my laptop out. Might as well get some work done, and I sure as shit could use the distraction.

14

HENRY

I should have told her about my hang-up with having my clothes in the bathroom before I started stripping, but I had hoped she would take the hint and give me some privacy. Instead, Mia's baby blues sparked with curiosity, which is the last thing I need. Not when I'm already struggling with Greer and Beck and Dawson all being interested in her.

I shouldn't care.

I shouldn't get involved.

And I definitely should not have noticed the way she flinched when I slammed the door.

What happened to her?

I asked Gordy if he could link any social media accounts to Mia's ex, curious if he had finally let her go since moving a few states away. Gordy found two. Mia blocked one, but the other is a fake account tied to one of Shorty's email addresses. The handle is hattrick69. Mia wouldn't know it belongs to her ex, but he has liked every post. Every video. Every fucking comment. And there is nothing I can do about it. After sharing his findings, Gordy asked if he should delete the account, but I'm afraid Shorty will only create a new one. Instead, I told Gordy to let it slide but monitor Shorty's activity. At least he has kept his distance--physically, anyway--since graduating from LAU despite following her online. Hopefully, it stays this way.

~

THE GAME GOES TERRIBLY, AND WE LOSE. ERIKA apologized--again--for the sleeping arrangement, and the hotel reimbursed us for our room. I don't need the money, but I appreciate their determination to make things right.

After spending the rest of the night in the hotel bar, I head upstairs, unable to avoid my room any longer.

The bathroom door is closed when I walk in. The familiar sound of running water confirms Mia is probably taking a shower. After changing into a pair of sweats and a T-shirt, I stare at the stack of extra bedding the hotel delivered to our room in case we changed our minds about sharing the bed, unsure what to do. The idea of sleeping on the floor makes me feel like a bolt of lightning is penetrating my chest, but the idea of sleeping next to Mia is even more precarious.

I should have had another shot.

Tonight might be an inconvenience for my sanity, but it was the lesser of two evils. The idea of Mia sleeping next to Beck or Greer is even worse.

The shower cuts off, and I force myself to move, grabbing the maroon blankets from the stack on the credenza. I spread them on the dark industrial carpet. Shivers climb up my spine at the prospect of sleeping on it for the night, but I ignore them.

I definitely should have had another shot.

I don't like germs. And hotel floors are covered in them. Thankfully, years of therapy have reined in my obsessive tendencies, making most of them bearable. Usually. Bathrooms are still a trigger, though. Urine. Shit. Vomit. I almost shiver. At least the carpet doesn't smell.

I'll be fine.

With the bed separating me from the bathroom, I sprawl on the floor and stare at the ceiling, willing myself to fall asleep and get the next eight hours over with.

Quiet footsteps pad across the room, and Mia calls out, "Professor?"

"Not your professor anymore," I grumble from the floor.

"Where are––*oh*." Her head peeps around the top of the mattress. The bathroom light casts shadows around her nearly naked body. "What are you doing?"

I close my eyes. "Trying to sleep."

"On the floor?"

"Apparently."

"Okay. Come on, big boy." She taps my shoulder and offers her hand, but I don't take it, too distracted by the towel wrapped around her lithe frame.

"Where are your clothes?" I ask as her hand hangs between us untouched.

"I forgot to take them into the bathroom with me. Now, will you please get in bed like a normal person so I can grab my pajamas and go to sleep?"

Realizing I'm blocking her from reaching her suitcase in the corner of the room, I take her offered hand and stand. My legs feel like rubber, thanks to the alcohol swimming in my veins, but I barely notice. I'm too distracted by the scent of coconut clinging to her damp skin.

Fuck.

She takes a shallow, unsteady breath, and her breasts brush against my chest. The slight caress shoots straight to my groin. Her gaze drops to the ground, and she tiptoes around me. My dick stirs in my sweats, but I step aside.

Dangerous.

The girl is dangerous.

A lamp rests on the nightstand. I flip it on so she can search through her luggage easier.

Her long, lean legs are missing the same ink wrapped around her arm and shoulder. Her long blonde hair is still wet, hanging in thick strands down her back as she rummages through her suitcase, pretending I didn't feel her nipples against my chest.

The image in front of me is such a stark contrast to the girl I've come to know, I'm fucking speechless. Her face is free from her usual dark makeup. That alone makes her look like a stranger. No thick upper lashes. No concealer hiding her freckles. Earrings still adorn the shell of her ears, but otherwise? Nothing. It's as if the armor she is used to shrouding herself in has finally been removed, giving me a glimpse of a stranger. I've seen pictures of her from before her father died. She was a cheerleader. With golden highlights. Natural makeup. And a cheerful personality. After everything went down, she lined her eyes in black, dyed her hair a silvery shade of blonde with black underneath, tattooed her skin, and became obsessed with piercings.

So. Damn. Different.

I don't prefer one look over the other, but the glimpse of the girl from before her dad's death is...*staggering*.

Clutching a white T-shirt and black panties against her chest, she turns around and catches me staring at her. I should turn away. I should pretend the window is suddenly fascinating. I should turn the light off and lay back on the ground so I can sleep the alcohol off. Instead, I hold her gaze, waiting for her to make the next move.

"What are you looking at?" she asks. It isn't an accusation. It's genuine curiosity. As if she can't believe I might be looking at her in her natural state.

99

My hands itch to grab her. To tangle my fingers in her long hair, wrap it around my fist, and work off my frustration. At Scarlett. At Shorty. At tonight's loss. At the fucking hotel for screwing up our reservation. I'm so amped up, the voice of reason is long gone, leaving me on the precipice of making a huge mistake. Unclenching my hands at my sides, I force them apart one finger at a time while her eyes hold mine.

"Is there a problem, Boss?" she quips.

"Didn't know you had freckles."

"Oh." Her fingers brush against the bridge of her nose, and she drops her hand back to her side. "You should sleep in the bed. I can stay on the floor."

"Not going to happen."

"I'm used to roughing it, Professor. You, on the other hand..." Her brow arches as she scans me up and down.

"Are you always a brat?" I ask, more amused than I should be, but I can't help it. Maybe it's the alcohol, but I like the snark. The dry sense of humor. The sharp tongue and the no-bullshit attitude accompanying it.

Her arms fold, pressing her breasts together. My mouth waters.

"Are you always this stubborn?" she returns.

Tearing my attention from her cleavage, I order, "You're taking the bed, Mia."

"Fine. You're taking it with me."

"Not a good idea."

"I'm not gonna jump your bones or anything if you're worried about it. I'm not looking for someone to date. A good fuck, maybe, but I have a feeling you're too uptight to make me come, so--"

"You think I can't make you come?" I demand.

She bats her blonde lashes at me. "I'm not your type, remember?"

I catch myself staring at the terry cloth knot tucked between her tits and clear my throat.

She has no fucking clue.

The things I could do to her.

The way I could make her feel.

But it's a bad idea.

For both of us.

Even inebriated, I know it's true.

"You're right," I lie. "You're not my type."

"Then what's the problem?"

"No problem at all."

"Good," she says.

"Good."

"Good," she repeats, huffing and marching to the bathroom. Against my better judgment, I slip beneath the covers on the bed and stare at the ceiling like I was when she exited the shower.

I'm curious.

Fuck me, I'm curious.

And I haven't been curious about anyone in years. Even Scarlett was nothing but a distraction. A pretty and convenient one, but a distraction nonetheless.

Mia?

She's fucking gorgeous. But convenient?

Hardly.

Sleeping with her would be a terrible idea. Even contemplating it is dangerous. And considering it while sleeping beside her in this bed? It's practically suicide.

But making her come? For only one night because she thinks I can't?

The bathroom door opens a few minutes later, followed by the sound of rustling cloth. The bed dips as she slides under the comforter, drags it up to her chin, and slips a hot pink eye mask over her face.

Seriously?

She sleeps in one of those things?

It clashes with the badass persona she wears like a second skin, but it only feeds my curiosity. My interest. I bite back my amusement as I take her in beside me. I don't comment on it, choosing to flip the lamp beside the bed off instead.

She shifts beside me and lets out a slow breath. The soft sound shoots straight to my dick, and I give into it. Letting it wash over me. Letting it spur me on. I blame the darkness. The scotch. The shit week. The loss of tonight's game. The knowledge that Mia isn't like others, which she's proven time and time again.

"You're looking for someone to fuck?" My voice cuts through the silent room.

"Buchanan," she whines. "Go to sleep."

"It's what you said, right? You're not looking for someone to date, but someone to fuck is on the table?"

"Can we drop it, please?"

"You really think I can't make you come?"

Shoving her eye mask on top of her head, she shifts onto her side, rests her weight on her elbow, and looks at me. It's dark, but the moonlight filters through the hotel window, making her the sexiest thing I've ever laid eyes on. Every inch. Every freckle. Every curve.

"I was spouting off bullshit, okay?" she huffs. "It's what I do, so ignore me."

Ignore her?

Does she have any idea how impossible it is? How much she intrigues me? Gets under my skin? Drives me insane? And she thinks I can simply...ignore her?

"Put your sleep mask back in place," I order, lifting the sheets and dipping my head beneath them.

Her breath hitches, but she doesn't move as I maneuver myself closer to her.

"Buchanan, what are you doing?"

"Spread your thighs for me," I grit out. The sheets are already warm, having stolen her body heat as she shifts slightly beneath the comforter and makes room for me.

"Buchanan," she repeats. The warning is on the tip of her tongue, tainting my last name, but she opens her legs a little more, and I slide to the bottom of the bed, settling between her thighs.

"You should know I don't appreciate being underestimated." Only a thin scrap of black lace covers her pussy, and I breathe her in, committing her scent to memory. I'm unsure if I'm drunk on scotch or if Mia is the one leaving me dizzy, but I don't question it. My mouth waters even more, and my dick strains against my sweats, the last of my logic dissipating into thin air as my meal lies in front of me. I lean closer, sucking her lips through the flimsy fabric, and she squirms.

"Wait." The word is nothing but a breath, yet it cuts through the alcohol, and I pull back a few inches. Waiting.

Her breathing is unsteady, and her hips shift slightly in front of me as if she can't help herself. As if her body wants me even if her mind doesn't.

Trust me, Mia. The feeling's mutual.

"Are you drunk?" she asks.

"Buzzed," I counter.

"So, drunk," she clarifies.

"Not drunk enough to regret this."

She squirms beneath me again, and I nip at her inner thigh but don't move closer to her pussy. Not unless she gives me permission.

"One night only," she whispers. "And we never speak of this again. *Ever.* Understand?"

"I hear you loud and clear, Brat."

I spread her legs even wider and massage small circles

along the divots between her thighs and underwear with my thumbs. She relaxes instantly. I haven't been this interested in foreplay in a long time. In making a girl come. In rocking a girl's world simply to prove I can. I blow softly against her center, testing how sensitive she is. Mia's hands find the back of my head.

"Lick me." She lifts her hips and pushes my face against her as if she's already aching for my touch, and I revel in the power as I hook my thumb along the thin black lace and push it to the side. It's too dark to see much beneath the covers, but the lack of light only heightens my senses. My curiosity. My desire. I slowly suck on her lips again, this time without the barrier of her thong, letting her scent wash over me and drive me insane.

And I *am* being driven insane.

Since the moment I heard her name. Since the moment I saw it on my class roster. Since the moment she poured my first drink at SeaBird and countless times after. This woman makes me crazy, and now, I want to do the same. I want to drive her wild. To make her unhinged. To make her come harder than ever. I nibble on her pussy, but I don't dive in. Instead, I wait. For her desperation to take hold. Her need. A soft mewl echoes from the other side of the sheets, and her thighs tense with anticipation.

"So help me, Professor, if you don't lick me--"

I lick at her center, swiping at her juices with the flat of my tongue.

"Yes, just like that," she whimpers.

If you insist.

She's already drenched and tastes like fucking heaven as I lick her again. Spreading her folds with my fingers, I kiss her deeper, dragging my tongue along her slit and dipping it inside her. Honey. She tastes like honey. Sweet. I find her clit and nibble it softly, grinding my dick against the mattress. I want to be inside her. Mark her. Claim her. Fuck her into oblivion. My self-restraint slips further and further from my grasp with every passing second as I eat her, shoving my hands beneath her and lifting her to my mouth.

"Fuck, Boss," she rasps. "So good."

Setting her ass back down, I slip my finger inside her. She's velvety and smooth and so damn wet I can only imagine how good it would feel to have my cock inside her. To feel her squeezing it instead of my finger. I flick the tip of my tongue against her nub again, letting her juices soak my hand as she grinds against me.

"*Really* good." Her grip tightens in my hair as her moans fill the air. She tugs at the roots and hooks her legs around my shoulders, anxious to come. To fall over the edge.

Her muscles quiver beneath my touch, and I quicken my pace, thrusting my fingers in and out of her, pressing my opposite hand against the soft skin above her pubic bone. Latching onto her clit again, I suck softly, savoring her taste as my dick turns to steel.

Fuck, I want this. Want her. Even if it's only for one night. Even if it's only to prove I can make her come. Even if this is all I ever get. A taste. It's the most pleasurable hell a guy could ask for, and I want to drown in it. To drown in her.

"Fuck!" She grabs onto the sheets on either side of my head, fisting the white fabric as her hips lift over and over, meeting my mouth until air is a luxury, one I don't need. Not now. Not with Mia's pussy pressed against my tongue.

She comes with a scream, and it's the hottest thing I have ever heard in my entire life. Her muscles go limp as I crawl up her body, pressing kisses along her belly, finding her lips parted and her sleep mask still firmly in place.

I want to bury myself inside her, but I won't. Not tonight. Not like this. Not when I already crossed a line. I might be buzzed, but I'm not stupid.

Leaning forward, I brush my lips against hers and murmur, "Good girl."

"Condom?" she whispers.

I shake my head. "Told you I could make you come."

She reaches for her sleep mask, but I keep her hand in place.

"Don't ever question me again." I let her hand go and shift onto my side of the bed. "Goodnight, Brat."

"You're serious?"

"Get some rest."

Her tongue darts out between her lips, but she gives in and whispers, "Goodnight, Professor."

Then, I sleep.

Or at least try to.

It's not exactly easy, considering my dick is wide awake, and she smells like heaven. Seriously, what kind of body wash is she using? Coconut...something.

I roll over onto my opposite side and squeeze the base of my cock roughly while listing off my entire roster before finally falling into a restless sleep.

15

HENRY

She's still asleep when I wake up. Her soft snores and constant shifting made it almost impossible to get any rest. Or maybe it's because I've been too amped up to sleep after lying in bed with Mia's taste on my tongue. Regardless, I gave up an hour ago. Instead, I ordered room service, took another shower, and am now answering emails. There are a lot of them. But the one from my father grabs my attention, and I open it against my better judgment while sipping my black coffee. He saw the score from last night's game.

Fucking great.

Like a bloodhound, Mia lifts her nose into the air, and the mattress shifts as she shoves her pink eye mask onto the top of her head.

"Do I smell coffee?" she croaks.

I nod.

"Did you get me any?"

"Didn't know if you wanted any," I tell her, but it's a lie. I considered ordering some but decided against it, unsure how she would take the gesture and unwilling to find out, especially after last night.

I should regret what we did, but I don't. Besides, it didn't mean anything. I didn't even orgasm. I simply proved I could make her come. But she was right. It was a one-time thing, and I need to make sure we're both on the same page. I need to be sure I don't treat her differently simply because I now know what she tastes like.

"Didn't know if I wanted any coffee?" she repeats with a gasp. "Um, did Grizzly Adams have a beard?" Without waiting for me to offer it, she snatches the mug from my grasp and takes a sip, smiling against the rim of the cup as the coffee hits her taste buds. "Mmm. Thank you." Handing it back to me, she stands and lifts her hands over her head, stretching and yawning, giving me a glimpse of the thigh tattoo hidden beneath the hem of the towel last night.

Apparently, she does have tattoos in locations other than her arm. Interesting. I was too preoccupied with her little whimpers of appreciation to notice last night.

When she catches me staring, she murmurs, "Like whatcha see, Boss? Because from what I recall, we both agreed to one night only."

"It still stands." I take a sip from my mug. A voice inside my head notes she drank from the cup, too, but I don't mind. If it was anyone else, I would.

I can feel her watching me. Waiting to see if I'm going to fall at her feet and beg her to fuck me or some shit. Instead, I set the coffee down and reread my father's message. Along with his note about the game, there is something about budgets and a family dinner and a few referrals for B-Tech Enterprises I should keep an eye out for, but almost none of it sinks in.

"I'm gonna go for a run," Mia announces.

I tear my attention from the computer and look up at her. "A run?"

"Is that a problem?"

"You don't know the city."

"I'm pretty sure I know how to read a few street signs."

"There's a marathon going on."

"I think I can handle staying away from a large group of people, Buchanan." She grabs her running shoes from her suitcase.

"Are you bringing your phone?"

"Are you my father?" she counters.

"I want to keep my employees safe."

With the sneakers dangling from her fingertips, she crosses her arms. "So if I were Beck, Thorne, Greer, Taylor, or Mortinson, would you be saying the same thing?"

"Depends," I return. "Are you running with them?"

"If I was, would you be jealous?"

I turn back to my laptop and don't look at her again. "Have a fun run. Don't get caught in a marathon or anything."

"Gee, thanks." She rummages through her luggage for a few minutes. Disappearing into the bathroom, she returns wearing a pair of black shorts and a matching sports bra. Her hair is pulled up into a high ponytail, but her face is still free of makeup as she fiddles with her earphones.

She's the sexiest thing I have ever laid eyes on.

And knowing what she tastes like?

My hard-on practically weeps.

Without bothering to say goodbye, she leaves the room as I attempt to focus on my emails once more, but it's fucking impossible because all I see is her.

~

IT'S BEEN FIFTY-SEVEN MINUTES. I DON'T KNOW HOW LONG Mia usually runs, but it doesn't ease the worry as I try to keep myself busy while avoiding the time on the right corner of my laptop like it's the Plague.

After another thirty minutes, the hotel room door opens, revealing a sweaty Mia. She's squeezing something against her palm, looking as if she's been caught with her hand in the proverbial cookie jar.

I cock my head. "What's in your hand?"

"Uh..." She looks down at the wad in her grasp and tosses it toward her luggage. Over the past several hours, it has slowly turned into a lump of laundry in the corner of the room. The girl is messier than a teenager.

"It's nothing," she announces. "I'm gonna shower."

I lean over in my chair and pick up the wad of red, white, and blue ribbon, lifting it until it unravels. *Thirteenth Annual Creekside Marathon* is stamped on the front of a silver medallion.

"Hey, that's mine!" She reaches for the medal, but I keep it from her grasp.

"You were gone for eighty-seven minutes," I tell her.

"You timed me?"

"Did you run an entire marathon in eighty-seven minutes, Mia?"

Her lips are nothing but a slash of pink against her unreadable expression as she crosses her arms. She does it a lot when she's flustered. The tinge of pink in her cheeks is a nice touch.

"It's what? A three-and-a-half-minute mile?" I suggest. "I knew you were in shape, Brat, but I didn't think you were quite so fast."

Shoulders slouching, she mutters, "Okay, I didn't run a marathon."

Tongue in cheek, I fight back my amusement. "So why do

you have a medal for one?"

"I may have...."—she clears her throat—"*accidentally* stumbled onto the course during my fourth mile."

"Accidentally?"

Her lips purse even more. "Okay, you were right. I got a little lost and wound up in the middle of a marathon. Well, *middle* might be a stretch," she clarifies. "It was more like the last tenth of the marathon, but––"

"What happened?" I demand.

"I was running and got a little turned around," she mumbles, playing with the end of her ponytail while looking everywhere in the room except where I'm sitting.

"And?"

With a huff, she flings her ponytail back over her shoulder and folds her arms. "And, the next thing I know, I take a right turn and find a big balloon arch a quarter mile down the road. At this point, I'm thinking I should probably get off the course, ya know? So, I try to climb over the barriers, but they're lined with people cheering for everyone. Instead of letting me through, they tell me I'm almost there, and I can't quit now while pushing me back onto the road."

Amusement simmers beneath the surface, but I keep it in check as I close the laptop on the small hotel table, giving her my full attention. "What happened next?"

"I crossed the finish line, and someone handed me a cookie and put a medal around my neck."

"So, you cheated," I muse.

"I didn't cheat. I didn't even sign up in the first place."

"Did you tell them?"

The girl has the decency to look sheepish. "Well, no."

"Why not?"

"Because the cookie looked really good, and––"

I snort.

"Oh, shut up. It was chocolate chip. We both know no one turns down chocolate chip."

"I prefer oatmeal raisin," I counter.

She snorts. "Of course you do. Regardless, I...just got a little lost."

"So you should have listened to me," I point out.

Her nose scrunches. "Okay. I should've listened to you. Happy now?"

"Quite." I hand the medal back to her. "Will you have enough time to shower before our flight to Michigan?"

"Yup. Planning on it. Did you already shower?"

"Yes."

"Good. 'Cause if I have to see you walking around half-naked again, I might lose it." As the words leave her lips, her eyes slide down my body. I doubt she does it on purpose.

No, the girl would never. And for some reason, it makes me want to push her against the wall and fuck her into oblivion.

But what's worse? The black sports bra, toned stomach, and ink swirling on all of her smooth skin on full display in front of me. I never liked tattoos. Not on myself. Not on others. But on Mia? I want to study them. Ask about them. Why she got them. Which one is her favorite.

One. Night. Only.

When she catches me staring, she pops out her hip. "Is there a problem, Buchanan?"

"No problem." I tear my attention from her toned stomach and reopen my laptop. "I'm going to get back to work."

"Have fun."

The bathroom door closes a minute later, and I breathe out the oxygen held hostage in my lungs.

Yeah. I need to get on our flight and leave Creekside behind me as soon as possible.

16

MIA

"Come on!" I yell as a defender from the Blazers slams Colt against the ice. I glance down at my camera, confirming Colt's centered on the screen. Yup. I'm capturing the whole thing on video. It'll be great for views. Not so great for Colt's shoulder and face. Poor guy. He'll definitely be feeling it tomorrow. Good thing hockey players wear helmets.

Pissed, Theo and Mortinson, one of the Lions' defenders, race toward the scuffle near the glass and body-check the guy like they're wrecking balls, peeling him away from their teammate. A few more Blazers rush toward the chaos, and a brawl starts within seconds. The referees blow their whistles and break the players apart.

It's freaking social media gold.

Afterward, the next play begins, and I stop recording, checking the footage with a sly grin. I'm gonna have to send this bad boy to Blakely because this makes her fiancé look *hot*. Once the replay is over, I lift the camera and catch a few players being escorted to the penalty box, thanks to the fight. A voice in the crowd behind me catches my attention.

"Hey! Hey, you!"

I peek over my shoulder to find a forty-something-year-old man staring at me. A red and yellow Blazers jersey is stretched across his beer belly, and he's balancing a plastic cup filled with amber liquid.

Yeah, I most definitely do not recognize the dude. Convinced he's calling for someone else, I turn back toward the ice and raise my camera into the air.

"Mia, right?" he yells. "You're Mia?"

Fear clogs my throat, but I don't look at him again. I keep my eyes glued to the rink, the players blurring together in a mess of orange, yellow, black, and white. This has happened before. Only a few times, and not since I started working with the Lions, but still. I know how it plays out. Thanks to Shorty outing me, someone connects my OF account to my other social media platforms after a quick Google search of my name. And when they see me in public, they ask for a photograph, or a private show, or…something. I tell them no, and they throw a fit, become aggressive, or call me a slut, a whore, or any other not-so-clever name they can think of. But now is not the time.

"Yeah, you're Mia!" the stranger decides. I swear I can feel him stalking down the steps and heading toward me. A barrier separates the players' bench from the stands, but it doesn't make me feel any better. I don't know how, but some strange, innate instinct tells women when a predator is nearby, and I feel it right now. I feel it from the top of my head to the tip of my toes. The discomfort catches in my chest and sinks lower in my gut, making me nauseated. Cotton forms in my mouth as I keep my eyes on the camera, but the image continues blurring into a mess of colors, losing focus while Colt slaps the puck toward Wells, the right wing, fifteen feet away from me.

"Hey, baby! Stop ignoring me! I just wanna talk!" the stranger calls.

My spine is like a steel rod.

"Come on! I wanna know if you'll lift your shirt for me!"

Turning on my heel, I rush down the tunnel to the locker room, my pulse thrumming faster and faster with every step as his words echo through my mind.

I should be out there. I should be filming. I should be--

Angry roars explode from where I came from, and I hang my head. I missed something. I don't know what it was, but the Lions pissed off the home team. They could've scored or blocked a shot or started a fight or...*something*, and I missed it. I won't have the footage for later. I won't be able to use it to promote the team.

"Fuck," I seethe under my breath as I drop my camera, letting it hang from the strap around my neck. Shoving my hands through my hair, I push it away from my face and attempt to steady my breathing.

I should go back. I should ignore him. It's not like he could've reached me, anyway. It would've been fine. I'm safe. He can't touch me. Not when there are so many people around. He probably wouldn't touch me anyway, even if I *was* alone. Not all guys are Shorty. Not all guys are out to get me.

It's fine.

I'm fine.

"Does Buchanan pay you to be in here during a game?" a cold, detached voice demands. It mingles with the familiar sound of shoes on concrete.

My spine straightens as I balance my camera in one hand and face the culprit.

Seriously?

The guy hasn't said two words to me since our initial

meeting in the arena at my first practice, and now he shows up? Jeffry needs to get laid--and soon--because the stick up his ass is starting to get on my nerves.

"I needed to use the restroom," I tell him.

"You missed the highlight of the game because you couldn't hold your bladder for three more minutes until the period ended?" Jeffry challenges with his hands shoved into his pockets. "You really think that'll fly with the board when they find out?"

Man, I want to punch him.

Instead, I raise my chin and hold his gaze. "It won't happen again."

"What won't happen again?" Buchanan interjects.

Seriously? Is the locker room the place to be tonight or something?

"She missed one of the game's biggest highlights," Jeffry explains. His tone is thick with condescension.

Buchanan's stone-cold gaze turns from Jeffry to me. "Is there a reason you aren't where you're supposed to be?"

Is there a reason you *aren't where you're supposed to be?* I want to spit back at him, but I close my eyes and count to three as all the reasons why I'd be smart to keep this job flash through my mind. It doesn't matter how much I want to reach out and smack Jeffry across the face. I need to keep my impulses in check.

Need. Not want. *Need.*

Breathe, I remind myself. Peeling my eyes open, I paste on a smile. "I needed to use the restroom. Like I said, I'm sorry. I'll make sure to not drink as much water before a game from now on. It won't happen again."

Silence follows my excuse as Buchanan's eyes thin. It's like he doesn't believe me. To be fair, I wouldn't believe me, either. But right now, I don't give a shit. I need to get back to the rink. I need to do my job. I need to be stronger than this. To not let random assholes affect me.

"Everything okay?" Buchanan prods, watching as I shift my weight from one foot to the other. His question isn't warm. But it isn't necessarily cold, either. It's...detached. Bland. But with a sharp undertone hinting he almost cares. *Almost.* If I didn't know him better, I might even believe him. But I do know him. And if there's anything I've witnessed more times than I can even count, he's all about the bottom line. All about the rules and how they must be followed. All about the job and how it must be completed. No. Matter. What.

And the fact I'm in the locker room instead of filming more content for the Lions? Well...I dropped the ball, and we both know it. Which means I better have a good excuse locked and loaded if I don't want to piss him off. Too bad I can't give him one.

I force myself to nod, answering, "Everything's great, grand, and wonderful. Now, if you'll excuse me..."

Without a backward glance, I head to the rink as the buzzer sounds, ending the second period.

The team ambles past me before I even have a chance to reach the bench, but I don't follow them back to the locker room. My feet stay rooted to the concrete inside the tunnel. Because I don't want to face Buchanan or Jeffry again. But I don't want to go to the rink by myself, either. It's stupid, but I can't help it. The desire to blend in. To not be seen or noticed. Not when my head is a jumble of regret, guilt, and...fear.

Is he still out there?

Is he waiting for me?

Once the next period starts, I keep to the shadows, avoiding the stands as if my life depends on it, only casting a peek into the crowd when I can't take the niggling sensation in the back of my mind for another second. Thankfully, the guy's gone.

If only he'd taken the heebie-jeebies he gave me with him.

17

HENRY

With her iPad in one arm, Erika walks into my office, announcing, "Quite the game last night."

Jeffry is already seated across from my desk. We flew in from Michigan early this morning, but there is still plenty we need to catch up on.

"The game was fine," I agree. We won during the last fifteen seconds of the third period. It almost takes away the sting from the Creekside loss.

"And the videos Mia is posting seem to be bringing in quite a bit of traction," Erika mentions.

"Too bad she missed two of the best plays in the whole Michigan game," Jeffry counters.

As Erika continues toward her seat across from my desk, she argues, "Personally, I don't blame her for needing a minute to herself after all the goading from that man."

I freeze, the words washing over me like a frigid bucket of water.

"What man?" I sit forward in my chair and lace my fingers in front of me.

"The man in the stands," Erika clarifies. She casts an awkward look at Jeffry as if hoping he'll take the hint and fill me in, but he stays quiet, so she turns to me again. "The one who wouldn't stop leering at her? And the awful things he was yelling at her? Well…" She clutches the strand of pearls around her neck. "Needless to say, I don't blame Thorne for putting him in his place and making him leave."

What. The actual. Fuck?

Someone was leering at her? Someone was making her uncomfortable?

"When did Thorne make him leave?" I growl.

"Right at the end of the second period. After Mia disappeared down the tunnel, Dawson pulled Colt from the ice as Theo was escorted to the penalty box, and he let the guy have it."

Scratching my jaw, I replay the scenario from the locker room. It was a fluke I was even in there, but when I walked in on Jeffry and Mia, my blood boiled at the way he was speaking to her. But what's worse? I couldn't figure out the reason behind my frustration.

He was right. Mia should have been at the bench.

Or was he overreacting?

I didn't have enough information to analyze everything properly. It was even more muddled when I found myself caught between being Mia's boss and the guy who fucked her with his tongue the night before.

But knowing there was another factor involved? A key factor as to why Mia didn't want to be at the bench?

I glare at Jeffry as the pieces fall into place. "She said she needed to use the restroom."

He lifts his hands in defense. "That's what she told me."

"You were at the bench around the same time," I remind him. "And if Colt overheard what he was saying while his face was slammed against the glass, I have to assume you overheard the man's comments as well."

"Well, I uh--"

"Am I wrong?" I growl.

"I was too busy focusing on the game to pay attention to..." His voice trails off as my mask of indifference slips, revealing my fury. Jeffry gulps, tugging at the top button on his shirt like it's suffocating him.

"Did you or did you not hear what the man was saying to her?" I boom.

Tremors run along his bottom lip as he shakes his head furiously. "You know how fans can be when they've had one too many beers. Honestly, I didn't think much of it, but when I noticed she was missing, I went looking for her and found her in the locker room a few seconds before you did."

The coward's squabbling. Grasping at straws. Attempting to fabricate a scenario where he doesn't look like a dipshit. But I know Mia. She has thicker skin than most. Which means whatever the stranger was saying had to have been bad. Or at least triggering.

Swallowing thickly, my attention slides to Erika. "What was the guy saying?"

"Well, uh, he told her he wanted her to lift her shirt, and--"

"And he wasn't escorted from the game?" I demand. The last of my patience snaps like a rubber band, and I shove to my feet, causing my desk chair to fall.

It crashes against the floor, making Jeffry flinch, and he blubbers, "W-well, I--"

"Did you hear him say this, Jeffry?"

His entire body shakes as he lifts his shoulders into a shrug. "Not the specifics."

"You're fired," I grit out.

His eyes bulge. "Sir, you can't--"

"I can, and I did. Get out of my office. *Now*."

"But you need me," he argues, unwilling to move his ass off the leather chair across from my desk.

I press my clenched fists onto the top of my desk, shifting forward while reminding myself of the repercussions if I give into temptation and throw Jeffry out of my office with my own two hands. "Erika, get security," I order without tearing my stone-cold gaze from the weasel in front of me.

Without a word, Erika stands and rushes out of my office, her one-inch heels tapping against the hard floor as she leaves.

Once she's gone, I unclench my fists, forcing my hands to relax on the desk separating me from the sniveling slug still in my office. I lean over him but keep my voice deathly controlled. "I suggest you listen closely, Jeffry. If you ever step one foot into B-Tech Enterprises or any of its subsidiaries again, not only will you be blacklisted from its ventures, you'll be blacklisted from any reputable business in the entire state. Do you understand?"

"But I didn't--"

"You fucked up on multiple fronts, Jeffry," I tell him. "For starters, you led me to believe Mia was knowingly dropping the ball when it was the furthest thing from the truth. Second, you didn't defend an innocent woman from being catcalled and humiliated in front of countless people. And third, you threw her under the bus at the first opportunity, all because you can't handle her having more influence on the Lions' community than you do. You've been biased since the beginning, and now you're out of a job because of it. You have thirty minutes to clean out your desk. Once the time is up, your things are going in the trash, same as your career."

The sniveling asshole looks like he's about to cry. He stands and rushes out of the office. I watch him leave, pick up my phone, and call Erika to tell her to schedule a few interviews. Apparently, I have another position I need to fill.

But the real question I can't let go involves a mysterious blonde who refuses to let me in or ask for my help even when her own safety is at risk. And it's a problem. One I need to fix as soon as possible.

18

MIA

"Hey, sorry I'm late," I apologize to Sammie as I slip behind SeaBird's bar.

"No worries," she returns, watching me wrap a small black apron around my waist while a customer asks for a gin and tonic. "You okay here?" she adds, throwing the order together like she can do it in her sleep. She's been bartending for so long she probably can.

"Yeah, I'm good," I answer. "Thanks again for covering for me. And I really am sorry I'm late. I thought I could sneak in a quick nap before my shift, but--"

"Not a big deal. Hawthorne had to stay to watch the band anyway," Sammie tells me as she sets another order--this time, an Old Fashioned--in front of a guy who looks like he's at least eighty.

"Thank you, m'lady," he acknowledges as he lifts the drink in a silent cheers and takes a sip.

"You're welcome." She gives him her back and mouths to me, *That's his fourth one.*

"Noted," I quip, wiping my hands on one of the clean dish towels. Then, I get to work.

Sammie leaves with Hawthorne a few minutes later. I'm not sure how much time passes when another faceless customer takes a seat at the bar and asks for a BudLight. Kind of a boring choice compared to all the IPAs we have on tap, but I reach beneath the bartop, grab a bottle, pop the lid off, and set it in front of him.

"You're Mia, right?" the stranger asks.

The words alone feel heavy. Like they add a pair of sandbags to my shoulders as I look at the guy again, my eyes squinting.

Yup. I definitely don't know him.

Again? Really?

I shouldn't assume he recognizes me because of my OnlyFans account, but after the shitshow at the game last night, I can't help but feel on edge.

Barely containing my annoyance, I reply, "Yup." I head to the back for another bottle of Bacardi. When I return, the asshole's still there and looks to be hitting on a random group of girls. They ignore him and move to the dance floor.

Shamelessly, he checks them out as I slide behind the bar again, grateful he's distracted. Unfortunately, the usual evening rush has died down a bit, and I'm not sure how long it'll last as I try to keep myself busy on the opposite side of the bar.

A few minutes later, he flags me down and asks for another beer.

I set it in front of him, but before I can dart away, he says, "I'm Darryl, by the way."

Great. Now the guy wants to have a conversation.

"Hi, Darryl." My tone is clipped, but I don't give a shit. I doubt he'll give me a tip, anyway. After wiping my hands on my apron, I pick up an empty glass, attempting to look busy as I avoid his gaze entirely. "Need anything else?"

"I know your friend."

I glance up at him and back at my hands. "What friend?"

"Name's Shorty."

The tumbler slips from my fingers but lands on the counter, saving me from picking up any broken glass.

Fuckity, fuck, fuck, fuck.

Of course, he knows Shorty. Of course, Shorty would have something to do with a random stranger approaching me. Of course, he'd find a way to mess with my brain even when he's hundreds of miles away.

Picking the tumbler up again, I squeeze it in my palm. I'm surprised it doesn't break from the pressure as I try to figure out how to end this conversation as quickly as possible without offending the asshole or making things worse. Okay, I don't actually care about offending the guy, but causing a scene and giving Rhodes more work than he bargained for isn't on my to-do list. Which means I need to tread lightly.

Tread. Lightly, I remind myself.

"That's nice," I tell Darryl, then give him my back.

"Yeah. I've known him for a while now," he calls out.

Annoyance simmers beneath my skin as I face him again. "Doesn't Shorty live in Ohio now?"

"Sure does. I do too."

"Good for you." My sarcasm is thick, but I don't bother to hide it because when it comes to Shorty? Well, it's never good, and I've learned to steer clear.

"Yeah. I sell pest control, so I travel all the time," Darryl continues.

"Cool." I fill the glass I'd been throttling with Diet Mountain Dew and vodka, remembering the order I'm supposed to be preparing for the leggy blonde on the opposite end of the bar top.

Oblivious, Darryl adds, "Yeah. When he found out I was coming here, he told me I should stop by."

"How nice of him."

"Yeah. He's a good dude."

Sure, he is.

"Mm-hmm." I start to walk away, but he keeps going.

"Said you like it rough."

The last of my restraint fizzles, and I set the glass on the counter, my head cocked. "Excuse me?"

"Yeah. Said you like it rough, and for fifty bucks, you'd be willing to suck my dick."

My jaw drops, and my brain attempts to catch up with the screwed-up turn this conversation has taken, but I'm lost.

Did Shorty really send him here to say that to me?

It's been almost two years since we broke up. He signed with the Tumblers after graduation, and I haven't seen him since. Not physically, anyway. I've seen him splashed across the media with different girls on his arm more times than I can count. He's never personally reached out, yet he still finds a way to be an ass any chance he gets.

Ya know, like tonight.

Honestly, it makes me want to neuter him.

"So what do you say?" Darryl pushes. He digs into his wallet and slides a crumpled-up fifty onto the counter. It looks like it might disintegrate at any second. "Should we go out back or--"

I splash the vodka and soda into his face, and he nearly falls off his barstool. "What the fuck?"

"That was for you being an ass," I spit. "Now, leave."

He lunges for me, reaching across the bar, but he's tugged back and slammed onto the seat.

"I'm going to need you to apologize," a low voice growls. The sound makes my stomach tighten, and my attention snaps to Buchanan a few feet away.

When did he get here? And how much did he overhear?

Embarrassment floods every inch of my body as I murmur, "Professor--"

"Not now." His voice is dark and thick with full-blown rage as he tightens his hold on the back of Darryl's neck, forcing him to his feet.

"Whoa." Darryl wipes the sticky drink from his face and raises his hands in defense. "You her pimp or somethin'? Look, I'll give you another fifty––"

"She is *not* a prostitute," Henry spits. "Now, apologize and get the hell out of here."

"Fuck you, man. I'm not leavin' until I get my dick––"

With Henry's grip full of Darryl's worn flannel shirt, he punches him in the stomach. Darryl's body sandwiches in half from the impact. The air whooshes from his lungs as Darryl blindly reaches for his beer bottle on the counter. Henry stands above him, assuming he's made his point.

The movement happens so fast, I'm not even sure what I'm witnessing. "Henry!" I yell in warning.

The asshole is too quick. He slams the bottle against Henry's head. The thud makes my stomach roll, but Buchanan recovers quickly, ramming his fist into the stranger's nose, cocking his arm back for another hit when SeaBird's bouncer shoves himself between Henry and Shorty's friend.

"What the fuck is going on?" Rhodes shouts while the rest of the customers create a half-circle around the chaos, giving themselves front-row seats. After all, it's not every day they witness a bar fight. And when the bartender is the cause of said fight?

Yeah. It's a real treat.

Rhodes, however, looks like he's about to throw Buchanan and Darryl over his shoulders for causing such a scene, and I can't let Henry take the fall for it. Not when it's my fault in the first place.

"Stop!" I yell, pointing at Henry. "This guy did nothing

wrong." My gaze shoots to Darryl. "That guy, however, is banned for life."

With a nod, Rhodes lets Buchanan go and grabs Shorty's friend beneath his armpits. He drags him toward the exit like a sack of potatoes and tosses him outside onto his ass.

The silence following is palpable.

I can feel everyone's eyes on me. Watching me. The shit-show. The aftermath. Everything. But I hardly notice. Because a cut above Buchanan's left brow from the glass bottle he'd taken to the head looks gnarly. Blood trickles down the side of his face, framing his dark eyes, and drips off his chin onto his white button-up shirt, staining the crisp material.

He's hurt.

And it's all my fault.

A clean dish towel hangs beneath the counter, and I grab it, rounding the edge of the bar. I press the white cloth to Buchanan's wound before he has the chance to let self-preservation sink in and leave. Henry hisses softly, but he doesn't pull away as I seep up some of the blood with the towel.

There are so many things I want to say.

I'm sorry. I can take care of myself. Thank you. Why are you here?

The list is endless, but none of them feel right. None of them fit. But the silence? It's even more grating. More unbearable. And I'm not sure I can take another second of it.

"Come on," I murmur. "Let's get you taken care of."

There are too many eyes out here. Too much attention. It makes me squirm as I continue pressing the white cloth to the cut above Buchanan's eye.

"I'm fine," he grunts.

"Will you listen for once?" I finally steal the courage to look him in the eye while avoiding the curious stares around us. "I'm trying to help you."

I can see the indecision in his gaze. The stubbornness. But surprisingly, he gives in and follows me down the hall and into the breakroom.

It's nothing but a small square room with a fridge, a small set of lockers, a few cabinets lining the wall, and a folding table in the center. It's quiet here. And away from curious stares. Which is exactly what we need.

"Sit down," I order. My tone is bossy, even to my own ears.

Grudgingly, he plops onto the edge of a metal folding chair, looking less than comfortable as he stares at the crumbs scattered on top of the table. Rhodes is shit at cleaning up his dinner, and I have a hunch the mess bothers Henry. Since our stay at the hotel in Creekside, I've started noticing things about him. About the way he carries himself. About the way he washes his hands.

About the way he zeroes in on messes while trying to maintain his composure. Like right now. When he's clearly uncomfortable. If only I could figure out if it's because of a crumby table or a throbbing headache.

"Hold this," I tell him.

Buchanan takes the pink-stained dishcloth from my grasp and keeps it pressed against the cut above his eye while I wipe the little crumbles from Rhodes' PB&J into my hand, cleaning the space and washing my hands in the kitchen sink.

"Better?" I ask.

"I'm fine," he argues.

"Sure you are." Closing the distance between us, I take over washcloth duty again and slowly peel it away from his head so I can examine the damage.

Yikes.

The cut is pretty deep and still bleeding. But head wounds tend to bleed a lot, so maybe it's not too terrible?

"How bad is it?" he asks, shifting slightly in his chair.

I grimace and shrug one shoulder. "Semi-deep, but nothing crazy. Pretty straight split. Let me see if we have any superglue."

I start to step away from him, but he grabs my wrist, keeping me in place. "Supergluc?"

"Unless you want to go to the hospital for stitches," I offer. "Since the cut is on your face, it might not be a bad idea. I can pay for your Uber or..." My voice trails off, and I look down to where he's holding me. His long fingers are wrapped around my wrist, and his thumb is drawing gentle circles along the inside. It feels good and sends tingles up my arms, no matter how inappropriate it is. Because he shouldn't be touching me like this. Not when we agreed to one night only. Not when he's my boss.

When Buchanan notices what he's doing, he lets me go and sets his palm on the table. His knuckles are red and split from hitting Darryl, but since they are the lesser of the two injuries, I don't comment, making a note to grab him an ice pack from the freezer in a minute.

"Superglue is fine," he grumbles.

His injury. Right.

My eyes flick to his. "It might scar more."

"Chicks dig scars, don't they?"

My mouth twitches. I can't decide if he's being serious or if the guy actually has a sense of humor. "Yeah. We do." I grab some ice and wrap it in a paper towel, offering it to him.

"For your hand," I clarify.

He looks down at his bruised knuckles and nods, pressing the DIY ice pack against the back of his hand. I can feel his eyes on me as I search the cupboards along the back wall for the rest of my supplies, our silence growing more and more stifling with every passing second.

But part of me wonders what would've happened if he wasn't here. If he hadn't stepped in.

Rhodes would've intervened, I'm sure of it.

And if he had, he'd be sitting here, letting me tend to his wounds with a smart-ass comment on the tip of his tongue instead of the angry businessman who looks downright lethal. And I wouldn't have any flutters in my abdomen. I wouldn't feel flushed. My heart wouldn't be thumping out of my chest. I wouldn't feel embarrassed about what he may or may not have overheard. Why? Because Rhodes wouldn't care either way.

Buchanan, on the other hand? I'm not so sure.

When I find a tiny tube of unopened superglue along

with some alcohol wipes and a dinosaur Band-Aid, I set the tools on the table and ask, "What are you doing here anyway?"

He shifts in his seat, keeping his unwavering attention on his busted-up hand. "Came to ask you something."

"Ask me what?"

His features pull as his eyes meet mine, causing another flutter low in my stomach.

"I want to know why you didn't tell me someone was harassing you at the last game." His gaze is so sharp I'm pretty sure it can cut glass.

My head falls.

I don't want to do this. I don't want to talk about this. I don't want to acknowledge the situation or how I handled it. I only want it to go away. I want everything to go away.

But the funny thing about bad decisions? Their consequences always follow. Like dating Shorty. Or creating an OF account. Or giving all my money away until I need to take handouts, no matter how much I despise them.

"Mia," Buchanan warns.

I fuss with the First Aid supplies, arranging them on the table in a straight line. "Because it didn't matter."

"Didn't. Matter?" he rumbles.

"I shouldn't have left the game in the first place."

"You should feel safe at your job."

"I'm a woman." With my teeth, I rip the corner of the alcohol wipe package, pull the small square out, and remove the stained washcloth from Henry's head one more time. "I should feel safe everywhere."

"Yeah. You should."

"If only life was a Disney movie, right? Don't worry. It won't happen again. Next time, I'll stay and make sure I don't miss a second of the game."

His jaw is locked tight, and he shakes his head. "I don't

133

give a shit about the game. I give a shit about you not telling me what was really going on."

"Yeah. Well." I lift my shoulder. "Sorry."

He stays quiet, those dark eyes bouncing around my face as if searching for all my secrets, though he isn't stupid enough to believe he'll actually find them.

Still, he doesn't believe me. To be fair, I don't believe me, either. I'm not sorry. I don't trust the guy. I don't trust anyone.

So, sue me.

"Why was he propositioning you?" Buchanan tilts his head toward the front of SeaBird, hinting he's talking about the Darryl incident instead of the stranger at the last game.

Because I have two incidents worth discussing in the first place.

Good one, Mia.

I bite the inside of my cheek, my frustration oozing from my pores. I let out a soft breath and admit, "Because my ex is an ass."

"Shorty?" he clarifies.

I should be surprised he knows my dating history--and part of me is--but the other part? I guess I suspected it. Buchanan's always kept an eye on me. Looking out for me from a distance. But actually discussing my asshole ex with me or asking me anything personal in general is new. I don't like it.

"Can we not do this?" I ask. "I appreciate your help tonight, but airing out all my dirty laundry doesn't exactly sound like a great way to end my evening."

Again, those dark eyes pin me in place, and tension lines my stomach.

He gives in and dips his chin. "I can be patient."

I scoff as relief spreads through me. "You really think with enough patience I'm gonna cave and open up to you?"

"I guess we'll have to wait and see."

"Mm-hmm," I hum, grabbing his chin and tilting his head toward me so I can get a better look at his cut. "Ouch."

"Is it still that bad?"

"I mean, you'll survive," I quip. "But seriously. Thank you for tonight."

His eyes dart to mine. "You're welcome."

I press the alcohol wipe to the cut above his brow, and he hisses.

"Shit. Sorry," I apologize, leaning in further to examine his cut more closely. The space around us crackles as I wait for the slight burn from the alcohol to ease. Feeling the shift in the air, I slowly pull away to find Henry staring at my mouth. And the heat in his eyes? Pretty sure they could turn a glacier into an inferno in two seconds flat. My tongue darts out, and I moisten my bottom lip and clear my throat.

Focus, Mia.

Twisting off the superglue lid, I murmur, "Don't move. This might sting a little."

Thankfully, the cut has almost stopped bleeding. I drip a bit of superglue into it, grimacing as I examine the damage. It's probably close to an inch long and will definitely scar. He's right, though. Pretty sure it'll only make him look more rugged. More appealing.

Like the asshole needs help on that front.

Once the glue is in place, I squeeze the wound closed carefully and admit, "Didn't know you could throw a punch."

He chuckles. "I guess we've both made some assumptions about each other, haven't we?"

"Yeah. I guess we have." Making sure the glue has dried, I slide my hand down the side of his face. The slight five-o'clock shadow tickles my fingertips as they linger on his heated skin. But I don't pull away. I don't stop touching him. I should. I know I should. But I don't.

What is wrong with me?

I should not be touching my boss' cheek like this.

I should not have let him go down on me at the hotel, either, but I've always been a sucker for bad decisions, so why stop now, right?

The same crackling taints the air around us as he moves closer, his breath caressing my lips and his head tilting up until less than an inch of space separates his mouth from mine. My heart fucking gallops faster and faster as I realize exactly what's going to happen if I don't move. If I don't pull away. If I don't put some much-needed distance between us––both figuratively and literally.

He's going to kiss me.

Henry Buchanan is going to kiss me.

Henry. Fucking. Buchanan.

And it won't be like it was at the hotel. It won't be something I can shove in a box and label it as a one-time thing. Because this would make it twice, even though the kiss at the hotel was barely a brush of our lips. And two is close to three. And three is…a habit. A really. Bad. Habit.

He smells like pine trees.

My eyelids flutter as the scent wraps around me.

Damn, he smells good.

Like, really good.

Like the forest and Christmas and happiness and––

His head tilts even more, and I swear I can already taste him on my tongue.

I want to kiss him.

I want to thank him for intervening today.

I want to climb onto his lap and fuck him right here. Right now.

I haven't been fucked in so long.

Not since Shorty.

I haven't wanted to. Not really. Not since before the hotel.

Having a guy backhand you mid-thrust simply because you were talking to a guy earlier at a party will do it to a girl.

I still can't believe I trusted him. Shorty. Can't believe I kept going back. Can't believe I was jealous when I saw him with other girls, or that part of me wanted to stick it out with him because he said he loved me.

I trusted him.

With my body. My mind. My soul.

And he tore me to shreds.

And if I was stupid enough to trust a guy like Shorty, who's to say Henry will be any different?

Hello, issues.

He leans even closer, the seconds ticking by in slow motion until I can practically see the entire situation unfolding from a distance. Like it isn't me who's about to be kissed by a billionaire. But someone else. Someone who deserves to be kissed by Henry Buchanan. And I want to hate her for it.

On instinct, I turn my head at the last instant, and his lips skate across my cheek. A shot of disbelief punches into me.

Shit.

Why did I turn my head?

Did I just reject him?

"I don't— " I shake my head. "I mean, I do, but I--"

"You're right." He backs away from me as if I'm a loaded gun aimed directly at his chest. And I know I've hurt him. I know I've embarrassed him. I know I've messed this up. Even when there isn't a *this* in the first place.

There isn't an *us.*

So we fooled around at a hotel one time. Big deal. He was buzzed. I was horny. Wham. Bam. Thank you, ma'am.

Well, technically, we didn't *bam*, but... He's my boss. He's a freaking billionaire. He's my opposite in every. Single. Way.

So why did he try to kiss me? And was it a mistake to reject him?

How is this even happening?

"Boss," I start, but he stands from the folding chair and smooths out his blood-stained shirt.

"I should be going."

"Buchanan, wait. Let me explain."

"There's no need to explain. We agreed to one night only. The night has passed. Make sure Rhodes walks you to your car. And thanks for…" He points to his forehead and drops his hand to his side. "Goodnight, Mia."

"Henry…"

The breakroom door closes behind him, and I drop my head back, staring at the textured ceiling. "Dammit." Regret pools in my stomach.

What was I thinking?

And why the hell do I feel like I screwed something up when we both know crossing the line together––again–– would be a terrible idea?

20

MIA

A shton, one of SeaBird's managers, insisted I go home after the shitstorm with Darryl, and I didn't argue. Not because of Darryl. But because of the *almost* kiss I shared with Professor Fucking Buchanan.

The phone starts ringing as I press it to my ear, desperate to talk to someone who might make some actual freaking sense of the situation. A few seconds later, Ashlyn's voice echoes through the speaker.

"Hey, this is Ash. I can't come to the phone right now. Please leave a message, and I'll get back to you as soon as––"

I end the call without letting the recording have a chance to complete and dial Blake's number.

I shouldn't. She's probably having hot and sweaty sex with Theo since this is his first night home, but I can't help it. I need to talk to someone before I lose my freaking mind.

Sure enough, a robotic voice sounds a few rings later, notifying me the person I am calling has yet to set up her voice mailbox.

I hit end and push Kate's number.

It rings four times, and a groggy voice answers, "Hello?"

KELSIE RAE

I check the time on my phone and grimace. It's only eleven, but Kate's always been an early bird and is usually in bed by ten. With her pregnancy, she's even worse. "Shit. I didn't realize it was so late. Sorry—"

"What's up?" Kate interrupts.

"Nothing. Go back to sleep. I'll talk to you in the morning."

"You sure?" she croaks.

"Yeah. I'm sure." I scrub my hand over my face. "Sleep tight, Kate."

"Okay," she mumbles. "You too."

The call ends, and I puff out my cheeks, dropping my phone into my lap and staring blankly at the ceiling in my apartment.

He's up there.

Or at least, his penthouse is.

It's weird to think only a single floor separates us.

What's even weirder is the fact I could knock on his door if I wanted to, though I doubt he'd answer. Especially after I rejected him earlier.

Actually, scratch that. The bastard doesn't have a door. He has an electronic key for the elevator leading to his penthouse because he's too classy for regular doors. It's one more reminder of how different we are. How stupid it would be to entertain anything more with him.

But the almost kiss?

Fuck me, it would've been so good. I know it. I freaking *know* it.

I could really use Ash or Blake or Kate right now. Especially after a night like tonight.

Sometimes it sucks. Being the last one standing. The last one without a significant other. The last one single and alone. Normally, I don't mind. It's not like I want a relationship with anyone, and my friends are happy. So damn happy it's nauseating most days. But they deserve it. Happiness. They deserve it more than anyone.

And I like being alone. I don't have to pretend everything is okay when I'm alone. And I sure as shit don't have to worry about someone stabbing me in the back when I'm by myself. But nights like tonight? Well, it feels sort of melancholy, and it kind of sucks.

Since I'm out of gin, I guess my friends Jim Beam and Jack Daniels will have to comfort me. Pushing myself up from my ugly flower chair in the center of the family room, I head to my kitchen and rummage around in the cabinets. Twisting the cap off with a flick of my fingers, I bring the Jim Beam bottle to my lips and take a long pull.

Warmth spreads down my throat, settles in my chest, and plunges lower. The liquid heat warms my stomach, and I smile against the glass rim, taking another swallow.

I don't drink often. Okay, that's sort of a lie. I drink about as much as every other college student, but getting wasted? I save that particular vice for special occasions, and if the familiar buzz humming beneath my skin is anything to go by, apparently, tonight fits the bill.

After another long swallow, I head back to the floral chair and plop onto it, grabbing my laptop and Googling Henry Buchanan against my better judgment. I don't know why I do it. To torture myself, I guess.

Yup.

He's as attractive as always.

Strong jaw.

Straight nose.

And the way he punched a guy today? I bite my bottom lip, the memory making me squirm in my seat.

Yeah. It was hot. Like, really hot.

I never thought a guy like Henry, a guy so controlled and stern, could lose it the way he did.

I wonder what it would've been like to kiss him. Not like the barely-there brush of his lips at the hotel, but a real kiss. If it would be soft or hard. I bet he's a terrible kisser—too stiff and forced. Then again, the entire hotel incident was *not* stiff or forced. No, it was freaking incredible. Like, mind-blowingly good.

Pressing my thighs together, I examine the photo more closely, magnifying his full lips.

He has sexy lips. I wonder what they taste like *before* some solid oral sex. Like mint? Or Pappy Van Winkle?

I snort and take another pull from the bottle. It ain't no Pappy's, but Jim's never done me wrong.

Pretty sure Jim and Jack are the only two men in my life worth keeping. Well, them and Ben & Jerry. I love me some good ol' Ben & Jerry.

If only they could turn me on like the man staring back at me from my laptop. I wish I could've told him why I didn't kiss him tonight. Why I turned away. I wish he hadn't assumed it's because I'm not interested in kissing him when it couldn't be further from the truth.

I'd love to kiss him.

To tease my tongue against the seam of his lips. To feel him pressed against me.

My clit pulses, and I almost moan as I take one more shot from the bottle.

Yeah, I'm gonna be fucked tomorrow if I keep this up.

I snort as the thought flutters across my mind.

If only I could get fucked tonight, too.

Keeping my laptop open, I set it on the ground, vowing to purchase a coffee table one of these days. Buchanan's stone-cold stare pins me in place, and I spread my legs, slipping my hand between my thighs.

"Mmm." I look at the ceiling, then back at the screen and the eyes shining out at me. Cold. Calculating. Fucking frigid.

What I wouldn't do to see them heat up one more time like they did in the breakroom. I wonder if they would heat up again if he saw what I was doing right now. The button on my jeans pops, and with a quick tug of my zipper, I slip my hands into my thong, playing with my clit while imagining it's Henry's fingers instead of my own.

Yeah...I should *not* be doing this. But since I'm the only one here, I do it anyway. I can't help myself. I like sex, and this is my only option, so it'll have to do.

I picture myself riding the elevator to the top floor and asking him to kiss me. To push me up against the wall or to my knees.

I rub my clit a little faster, eliciting another moan to slip past my lips.

"Fuck," I whimper.

I could always call him and ask for his elevator key. My phone rests on the arm of the chair, and I pick it up, finding Buchanan's name in my contacts folder. My thumb hovers over the call button as I continue playing with myself, my skin feeling hot and flushed with every pass of my fingers. I wonder if he'd like it. Seeing me like this. Knowing I'm thinking about him. Knowing I could use a solid fuck right now if it didn't include feelings or expectations.

Don't be stupid, the voice of reason slips past the comfortable haze from the alcohol, and I set my phone down while continuing my assault with my opposite hand.

It's a stupid idea, but the thought of making him finish what he started in SeaBird's breakroom sounds better and better with every slight brush of my fingers.

His fingers.

My head falls back, and I stare at the ceiling once more.

"You gonna fuck me, Henry?" I whimper, closing my eyes and imagining him caging me in with his strong arms, his dress shirt nothing but a rumpled mess on the floor as he

143

pushes his thick cock inside me over and over again. "You gonna make me come?"

My orgasm toys with me, and I spread my legs wider, my thighs pressing into both sides of the ugly ass chair. My breath hitches as I slip my index finger inside of me, pumping it back and forth. But it's too small. Too dainty. I need Henry. I need his dick. His gruff voice whispering in my ear. The possessive way he says my name.

"Come on, Henry," I plead under my breath. "Fuck me. Fuck me harder. *Ah.*" My mouth falls wide as I come on my finger, moaning his name and letting the rush of euphoria wash over me.

Shit, that was good.

I love a solid orgasm. To be fair, who doesn't? But this one? It might be the best one I've had since his head was between my thighs in Creekside.

Slowly, I come back down to Earth, my muscles melting into the lumpy cushion as I pant, "Fuck," and open my eyes. My phone's resting on the edge of the armchair. Its screen is shining back at me, along with Henry's name and the seconds ticking by with a connected call.

Eyes bulging, I scramble for the phone, stabbing the red *end* button. Covering my mouth, the severity of my situation hits like a damn wrecking ball.

He heard me.

He heard me moan his name as I fucking masturbated to him.

No, no, no, no, no.

This can't be happening. Not after the hotel. Not after SeaBird. Not after I rejected him. I seriously might die from embarrassment if what I think just happened *actually* happened.

I'm so screwed.

21

HENRY

"**Y**ou gonna fuck me, Henry?" Mia's voice is soft and sultry. A whisper. A plea. I tilt my head to the side, convinced I'm hallucinating, as I hold my phone to my ear.

"You gonna make me come?" she continues, sounding like a fucking porn star.

"Mia?" I growl. But the voice is too far away. Like the phone's been set aside. Like she isn't talking to me. She's simply letting me witness her inner dialogue. Treating me like a fly on the wall, and fuck, what I wouldn't give to see her right now like this.

"Come on, Henry," she pants. It's mingled with a quiet rustling of fabric. "Fuck me. Fuck me harder. *Ah.*"

My dick jumps as I register her gasp. I hold my breath, soaking up her tiny whimpers. She's coming.

Fuck, she's coming.

And she's moaning my name. The combination makes me harder than a steel pole as I sit on the couch with my laptop on my knees and a tumbler of whiskey resting on the coffee table in front of me.

I stay quiet, listening to her heavy breathing. She slowly comes down from her euphoria as more rustling sounds and the call ends. My mind short-circuits as I try to piece together what happened and why the hell I was privy to witnessing it.

Did she mean to call?

I'm not sure.

After she turned me down a couple hours ago, the last thing I expected was to see her name flashing across my phone screen. I almost didn't answer. Too frustrated by what happened in the breakroom to think straight but too curious to send the call to my voicemail. Part of me wishes I had, so I could listen to Mia's soft whimpers of pleasure over and over. It's the hottest thing I've ever heard, even if it doesn't make any sense.

I set my computer on the coffee table and squeeze my dick through my slacks. It doesn't ease the ache. It only drowns out my voice of reason. Knowing I'm a sick sonofabitch, I pull up the photos Gordy sent me a while ago, hating how I wasn't strong enough to delete them in the first place.

She's perfect. Every inch. Every curve. Like she was made for me. Shit, I can still remember what she tasted like. Her thighs on either side of my head. Her fingers tangled in my hair. Her scent. Her smooth skin.

Shoving my boxers down, I pull my dick out as her voice echoes through my mind.

"You gonna fuck me, Henry?"

I squeeze the base and run my palm along the shaft.

"You gonna make me come?"

"Yeah, baby," I groan. I pump my hand faster, studying the tiny dimples right above her ass in the photograph. She's wearing a lacy thong. The slip of red material disappears between her ass cheeks. I stare at the curves, my mind going crazy with everything I want to do to her. I can almost picture her bent over, her long blonde hair wrapped around my hand as I thrust into her from behind.

"Fuck me," she whimpers. "Fuck me harder--"

I come in my hand, the ropes of white painting my stomach and staining my shirt as I drop my head back to stare at the ceiling.

Fuck me.

What the hell was that?

22

MIA

My skull is throbbing as I roll over on my bed, shove my eye mask onto the top of my head, and check my buzzing phone. Ashlyn's calling. With a groan, I slide my thumb along the screen and croak, "Hello?"

"Dude. It's one in the afternoon. Don't you have a game in a few hours?"

Another groan slips out of me, but I don't answer her. She's right. The Lions are playing in their new arena, and I need to be there.

"Any chance you might want to drive together so I can go home with Colt after the game?" she asks.

Sometimes I like to head over early in hopes of filming as much content as possible, but since I'm still behind on editing from the away games, I decide missing one warm-up session isn't the end of the world.

"Sure," I answer her.

"Perfect. Sorry I missed your call last night, by the way. What's up?"

My bottom lip juts out at the reminder of everything

that's happened within the last twelve hours. I push myself up and rest my back against my bare bedroom wall.

"Mia?" Ash prods, sensing my discomfort. "You okay? What happened?"

"I did something stupid."

Knowing I rarely fess up to my mistakes, she hesitates, and I swear I can hear the disappointment in her voice as she replies, "What did you do?"

My fingers pinch the bridge of my nose while I debate where to begin. "It's a long story."

"So spill," she pushes. "Actually, don't. I have a feeling I need to hear this in person. You take a shower, and I'll grab you a coffee from The Bean Scene. Send me your address."

I grimace. "Ash…"

"Dude. You gotta show me your new place at some point. What? Are you living under a bridge or something?"

She's right. It's not like I can avoid showing her my insanely nice apartment for the rest of my life, and she's my best friend––heaven help her. Might as well get it over with.

"Fiiiine." I rattle off the address.

"Perfect. I'll be over in twenty."

"Okay."

"Want me to invite Blake and Kate?" she asks. "Actually, never mind. Blake's shopping for furniture with Theo, and Kate has a doctor's appointment. I'll see you in a bit, okay?"

"Yup. See you."

I hang up the phone, only to have it ring in my palm a second later.

Seriously. Two calls in one day? I'm never this popular.

I don't recognize the number but answer it anyway.

"Hello?"

"Hello, this is Erika, Dr. Buchanan's assistant."

"Oh." I frown, curious if I'm about to be fired over the

149

phone after last night's events. I shift my phone to my other ear, preparing myself for the inevitable. "Hey?"

"Hey," she repeats. "I'm sorry to bug you, but I wanted to reach out and apologize again for the hotel incident––"

With a sigh of relief, I cut her off. "Seriously, you have nothing to apologize for. Stuff happens."

"I know, but it was super nice of you to take one for the team and all."

I bite the inside of my cheek, remembering coming against Henry's mouth as my own sordid version of taking one for the team, but I stay quiet.

She has no idea.

"Anyway," she continues. "I also wanted to call to let you know you'll be reporting straight to Dr. Buchanan from now on. He seems to be taking a liking to everything you're doing. Since you're already sending him all of your videos and such, we figured it was easiest this way."

"Wait, what happened to Jeffry?"

"He's been let go."

My eyes bulge. "Let go?"

"Yes. I'm afraid Dr. Buchanan didn't appreciate Jeffry undermining your abilities or creative vision, and after the stunt he pulled during the game against the Blazers? Well, I'm sure you understand."

My lips part, but I clamp them shut, unsure of what to say.

"We've hired someone else as head of public relations, but you'll rarely see her," Erika adds. "If you have any other questions, don't be afraid to reach out, Ms. Rutherford."

"Of course," I reply. "Uh, thanks for letting me know."

"Have a good afternoon," Erika quips.

The call ends.

I OWN ONE TOWEL. ONE. TECHNICALLY, I HAD TWO BEFORE the move, but one of them disappeared somewhere between the townhome I shared with the girls and the new apartment. I have a feeling it might be in Tukani's truck since he let me borrow it so I could move all my things in, but it doesn't matter. Now, I have one towel. It's pink and fluffy and smells like laundry detergent. I run it over my wet hair when a quiet knock sounds from the front of the apartment.

Until now, I haven't invited anyone to see my new place. I didn't feel like I should after they found out how dire my financial situation was not so long ago. If they knew how much money I made online before giving it all away, they'd probably shit their pants.

I've tried to analyze my money issues, but I still don't understand why I can't save any. Why it leaves me itchy anytime I have more than a few hundred dollars to my name. Why I feel the need to give it all away. But if I can't understand, how can I expect others to?

I could always blame my dad. Maybe if someone had thrown him a bit of cash, he wouldn't have borrowed it from the man who killed him.

Regardless, money issues are the least of my problems after the hotel incident and last night's debacle.

Yup. An entirely new shitstorm is brewing and currently swallowing me whole. I made it ten times worse when I freaking masturbated while on a call with my boss.

Shoving the thought aside, I walk down the short hall and open the front door. With two iced lattes in hand, Ash grins at me. "Dude, you have a doorman."

"Pretty sure you already knew that little nugget," I remind her, pushing the door open the rest of the way.

Ash steps inside, letting out a whistle as she takes in the place. I guess I can't blame her. It really is crazy nice. She's probably thinking the same thing I did when I first saw the apartment. It belongs in a freaking magazine. Or at least, it would if it wasn't for the secondhand furniture ruining the whole photo-worthy vibe.

"Not too shabby," Ash announces as she takes in the kitchen, ten-foot ceilings, and stone fireplace on the opposite side of the room. "Although, you could use a few more pieces of furniture." She motions to the empty space where a kitchen table belongs and the worn armchair in the center of my otherwise bare family room. "And a TV."

"My laptop works very well, thank you very much." I grab the latte from her hand and take a long sip. "Ah. That's the stuff."

"So?" she prods. "What's going on?"

"Nothing," I lie, but she wiggles her index finger back and forth.

"Nope. No backing out and keeping me in the dark, missy. Tell me all the things."

"Who says there's anything to tell?" I question.

"Do you really think I forgot your cryptic little comment on the phone? And even if you hadn't said anything, I know you. No matter how much you love me, you're not one to call me out of the blue just to chitchat, so spill. Any more stalker issues? Colt told me about what happened at the game."

"Tell Colt he's officially on my shit list," I announce.

"Why? Because he's being a good friend and keeping an eye on you?" She folds her arms, careful to keep her latte from spilling down her chunky knit sweater. "Or is it because he's being a good boyfriend by keeping me in the loop when it comes to my best friend who, for better or for worse, sucks at communication?"

My lips purse, and I take another sip of coffee. "Both."

Her mouth lifts with a ghost of a smile, but she doesn't give in. Instead, she doubles down on her sleuthing efforts. "So? Tell me everything."

"So…" I lick my lips, deciding to get this over with because no matter how much I hate it, I really could use her advice. "One of Shorty's friends came to visit me at SeaBird last night. Apparently, Shorty told him I'd be willing to suck his dick for fifty bucks—"

Her gasp cuts me off. "You're joking."

"I'm not even to the crazy part yet," I mutter, replaying the night for the thousandth time. "Buchanan overheard the asshole's proposition and punched the guy, but the guy knocked Buchanan in the head with a beer bottle. Thankfully, the bouncer intervened and threw Shorty's buddy out while I took Buchanan to the breakroom to clean him up. And as I was supergluing the gash on his head, he leaned in and tried to kiss me."

"Professor Buchanan kissed you?"

"*Tried*," I emphasize. "Well, technically, I guess he did *kind of* kiss me when we were in Creekside," I ramble. "But I'm talking about last night--"

"Hold up." She raises her hand. "Buchanan kissed you when you were in Creekside?"

My nose scrunches with embarrassment, and I drop my chin to my chest, avoiding Ash's scrutiny. "Technically? No. It was more of a hot brush of the lips kind of thing."

"*When?*"

"We may have had a quick little…*session* while sharing a room during the away games, but we both agreed it was only a one-time thing, which is why, when he went in for the kill last night, I turned at the last second and--"

"But he's a babe," she argues.

"Yeah. A babe I have nothing in common with *and* has a penis, which we both know I've sworn off altogether, thanks to my shitty taste in men."

Attempting to keep up with the chaos of my life, she takes

a sip of her latte and licks her lips. "Okay, yeah, but Buchanan isn't a shitty guy."

"For now," I quip.

"What do you mean?"

"Well, let's look at my past, shall we? Either, A—I have terrible taste in men, and they're all shitty from the beginning, but I don't recognize it. Or, B—they're actually awesome dudes, but as soon as I start dating them, they turn into selfish assholes. Either way, it doesn't exactly bode well for me. I'm not about to make the same mistake by dating my boss only to have it blow up in my face."

"So, the one-time thing in Creekside doesn't count?" she argues.

"We agreed––"

"It was only a one-time thing," she repeats, mimicking me. "Yeah. So you said. And I would believe it if he hadn't tried to kiss you last night."

"Which is why I turned away," I remind her, "to uphold the *one-time thing*."

"Okay, let's pretend the hotel scenario never happened, shall we?" She flicks her blond hair over her shoulder. "Are you saying you *still* wouldn't date Buchanan because you're convinced it'll blow up in your face?"

"Uh, yeah?" I look at her like she's a crazy person. "And when it does, I'll be out of a job, which was hard enough to find in the first place, thanks to Shorty."

"So you're not going to date...ever again?" she asks. "Are you kidding me right now?"

"I don't know why you're surprised," I point out. "I haven't dated in almost two years."

"Well, yeah. But I figured it was because you were busy finishing school and distracted with trying to find a job. I assumed you'd give dating another try as soon as you found some stability."

Yup. The girl's delusional.

My shoulder lifts, and I shake my head back and forth. "Well, I'm not going to."

"Ever?"

"Ever," I confirm.

"But being in a relationship is awesome."

"For you, sure. But for me?" I shake my head again. "Yeah, no. Not so much."

"Just because you've had a few bad experiences--"

"Ash, I didn't call to talk about my dating life," I interrupt, rubbing at my temple while attempting to ward off my impending headache. "I called to talk about the shitshow which transpired last night."

Her brows dip in the center as she eyes me warily. "You already told me--"

"I didn't get to the worst part," I mutter, scrubbing my hand over my face. I'm defeated. Embarrassed. Overwhelmed. My cheeks puff out, and I let out all the pent-up oxygen in my lungs in hopes of it helping me breathe a little easier.

It doesn't do shit.

"Wait." Ashlyn takes another sip of her drink, as confused as before. "There's a worse part than you hooking up with your boss, then rejecting him when he leaned in to kiss you after being super chivalrous and beating up a guy for propositioning you in the middle of a bar?"

My shame threatens to swallow me whole, but I hold Ashlyn's gaze. "Yup."

She blinks--twice--attempting to maintain her composure. She drops to the floor in the middle of the entryway and pats the ground beside her.

Giving in, I sit and cross my legs in front of me.

With a satisfied nod, she prods, "Well? What's the worst part?"

"After the almost kiss, I came home, got drunk, and Googled pictures of Henry. I decided to"--I clear my throat--"take care of a few things downstairs and somehow wound up butt-dialing him, so he overheard the whole thing."

Her jaw drops. "Shut. Up."

"Yup."

"You're serious?"

"Yup," I repeat.

"And you're sure he overheard the whole thing?"

I replay the night and how everything transpired while fighting through the fog left by my alcohol indulgence and give Ash a nod. "I mean, the call was connected for a solid two minutes, so I don't know how he couldn't have overheard."

"Well..." She clicks her tongue against the roof of her mouth. "Maybe it went to his voicemail?"

"Like a voicemail is any better," I laugh, but it comes out almost maniacal. "Let's give the guy an opportunity to replay my most embarrassing moment over and over, shall we?"

"Maybe he hasn't listened to it yet," Ash suggests. "Maybe you can steal his phone and delete the voicemail."

"And if it wasn't a voicemail?" I ask. "What then?"

"Then, Henry Buchanan most definitely heard you masturbate last night." She shrugs, taking another sip of her latte. "I bet he thought it was hot."

A pathetic laugh slips out of me as I drop my head back to look at the ceiling. "You're ridiculous."

"I'm just saying..."

"He's said it himself. I'm not his type," I argue.

She quirks her brow. "Did he say you weren't his type before or after you hooked up with him and then tried to kiss you?"

At a loss for words, I pick at the lint on my tank top,

praying I can miraculously learn how to become invisible in the next two seconds or less.

"Exactly," Ash says triumphantly. "He wants you."

"For a fuck, maybe."

"You mean *another* fuck," she corrects me.

"Technically, he only went down on me, then called it a night."

"So you guys didn't go all the way?" Ashlyn confirms.

"No? And even if we had, Buchanan can't be blind enough to think we'd ever be anything more than a good fuck." I hesitate. "Actually…"

"Mia, I know that look." She wags her finger at my face. "Don't even think about it."

"Think about what?"

"I know you. And whatever's going on in your gorgeous little brain is a bad idea." She wiggles her finger an inch from my nose all over again, but I bat it away.

"*Little* brain?" I challenge.

"Okay, massively awesome brain, but you know what I'm saying."

"What's so bad about a solid fuck?" I ask her. "You know. So I can get it out of my system."

"And the first sexcapade wasn't enough to fill your appetite?"

"Well, since nothing was technically *filled*––"

"Ew." She shivers and shoves at my shoulder, pulling another laugh from me.

"Come on. Is it such a bad idea?" I ask. "It's not like he looks at me as if I'm actual relationship material."

The girl looks at me like I've lost one too many brain cells and shakes her head. "One, you don't know how he looks at you. You might be surprised. And two, it's not a bad idea. It's a *terrible* one, Mia. You said so yourself. You two work together."

"Well, yeah, but––"

"No buts," she interrupts. "Seriously. For someone who gives amazing advice, you're shit at taking it. Don't be stupid, Mia. Don't self-destruct." Her look is pointed and makes me shift uncomfortably beside her.

"Okay," I concede, desperate to bypass her inevitable lecture more than I'd like to admit. "You're right. And as you so eloquently pointed out, I'm not great at making smart decisions, but staying as far away from Henry Buchanan as humanly possible is probably a good idea."

"Exactly," she agrees, practically preening with how I've listened to her advice for once in my life. She adds, "PS, was it really your most embarrassing moment?"

My forehead wrinkles with confusion. "Huh?"

"Henry potentially overhearing you," Ashlyn clarifies. "You said it was your most embarrassing moment."

"Oh. Uh." I run a quick mental checklist. Shrugging one shoulder, I answer her. "Probably."

"Like, including the OF account and Shorty blasting your name to the entire world on the internet?"

"Honestly?" I hesitate again, nibbling the edge of my straw. "Yeah. I knew what I was posting through the OF account would reach a lot of people, and I knew it was for money. But having Buchanan overhear me say his actual name when I...ya know... It was meant to be private, and it wasn't."

With a sympathetic nod, she reaches over and squeezes my knee. "Well, if it counts for anything, I bet Henry almost jizzed in his pants when he heard you."

"Ashlyn!" I screech. "Who are you, and what have you done with my best friend? Actually, never mind. You've been hanging out with Blakely while the boys have been away, haven't you." It isn't a question. It doesn't need to be. Ashlyn's dating Blakely's older brother. Of course, they're going to grow closer. The thought stings slightly, but I shove the unwarranted jealousy aside and stand. "Thanks again for the coffee. I should probably finish getting ready."

"Okay. I'll hang out here until it's time for us to leave."

Slipping my phone out of my back pocket, I check the time and nod. "Perfect. I'll be out in twenty."

I head down the hall to my bedroom.

23

MIA

I'm able to avoid him for the entire game. Well, *avoid* might be a stretch. Truth be told, I haven't seen him yet, despite feeling like an owl with a rotating head in search of a man who looks hella good in a suit. But I haven't had any luck spotting him. Or maybe luck *has* been on my side for once in my life since the idea of facing him after my butt dial is absolutely mortifying.

The guy usually watches the game while schmoozing associates in the suites with a buffet of crab legs and escargot. Okay, I technically don't know if they serve crab legs and escargot in the suites. Still, it's how I've always imagined the buffet is stocked, along with classical music playing in the background.

Classy, I know.

Unfortunately, my luck has run out.

Resting my camera against my shoulder, I attempt to ignore Buchanan standing at the edge of the stage during the post-game interviews. Instead, I focus on Colt and Theo. They're sitting in the front of the room on a large platform, surrounded by cameras and answering questions with the

160

rest of the Lions lineup. I should probably be filming this in case someone says something clever, but I'm too distracted. My eyes dart in Henry's direction, despite my best effort. He looks good up there. He commands the entire room without even needing access to a microphone. He's more hands-on than a lot of the other owners in the industry. A lot more present. Hell, some don't even bother attending the games, yet Buchanan insists on traveling with the team. He doesn't seem like someone who does anything half-assed, so I'm not sure why I thought this would be any different. I tear my attention away from his strong hands toying with the edge of his suit. He has attractive hands. Like...stupidly attractive. It's a problem. I need to focus. Focusing would be much easier if Buchanan wasn't onstage looking like a solid snack.

"Yeah, I think the Lions played really well despite the loss," Colt answers, though I was too distracted to hear what the interviewer asked. "Once we make a few changes to our offense, I think we'll be able to close out the next game with a win."

"And how do you know the lyrics to every Taylor Swift song?" another reporter prods, lifting his pen into the air.

With a low chuckle, Theo leans back in his chair, spreading his legs wide beneath the coffee-colored table and waving his hand for Colt to continue.

"Our social media manager insisted we play it during warm-ups for the past few weeks," Colt answers. "Guess the lyrics kind of sunk in."

Beck's sitting on Colt's left and leans closer to his mic, adding, "Yeah, she said it helps us memorize the words so we're ready to lip-sync whenever she wants us to."

"Either Mia's a genius or a sadist," Greer pipes up dryly. "None of us are sure which one."

The reporters laugh along with the players, and my mouth lifts as I drop my gaze to the ground. These boys. I kind of love how they've claimed me. And how they willingly go along with my shenanigans these days.

"Ah, so this Mia is the mastermind behind all your videos," another interviewer states. "May I ask how much time she requires you to spend filming silly videos instead of practicing actual hockey?"

Silly videos?

My brows tug, but I force myself to let the words roll off my shoulders.

I'm not the only one who hears it. The hint of condescension. Greer and Beck share a look, each of them shrugging. "Depends on the video. Nothing crazy, though."

The reporter taps the edge of her recorder against her chin and adds, "Do you think if you spent more time focusing on practicing instead of being distracted by your social media manager's desire to boost your online presence, the outcome of tonight's game would have been different?"

My gaze narrows along with the rest of the team's as I digest the reporter's thinly-veiled accusation posed as a question.

Is she seriously blaming the loss on me?

Dude. I wasn't even on the ice.

You gotta be kidding me.

Whatever earlier amusement had been present evaporates from Colt's features, and he demands, "Are you suggesting we lost the game because of Mia?"

"I'm saying the Lions have quite the social media presence, and I'm curious if the trade-off is worth it," the woman explains. "Do more followers online equal more losses on the ice?"

Colt's scoff echoes throughout the silent room, and Theo sits up fully in his chair. He reaches for his mic like he's about to lose his shit on the woman, but something grabs his attention from his periphery, and he hesitates.

Henry's determined stride catches us all by surprise as he closes the space between him and Greer's microphone, lifting it to his mouth. "In case you missed it, our social media manager didn't play in the game tonight, so I'm not sure how you can insinuate the loss was her fault."

"I'm saying––"

"I suggest you spend a little more time learning how hockey works before attacking my staff," Henry interrupts. I stare at him, willing him to look at me, but the bastard keeps his attention zeroed in on the reporter with a stick up her ass like I don't exist. Like he isn't talking about me to a bunch of people. Like he isn't defending me. "Mia Rutherford is great at what she does and has gained more support for the Lions in the last few weeks than any of your articles."

Again, the reporter opens her mouth to argue, but he cuts her off. "Does anyone else have any further questions about the game? Or are we finished?" His sharp gaze falls over the crowd in front of the stage as he waits for a reporter to say something. When no one utters a single syllable, Henry sets the microphone back in its stand in front of Greer and strides off the platform and out of sight.

Whoa.

Now *that* I wish I'd caught on camera. I'd probably watch it and get off to him all over again.

Yeah, super healthy idea, Mia.

I shake the thought off and attempt to focus on the rest of the post-game interview. It goes by without a hitch, and when the guys all stand, I click the lens cover back onto my camera and head toward the exit. I grabbed my camera bag when the players were showering before the interviews, and with them finished, I'm ready to call it a day.

Almost everyone has trickled out of the arena as I head to my car. It's dark now. The last of the sun has already slipped beneath the horizon. I parked under a lamp post, knowing I wouldn't leave until after dark. And if I've learned anything from my precarious situation with stalkers, it's light is my friend. And so are crowds. Unfortunately, the latter is a little sparse, so I pick up my pace.

When my beat-up car comes into view, I stop short, recognizing the dark figure leaning against the driver's side door, one ankle crossed in front of the other with his hands in his pockets. Yup. I'd recognize those broad shoulders covered in Armani anywhere.

At least he isn't a serial killer, right?

Forcing my feet to work, I head toward Henry Buchanan, despite the fresh wave of embarrassment rolling over me. I tug the strap of my camera bag further onto my shoulder while digging into the front pocket for my keys.

This is awkward.

I want to know if he heard me last night. I want to know if he was on the phone or if my moans are hidden in a copious amount of voicemails he's never bothered to listen to. I doubt a man this uptight would leave a single one unanswered for more than three minutes.

Which is just great for me.

The real question is, why the hell is he waiting for me at my car?

What if he fires me?

Sure, Erika could've done it for him when she called earlier this morning, but still. Maybe he wants to do the deed himself.

What if he lectures about appropriate behavior between colleagues? Hell, we aren't even colleagues. He's my boss. My boss's boss. My boss's boss's boss? Honestly, I don't even know the hierarchy, but it doesn't matter anyway. I crossed a line, and we both know it.

But he crossed it first.

He shouldn't have tried to kiss me.

He shouldn't have slipped his head beneath the covers in Creekside.

He shouldn't have made me come harder than any of my previous partners.

Yup. This is his fault.

All. His. Fault.

He's the one who got the ball rolling. Who sparked my imagination. Who made me curious.

The familiar click of the doors unlocking is barely heard over the buzzing in my ears as what if's and finger-pointing wreak havoc on my sanity. Henry lifts his head, and his eyes meet mine.

Man, he's beautiful. Dangerous. But beautiful.

The danger should remind me why I need to stay away, but it only draws me in more.

"Can I help you?" I ask, feigning confidence.

"Why did you reject me at the bar, then call me so I could hear you say my name when you came on your fingers?" he demands.

Wow.

So he *did* answer the call.

I knew the guy was blunt, but did he really just lay it all out there like this?

What am I thinking? He's Henry Buchanan.

Of course, he did.

24

MIA

"**W**hy did you reject me at the bar, then call me so I could hear you say my name when you came on your fingers?"

Regret swells in my stomach as I replay Henry's comment, unsure what to do or say in this moment. Not when he's looking at me like this. Cold. Detached. And... determined? Yup. Determination is the underlying emotion in those dark eyes. He wants answers. And I have a feeling he won't let me off the hook until I give them to him.

Clearing my throat—and rejecting Buchanan's opportunity to catch me off guard—I challenge, "Who says I wasn't using a toy? Ya know, if I hypothetically owned one."

"I didn't hear any vibrating last night." He shrugs his broad shoulders and shifts to face me fully. "Tell me why you turned away."

"From the kiss?" I question.

His chin dips.

"We agreed our little hotel adventure was a one-time thing. Kissing you in SeaBird would've made it a *two-time* thing. And a *two-time* thing feels a hell of a lot like dating.

166

And dating? Well, as I've stated before, I'm not interested in dating anyone."

"Only finger fucking yourself while imagining it's me." He pushes away from my car and strides closer to me. The confidence in every freaking footstep makes my heart rate thrum faster and faster. My attraction to the bastard is practically driving me insane.

When he reaches me, the toes of his loafers nearly touch the front of my sneakers. It's a stark reminder of the different worlds we come from. I tilt my head up and ask, "Are you always this direct?"

"I think we both know the answer to that." His fingertips brush against my forehead, following my hairline and tucking a few strands behind my ear. A shiver of anticipation races down my spine, but I don't move an inch.

"Do you want to know a secret, Mia?" he whispers.

I stay still, drowning in his scent as my tongue darts out between my lips. I blame the man in front of me. It seems he has a habit of making all logic evaporate into thin air anytime he's around.

"I might have given you a preview of how hard I can make you come while we were in Creekside, but whatever fantasy you created up here?" He taps the side of my temple with his forefinger. "It doesn't remotely compare to the real thing."

My attention drops to his lips. I lean away from his touch, but I don't back away. Not fully. Honestly, I'm not sure if I can.

"Someone's cocky," I note.

"Confident," he clarifies. "Do you want to know another secret?"

Ignoring the warm caress of his breath against my cheeks, I suck my bottom lip into my mouth before forcing out, "What?"

"I'm glad you rejected me in the breakroom."

The sharpness of his words makes me flinch, and I step around him, heading to the driver's side door as I grasp my keys in my shaking hands. "I didn't--"

"You did. But don't worry." I swear I hear a smirk in his voice. "Hearing you say my name as you came last night took the sting away." He follows me back to the car and steps even closer, causing my stomach to press against the door as he cages me in. "Despite my best efforts, you've piqued my curiosity, Mia."

I twist around to face him. "I hate to disappoint you, but I'm pretty boring."

"Go on a date with me."

"You just got out of a relationship," I remind him.

"I'm aware." His molars grind, but he forces his jaw to relax. "While the timing may not be perfect, when I find something I want--"

"Some*thing*?"

"Some*one*," he corrects. His fingers skate along my arm and brush against my wrist, reminding me exactly what it feels like to have them inside me. "Go out with me."

"I'm not interested."

"You sounded interested last night."

"I was interested in coming, not dating," I argue.

"So, you can fantasize about me, but I'm not allowed to buy you dinner?"

"Nope."

His fingers flex around my wrist. "I like you, Mia. And despite your words, I think you like me too."

I lift my chin and take in the shadows striking against his sharp features from the light post above us. This man is dangerous. You can feel the power radiating off of him. He's like a shark. The way he moves. So smooth, yet predatory too. Like you know he could strike at any second, ripping you apart with a single bite, and it would happen so fast, you wouldn't even see it coming. I want to touch him. To study him. To push him to see what happens. To see if he bites. Even when it's a bad idea. Even when we both know he could tear me to shreds in an instant.

"Tell me I'm wrong, Brat," he pushes. The nickname isn't laced with malice. Hell, it's practically a caress. "Tell me you don't like me."

"My body likes you," I concede, choosing to stare at the dark sky above us instead of his eyes. "But it doesn't mean I'm interested in dating you."

"And what are you interested in?" He leans even closer until his lips brush against the column of my throat. It's like he knows he has me exactly where he wants me. Desperate and needy. Horny. Practically putty in the bastard's hands.

I bite back my moan of frustration, tilting my head up, giving him better access to my exposed neck as I choke out, "Fucking." I swallow. "I'm interested in fucking."

"Let me take you out."

"No."

He lets go of my wrist, trailing his hands along my waist and cupping my sides, making me feel small and delicate. "Why?"

"Because you're my boss."

"We both know I'd never let a personal relationship affect the way I run my company. You're an asset to the Lions whether or not we're together." He runs his nose along the column of my throat, making my knees weak. "Go out with me."

"Not. Interested," I whisper, but I can feel myself wavering. My resolve crumbling.

"If I touched your pussy right now, I think I could prove otherwise."

My lips lift despite myself. "We've already discussed my body's interest in yours."

"So my mind repulses you?" he challenges, then sucks the patch of skin right beneath my ear into his mouth.

Dammit, this guy is way too talented with that thing.

My pulse races, and I try to steady my breathing, but it feels like he's stolen all the oxygen available, and my only option is to kiss him if I have any hope of convincing my lungs to work ever again. But I don't. I won't. I *can't*.

Squeezing my eyes closed, I lean my back against the car and let it take my weight, knowing my legs might give out at any second as my fingers press into the cool metal to keep from reaching out and tugging Henry closer. "If I say yes, it shows I'm interested in dating you, which means you'll immediately turn into an asshole, and I really don't want you to be an asshole."

He hesitates, pulling away an inch or two as his eyes narrow, studying me with interest. "Who says I'll turn into an asshole?"

My eyes open. I look up at the night sky. The stars twinkle above us, and the moon is big and bright as I admit the truth. The one that's haunted me since my father died. Even before. When my dad would promise to take me out for ice cream, and I'd wait on the curb for hours, not even caring he was late. And when he'd call a week later with some bullshit excuse as to why he didn't show up, I'd eat it up, denying the truth and agreeing the next Saturday would work for me too. Yeah. My penchant for assholes started long before my dad died. He was the one who started it all, then he was ripped away from me, leaving an unfillable hole in my chest no matter what I did.

"Who says I'll turn into an asshole, Mia?" Henry repeats. His tone is softer now. Warmer, maybe.

With a deep breath, I whisper, "Me. Because I'm only attracted to assholes."

I can feel his amusement against my skin, and it surprises me. The amusement. But it's not at my expense. It's more like I surprised him, too, and he's rarely caught off guard.

"So, you're refusing to go out with me because you're afraid I'll turn out to be an asshole?" he questions.

"Yes."

"I'm already an asshole, Mia."

"I know," I whisper. The tightness in my chest eases. Because it's true. He is an asshole. So much so, I should be running for the hills. Yet here I am, letting him nibble on my throat as desire pools low in my belly.

"But I don't want to be an asshole with you." The same warmth seeps into his confession, and I swear I might dissolve entirely.

My eyes close again, and I fist my hands at my sides, desperate to touch him, while knowing exactly how bad of an idea it would be if I allowed myself to give in. "I know."

"Let me take you out," he repeats, continuing his assault on my sensitive skin.

"I can't."

"You're making this difficult, Brat."

"I know." My lips lift, and I squeeze my eyes shut even tighter, lost in the feel of him. He's everywhere. His hands. His scent. His mouth. He presses his knee between my thighs while pinning my upper body in place with his own. The heat from my core warms his slacks, proving how weak I am for him.

And dammit, I *am* weak.

So damn weak, I'm about to make a huge mistake, but I'm too turned on to give a shit.

"I have a proposition for you," I tell him. My fingers find the lapel of his suit, and I tug him closer.

He tightens his grasp around my waist and lifts his head from the crook of my neck to look down at me. "What kind of proposition?"

"Friends with benefits."

He cocks his head. "Are we friends?"

"Okay, frenemies with benefits," I clarify. My hips shift slightly against his thigh.

Yup. Pretty sure I could come by humping this guy's leg in the middle of a parking lot.

Super classy, I know.

"You want me to fuck you," he surmises while lifting his thigh like he knows exactly what I'm thinking.

My breath catches, and I nod. "Yes."

"But you don't want me to date you."

"Isn't sex the only thing guys really want anyway?" I challenge.

Grasping my chin, he lifts my head up. "You think the only reason I asked you out is so I can fuck you?"

"Am I wrong?" I shamelessly roll my hips even more, but he drops his knee an inch, leaving me desperate. "Professor," I warn.

He lets my chin go. "I can get sex anywhere, Mia."

"But you want it with me, right?" I tug him toward me again, attempting to melt a bit of the iciness between us. It's weird how there's even any ice between us in the first place. I just asked him to sleep with me without any strings attached. I assumed he'd be jumping for joy. Instead, he looks torn. Hell, he looks almost offended.

"We all have needs, Professor." I lift my chin without his prompting and meet his eyes. Sliding my hand down his torso, I toy with the button on his slacks.

"So you want to be fuck buddies," he concludes.

"Yes."

"But we aren't buddies. You work for me."

"Fine. We'll be fuck associates," I offer dryly. My hand travels a few more inches south until the head of his cock jerks beneath my palm.

"This is a bad idea," he grunts.

"You're one hundred percent correct." I squeeze him one time and let him go. "But if you're not sure--"

"What are the ground rules?" he growls.

I rise onto my tiptoes and nip at his bottom lip. "Well, for one, you can't fire me when this ends."

"Done." He bunches the sides of my shirt in his fingers, and the cool metal from my car hits my lower back when I arch my chest into his. "Two," he continues. "While we're in this arrangement, neither of us will have sex with anyone else." His grasp on my shirt disappears, and his hand finds my neck. He tilts my head up to his, commanding my full attention. "Understood?"

"Yes," I whisper.

"Three." He squeezes my throat softly but doesn't let me go. "You aren't allowed in my penthouse. Sex in hotels only."

"Sounds expensive," I note.

"I think I can afford it." His mouth lifts. "But if you prefer, I'm open to your place, as well, if you're comfortable."

"But not yours?" I ask.

My carotid artery thrums against his thumb as he rubs it back and forth along my skin. Playing with me. Like he already knows exactly how I like to be touched, and he's nailing his demonstration.

"I'm particular about my personal space," he tells me.

"Scarlett never stayed at your place?"

The rhythmic brush of his thumb ceases, and he lets my throat go, trailing his hand up and onto the nape of my neck. He tangles his fingers through the strands of my hair and tugs roughly, bringing my mouth an inch from his. "Scarlett and I lived together for over a year."

"Oh."

"Scarlett and I were *dating*." He tugs my hair one more time and bends closer. "She was interested in more than my dick. At least for a little while."

"And your money, right?" I quip but quickly snap my mouth shut. "Shit, I'm sorry, I didn't mean——"

"Rule number four," he interrupts, dropping his knee from between my legs. "No lies. If you're unhappy with the arrangement, you end it."

"Agreed," I whisper.

"Good."

He gives in and nibbles at the corner of my mouth, teasing me while postponing our inevitable kiss. It messes with my head. Leaving me aching in all the right places and seconds from jumping up and wrapping my legs around his waist right here. Right now.

"Should we make rule number five the cliched no falling in love decree?" I twist my head toward his in hopes of making my needs clear.

Kiss me, dammit!

Instead, he pulls away slightly, his eyes darker than ever. "I don't think it will be a problem for you, now, will it?"

My attention drops to his lips barely a breath away. I shake my head. "No problem."

"Then I don't think it's necessary." His grip is tight as he slides his other palm along my lower back, splaying his massive hand against the swell of my ass. Heat spreads from his touch and down to my core as I replay his words. The obligatory no-falling-in-love decree won't be necessary because there's no chance of us actually falling in love? Or did he decline my suggestion because he knows my heart's too petrified to beat for anyone after all the shit it's been through?

Does it even matter?

I'm getting exactly what I want.

Sex with Henry.

No strings attached.

No feelings.

Simply a few solid orgasms.

I lift my head and meet his gaze. Waiting to see if he'll actually go through with it. If he'll actually kiss me out in the open parking lot. Which would be a terrible idea. One of many.

Most of the cars are gone, but there are still a few vehicles scattered around. Someone could spot us.

His attention drops to my lips. "Pull away, and we'll pretend like the last two days never happened." He leans even closer, his hot breath kissing my lips. "But if you let me kiss you, it isn't going to stop here. I will take you to the nearest hotel, spread you out on the bed, and taste every inch of you while comparing it to the hotel in Creekside. Because fucking hell, Mia, I've been craving you ever since. Tell me you understand."

Pressing my thighs together, I whisper, "I understand."

"Good girl."

25

MIA

Henry takes his time. The tension is stifling and makes me want to rip off my clothes until he finally gives in and kisses me. As soon our mouths connect, his hand slides down, and he cups my ass. The contact is almost more than I can bear, sending a zing of excitement to take up residence in my core. I tug at the edge of his suit and pull him closer, dragging my tongue against his. My shirt rides up a few inches. The cool metal of my car presses against my back as he tangles his fingers in the hair at the nape of my neck and tugs. Shivers race down my spine, my thighs spreading on their own accord, and he shoves his knee between them like before. This time, I shamelessly grind against him. The pressure and friction, combined with the foreplay from the past few minutes, make me desperate. My heart pounds against my ribcage as he rips his mouth from mine, slips his hand from my ass, grasps the handle, and opens the back door of my car.

"Get in," he orders.

I slide inside, and he follows right after me, smacking my ass and encouraging me to straddle his lap.

"I thought you said you were gonna take me to a hotel," I argue as my fingers find the button on my jeans, and I slide them off. His chuckle is dark but thick with desire as he watches my movements. His own hands follow suit, tugging at the top button of his slacks. When his very hard erection pops out, my eyes widen, and I take him in.

Yeah. I was right. The dude is hung.

My tongue runs along my bottom lip, but I restrain the urge to bend down and lick him like a lollipop. I rip my attention from his massive dick and meet Henry's eyes. "Do you have a condom?"

He nods. "I'm clean."

"So am I, but it doesn't mean I'm going to sleep with you without protection."

"Good girl." He pulls a condom out of his wallet, but I take it from his grasp, ripping the package with my teeth and rolling it on. My fingers trail down the mushroom head as I straddle him, keeping my center lifted until he's lined up with my entrance.

Am I really doing this? Are we really doing this?

His grip is tight on my waist as I slowly pump him with my hand, teasing him as all the reasons why this is a terrible idea flutter through my mind. Too bad I don't give a shit.

Ashlyn's right. I might be great at giving advice, but taking it? Not so much.

"I should warn you," he grumbles. His dick jerks in my palm. "I like being in control."

I almost laugh but hold it back as I continue my assault, grinning shamelessly at him. "And this is killing you, isn't it?" I guess.

His attention shifts from where I'm teasing his cock to my eyes. His own are hot with desire, leaving my skin flushed with anticipation. "Let's just say, if you aren't careful, I'm not afraid to take you home and smack your ass."

I grin, rubbing the head of his dick along my slit as I roll my hips without lowering myself onto him. "You mean, take me to the nearest hotel," I remind him. "Sounds like a solid round two to me."

He grabs my waist and holds me in place. Shoving his hips up, he thrusts into me. I gasp at the intrusion and almost see stars as my hand flies to his shoulder.

"Shit," I breathe out.

Once he's fully seated inside me, the delicious stretch makes me nearly come on the spot, but I fight it off, enjoying this way too much to let it be over so quickly.

My eyes roll back in my head. "Fuck."

His own breath catches, and he gives me a cocky smirk. "Ride me, Brat. Let me feel you."

Slowly, I shift in his lap, riding his dick while appreciating every single nerve he's touching and how good it feels. Seriously. Masturbation is great and all, but there's nothing like the real thing. Not when the guy knows how to pleasure a girl.

I continue riding him, slipping my hand between us and playing with my clit while he sucks on my neck, peppering kisses along the sensitive flesh and scraping his teeth against my collarbone. The sharp sensation makes my stomach dip and leaves me breathless. I knew it'd be good. Sex with Henry. But this? This is more. It's better. So much better. His hands find the hem of my shirt, and he shoves it up, squeezing my breasts as my orgasm starts to crest. He must be able to feel me tightening around him because a low grunt rumbles through his chest as he leans his head back, watching me ride him.

"Fuck." He squeezes my breasts tighter, brushing his thumbs against my sensitive nipples. "Milk my cock, baby. Come for me. Come for me now."

My mouth opens wide as I orgasm, and he follows suit, his dick jerking inside me.

"That's it, baby," he murmurs. My back arches as I push myself into his hands. "That's it."

Before I have a chance to come down, he slips out of me and tosses my body onto the center console. Spreading my thighs wide, he bends down, licking my core, not even giving my brain a chance to catch up.

"Boss," I pant. My fingers find his hair on their own accord, and I grind myself against him. "Fuck, Professor."

He shoves his fingers into me and pumps them back and forth while his mouth latches onto my clit, rubbing the tip of his tongue against the nub.

Seriously. Is this guy trying to kill me?

But what a way to go.

I spread my legs wider and lean back, placing my hands on the front seats for balance, knowing I'm seconds from another orgasm.

"Yes. Yes. Yes." I chant the words as he scissors his fingers back and forth while nibbling my clit, sending my body spiraling again. I come on his tongue with a moan, but he doesn't stop. Not until I push him away from my sensitive center, my chest still heaving.

"You," I pant, "are something else."

He grins, wiping his mouth with the back of his hand and slipping the used condom off. Tying a knot in the top, he slips it into his suit pocket and pulls his pants up the rest of the way.

"And you," he murmurs once he's back to his usual collected self. He leans forward and kisses me again. I can taste myself against his lips, and my core clenches at the memory of how incredibly talented his mouth is. He pulls away and continues, "Are exactly how I remembered." He kisses me another time. "*Perfect.* I'll meet you at your place? Or would you prefer a hotel?"

"You can go again?"

"Mia, I told you. I have a one-track mind, and I'm only getting started."

Well, okay then.

I grin and peck his lips again. "My place, it is."

26

HENRY

"**M**ake yourself at home," Mia suggests as she opens the door to her apartment and steps inside.

I shrug out of my suit jacket, fold it over my arm, and take in her living space. Mia's apartment is as bare as when I first toured it to ensure it was livable for her. There is nowhere to hang my jacket or set it down on...anything. There's nothing but an old--and likely moldy--chair in the center of the family room, a couple pairs of shoes beside the door, a box of Captain Crunch on the counter, and a few dishes scattered along the kitchen island. Otherwise, you would think the place was vacant.

"Where is your furniture?" I ask.

Mia peeks over her shoulder at me and smiles coyly. "I have a chair."

"You have a flea-infested lump," I counter.

Her smile spreads. "Yeah, but it has flowers on it."

"Which are probably what attracted the fleas."

With a roll of her eyes, she approaches me, drags her hands along my pecs, slips her arm beneath the fold of my suit jacket, and tosses it onto the kitchen island. I bite back my groan, knowing it probably landed on a pile of crumbs. It's a good thing she's cute, or I would probably smack her ass for it.

"Are we here to discuss my lack of furniture, or are we here to scratch a few more itches?"

I glance at the worn armchair again. "As long as you aren't itchy because of the fleas."

Another laugh slips out of her, and she shakes her head. "None of my other conquests have complained."

Conquests?

She's only lived here for a month or two, and as far as I know, she hasn't had any recent conquests, so what the fuck?

I shouldn't care what she does with her time outside the office or who she's slept with. It's none of my business. Or it wasn't. But now we're sleeping together, and I'm curious. More curious than I would like to admit. Even if the idea *does* piss me off.

"You've brought someone here since moving in?" I ask, forcing my tone to stay even.

Her lips press together as if she doesn't want to answer me, as if she's considering lying to me. "Unfortunately, I've been a little preoccupied with work."

"Too preoccupied to invite someone to your place?"

"Or to buy new furniture," she adds.

The tightness in my chest eases almost instantly. "So, no one but me."

"Only you." She hesitates, then a grin spreads across her full, pink lips. "Well, other than your mascot."

A low growl rumbles through my throat, and I step toward her, but she mirrors my movement, keeping herself just out of reach.

"Are you telling me I need to hire a new mascot?" I demand.

"Are you telling me you'd fire Leo the Lion all because he potentially got in my pants?"

My head cocks. "He's barely nineteen."

"Maybe I like 'em young."

"And he never takes his costume off."

"Maybe I have a thing for role-playing." Her grin makes my gut clench.

She throws her head back and laughs. The sound is loud and boisterous, giving me a glimpse of the girl from before. Before her father died. Before she was too overwhelmed with the shit hand life dealt her to enjoy the little things. I like it. A lot.

"You should see the look on your face," she tells me, nearly lost in a fit of giggles.

"I don't like the idea of someone touching what's mine."

She sobers slightly, dragging her long hair over one shoulder and giving me a shrug. "It's a good thing I'm not yours, then, isn't it?"

"Our arrangement says otherwise."

"Even though I promised not to sleep with anyone else while we're hooking up, it doesn't mean I belong to you, Professor."

"Not your professor anymore," I remind her.

"I'm well aware, Captain Obvious," she snarks. "However, since we're discussing our arrangement, I thought of another rule on the way over here."

"Which is?"

"No one can know about us."

Her proposal makes me feel like I'm her dirty little secret. A sharp ache pricks my spine. "Mia--"

"I'm serious." She lifts her chin in defiance. "I don't want you going all overprotective macho man on me at the rink or anything simply because one of the players talks to me and you don't like it. Understood?"

"Afraid Leo the Lion will find out we're sleeping together?" I question.

Another grin touches her lips. "Exactly."

The girl is infuriating.

The way she's playful and flirty and stubborn. So damn stubborn. But I know her. I know if I don't agree, she'll ask me to leave. It doesn't matter how hot the sex is or how much her body craves mine. She is already on the fence. Already unsure whether or not our arrangement is a good idea.

Then again, so am I.

I need to play this carefully.

"Fine," I concede. "Although, I *definitely* need to find a mascot replacement."

Another breath of laughter slips out of her. "Oh, really?"

"Mm-hmm. And a replacement for your ugly ass floral chair."

She glances at the chair in question and crosses her arms. "Maybe I like the ugly ass floral chair."

"No one likes the ugly ass floral chair," I counter and step closer. "I'm also going to be a replacement for your vibrator."

"Who said I have a vibrator?" she quips.

"A girl like you knows how to take care of herself," I note, prowling closer.

Her eyes soften slightly, but she takes another step back. I doubt she realizes how close she is to the wall behind her.

"I knew you were smart, Buchanan."

"Just because you can take care of yourself doesn't mean you should push everyone who wants to help away."

Her back hits the wall with a soft thump, and her lips part on a gasp.

"Nowhere else to run, Brat," I rasp, grasping her waist.

She reaches up and hooks her arm around my neck,

tugging me closer to her. "Does this look like I'm running? Like I'm pushing you away?"

I shake my head, her scent driving me insane as my hands flex against her sides.

"Didn't think so," she quips. "Now, fuck me."

"Here?"

She nods.

"You aren't going to invite me to your bedroom?"

"If you think the chair's bad, you'll probably have a heart attack when you see my mattress."

"Then, I guess it's a good thing I don't need a bed to fuck you properly."

"A very good thing," she agrees, lifting her head until barely a breath of space separates her mouth from mine. I can almost taste her. Her mouth. Her pussy.

The memory from the car earlier is like gasoline to a flame. It ignites every inch of me. I grab beneath her ass, hook her legs around my waist, and spread her wide. Heat seeps from the apex of her thighs as I give in, grinding into her. My body swells at the thought of round two and exactly what I plan to do with her.

Yes. This is a very good thing. So good, I'm not sure my mind will ever be able to placate my lust long enough to consider my own well-being when it comes to Mia Rutherford.

27

MIA

It's amazing. What good sex can do for a girl. There's a pep in my step and a flush in my cheeks whenever I think about my arrangement with Henry, no matter how unconventional it is. The reminder I don't have to deal with Jeffry while on the job is basically the icing on an already delicious cake.

Halle-freaking-lujah.

It's going to be a good day, and I've finally given myself a chance to actually enjoy my job for the time being.

It's weird.

Enjoying something.

Life in general, even.

Part of me is waiting for the other shoe to drop. For reality to crash into me. The other part? I'm soaking up the good stuff as long as it lasts because I'm not naive enough to believe this doesn't come with an expiration date.

Still.

A few solid orgasms last night.

A fun job.

A chance to travel.

And zero creepers breathing down my neck.

Yup.

I'm calling it a win.

"All right, hit the showers," Dawson yells when the team crosses the red line on the opposite end of the rink like their lives depend on it. Plumes of ice crystals spray across the goal as they each stop short, the players' chests heaving from exertion.

"Actually," I call out as the Zamboni appears and starts zamming the ice. "Do I have any volunteers willing to lip-sync a trending song for me? The video's only ten seconds, so it shouldn't be too terrible. Any takers?" I press my hands into a prayer gesture and give them a syrupy sweet smile, knowing at least one will cave with enough begging. "Pleeeease?"

With his glove-clad hand raised in the air, Beck heads toward me by the benches. "I can help."

"Perfect. Anyone else?" I scan the already-tired players, their hair dripping with sweat as they skate toward the bench, but no one else speaks up. Another beat of silence passes, and I add, "Bueller? Bueller?"

"What song is it?" Greer asks.

I pull my phone out and play the song I plan to use. He bobs his head up and down with the beat for a few bars and gives me a thumbs up. "Sick beat. All right, I'm in."

"Perfect. Can I have one more volunteer?"

Mortinson, one of the defenders, lifts his hand. "Yeah, I'm in."

"Awesome, thank you!" The guys gather around me, preparing for my instructions while the rest of the team hangs out near the side of the rink, shooting the shit and waiting for their heart rates to finally slow after a particularly brutal practice, thanks to yesterday's loss.

Ignoring them, I announce, "Okay, so for this video, I

want to be in the middle of the rink and have everyone skate around me while lip-syncing the song. Like I said, super easy. Make sense?"

Again, everyone nods, and Beck offers his hand. "Do you need help onto the ice?"

"Yes, please." I take his gloved hand, and he chuckles, guiding me from the bench onto the freshly-zammed ice. Gratitude shines in my amusement as I stare at the slippery surface beneath my feet.

Yeah, this stuff is slick.

We shuffle slowly, moving along the blue line toward the center of the rink like a couple of snails. I clutch his hand even harder, knowing how much it would suck to fall right now. My camera hangs around my neck, swaying with every shuffle of my feet. I lose my balance and nearly face-plant on the ice. Beck's hands are on my hips almost instantly, steadying me with a sure grasp as my camera smacks him in the chest.

"Whoa, you okay?" he asks.

I nod. "Yeah, thanks."

His hands stay planted where they are, and he grins down at me as the Zamboni finishes smoothing out the ice. "Glad I could catch you."

My own amusement falls.

Shit.

I know this look. It's the look I've received a thousand times at SeaBird. The look I've dodged more times than I can count while attending LAU. The look telling me he's about to say something stupid, and I brace myself for it.

"Hey, so I was thinking..." His eyes catch on someone behind me, and he adds, "Go away, man. Mia and I need some privacy."

Uh, no, we don't.

"Mia doesn't mind, do you?" Greer chirps, continuing his circular path around us like the well-seasoned skater he is.

When I stay quiet, Beck shakes his head and clears his throat. "I was, uh, wondering if you wanna grab a drink with me after we're done filming today?"

Aaaand, there it is.

The line in the sand, separating us from friends to...*more*, and I have no desire to cross it.

Smoothing out the practice jersey across his pads, I avoid his gaze. "I can't. I'm sorry."

"Okay. Maybe next week or something?" he prods.

Grimacing, I pat his chest and shake my head. "Sorry, Beck, but I have a thing against dating hockey players."

A wrinkle forms between his brows. "Why?"

"I had a bad experience," I tell him.

"Ah, come on," Greer chimes in. "We're not all bad."

"You're right. You guys aren't bad at all." My head swivels from left to right, following Greer's path around us. "You're actually a group of really great guys, but--"

"If you're worried about it being forbidden because of a policy or anything, Erika gave us the green light last week," Beck explains. "Said if you're interested, they're not gonna stop you from dating anyone who catches your eye."

"And trust us. You've caught a lot of eyes on the team," Greer says while Beck laughs. "Yeah. Pretty sure most of the team would jump at the opportunity to take you out."

"Even Coach Dawson asked about you," Greer adds, reminding me of a teenager spreading the latest gossip during first period.

Dawson too?

Seriously?

"That's...nice of him, I guess?" I laugh and shake my head, unsure what the hell I'm supposed to say in this situation. I glance up at the box seats to find Henry staring down at me, his arms crossed over his broad chest, his expression unreadable. I don't know how long he's been watching, but I know this look too. It's still cold. Still detached. But there's a heat to it, as well. One simmering beneath the surface, threatening to steal my breath as he takes in Beck's hands on my waist and Greer slowly circling us with a wide grin on his face.

I wonder how this must look to him. What he must be thinking. Especially after last night. Hell, I can still feel him inside me. A slight ache sinks between my thighs.

Don't worry, Professor. I know the rules.

And I'm not planning to sleep with anyone else while our arrangement is still in place.

Tearing my eyes from his, I playfully bat Beck's hands away from my hips. Once he's satisfied I can keep my balance on the ice, he lets me go. I cup my hands around my mouth, calling out, "I have an announcement to make!" My voice echoes off the glass, ice, and every other surface in the arena. Most of the team is still hanging out near the benches. Coach Dawson and the rest of the coaching staff are also present, and their conversations cease as Dawson lowers his clipboard and looks at me.

Licking my lips, I continue. "I know this probably only relates to one or two people, but I think it's best if I clear the air with everyone." Keeping my balance, I rub my hands together and prepare myself for the inevitable. "So, I've been informed of this organization's hands-off approach to dating, hooking up, et cetera, et cetera. And while I appreciate their stance, I want to take two seconds to say I don't date. Not hockey players. Not coaches. Not coworkers. Not strangers. Not friends." I check each potential scenario off, one by one, with my fingers. "I. Don't. Date. *Period.* And this isn't an opportunity for anyone to prove me wrong or be the exception to the rule or whatever. This is my formal announcement stating all I'm looking for is friends." Fiddling with the strap of my camera, I keep my chin held high and add, "So...yeah. If anyone else was thinking about asking me out or anything, I'm really flattered, and you guys are all major catches, but it's not gonna happen. I'm sorry." My eyes find Henry's stoic expression despite my best effort as the apology slips past my lips.

He looks like a king up there. Above us. Superior, somehow. Like we're lucky to wipe the dirt off his loafers or something. Part of me hates how I gave in. That I proved my loyalty after only one fuck session. But I know what it's like to have zero trust in the opposite sex, and if the roles were reversed, I'd be grateful for the clarification. For the subtle show of loyalty and understanding despite our arrangement only being physical.

His chin dips with the slightest of nods, confirming his appreciation for my little impromptu speech. I lift my camera and rest it on my shoulder, turning back to the rest of the team. "Anyway, I'm done with my little speech." I give them a thumbs up. "Thanks! Now let's start filming, shall we?"

THE VIDEO TURNS OUT AWESOME. THANKFULLY, NONE OF THE guys batted an eye after my announcement, treating me the exact same way they did before my little speech while making sure they stayed respectful and as sweet as always.

It's nice. Refreshing, even. To have my opinions and wishes and boundaries respected.

Really refreshing.

Setting my camera into its black bag, I slide it onto my shoulder and head to the parking lot as the team showers after practice. It's still relatively early, but my stomach grumbles, begging for food. Mexican sounds nice. Some queso, maybe.

Oh, a smothered burrito would be perfect.

"Quite the announcement," a voice calls from behind me.

I glance over my shoulder and smile.

Pretty sure a slice of Henry Buchanan would soothe my appetite quite nicely, as well.

"You heard it, huh?" I ask though we both know he did. My steps slow, giving him time to catch up to me.

As his long legs eat up the distance between us, he prods, "Was it for me? The speech?"

My lips pull into a thin line as I deflect, "Were you jealous? Watching me with Beck and Greer?"

He steps closer to me with his hands in his pockets. "They want you."

"So?"

"So, yes," he clarifies. "It makes me jealous."

"Why?"

"Because I have no claim on you," he reminds me. "I was already turned down once."

"You were the one inside me last night."

"Last night, sure. But what about tonight?" he counters. "What about tomorrow?"

"You don't have anything to worry about, Professor. I might be against dating, but I'm a girl of my word. While we're in our arrangement, I'll abide by the rules we agreed to, including not sleeping around."

"Is that what the speech was for?" He tilts his head toward the arena across the parking lot. "To prove it?"

I want to say yes. To tell him I could see the jealousy in his eyes, even from across the stands. I could see the fear shining in them, wondering if I'm like Scarlett. If I'm not trustworthy. If I could stab him in the back like she did. Like Shorty did to me. But admitting I care about Henry's feelings is...personal. Too personal, considering our arrangement, so I pop my shoulder up instead and look down at the dark pavement beneath my feet.

"I would've made the speech regardless," I tell him. "Because even if you weren't in the picture, I still wouldn't be interested in dating anyone." I lick my lips and meet his gaze again. "But, yes. Now everyone knows my expectations, and there shouldn't be any issues."

The same heat flares in his dark irises as he stares down at me. "I think it was a wise decision."

"One of few," I quip dryly.

"I don't know about that."

I do, but I don't argue with him. Instead, I say, "I should probably go."

I take a step toward my beat-up car, but he grabs my wrist and holds me in place. Rocking back on my heels, I wait as his astute gaze flutters over the nearly empty parking lot. When he's satisfied we're relatively alone, he tugs me closer, invading my personal space and letting his chest brush against mine. The innocent friction makes my stomach clench with anticipation, reminding me of last night. Images of his sweaty body hovering over mine as he thrust into me over and over again make my thighs press together, but I don't move a muscle. I simply wait. For what, I'm not sure, but I do. I stand there, replaying every moment, every kiss, every bite, every touch, until I realize I'm barely breathing. Forcing the air from my lungs, I hold his expectant gaze.

He leans down and whispers, "Meet me at The Grand Hotel on Baker Street in fifteen minutes."

"Who said I'm available?" I ask, my voice breathless.

Amusement sparks in his eyes. "Are you available for a few orgasms this evening, Ms. Rutherford?"

My core clenches, and a laugh bubbles out of me. "I mean, when you put it that way..."

His hand slips beneath the strap of my backpack hanging at my side and grips my waist. The possessive touch nearly makes me melt on the spot as he tugs me against him fully, plastering our fronts together. His hard length swells, pressing against my belly, and he growls, "Good girl."

28

HENRY

I t's been three weeks. Three weeks of solid fucking and no strings attached. For her, anyway. Mia has only invited me to her place once or twice. Still, between the locker room after hours, her car, and the Baker Street hotel room I booked for the next month, we've found plenty of time to hook up and scratch each other's itches.

Well, our physical ones. Emotionally? She's keeping her distance. I don't dare push her. If I do, she'll run.

I've watched her lately. Even more so than before. The way she keeps people at a distance. The way she deflects any personal questions, choosing to reply with a question of her own instead. She's a puzzle. One I want to piece together.

But not yet.

Because in her eyes, we're only fucking.

She doesn't want it to change.

But I'm patient enough to take things slowly.

I remind myself of this as I follow Mia and the rest of the team outside, keeping my distance. I don't want to look too eager. Too possessive. Too interested. But seeing her surrounded by hockey players who would love to see her naked tests my patience despite her speech at practice a few weeks ago. I see the way they look at her. The way they want her. The way they are pulled to her.

The Wisconsin air is cooler than in Lockwood Heights. Mia rubs her hands up and down her jacket-covered arms. She's laughing at something Theo said. Beck steps around me and catches up to them in the parking lot.

The Lions just finished playing the Brawlers, and the team is buzzing from the victory.

"You guys go ahead," Mia replies to whatever Theo says. "I think I'm gonna head back to the hotel so I can get some editing done."

"You sure?" Beck prods.

"Yup. I'm sure. Thanks, though."

"Colt and I will walk you back," Theo offers.

"You guys, I'm fine." Mia shoves at his shoulder playfully. "It's like a five-minute walk."

"Ash and Blake would kill us if we let you walk alone," Colt reminds her.

"Then it'll be our little secret," she quips, breaking apart from the group and wiggling her fingers back and forth. "See ya."

Her pace is quick, creating a solid twenty yards between her and the rest of the group as Colt and Theo exchange a look, debating whether or not they should follow.

"I'll walk her back," I announce.

They look over their shoulders as if only now realizing my presence. "We'll take her––"

"She'll be safe with me," I interrupt, annoyed they even have to question it.

After exchanging another look, they both nod and tuck their hands in their front pockets, heading to the bar across the street while I pursue Mia. She has already doubled the distance between us, and I pick up my pace, watching her hips sway as she heads down the street.

The hotel is only a couple of blocks from the arena. Despite being in the middle of the city, it's quiet outside. Mia lifts her head, looking up at the stars. I'm too far to see if she's smiling, but I bet a thousand dollars she is. Her shoulders relax more and more with every step, the comfortable quiet helping her walls lower as she settles into herself. The real her. The one she keeps hidden from the rest of the world. Less than a block ahead of her sits a homeless man with a large, scruffy dog resting on the edge of the sidewalk. I lengthen my stride when I notice them, and Mia stops in front of them a few seconds later. She says something, though I'm too far away to hear what, and digs into her purse, retrieving her wallet.

Does the girl have a death wish?

I rush to catch up as she hands him a stack of cash, squats, and pets the ball of fur.

"Aren't you the cutest thing ever?" she gushes.

"Mia," I bark.

Her eyes find mine, and she frowns but doesn't stop scratching behind the flea bag's ear. "What are you doing here?"

My nostrils flair, and I glance at the man hunched near the brick building to our right. "Helping you back to the hotel."

"You're not celebrating the win with the team?"

"Figured I would have an early night." I shift on my feet. "We should probably get going."

"I'm fine, Professor. Just saying hello to my new friend here."

"The man or the beast?" I ask.

She smiles at the homeless man and looks back at me. "Both." After another quick scratch behind the dog's ears, she

KELSIE RAE

stands and brushes her hands against her dark jeans. "See ya later. I hope you can find yourself a hot meal."

"Thank you, miss. Thank you so much," the stranger returns. He pushes his stringy white hair aside and gives Mia a toothless grin.

Mia returns it with a smile of her own, turns to me, folds her arms, and waits for me to catch up the rest of the way.

When I do, we walk side by side toward the hotel, and I ask, "How much did you give him?"

She glances behind her, then tilts her head. "Does it matter?"

Reining in my annoyance, I grunt. "You should wash your hands. You don't know where the dog has been."

"I'll wash them when I get home, Professor," she quips. "Don't get your panties in a twist."

I don't comment, too irritated by her carelessness as we continue walking back to the hotel. Cars pass us by, and our feet scuff against the pavement. Otherwise, it's quiet.

"I bet you hate animals, don't you?" she mentions when we reach the crosswalk leading to our hotel.

I hesitate, surprised by her comment. "I don't hate them."

"You looked like you hated that one, and he was nothing but a big ol' sweetheart."

"I'm sure he was very nice." I press my hand against her lower back. "But it wasn't very wise to pet him. You don't know the dog. He could have bitten you."

"I asked the owner's permission first," she argues.

"And I'm sure he would have told you it was fine, even if it wasn't the case."

Her eyes thin. "You've never owned a dog, have you?"

"No, I haven't."

"Why am I not surprised?" she asks herself, then adds, "You're missing out."

"Oh, I am?"

198

With a nod, she looks both ways and steps onto the crosswalk. "Yeah, majorly. Dogs are the best."

"You don't have a dog," I remind her.

"I used to."

"Used to?" I hesitate. "What happened?"

"It's complicated." She shrugs one of her petite shoulders. "My dad got me one when I was a kid, but since my parents were divorced and my mom hates dogs, Pixie would stay with him. I only saw her when I visited. When my dad disappeared, my aunt started taking care of her before Pixie found her soulmate—aka my aunt's husband—and they've lived happily ever after ever since."

"Pixie," I murmur. My tone softens as I realize why I recognize the name along with its significance. "The tattoo."

Rubbing her thumb against the inside of her opposite wrist where Pixie's name is inked, Mia's eyes soften. "Yeah. It's for my dog."

"She's still alive, I take it?"

Mia nods. "Yeah. She's getting older, though. And let me tell ya, I'm going to be a wreck when she finally goes." She gives me a pathetic smile, and her eyes cloud at the thought alone. "The girl's been through everything with me."

This is the first time I've seen emotion from her. Real emotion. Without holding herself back. Without laughing it off or changing the topic. She loves the dog more than almost anything. I can see it. Feel it.

"Is she a big dog? Little dog?" I prod, more curious than I would like to admit.

"Big. Massive," she clarifies with another smile. This one is happier. Less tainted. "I got her at a shelter, so they don't technically know what breed she is, but there's definitely some Husky in there, and maybe some German Shepherd or Mastiff. I'm not sure. She's awesome, though. Super smart. Super active. And with the personality of a human."

"Sounds like you love her."

"I do. I love all dogs. But Pix?" Mia clutches at her chest. "The girl owns my heart."

"Why haven't you adopted another one since Pixie lives with your uncle?"

"Honestly?" She shrugs. "I dunno. I've never been a master at making wise decisions, especially big ones."

"You don't think you could handle it?"

"I mean, I *could*. I love dogs."

"Then why not adopt another one?"

She hesitates and peers up at the hotel in front of us. The cool air has turned her cheeks a soft shade of pink as she tucks her long silvery blond hair behind her ear. "I dunno? I guess if I've learned anything from my life, it's plans never work out, so why keep making them, ya know?" The strap of her black camera bag slips, and she tugs it back into place, looping her thumb beneath it as if lost in thought. "It's easier if I go with the flow and see where it leads. Besides,"—she blinks and looks at me again—"I'm traveling with the team now. It's not like I can hire a dogsitter whenever I go out of town, right?"

"I guess not," I mutter. I'm not entirely convinced as I open the hotel door for her. "Can I see it? The tattoo?"

We step inside, and warmth envelops us almost instantly. She leads me to the side and ensures we're out of the way. Lifting her hand, she shows me the inside of her wrist. My fingers graze the inked skin, copying the familiar font. It's her handwriting. I'm almost positive it is. Goosebumps break out along her arms as she glances up at me, unsure what to say. I don't blame her. She's scared and has more barriers surrounding her than the Pentagon. We never really talk about anything personal. Even our sexual encounters have been nothing but some solid fucking. But this? It feels more intimate somehow. And she doesn't know what to do about it.

"Do you have any tattoos?" she asks, then realizes she already knows the answer. She's seen me naked, and no, I do not have any tattoos.

My mouth lifts into a ghost of a smile as I stare down at her and explain. "Never found anything that meant enough. Is the Pixie tattoo your favorite?"

"I have a lot of tattoos, so I'm not sure." She looks down at the ink swirling along her arm, and I realize I am still holding her wrist. Still tracing the letters. Still memorizing the feel of her soft, warm skin.

Her tongue darts out from between her lips, moistening them. She murmurs, "This one is from a drunk night with Shorty." She points to a sloppy hockey stick. "This one"--her fingers graze a bouquet of daisies, and I peer closer, noticing a smiley face hidden between the petals--"is from my favorite tattoo artist's apprentice who had no idea what he was doing. Milo covered it for me with the daisies."

I brush my thumb along her forearm and examine each and every mark on her skin, pausing when I notice a small row of numbers along the inside of her bicep. I don't ask what it symbolizes. I already know. It's the day her father died.

"Do you still talk to him?" she asks. Her tone is quiet. Unsure. "Troy?"

The name makes me pause. "No." I shake my head. "Not after I found out what he did."

She nods.

"I really am sorry, Mia."

"Don't be," she rushes out. "My dad might not have deserved to die, but it was still his decision to mess with shitty people. He should've known not to trust his gut after falling into drugs and being in and out of rehab. That's on him."

"You don't think he was capable of making wise decisions simply because he fucked up in the past?"

"I think each of us is born with both moral and work ethic compasses, but only some work as well as others. Look at you, for example." Her blue eyes meet mine, and she smiles, yet it doesn't erase the sadness in her gaze. "Sure, you were born with money, but you didn't simply spend it until it was gone. You multiplied it. You trusted your gut. Became a professor. Bought a hockey team. Your instincts are spot on, even when they've seemed absolutely insane from the outside looking in." This time, the amusement soaks up a bit of her sadness and eases the ache in my chest. "Some call it luck. And it's probably a factor," she clarifies. "But it's also innately you. Your decisions brought you here. Yours. Not your father's. Not Troy's or any other asshole you've met. *Your* decisions. And my dad's?" Her shoulder lifts. "Sometimes, I wonder if it even mattered that Troy was involved with killing him. Maybe he would've wound up in the same place regardless."

Fuck.

I knew the girl was brutally honest, but assuming her father would have died regardless of his choices? It's the most callous statement I have ever heard.

"Is it why you don't trust your gut?" I ask.

She pulls out of my grasp. The familiar barriers rise into place as she stares down at her feet. "Who says I don't trust my gut?"

"You did."

Another pop of her shoulders is my only answer. She rocks back on her heels.

"What does your gut tell you about us?" I prod.

Her mouth lifts, and she runs her hand along my chest.

"It's telling me I could really use an orgasm in the hotel room."

Part of me wants to tell her no. Tell her she's safe with me emotionally and doesn't need to distract me with sex to end our conversation. The other part? It knows I'm not the one who needs the distraction.

Mia is.

Without giving a shit who could possibly see us, I tangle our fingers together and guide her toward the elevator. "Come on, Brat. I think I can offer my services."

She grins cheekily and loops her arm through mine. "Why, thank you, Professor."

2 9

MIA

My chest heaves as I pump my arms back and forth, rounding the last corner and finding the home stretch in front of me. The sun is hidden by gray clouds that finally decided to burst during my last half-mile. I'm drenched from head to toe. The water has soaked into my sports bra and spandex shorts, making me look like a drowned rat, but it feels good. The rain. It's cleansing, almost. A little chilly, but the idea of a hot shower spurs me on. I feel like I'm on top of the world. Like I can do anything. It's the endorphins speaking, but I soak the feeling up, grateful for the high running gives me. When my apartment building comes into view, I kick it up another notch.

Come on, Mia. You got this.

With a last burst of energy, I race to the front of the building, only beginning to slow once I've reached the entrance. Resting my hands on the top of my head, I bring my pace to an even walk, taking another lap around the skyscraper while letting my heart rate slowly return to normal. Sweat and rain cling to my skin as I steady my breathing, reach for the front door, and wave at the doorman as I head to the elevator. Once I'm on my floor, I search my shorts pockets for my apartment key, but it's missing. Patting the soaked spandex, I confirm I'm not hallucinating. I peek between my cleavage in case I'd hidden the key there for safekeeping.

Nope. As empty as the pockets.

My shoulders hunch in defeat, and I rest my forehead against the locked door to my apartment.

"Dammit, dammit, dammit," I mutter.

Goodbye, endorphin high.

Digging my phone out of my pocket, I pull up my text thread with Henry and send him a message.

ME

Any chance you know the superintendent's phone number?

PROFESSOR HOT SUIT

Why?

ME

I may have lost my key while running and need someone to let me into my apartment.

PROFESSOR HOT SUIT

Come upstairs.

ME

Pretty sure it's against the rules.

PROFESSOR HOT SUIT

Just get your ass up here.

Chewing on the side of my thumb, I read his message a dozen times, unsure what to say. We have rules. And they're there for a reason. But I'd also love to *not* be hanging out in the hallway until someone lets me into my apartment, so...

My phone buzzes with another message.

PROFESSOR HOT SUIT

You can wait up here while I make a call.

It's a bad idea. Toying with the rules. Especially after I opened up to him about my relationship with Pixie. He's been looking at me differently ever since. With actual interest. And not in my body like every other guy I've met. He's looking at me like he's interested in more. Or maybe I'm imagining it. No one knows about Pixie, though. Not really. They know of her, sure. But all the nitty-gritty details? Hardly. I've never told anyone about her. About how she saved me. How she saved my uncle. How much I miss her.

Yet, I told Buchanan.

The reminder leaves me on edge, and I type my response.

ME

I know how to use a phone, Buchanan. If you give me the superintendent's number, we won't break any rules.

PROFESSOR HOT SUIT

Stop arguing and get your ass up here.

Grudgingly, I head back to the elevator. For once, the button to the penthouse is lit up, indicating I can push it, so I do. It takes me to the top floor, and the doors slide apart, revealing a massive open floor plan with floor-to-ceiling windows and slate-colored walls. A pair of dark leather couches sit in front of a huge big-screen television hanging on the wall, along with a single closed laptop resting on the dark lacquered coffee table in front of it. Oh, and the fireplace? It's also gigantic. Like something out of *Beauty and The Beast,* a movie I loved to watch as a kid. I wonder if there's a hidden library in here somewhere, too, or servants to wait on you hand and foot. Probably. The fireplace is surrounded by gray stone and has a hand-carved wood hearth matching the warm mahogany floor.

And I thought my place was fancy.

Yeah, no.

It doesn't even hold a candle to his. Walking into the empty kitchen, I trail my finger along the white granite. It's as I suspected. Not a single crumb or speck of dust. The gas stove looks as if it's never even been used.

Yeah. It's official. If I didn't know Buchanan was loaded, I do now.

Rubbing my hands up and down my bare arms, I head to the enormous windows, taking in the heavy clouds and streaks of rain against the glass when Henry rounds the corner a second later from where I assume his bedroom and bathroom are located. His nose is glued to his phone as he types something quickly and slips it into his back pocket.

"He'll be here in an hour," he announces, looking up at the foyer. Finding it empty, he scans the rest of his apartment.

When his gaze lands on me, I clarify, "An hour?"

"It's Saturday. The building runs on a skeleton crew on the weekends." Amusement teases his lips. "Glad you made yourself at home."

"Can't blame a girl for being curious," I quip.

"Of course not," he returns dryly. "I'm sorry David doesn't have access to the spares. We had an issue last year and decided to make the superintendent and his backup the only two with access to apartments."

"Makes sense." I rock back on my heels, taking in the perfectly organized family room and kitchen from my fresh angle. *Are those...?* I tilt my head, examining the fluffy gray rug in the center of the family room. *Yup.* Those are vacuum marks. My mouth lifts with amusement.

"Something funny?" Henry asks.

I smooth my features and turn to him again. "Nope. Just admiring your place. It's nice."

"Thanks."

"And clean," I note.

"I like order."

My mouth twitches again. "I've noticed."

"Is it a problem?"

I shake my head. "Nope."

And it isn't. So, he has a thing against germs and likes having a clean space. Both of those are good things, aren't they? They're also a stark reminder I shouldn't be here.

We have rules, and for some strange reason, one of his involves my presence in his personal space.

"You look like you're freezing," he notes, watching as I rub my hands up and down my bare arms.

"It started raining during my run." I pull my sopping ponytail over one shoulder to keep it from dripping all over his floor. It doesn't help.

"Do you want to use my shower?"

My brows pull. "Are you sure it isn't against the rules?"

"We have an hour to waste. Might as well make you comfortable."

"I'm fine."

"Let me take care of you for once."

"I don't need anyone to take care of me."

"Humor me, Brat."

Without waiting for my response, he heads down the hallway he came from, and I follow until we reach a massive bedroom. There isn't a single fold in the comforter. The sheets are freshly pressed and tucked beneath the mattress. The carpet looks freshly vacuumed too. Part of me wonders if he cleans it himself or if he has a maid who takes care of everything for him. Probably both, considering his OCD tendencies.

The reminder of how opposite we really are amuses me, and I don't bother to hide it as I take in his perfectly primped room. I'm pretty sure he'd have an aneurysm if he ever saw my apartment.

Oh, wait.

He kind of did see it.

A large walk-in closet is on the left, and another archway leads to the master bathroom. I hesitate when I realize where he's taking me.

"Yours?" I ask.

He stops and faces me. "Is that a problem?"

"I guess I assumed you'd have a spare bathroom or something."

"Sorry to disappoint you."

"You've done many things, Professor. Disappointing me isn't one of them. *Yet.*" I pat his cheek as I slip past him into the bathroom. I'm greeted with white marble countertops, charcoal-colored cabinets, a tub big enough to easily fit two grown adults, and a long, rectangular shower surrounded by glass with two shower heads.

And I thought my bathroom was over the top.

It's crazy. And foreign. And a major reminder of how wealthy this guy is. So much so, it almost makes me uncomfortable. I was raised on PB&J sandwiches. On ramen noodles and tap water. Part of me wonders if Henry's ever tasted tap water or if the sparkling shit that tastes like ass is all he's ever consumed.

This is why I should've never come to his apartment.

It's too personal.

Too...intimate almost.

I don't belong here.

"You know what? I think I'll skip the shower." I turn around but run smack-dab into Henry's warm, hard chest.

He catches me around my waist and keeps me from stumbling. "Tell me what's wrong."

"Seriously, it's nothing."

"Mia." His tone brooks no argument. It's like a whip. A gavel.

And I know there's no way I'm getting out of this without having a conversation I really don't want to have.

I guess it's like he said. We have an hour to waste, right? Why not make it as uncomfortable as possible, shall we?

30

MIA

A voiding his gaze in the mirror, I take in the luxurious bathroom one more time. It screams Henry Buchanan in every way. Which makes sense, all things considered. Clean. Precise. Masculine. His cologne clings to the air. There isn't a single item on the counter other than a slim bottle of hand soap on the left side of the sink and a toothbrush placed carefully in its holder. A blue light shines on the bristles, sterilizing them.

Of course, he has one of those things. Part of me is curious how much it cost him. The other part? Yeah, I'm not sure I want to know.

"Mia," he warns when I've stayed silent for too long.

"It's not a big deal," I say.

"Then you shouldn't have a problem telling me why you look like you're crawling out of your skin."

"I'm not crawling out of my skin," I lie, peeking up at him. "It's...uh, sometimes I forget how wealthy you are."

His eyes harden. "Is my wealth a problem for you?"

"Since we aren't even dating, it wouldn't matter if it was, but no. It's not a problem," I lie. Again. "It's...different."

"Different?"

I drag my fingers along the fluffy gray hand towel hanging on the wall next to the sink, avoiding his penetrating gaze. "Yeah. Different."

"How so?"

Brushing my fingers together, I note the lack of dust in here, as well, while murmuring, "You and I are opposites, Professor. Sometimes it's hard to wrap my head around it. Why you're spending time with me. But then I remind myself it's for the awesome sex and poof." I paste on a fake-ass grin and look up at him. "Reservations gone."

He doesn't take the bait. He doesn't buy my forced amusement. Instead, his eyes thin, and he studies me in the same unnerving way, making me want to squirm.

"You have a thing about money, don't you." It's not a question.

"A *thing*?" I laugh and tuck a loose strand of hair behind my ear, but the bastard doesn't crack. He simply keeps looking at me. Piecing together way more than he has any right to.

"You don't like it," he pushes.

I gulp and lift my chin. "I don't like what it does to people."

"What does it do to people, Mia?"

"Makes them selfish. Desperate. Hungry. Lazy. Depends on what side of the coin you're on."

Grabbing my bicep, he forces me to face him, leaving a few inches between us. I'm not sure if he needs the distance or if it's for my own benefit.

"If you hate it so much, why did you sell pictures of yourself online?" he challenges.

"I'm not sure it's any of your business."

"My IT guy threw out an estimate as to how much money

you likely made after he took the photos down. It was no small amount."

I suck my lips between my teeth, not sure what to say while feeling more trapped than I'd like to admit. Other than Buchanan, no one's ever asked me this. No one's ever thought to ask me this. It's too personal. Too nosy. Too rude. But the answer is even more shameful. More stupid. Okay, not entirely. Selfless, sure. But stupid? Actually, yeah. Kind of. And admitting it to him? Financial guru with a side of Judgy McJudgerson? No, thank you.

An overwhelming need to defend myself falls over me as I cross my arms and raise my chin even higher. "I'm surprised you didn't hire a detective to figure it out for you."

"You still haven't answered me."

"I don't have an answer for you."

"So it simply..."--he steps closer, and my ass hits the edge of the counter as my hands press into his firm chest--"*disappeared?*"

"I guess so," I reply, refusing to give in or acknowledge the way his heart thumps against my palm or how the feeling shoots straight to my core.

His aggravation twists his handsome features, willing me to budge. To answer him. It's so strong, so consuming, I can almost taste it as I hold his angry stare. He's so used to getting what he wants it's like he didn't even think it was possible for someone to tell him no. To stand their ground.

"And your father's money?" he prods. "The money he borrowed to pay for your degree?"

"You mean the money that cost him his life?" I mock. "It barely lasted a semester." Unable to hold his gaze for another second, I look around the gorgeous bathroom again. "Unlike this bathroom. *This* is timeless, don't you think?"

His grip on my bicep disappears, but he doesn't back

away. And he doesn't stop looking at me. I can feel it. His eyes on the side of my face. "It's only a bathroom, Mia."

"But it isn't," I argue. "This entire building screams wealth, while I grew up in a studio apartment with my mom and a barely-there father, depending on whether or not he was on a bender."

The bastard looks like I've slapped him, but I don't apologize. Not for being too stubborn to open up to him. Not for assuming things. Nothing.

"You're angry with me," he decides, and his hands fall to my waist. "For growing up with wealthy parents who didn't struggle like yours."

I stay quiet. Confused by the adrenaline thrumming through me. The need to run away from this. From him. From the reminder of my past. Everything.

"Most girls love it," he murmurs through clenched teeth as he takes in the lavish bathroom with fresh eyes. "The reminder they are sleeping with a rich guy." There's an undercurrent of frustration in his words. Resentment almost.

"Like Scarlett?" I ask.

His gaze darkens as his ex's name slips past my lips. "Yes." He squeezes my waist again. "You never told me why you covered for her."

"You're right. I didn't."

Sensing my lack of remorse, he cocks his head. "Okay, Brat, I'll bite. Why did you cover for her?"

"Because it was none of my business."

"You lied to my face."

"I've lied to a lot of people's faces," I volley back.

"I don't like liars."

"Then it's a good thing we don't have to like each other to fuck each other, isn't it?"

He grabs my jaw, twisting me until all I can see is him. "I have another rule."

"So many rules," I muse.

"Don't lie to me. *Ever.*"

"We already have that rule," I remind him. "*If you're unhappy with the arrangement, you end it. Remember?*"

"I'm amending it," he clarifies. "No lies in general."

"Does it go both ways?"

"I don't lie to anyone."

"Ever?" I challenge. The guy has to be kidding me. Everyone lies. *Everyone.* Maybe not on purpose. And maybe not with animosity. But he can't tell me he doesn't lie.

He shakes his head.

"Even when you're conducting a business deal?" I press.

"Integrity is an integral part of success. In businesses *and* relationships."

"But we aren't in a relationship," I argue.

"My cock has been inside your body, Mia." The words make my skin hot, and I lick my bottom lip. "Multiple times," he continues. "It might not constitute an emotional relationship, but it does constitute a physical one."

"Fine," I mutter, attempting to keep my libido in check. "No lying."

"Good. Now, I'll ask you again. Why didn't you tell me Scarlett was cheating when I asked?"

My shoulders fall. "Seriously?"

"I want to know. Are you against cheating?"

"Of course, I'm against cheating," I seethe, blown away he has the audacity to assume otherwise. He has no fucking clue how much I hate cheating. How low it is. How despicable.

"But only when it's happening to you," he concludes, dropping my chin from his grasp as if he's disgusted.

I glower up at him. "Excuse me?"

"Tell me I'm wrong."

"You're wrong," I snap. "The reason I didn't tell you about Scarlett was because I knew I didn't have the whole story.

Did you cheat first and were better at hiding it? Were you abusive? Did you hit her?"

"I would *never* hit a woman, Mia," he growls. His tone is full of conviction, but it's woven with disbelief too. Like he's offended I'd even think it was possible.

I scoff, blinking away the sting behind my eyes, shocked by how quickly it hit. "Lots of guys say they would never hit a woman. Doesn't mean none of them are lying."

"I'm not lying."

"Yeah, well, I didn't know you well enough to make the call at the time, so I kept my nose out of Scarlett's business the same way I want other people to keep their noses out of mine."

My words hang in the air as he watches me, the wheels in his head churning. I have no idea what they're attempting to decipher. He wanted to know why I didn't tell him about Scarlett. Now he knows. Big deal. Let's move on.

"Tell me you believe me," he orders. There's a slight rasp to his voice. An undertone of conviction and need. The combination leaves me speechless. "Tell me you know I would never hit you."

The same burn hits my eyes with a vengeance, and I turn my head, unable to look at him any longer. Not when he's this close. When I can feel the heat of his body. The weight of his stare. The brush of his clean, minty breath.

"Do you really think so little of me?" he whispers. The harshness in his voice is gone. It's replaced with genuine curiosity.

And fuck me, I don't. I don't think so little of him. Call me crazy, but I believe the guy. And it's like he said, he's nothing if not honest.

"No." I sniff. "No, I don't think you'd ever hit me or anyone else."

Buchanan nods, his gratitude warming his normally lethal gaze. He reaches up and tucks the same loose strand of my hair behind my ear. His movements are cautious and controlled, and so is his voice as he prods, "Did he hit you, Mia?"

He.

We both know who he's referring to. It only makes my shame grow stronger. Bigger. Heavier.

Weak girls get hit.

Pathetic girls get hit.

Desperate girls get hit.

And admitting my ex hit me? To anyone, let alone Henry Buchanan? The man who holds the world in the palm of his hand?

Yeah, not gonna happen.

I swallow the ache in my throat and shake my head, forcing myself back to the present. Or at least attempt to. My vision is still blurry. The bathroom is fading around me, fighting with the image of Shorty's bedroom in the basement of the Taylor House and all the times he hurt me. Manipulated me. Slapped me around simply because he could. Because I was too weak to leave. Too desperate for his attention. Too pathetic.

A gentle touch grips my chin, and Buchanan turns me to face him again. "No lying, remember?"

A sad smile graces my lips as I process his words.

Lying is easier, though.

Maybe not all the time, but in this instance? Yeah, I think it's the safer route, and for two people who are only here to help each other get off, I'm pretty sure we've done enough talking for one day.

Rising onto my tiptoes, I press my lips against his in hopes of bridging the gap created by our conversation. "Do you want to shower with me?"

He hesitates, and I swear I can see a mask of confusion slip over his face as he looks down at me like I'm a stranger.

"Is that a no?" I tease.

"I see what you're doing," he murmurs.

"I'm asking if you want to shower with me."

"No, you're pushing me away."

A sour taste floods my mouth, and I grit out, "No offense, but I don't owe you anything. We aren't exactly friends, Professor."

"You're right. I'm nothing more than a dick to you."

He steps away, but I grab his arm and pull him back. "That isn't true."

"Then what am I?" he demands.

A vein pulses at his temple, and my lips part, but I don't know what to say.

What does he want from me?

He's Henry Buchanan. The one and only.

But if he expects me to say something else, he's sorely mistaken.

My chest heaves with pent-up irritation, though I keep my breaths steady, anxious to fix this.

"I mean, we're fuck buddies, right?" I tell him playfully.

"Right." The word is sharp as his frustration seeps from his dark irises, replaced with an indifference I feel deep in my chest. "We're fuck buddies."

"Exactly." I kiss the corner of his mouth, anxious to spark something--anything--in his hard stare. But he doesn't kiss me back. He only stands there. Practically a statue.

Come on.

Let's not make this weird.

Let's have sex and fix this.

Please?

Nibbling at the edge of his mouth, I let my hands slide

down his body, play with the ridge of his cock, and whisper, "And right now, I want to fuck."

My tongue slips between his lips, and I taste him again. Trailing my mouth lower, I lick the scruff of his five-o'clock shadow. The slight roughness makes my core clench as I imagine what it would feel like against my inner thighs. I smile against his stone-cold expression, silently begging him to let this go. To let me make this better.

"Please?" I whisper.

His hands on my waist tighten, but he pushes me away. Not much. Hell, it's barely a few inches. The rejection stings nonetheless. He stares down at me with the same cold indifference. Making me feel small and insignificant. The combination only heightens my insecurities.

"Except we aren't *buddies*, either," he rasps. "Are we." It isn't a question.

Feeling whiplashed, my heels hit the ground, and my mind races as I shake my head. "What?"

"If we were *buddies*, you'd tell me what happened."

"Buchanan, I'm not here to talk," I snap. "I'm here to fuck."

Slowly, he steps away from me. "Not today."

"What?" The word is nothing but a breath as it slips out of me. "You're seriously turning down shower sex with me?"

He lets me go and opens one of the drawers, retrieving a fluffy gray towel folded into perfect thirds. "Here. I'll leave some clothes for you to change into on the bed."

Then he leaves.

And I can't help but wonder if it's because I didn't answer his questions. Because I didn't open up to him. Because I didn't let him in. And I don't like it. Not one bit.

31

MIA

The superintendent dropped my key off while I was in the shower. I should be grateful for it. The opportunity to distance myself from Buchanan and our conversation, especially with how it ended. In a way, I guess I am. After slipping on the change of clothes he left for me on his bed, I went back to my place, but the relief I usually feel in solitude is missing. Instead, I feel...like a shaken-up can of soda. Like I messed up, and I don't know how to fix it, even when there's nothing to fix in the first place.

Part of me wonders if I should've told him the truth. If I should've opened up to him. If I should've told him I gave all my OF earnings to my uncle's charity instead of keeping it. If I should've admitted what happened with Shorty while we were dating.

Instead, I clammed up and pushed him away, making him feel like he's nothing but a dick for me to use.

I was weak. Pathetic, even. Too ashamed to tell him the truth or why I'm so resentful of the opposite sex.

Annoyance tugs at me. I should probably change into my

own clothing and wash Buchanan's T-shirt and sweats so I can return them. Instead, I lift the collar of his worn T-shirt to my nose and breathe in deeply.

It smells like him.

I used his body wash and shampoo, so my entire body is engulfed in his scent. But I like it.

I like it a lot, actually.

My phone rings, and I drop the collar of Buchanan's shirt like I've been caught doing something I shouldn't and pull my cell out of my pocket. Ashlyn's calling.

Pinning it between my shoulder and ear, I say, "Hey."

"Hey! Long time no see. Want to get together for a girls' night?"

Relief washes over me, and I nod. "Yeah, I'm in. Are Kate and Blake free too?"

"Yup! Do you want to come to my place, or do you want me and the girls to come to you?"

"Let's do yours," I offer.

"Still afraid to show your place to Kate and Blake?" Ash questions.

The girl knows me too well.

Reaching for the laundry detergent, I scoop a small amount into the machine and argue, "No, I just figured your place is closer to everyone else."

"Mm-hmm," Ash hums. "Sure."

"And your place has chairs and a couch," I add.

"Hey, if I can sit criss-cross-applesauce on the floor, I'm sure Blake and Kate can too."

"Okay, fine." I slap the washer door closed and lean my hip against it. "Why don't you guys come here?"

"Yay!" Her squeal makes me laugh, and I pull my phone away from my ear. "Okay, perfect. We'll see you in an hour. I'll call and let everyone else know."

"Fiiiine," I drag out, then hang up the phone and grudgingly strip off Buchanan's clothes, knowing Ashlyn will grill me if she finds me wearing them. After adding the small pile to the machine, I press the start button, head to my bedroom, and slip on some yoga pants and a Broken Vows T-shirt.

They don't smell like him.

My nose wrinkles when I place disappointment settling in my stomach.

Great.

AN HOUR LATER, THERE'S A LOUD KNOCK ON THE DOOR, AND I answer it. Ashlyn, Kate, and Blake are waiting on the opposite side and squeal when they see me.

"Hey!" Ash pulls me into a hug. "I've missed you."

"Yeah, seriously," Blake adds. "You need to stop traveling with the guys. It feels like we never see you anymore."

"Right?" Kate squeezes me softly. "We've missed you like crazy."

"I've missed you guys too," I admit. "Come on in."

Blake and Kate whistle as they take in the apartment while Ash watches me with a grin, knowing how uncomfortable the attention makes me.

Throwing me a bone, she lifts the grocery bag she brought with her into the air and says, "Look what I brought."

It's loaded with Ben & Jerry's, and I take it from her, setting it on the counter as Blake finishes her self-led tour and rummages through my drawers in search of spoons.

"So," Kate starts, leaning against the center island. "What's new?"

"Nothing much. Traveling, working, the usual. How 'bout you guys?"

Kate rubs her baby bump with a wistful sigh. "Everything's great. Mack and I had a doctor's appointment this morning and heard Baby's heartbeat again, which was surreal."

Sometimes, I forget she's pregnant. Thanks to the little nugget in her stomach, her entire world was flipped upside down, but Macklin and Kate have taken the whole thing in stride. Now they're engaged, living together, and doing everything in their power to make sure the baby's born healthy and strong despite Kate's epilepsy.

"That's awesome," I tell her. "I assume everything is going okay in the pregnancy so far?"

"Yup. Baby's growing exactly as he should be."

"*He?*" I ask.

"Technically, we're waiting to find out the gender until I deliver, but I have a feeling it's a boy," Kate replies.

"Aww, I'm super happy for you, and I'm also super happy he or she is healthy."

"Me too." She sighs. Her relief is so palpable it fills the room.

"How 'bout you?" I ask Blakely. "How is everything? How's Uncle Fen's foundation going? How's the house? Tell me all the things."

"It's all good," Blake answers. "The kids love coming and keep telling all their friends, so it's growing like crazy. I feel like we have at least one more kid show up every single time we have an activity."

"Aww," Ash gushes. With her elbows on the granite countertop, she rests her chin in her hands. "I love it."

"Me too," Kate agrees.

Blake nods. "Yeah, it's really fun to see. Crazy and chaotic but fun. Thankfully, the donations we've had over the past year have been super helpful. We should be able to afford another full-time person soon so we can split the kids into a couple more groups based on age. Then the five-year-olds aren't hanging out with the twelve-year-olds and so on." She reaches for the sack in front of me, drags it toward her, and pops the lid off a carton of The Tonight Dough. "Trust me, when all the kids are together, attempting to split the group into two teams for a game of basketball is laughable." I smile at the thought, and Blake bumps her shoulder with mine. "Ya know, if you weren't so busy, I'm sure Fender would love your help––"

"Yeah, I'm definitely too busy," I interrupt. "But I'm glad you've been receiving more donations."

"Me too. You have no idea how much they help."

She scoops a heaping bite of ice cream with her spoon and shoves it into her mouth as I ask, "And how's the house coming along?"

"It's good," she answers. "We're renovating one of the bathrooms, but as soon as it's finished, we want to have everyone over for a housewarming party. Are you guys in?"

"Yeah, of course," we all agree.

"Perfect." Blake grabs a few more spoons from the drawer and slides one to each of us.

"So, Mia, any update on the whole Henry front?" Ashlyn's perfectly plucked brow lifts as she takes the pint of mint chip ice cream from the bag and pops the lid off.

"What update?" Blake asks between a mouthful of ice cream.

"What Henry front?" Kate adds.

My gaze narrows, but Ash only grins. "Come on. You have to tell them."

"Oh, yes. Whatever it is, Ash is right," Blake agrees. "You have to tell us."

"Fiiiine," I pout but tell them all the gory details about my hook-up with Buchanan in Creekside, along with the rejection at SeaBird and butt dial from hell.

"And that's it. The end," I lie through my teeth with a sigh of exhaustion.

An unconvinced Ashlyn opens her mouth to call bullshit when Kate lifts her forefinger into the air.

"Pause. I have to use the bathroom," she announces. "But I really want to hear everything else, so don't keep going without me."

"Take your time," I tell her.

She heads down the hallway and finds the bathroom as I shove a bite of ice cream into my mouth, avoiding Ashlyn and her detective-worthy gaze beside me. To be fair, she isn't wrong in her unspoken assumption. There's a lot more I need to tell her. And I will. But only *after* I've had a shot––or five––so I can get through it.

Admitting I'm sleeping with my boss to myself is one thing. Admitting it to my best friends is an entirely different story. And after how this morning ended with Buchanan? The whole situation is even more of a mess, leaving me curious and uncomfortable and caught between the urge to end things as fast as possible and telling him every single detail about my past he wants to know.

Yeah. I'm a wreck, and I don't even know where to start.

Shoving another bite of cookie dough ice cream into my mouth, I lick the spoon, too lost in the clusterfuck of my life to notice the deafening silence surrounding me.

"There's more," Ash decides. "Isn't there?"

"Yup, definitely more," Blake agrees.

"There isn't more," I lie, grimacing from their scrutiny.

"Come on. Tell us," Ashlyn prods, then her eyes bulge. "Wait. Tell me you didn't do what I think you did."

I grimace harder, hiding my guilty expression behind the pint of cookie dough deliciousness.

"No freaking way." She shoves my shoulder. It isn't rough

by any means but still manages to get her point across, and I scrub my hand over my face.

"Yeah, I know," I mutter.

"Know what?" Blakely demands. "What just happened?"

"Wait, what'd I miss?" Kate asks as she walks back to the kitchen.

"Details. Now," Ashlyn orders.

"There isn't much to tell," I hedge.

"Mia," Ashlyn warns.

"Kate, how's the temperature in here?" I ask her. "Are you hot? Cold? I want to make sure you're comfortable since you're pregnant and all--"

"Nope," Ashlyn interrupts. "Sorry, Kate. You know I love you and want you to be comfortable, but Mia's using you as a scapegoat right now, and we're not done talking."

"Okay, fine," I snap. "After Buchanan asked me out and I rejected him, we agreed to a less traditional...arrangement, and--"

"So you went through with it?" Ashlyn interrupts.

My lips bunch on one side, and I mutter, "Maybe?"

"What the hell does *maybe* mean?" Blake demands. "Are you guys like, friends with benefits or something?"

"More like frenemies," I clarify. "Or at least, it started that way."

"And now?" Ashlyn prods.

"I'm not entirely sure," I murmur under my breath while searching my cabinets for a bottle of vodka. Those shots are sounding pretty good right about now. "I mean, yes. I'm definitely not crossing into relationship territory or anything, but the more we've hung out, the more we've gotten to know each other, and earlier today, things got a little more... personal, and instead of opening up to him like I should've, I was a bitch and deflected like I always do. Now, I don't know where we stand or how I should act, or anything else for that matter."

"So you've become friends," Kate concludes.

"Maybe?"

"Friends who bump uglies," Blakely adds. "Which means I was right!" Hands raised in the air, she does a twirl. "Booyah!"

With a flick of my fingers, the bottle cap on the vodka untwists and clatters to the ground, but I don't bother to pick it up. Instead, I pour some vodka into my ice cream container and give the concoction a swirl with my spoon. "I'm not sure what we are at this point, but I do know I feel bad despite not being able to put my finger on why, which makes everything awkward and weird and...a mess."

"No offense, but it became messy as soon as you proposed no-strings-attached sex with your boss," Ash tells me. She takes the vodka from my grasp and adds a splash of it into her own pint. "But since you've already crossed the line, you might as well enjoy it, and if it turns into something else, so be it."

Something else?

My expression sours, and I drop my spoon back into my ice cream, causing a few drops of the creamy vodka milk-shake to splash onto the counter. "I don't want it to turn into something else."

"If you didn't want it to turn into something else, you wouldn't feel guilty about keeping something from him," Ash points out.

"Ash is right," Kate adds. "You're a closed book to literally *everyone*, and you've never cared until today. Maybe it doesn't mean you're looking for an actual relationship with the guy, but it does mean you're starting to look at him like he's more than a random hook-up."

"Like maybe he's even your friend," Blakely adds. She

reaches across the counter and swipes the creamy splash on the counter with her finger, popping it into her mouth. "Oh, yeah, that's good." She pours some alcohol into her own half-eaten carton and gives it a stir while Kate grins.

"You're finding this way too amusing," I point out.

With a shrug, she chuckles and says, "Take it from the girl who did everything in her power to keep a guy at arm's length despite his determination to cross into the friend zone. It's not so bad if you give in and let it happen. Who knows? You might even wind up liking him."

"But I don't *want* to like him," I argue.

"Or maybe you're scared of what will happen if you do," Ash murmurs. "Regardless, having friends and letting them see you being vulnerable isn't a bad thing. In fact, I'd argue it's a really good thing."

"Debatable," I mumble.

"Or spot on," Blakely offers. "You should've seen one of the boys I teach at the foundation. He was a big, fat butthead to everyone for months until another big, fat butthead started coming. They got into a nasty fistfight, and I had to break them up, which was a real hoot, let me tell ya. But afterward, Butthead Number One had a breakdown and started crying in my arms, telling me how much he missed his mom, who happens to be in prison. Butthead Number Two witnessed the whole thing, and instead of giving him crap for it, he sat on the curb beside Butthead Number One and told him about his older brother, who's also in prison. They allowed each other to see their *vulnerable* sides," she emphasizes. "And what do you know? They became friends and are practically inseparable now."

"I think it's really great for Butthead Number One and Two," I tell her. "Although, I think you should probably give them new nicknames since they now get along and all."

"Meh." Blake shrugs. "They're still buttheads, only not to each other."

"PS, what didn't you want to tell him?" Ash prods.

Pressing my lips together, I shake my head. "Nothing."

"Obviously, you're lying," she returns. "So, you're really not going to tell us, either?"

The familiar weight of my past sits heavily on my shoulders as I stare at the alcoholic milkshake in front of me, my stomach squeezing. They know. I know they know. Maybe not the details, but they saw the bruises. Or at least some of them. But it doesn't mean we've ever actually talked about it. Not really, anyway. Shoving aside the memories earlier today was hard enough. Doing it again? With my best friends? My lungs burn.

"Hey," Ash murmurs, sensing my discomfort. She reaches over and squeezes my forearm. "I was joking. You don't have to tell us anything if you aren't ready."

"He asked if Shorty ever hit me," I whisper.

Silence.

I peek up at my friends and sigh. "Yeah."

"Shit," Blake offers.

A dry laugh slips out of me. "Yeah," I repeat.

"How did it even come up?" Ash asks.

"He wanted to know why I didn't tell him I knew Scarlett was cheating on him, but when I said I assumed I didn't know the full story, one thing led to another, and he could see my resentment toward the opposite sex, and it...came up." I shove my hands in my hair and push it away from my face, adding, "And then, because I didn't want to talk about it, I asked if he wanted to have sex again, and he said, *'I'm nothing more than a dick to you.'*" I mimic his words and puff out my cheeks. "Then, he kind of rejected me, and now, I have no idea where we stand."

"You need to talk to him," Ash announces. "Even if you

don't want to tell him about Shorty and everything, which I completely understand, I think he's probably hurt and feels like you're using him."

"I *am* using him," I say with a laugh, but it's pathetic at best. "I don't want a relationship, Ash."

"Yeah, but if you guys agreed to friends with benefits, you should probably make sure he feels like your *friend* while also reaping the *benefits* portion. Because if you don't, he's nothing but a free gigolo," Ash counters.

I snort. "He said the same thing. I mean, not the gigolo part, but the whole *if I'm not willing to open up to him, we aren't exactly friends*, part."

"He has a point," Kate interjects. "So be friends with him. See? Simple."

"Hardly," I mutter into my ice cream. "But enough about me. Can we *please* change the subject?"

"Oh, I've got something," Blake offers, turning to Kate. "How's pregnancy sex? Is it awesome?"

Kate's face turns into a cherry tomato. "You guys!"

And just like that, I'm off the hook.

MIA

Pacing my kitchen, I tap the corner of my phone against my chin. The girls went home a couple of hours ago, but I can't get our conversation out of my mind.

I've also decided Buchanan's setup with the elevator is genius. He doesn't have to worry about unwanted visitors. It's not like you can show up on his doorstep. No one can. Instead, you have to talk to his doorman or have his personal number to be let up to his floor. For a girl who really doesn't like people, it sounds like a dream.

Too bad being on the other side of the situation is biting me in the ass. I really don't want to call him, but I need to get this off my chest. And soon. Or I may very well go crazy.

Before I can talk myself out of it, I dial his number and lift my cell to my ear.

Ring. Ring. Ring.

"Mia?" his low voice answers.

"Hi."

He sighs. "Are you locked out of your apartment again?"

I snort. "No."

Silence.

"I was wondering if I could drop off the clothes I borrowed?" I add. "I don't have to come in or anything."

"Come on up."

The call ends.

Puffing out my cheeks, I grab the freshly-washed clothes from the kitchen counter and make my way to the elevator. Sure enough, the penthouse button is lit up, and I push it, riding to the top floor.

When the doors open, Buchanan's on the other side. His suit's missing, though. Instead, I'm gifted with Workout Buchanan, and damn. I think he's a solid competitor for my number-one slot in the spank bank. White T-shirt. Gray sweatpants. Damp hair.

"Take a picture. It will last longer," he quips.

With a smirk, I reply, "As an OF contributor, I can confirm this is indeed true."

Silence.

I tuck my hair behind my ear, not sure what else to say now that I'm here. In front of him. Wanting to be...*friends?*

"Can I help you, Mia?" he prods. It's detached. Cold. Robotic almost. Like before we started hooking up.

"I believe I owe you an apology," I announce, offering him his freshly folded clothes.

He takes the stack hesitantly but shakes his head. The sharpness in his gaze softens the smallest amount. "You don't owe me anything."

"Yeah, but I kind of do. I'm sorry I got weird."

"Don't apologize for shit like that."

"You're mad at me," I point out. "And I know I shouldn't care, but I think I do. And it's messing with my head."

His brows furrow. "So you're apologizing because it's messing with your head?"

"I'm apologizing because I don't like the idea of my

friends being mad at me, and somehow, during all of this, I've started to look at you like you're my..."--I clear my throat--"*friend*."

"Friend," he repeats, but the bastard's indifferent face doesn't waver, denying me even the slightest hint as to what he's thinking.

"Yeah," I breathe out. "Which is weird, 'cause you're kind of an asshole."

His mouth quirks, but he sobers. "I'm not mad at you."

"It feels like you're mad at me."

"Just trying to keep everything in check," he clarifies.

Everything.

As in, *us*.

And our arrangement.

Maybe we're more on the same page than I'd given him credit for.

"Me too." I stare at the white fabric stretched across his broad chest instead of the sharp gaze. It always manages to peel my protective layers away, leaving me more exposed than I'd like to admit.

He steps closer and touches my cheek, tilting my head up until our eyes meet. "I'm not like him. I'm not going to push you, especially when you don't owe me anything. I thought you knew me better."

"I do," I start.

He nods. "I'm here. I'm here in whatever way you need me to be."

"Even if it's only sex?" I ask.

His expression flashes with something, the familiar mask of indifference falling into place. The glimpse is too quick for me to analyze, and I cock my head.

His hand drops from my chin, and he nods. "Whatever you need, Brat."

"Thank you." I gulp. "But as long as we both agree there

233

isn't a relationship on the table, I want you to know I look at this"––I wag my finger between us––"like it's a two-way street, so I'm here too. To give whatever you need. Even if it's more than a few solid orgasms. Even if it means opening up to you a little more."

"Like *actual* friends?" he clarifies. "Not just fuck buddies?"

I nod. "I mean, buddy is kind of a synonym for friend, but yes. I think I've been focusing a bit more on the fucking portion while failing in the buddy department, which one of my friends pointed out may have made you feel like a gigolo, and it wasn't fair, so I'm sorry."

With a dry laugh, he shakes his head. "You told your friends about me?"

"Maybe." I lick my bottom lip. "Is that a problem?"

"Isn't it against the rules?" he prods.

"I guess I bent that one."

"And you told them we're having sex?"

I grimace. "Maybe?"

"Yes or no," he pushes.

"Yes."

"Then I say you more than bent it."

I bite the inside of my cheek, preventing my amusement from showing, and mutter, "Maybe."

"Did you tell them how much you like my cock?" His hands find my ass, and he pulls me into him.

"Am I in trouble if I say no?" A squeal bursts out of me as he tosses me over his shoulder and carries me to his bedroom. I land with a *thump* on the center of his mattress, ruining his perfectly made bed. He's on top of me in an instant.

"Hey!" I protest, shoving at his chest while ignoring how good it feels to be beneath him again. To feel him. Every. Single. Inch. Dragging my hands along his pecs and shoulders, I ask, "What about the rules? I'm not supposed to be in your bed, remember?"

"Fuck the rules."

"Professor——"

"For tonight," he clarifies. "Only for tonight. And only the one rule," he adds. "I still don't want you lying, and I still don't want you hooking up with anyone else."

"Well, since you're the one between my thighs, I don't think it's an issue." I squeeze my legs around him, proving my point.

"Good."

His arms cage me in on both sides, and I spread my legs even wider, cradling him against me. Having him nestled between my thighs dulls the ache from our fight. Honestly, I'm so happy he isn't mad at me I don't even need sex. A hug will do.

Brushing the hair away from my face, he murmurs, "I like your laugh."

"Oh, you do?"

He nods. "Especially when it's genuine."

"It's always genuine," I argue, but his eyes thin.

"No lies, remember?"

My smile softens, and I trail my hands along his back. "No lies."

"Good girl." He bends down, kisses my forehead, and slides down my body like a man on a mission, though I'm not entirely sure what the mission is.

Lifting my head, I watch him scoot lower, hooking his thumbs into the waistband of my yoga pants and sliding them down my legs. "What are you doing?"

"I only have one night to break the no sex in my apartment rule." He tosses my legs over his shoulders. "You really think I'm gonna waste it?"

In an instant, his mouth is on me, feasting on my folds as

his hands find my waist, and he hoists me up until nothing but my shoulder blades and head are touching the mattress while he's on his knees.

"Holy fuck--" My words are lost on a moan. Shivers break out along my skin, and his groan fills the air.

I've had makeup sex before.

Lots of times, considering my tumultuous relationship with Shorty. But I've never had friends-with-benefits sex after an argument.

Yup. It's pretty freaking incredible.

His tongue dips into my center, then circles my clit as my heels dig into his shoulders. I'm desperate for leverage. For friction. For...everything.

"Yes," I chant. "Yes, yes, yes. Lick me, Professor. Lick me good. You have no idea how amazing this feels." I squeeze my eyes shut, fisting the sheets at my sides before the heat from his mouth disappears, and he flips me over.

"Ass up," he growls.

With my face pressed against his pillow, I shove my butt into the air as the familiar rip of a condom wrapper echoes through the air. The sound has never sounded sweeter. Because I need this. I need him. I need the reminder our arrangement is still in place, and he hasn't rejected me or replaced me. Not yet. Not when I'm not ready to give this up. To give him up. His hands grip my waist, and the head of his cock plays with my dripping entrance.

I press into him, but he pulls away, forcing a groan of my own as I peek over my shoulder. "Professor--"

"You want this?" he asks, dragging his dick to my clit and pressing into it.

My eyes nearly roll back in my head, but I keep them focused on the man behind me. "You know I do."

"How much?"

"You want me to beg for it?" I ask.

"I want you to know it's my dick doing this to you. My tongue. My fingers. My cock. *Me*."

"Yes, you," I breathe out.

"Then say my name." He rolls his hips against me again, and I squeeze my eyes shut. "Not Professor," he spits. "Not boss. Not Buchanan. But my name, Mia."

"I call you by your name all the time, *Professor*," I say, testing my luck.

The sharp sting of his hand slapping my ass makes me whimper. Then his hands are on my waist again, pinning me in place.

"Not when we're together," he argues. "Not when we're like this."

My expression twists. "You promised me an orgasm."

"And you promised me I'm not simply a dick to you," he grunts. "I'm a person. A friend."

"I don't say my other friends' names while orgasming."

Slipping the head inside me, he retreats and smacks my ass a second time, pulling a moan from my throat. "Dammit, Boss! Just fuck me!"

"Say my name, Mia." His fingers find my entrance. He dips them softly inside me, brings them to my clit, and rubs it in slow circles, making it almost impossible to think straight, let alone have an actual conversation.

"Admit no one makes you feel like this but me," he rasps.

The sensation overwhelms every single inch of me until I'm convinced I might actually cry if I don't orgasm soon. "Dude, stop torturing me. Can we please--"

"Say." His fingers scissor back and forth. "My." He crooks them and rubs in a slow circle along my inner walls. "Name."

"Fine." I arch my back, desperate and more turned on than I've ever been in my entire life. "Fuck me, Henry."

His hand retreats, replaced by the head of his cock. "Say it again." Then he waits.

"Fuck you, Henry."

I swear I can hear the amusement in his voice. "That's what I want *you* to do. Come on, Mia. Let me in. Let me know when you're with me, you're with *me*."

My unsteady breaths mingle with his controlled ones, and I whisper, "I'm with you, Henry. You know you're the only one who makes me feel this way. *Please*."

"Good girl." He thrusts into me but keeps me in place, preventing me from jerking forward from the intrusion as I stretch around him. And I nearly come on the spot as he moves his hips back and thrusts into me again.

"Yes. Fuck, Henry, yes," I praise. "You seriously have no idea how good this feels. Keep going. Don't stop. Please don't stop." My rambled words tumble out of me as he pistons his hips over and over again. My skin grows hotter, sweat breaking out along my spine and forehead while I chant his name. Henry. Not Buchanan or Professor or Boss. But Henry. The one and only.

And I come. Bliss radiates from every inch--every fiber--of my body.

"Milk me, baby. Let your pussy suck me dry."

His firm grasp on my hips keeps me in place as I clench around him, and Henry groans. His cock pulses inside me as his body folds on top of mine.

Fuck.

He has no idea how good sex life is with him compared to every other guy I've been with. If he did, he'd probably use it against me. But he wouldn't. I know he wouldn't. He wouldn't use anything against me. And it's scary as shit.

I'm glad we're okay, though. I'm glad we can keep doing this. Glad he can keep making me feel this way.

As I slowly catch my breath despite being squashed by his massive body, I mutter, "You're a good friend, Henry."

His chest rumbles with amusement against my back.

When he shifts onto his side, he pulls me into his chest. "You're a good friend too, Mia."

I stretch beside him. "You also have a really nice mattress."

His chuckle warms my insides and turns them into goo. "You don't? Actually, don't answer. Of course, you don't. We should probably fix your mattress."

"Meh, I'm fine."

He drops a kiss on the top of my head, but I'm too exhausted to give him shit for it. "Sure you are."

33

MIA

We lose the next game at home, and the team decides drowning their sorrows at SeaBird sounds like a pretty good way to erase the loss from their minds. Thankfully, I have a shift tonight, so I'm happy to serve them to their hearts' content, putting everything on my tab despite it being a shitty financial decision.

I get it.

What it's like to lose.

And after all the work they put into tonight's game and the shitty calls made by the refs? They've earned a little alcohol to drown out the pain.

Henry's here too. We haven't spoken much. I've been too busy doing my job, and he's been doing the same, chatting with the team, letting them bitch about tonight's turnout.

The man's a sex god, and while the team might wanna drown out the loss with alcohol, I'd rather drown it with orgasms. Preferably ones delivered by the one and only. He's busy clinking glasses with Colt and Theo when his eyes find mine. A familiar heat simmers behind them, hinting he might be thinking the same thing.

With a smile, I lift my chin in a silent hello as I pour tequila shots for a group of puck bunnies when my phone begins ringing in the black apron tied around my waist.

Curious, I wipe my hands on a dishtowel and pull my phone out.

Uncle Fen's name flashes across the screen, and I slide my thumb across it. "Hello?"

Silence.

I plug my ear with my opposite hand and close my eyes as if the lack of sight will heighten my hearing, but it does nothing to block out the chaos surrounding me. "Hello? Uncle Fen?"

"Hey, Mia," Fen answers.

"Hey. What's up?" I ask. "Everything okay?"

"Mia, honey," Aunt Hadley chimes in. They must have me on speaker.

Pressing a finger to my pierced tragus in an attempt to quiet the chaos around me, I say, "Okay, you guys are officially freaking me out. What's wrong?"

"Pixie's gone," Uncle Fen chokes out.

Like a sucker punch to the gut, the words hit me hard, and the air whooshes from my lungs. "W-what did you say?"

"Pixie," Aunt Hadley repeats. "She's gone, Mia."

A low buzz echoes in my ears as I stumble around the edge of the bar, praying I'm hallucinating. I head toward the breakroom but only make it as far as the hallway when my legs threaten to give out, and I lean my side against the rough brick wall. "W-what happened?"

"We're not sure." Uncle Fen sighs. "We left her on the bus during the concert so she could sleep, and when we got back…"

I rub at the center of my chest, but the ache doesn't go away. It only grows, leaving me breathless and broken.

No. No, no, no. Not Pixie. Not her.

"Mia, I'm so sorry," Uncle Fender says. "I know you trusted me to look after her, and--"

"You were the best thing for her." I blink back my tears and tilt my head toward the ceiling, willing the moisture to go away. "I was...I was really hoping I would've had a chance to say goodbye or at least been warned the end was coming, ya know?" I wipe beneath my nose with the back of my hand and let it fall to my side as if my arm weighs a thousand pounds. "Fuck."

"I know," Aunt Hadley murmurs. I'm not sure if she's comforting me or Uncle Fen. After all, Pixie is one of the reasons Fender's sober now. He must be feeling the loss as badly as I am. And it sucks. It really freaking sucks. She was my dog. My baby. Proof my dad wasn't always an asshole. Proof he could be thoughtful. Genuine. And now, she's gone.

My body shakes, and I nearly choke on the sob caught in my throat but manage to swallow it back.

Not here.

Don't lose your shit here.

"Don't know what I would've done without her," Fender grits out. "Can't believe she's gone."

"I gotta go," I whisper.

"I'm so sorry, Mia," he returns.

"I know."

I hang up and lean my head against the rough wall. My emotions are a jumbled mess of heartache and regret. I should've been there for her. I should've gone to see her more. I should've told Fender to go fuck himself and taken her back to my apartment. I should've done a lot of things. But she's gone.

She's gone.

"What's wrong?" a low voice asks from behind me.

I clear my throat, but the golf-ball-sized lump doesn't ease up. It only chokes me more until I can't breathe. I can't fucking *breathe*. The sob I'd been holding back bursts free, the pain hitting like a tsunami. Arms encircle me instantly, and I squeeze my eyes shut. It's like heavy, jagged rocks have been shoved into my chest, and the sharp weight is more than I can bear.

"Mia, what's wrong?" Henry demands, turning me around and making me face him.

I shake my head against his hard chest, unable to think the words let alone speak them out loud.

"Tell me, Mia, or I swear to God I'll rip this place apart until I find out––"

"Pixie's gone."

His hands freeze against my back. "What do you mean gone?"

"She's gone, Henry. She died." Another sob breaks free, and my chest heaves. "She's gone, and I didn't get to say goodbye. And I know she's just a dog, and I know she was old and she wasn't going to live forever, but it fucking sucks, Henry. Why does everyone leave? Why does everyone have to die?"

He squeezes me tighter, then guides me down the small hallway toward the exit. "Come on."

I shake my head and try to shrug out of his hold. "I have to work, I have to––"

His grip tightens. "I'll take care of it."

I'm too exhausted to protest. Too exhausted to put up a fight. Instead, I go with him, my legs nothing but spaghetti noodles as I lean against his unyielding frame and let Henry take my weight. When we reach the streets, the cool air knocks some sense into me, and I take a shuddered breath, wiping at my tear-stained cheeks.

"Fuck," I mutter under my breath as I see my mascara-streaked fingers. I must look like a mess.

Get a grip on yourself, Mia.

"Come on," Henry repeats, but I pull away from him.

"I'm fine."

"Mia--"

"It's just a dog, Henry." The words leave a bad taste in my mouth, but he wouldn't understand. He doesn't even like animals. He probably thinks I'm an idiot for crying over something so trivial. And honestly, he's not wrong. I'm being ridiculous. I release another shuddered breath and try to reel myself in.

Breathe.

I dig my fingernails into my palms, praying the biting pain will ground me.

Just fucking breathe, Mia.

"It's not *just* a dog," Henry argues. "It's *Pixie*." He reaches for my hand again, and this time, I'm too weak to fight him. To be strong. To be indifferent or to put on my proverbial badass mask.

God, it's Pixie.

She's gone.

And she's never coming back.

Another sob escapes me. He leads me to a shadowed corner at the edge of the parking lot where we can find an ounce of privacy and wraps me in a hug.

"Sh... " He rubs his hand up and down my back. "What can I do? Can I drive you somewhere? Fly you to wherever she is? How can I fix this?"

"You can't fix this," I whisper. "She's gone. And there's nothing we can do about it." My bottom lip trembles, and I squeeze my eyes shut again, praying with enough effort, the force will block out the world entirely.

It doesn't do shit. She's still gone. She's still dead.

"I'm so sorry, Mia," Henry rasps.

My hair sticks to my tear-stained cheeks, so I push it away, staring blankly at the ground beneath my feet. I need the numbness to take over. I need it to take over so I can stop feeling like I'm being ripped apart. Like I'm being torn to shreds. But it's useless. She's gone.

"I should've spent more time with her," I cry. "I should've given her more treats. Taken her on more walks whenever Fender was in town. I should've--"

"You were there when she needed you, and then, you were more selfless than anyone would have expected you to be when you realized your uncle needed her more, and you let her go."

I let her go.

"I hate it. I hate how I let her go. I hate how I loved her in the first place. I hate this feeling, Henry. I hate it so much."

Pulling me into his chest again, he rubs his hand along my back. "She loved you, Mia. I didn't even have to see you two together to know it."

Another sob practically tears me apart, and I shake my head back and forth.

"Fuck," I cry. "Fuck, fuck, fuck."

"Sh..." His lips brush against the top of my head. "Sh... Come on."

~

I FELL ASLEEP IN HIS BED.

It's against the rules, but I did it anyway.

And it's nice.

Being held.

I'd almost forgotten.

My face feels swollen when I finally open my eyes. I press my hand to it and pull away from Henry's chest, sitting up in his bed, the sheets pooling around my waist. The morning light filters in through the windows along the outer wall, but I can't appreciate it. The numbness I'd been begging for has finally reared its ugly head, and I'm exhausted. With my back pressed to the headboard, I stare blankly in front of me, not sure what to do or say after last night and my not-so-little emotional breakdown.

A few minutes later, Henry shifts beside me, his strong arm reaching across the mattress, searching for me. When it hits my knee, a frown tugs at his lips, and he opens his eyes. They're lighter than normal. Less guarded, maybe. Apparently, cut-throat Henry takes a few minutes to wake up, but I like the sleepy one beside me.

"Hey," he grumbles, pushing himself up and mirroring my position.

"Hi."

He covers his yawn with a hand, then scrubs it over his adorable bedhead. "How are you feeling?"

"Fine," I lie.

I know he knows. I know he can see it in my eyes. I know he can feel it in my vacant stare. I'm lying. I'm not fine. It's stupid, but I'm not fine at all. I'm heartbroken. And I haven't let myself feel anything, let alone heartbreak, in a long time. Peeling back those layers and allowing myself to *feel* is even worse than I remember, and I hate it. The vulnerability. The sharp pain. The helplessness.

"I should call you out for breaking one of our rules," he mutters, eyeing me warily, "but I think you've earned a pass."

A pathetic laugh slips past the numbness, and I shake my head. "Gee, thanks."

Squeezing my knee softly, he offers, "Why don't you take a hot shower?"

I nod. "Okay."

~

THIRTY MINUTES LATER, STEAM BILLOWS FROM THE SHOWER door as I push it open. Fog blankets the mirror, and a hot latte sits on the bathroom counter. I'm not sure when Henry snuck in here to deliver it, but I'm grateful. For his thoughtfulness. His sweet gesture. Beneath the cup is an envelope. Carefully, I pick it up and turn it over, pulling the photo out. It's me and Pixie.

"Pix." Another shuddered cry catches in my throat, and I bite my bottom lip, running my fingers over the glossy image. I open the door, taking the photo and paper cup into the bedroom. Henry's sitting at his desk in the corner of the space. His laptop is open in front of him, and his fingers click away as he answers emails. Like he didn't rock my world. Like he didn't go above and beyond last night and this morning. Like he didn't hold me for eight hours as I cried against his chest.

Pressing my shoulder against the doorjamb, I ask, "Where did you get this?"

He looks up at me, his expression unreadable. "Gordy found it. You posted it on Instagram a few years ago."

My hands shake as I lift the photograph, studying it again. We're in a park, surrounded by green grass. The sun is high and bright above us. Her tongue is lolled out on one side, and I'm grinning like a lunatic with my arms wrapped around her.

He's right.

I remember now.

"I forgot about this picture," I whisper. "Thank you."

"You're welcome."

He turns back to his computer and keeps working.

"Hey, Henry?" I whisper.

The rhythmic typing from his computer quiets, and he looks up at me again.

"The OF money?" I bite the inside of my cheek, hating

247

how vulnerable I feel but too stubborn to back out now that I've opened my big, stupid mouth.

His gaze softens. "What about it?"

"I donated it. All of it. Over four hundred thousand dollars." I laugh at the stupidly high amount and lick my dry lips. "Last year, my uncle opened Boost Youth Foundation for struggling kids with absent parents. He asked me to help volunteer. I did for a while. Part of me really liked it. The other part? It was hard. Being around them. Every time I looked into their sad little faces, all I could see was me as a kid. But they needed help, ya know? So much help," I whisper. "So I figured out a different way to contribute. A different way to provide what they needed since I couldn't be around them without feeling sorry for myself." I take a sip of my latte, but it doesn't rid my tongue of the sawdust feeling. "That's where the money went. To Boost."

He nods, absorbing my confession with pinched brows. "Why didn't you keep any for yourself? At least enough to pay off your student loans?"

"You were right. I do hate money," I whisper. "I hate what it does to people. How it changes them. How it can rip families apart, even with the best intentions. How people kill for it. How people die for it. It terrifies me."

"So, it's easier to give it away and scrape by without it?" There isn't any judgment in his question. Only genuine curiosity. A desire to understand. To see things from my perspective.

"I guess so." I look down at the picture in my hands and lift it in the air. "Thanks again."

And I disappear back into the bathroom.

34
MIA

My eyes are still swollen when my alarm sounds on Monday morning. Shifting onto my side, I reach for my phone to turn it off when I notice a text from Henry.

PROFESSOR HOT SUIT
Take today off.

ME
Not necessary.

PROFESSOR HOT SUIT
I think it is.

ME
Boss...

PROFESSOR HOT SUIT
Brat...

ME
Seriously, I'm fine.

> **PROFESSOR HOT SUIT**
>
> It's okay to not be fine every once in a while, Mia.

For everyone else, sure. For me? Well, I don't have the same luxury.

Nibbling on my thumbnail, I draft a dozen responses in my mind when another message pops up.

> **PROFESSOR HOT SUIT**
>
> Take the day off.

> **ME**
>
> I don't like handouts, remember?

> **PROFESSOR HOT SUIT**
>
> It isn't a handout. You have one week of bereavement leave written in your employment contract. Take it.

> **ME**
>
> Pretty sure when HR wrote the fine print for the policy, it didn't include animals, Professor.

> **PROFESSOR HOT SUIT**
>
> Not your professor anymore.

> **ME**
>
> My point stands. She was a dog, not a human.

> **PROFESSOR HOT SUIT**
>
> She was family. But if you need me to bring Erika into my office so I can update the policy simply because you're being stubborn, I will.

> **ME**
>
> Now you're being ridiculous.

PROFESSOR HOT SUIT

No, I'm being thoughtful. There's a difference.

ME

Does this updated bereavement policy affect everyone?

PROFESSOR HOT SUIT

If I say no, will you come into the office this morning?

ME

I think we both know my answer.

PROFESSOR HOT SUIT

Fine. If it convinces you to take time off to mourn Pixie properly instead of shoving your feelings in a box, so be it. I'll ensure everyone on the payroll understands their bereavement time now includes four-legged family members.

ME

So you're saying you have something against fish and snakes?

PROFESSOR HOT SUIT

You're lucky I had to fly out to San Francisco today, or I'd come over and smack your bratty ass.

I glance at the ceiling where his penthouse is located, surprised by the tightness in my chest when I realize he isn't up there. He isn't close.

ME

You're in San Francisco?

PROFESSOR HOT SUIT

Unfortunately, yes. Had to fly out this morning for an emergency meeting. My brother-in-law was supposed to go but asked if I could cover for him at the last minute. However, I would have delivered your breakfast in person if I wasn't.

My brows crease when a knock sounds from the front of the apartment.

Curious, I slip from beneath my covers and pad down the hall, opening the front door.

On the floor is a brown paper sack with The Bean Scene's logo stamped on the front, along with a white paper cup. The comforting scent of coffee filters through the air as I bend down, pick the goodies up, and peek inside the bag. There's a chocolate croissant and a small stack of BluRay movies. No note, though.

"What the hell?" I mutter under my breath. One by one, I pull the blue cases out and examine them more closely.

It's a collection of Tinkerbell movies.

"What the hell?" I repeat with a laugh. Flipping the first BluRay around, I read the synopsis on the back, yet it doesn't give me any clue as to what Henry was thinking when he picked these out for me. Or at least, I assume they're from him.

My phone buzzes in my hand, and I bring everything inside, setting the contents on the counter.

PROFESSOR HOT SUIT

Figured you could use a treat and some solid entertainment to help you get by without me.

ME

Tinkerbell movies are solid entertainment?

PROFESSOR HOT SUIT

My niece loves them.

ME

You have a niece?

PROFESSOR HOT SUIT

I do. She's five and also has an obsession with all things pixie.

My mouth curves as the familiar burn sparks behind my eyes.

So that's why he sent them to me. Pixie.

ME

I bet you're a good uncle.

PROFESSOR HOT SUIT

I'm the best. Now, enjoy your breakfast while watching the movies. If you decide your laptop isn't big enough for you to fully appreciate the cinematic adventure you're about to embark upon, tell David. He'll let you into my apartment, and you can watch it on an actual television.

My heart pitter-patters away. I don't dissect it or over-think my response to his thoughtfulness. Honestly, I'm too exhausted to care. I want to curl into a ball and marinate in my sadness, no matter how pathetic it is. Watching cheesy cartoons while sipping coffee and nibbling on a chocolate croissant sounds like a pretty freaking good way to do it.

ME

I'm only giving in because you're basically forcing me to.

PROFESSOR HOT SUIT

I suggest you start with the NeverBeast one. It's my favorite.

> **ME**
> You've seen them?

> **PROFESSOR HOT SUIT**
> I told you. I'm the best uncle ever.

> **ME**
> I believe you.

I hit send and wipe beneath my eyes, surprised at how something so simple can make me feel weepy. He's being so thoughtful. So sweet, I don't know how to handle it.

Before I can talk myself out of it, I type another response and send it his way.

> **ME**
> Thank you, Henry.

> **PROFESSOR HOT SUIT**
> Don't mention it.

I TOOK A WEEK OFF. FROM EVERYTHING. NO ONE IN THE LIONS organization batted an eye, and Sammie was cool with it too. I have a hunch Henry reached out to both of them, telling them my situation.

He's been gone all week but has made it his mission to reach out every single day. With texts, coffee delivered in the mornings, and dinners in the evenings. He even sent a copy of *Marley and Me* this morning and told me to press play at eight o'clock tonight. I wanted to ask why but restrained myself, following his instructions to a T. By 8:05 pm, I received a text from the devil himself.

> **PROFESSOR HOT SUIT**
> Based on the opening music, this might be a mistake.

> **ME**
> Opening music?

I look around my empty apartment and type another response.

> **ME**
> Wait, are you watching Marley and Me too?

> **PROFESSOR HOT SUIT**
> Why else would I ask you to start it at 8 pm?
> I had to finish up a meeting. Can you hit
> pause and answer the door real quick?

Sure enough, a knock sounds, and I set my laptop on the floor in front of my armchair, heading to the front door. The familiar scent of buttered popcorn causes my mouth to water as soon as I open it and check the empty hallway.

He didn't.

He *did*.

Of course, he did.

Picking up the large buttery carton, I pop a kernel into my mouth while heading back inside. Once I'm in my seat again, I tuck my feet under my bum and text Henry.

> **ME**
> Nice touch, Boss.

> **PROFESSOR HOT SUIT**
> Glad I can be of service. Ready to push play
> again?

> **ME**
> Yup.

I push play on my laptop a second later. We continue exchanging text messages during the movie. Some are funny. Some are more depressing. But they're all genuine. All thoughtful. And by the time the end credits roll, another message pops up. This time it's a photograph of a dozen wadded-up tissues scattered along white sheets. He must've been watching the movie in his hotel room.

PROFESSOR HOT SUIT

I was right. This was a terrible idea.

I laugh between my blubbering and send him a picture of my own pile of wadded-up tissues scattered on the hardwood floor.

ME

Ya think?

PROFESSOR HOT SUIT

I'm sorry. Seriously. I had no idea what I was getting us into. There was a cute photo of a dog on the cover, and I thought it would be a good distraction.

ME

You're forgiven. And honestly, it kind of felt good to cry.

PROFESSOR HOT SUIT

It feels good to feel sometimes, doesn't it?

ME

Maybe. When do you come home?

PROFESSOR HOT SUIT

Tomorrow.

ME

Oh.

PROFESSOR HOT SUIT

Can I see you when I get home?

I chew on my thumbnail, indecision tearing me in two, but I force myself to respond.

ME

Okay.

PROFESSOR HOT SUIT

Look at that. You agreed to something without me pulling your teeth.

ME

Don't rub my nose in it, or I might change my mind.

PROFESSOR HOT SUIT

I wouldn't dream of it. Goodnight, Mia.

ME

Goodnight, Henry.

3 5
MIA

"Yes, yes, yes," I chant as Henry's weight pushes me into the mattress, and his body connects with mine. It's been six days since I've felt him inside me. Six. Days. I had no idea how much I'd missed it. The feel of Henry. But after I received a text from him an hour ago informing me he was home and asking if I wanted to come up to his place, I practically ran to the elevator. As soon as the doors slid open and he came into view, I jumped onto his toned body, and he carried me into his bedroom, ripping at my clothes like a starving man.

Now, here I am, my clothes tossed around his otherwise spotless room and my muscles sore from being bent in a dozen different positions. But I love it. The rush. The chemistry. The smells and sounds and familiar ache. There's a strong possibility I won't be able to walk afterward, but I'm here for it. Raking my fingers against his back, I wrap my arms around him as we race toward our orgasms.

Well, technically, it's my third, but who's counting?

Within seconds, warmth spreads from my core and out to my limbs, leaving me nothing but a limp noodle as we both come. When he finishes, his muscles give out, and he collapses onto me, catching his breath and practically smothering me under his weight.

With a laugh, I tickle his back for another second. He climbs off me and stares at the ceiling.

"Fuck," he grunts.

I grin. "Yeah."

"You hungry?"

Shifting onto my side, I prop my head on my hand and take in his sexy profile. I like him like this. Right after sex, without a lick of clothing to hide his body. It's when I'm gifted with a glimpse of the real Henry. The one locked away during business deals. The one hidden from media and news articles. The one few people ever meet. When his guard is down and the stresses from running an empire are set aside, even if it's only for a few minutes.

I've missed him.

The thought scares me, but I'm too satiated to care. To get up and walk out of his apartment now that he's home again. Now that he's here.

"Mia?" he prods, turning his head and holding my gaze.

I bite my bottom lip, stopping myself from nodding as I ask, "Does food constitute a date?"

"Everyone has to eat, Mia. Even *friends.*" He smirks. "The question is, are you hungry?"

My stomach grumbles, giving me away. "I could eat."

"Good." He shifts back on top of me and kisses the tip of my nose. "What sounds good?"

"Hmm...how 'bout pizza?"

His mouth quirks. "I haven't had pizza in a long time."

"Why not?"

He shrugs but climbs off me again, his feet landing on the wood floor. He strides across the room and disposes of the condom in the trash.

"Do you have a thing about pizza too?" I ask.

"A *thing*?" he questions, glancing over his shoulder at me while giving me the perfect view of his sexy back and ass.

Seriously, I could take a bite out of his ass.

"Eyes up here," he adds.

Blinking slowly, I repeat, "Ya know, a *thing*. Like showers and suits and germs and cleanliness and all that jazz."

"And like your *thing* with money and relationships and handouts and--"

"Okay, okay,"--I raise my hands in defense--"you've made your point. We all have our *things*. I won't pry."

His triumphant smirk makes me press my thighs together.

"Order whatever you want, and I'll eat it. My wallet is on the nightstand. Give them my credit card number."

"I can buy," I start.

"Don't argue with me."

I bite my tongue, preventing me from doing exactly that. Dialing the nearest pizza place, I order a large pepperoni pizza with breadsticks and cinnamon twists on the side. I slip Henry's discarded dress shirt on and button it, rolling the sleeves up to my elbows while heading for the kitchen. A buzz on the intercom system greets me as I approach his foyer. Assuming it's the delivery man, I push the accept button, and the elevator opens a minute later.

It's not a delivery man.

Nope.

It's Scarlett.

Standing in the foyer, staring at me like I'm a piece of shit on her five-hundred-dollar shoes.

Well, I *am* wearing her ex's dress shirt, after all.

Tugging on the long white sleeves, I cover my tattoos and fold my arms. "Uh, you're not the pizza guy."

"Who are you?" she snaps.

"I'm Mia," I reply. I can't decide if I should play this out as friendly or hostile. Henry and I aren't necessarily together, and I have no reason to be jealous of his ex showing up at his door, but he's also been anti-sex-at-his-house until recently.

Is she the reason why?

The idea stings. Hell, it burns. Like duct tape being ripped off bare skin, leaving me red and raw and way more sensitive than I'd like to admit. Especially after his thoughtfulness this week. His sweet texts. His little gifts. His well-thought-out non-date night.

The reality is, it isn't any of my business. We aren't dating. We're friends. And everything he did for me this week? It's what a good friend would do. *Friend.* With a capital F. Nothing more.

"*Mia.*" Scarlett says my name is if she's tasting it and clearly doesn't like the flavor. She squints at me. "I recognize you."

"I work at SeaBird."

"You also follow Henry's hockey team around like some groupie, right?"

"I think they're called puck bunnies," I clarify, keeping my hostility in check no matter how much I want to go Carrie on the bitch. "But no, I'm––"

"I've seen your pictures," she interrupts. "And I have to say, despite most of the images being grainy, the real thing is still quite the disappointment compared to the photographs."

Aaaand all bets are off.

With a sweet smile, I drop my folded arms and rest one hand on my hip. "Yeah, I'll have to give you the editor's contact info, so you can take full advantage. Then again, I haven't seen any photos printed of you in…" I tap my finger against my chin, "Over a year now? Yikes, Scarlett. Especially considering the fact you're a model and all. Is business a little slow?"

Oof. I'm a bitch. But I can't help it. Not after the week from hell I've had, and not when someone like Scarlett thinks she can push others around. If she's treating me like this, I can only imagine how she treats people who don't have an acid tongue to defend themselves like I do. Besides, she started it.

Ashlyn would tell me to be the bigger person if she was here. I take a deep breath and attempt to do exactly that when Scarlett demands, "Is there a reason you've been hanging around the Lions lately?"

"I'm actually their social media manager, but—"

"So you're sleeping your way to the top?" Her eyes trail down my body. She looks less than impressed. "I'm surprised Henry would stoop so low. After all, he's never been a fan of trash in his apartment."

Did she just call me trash?

"You're right," I reply. "So you should probably leave before he gets out of the shower and realizes you're here instead of the pizza."

"Is there a reason you're in my apartment?"

"You moved out a few months ago, sweetie," I remind her.

"And yet, it's clear you've been keeping my side of the bed nice and warm until I decided to return."

"*Decided* to return?" I laugh. "He broke up with you. Not the other way around."

"Is that what he'd like you to believe? He was through with *me* first?" Her giggle grates on me. She adds, "Oh, honey. You have no idea."

"Are you talking about the fact you cheated on him?" I clarify. Her silence is deafening as I step closer to her. "You're right. You might've slept with someone else first, but only because you were too much of a coward to break it off beforehand."

Her eyes widen. "Excuse me?"

"I hate to break it to you, Scarlett, but cheaters are cowards. Weak. Pathetic. Cowards." I step even closer and tilt my head up, holding her glare. I've never felt short, but being barefoot compared to her willowy frame and four-inch heels, I'm definitely dwarfed by the bitch. However, I'm too stubborn to back down.

"So he told you I cheated, huh?" she muses. "Sounds like he can't stop thinking about me."

"No, I saw firsthand how you cheated. Like I said, I work at SeaBird, which we both know happens to be one of your favorite places to hang out when you're feeling horny. Too bad none of the guys you ever landed even held a candle to your billionaire ex, huh?"

"So you're the one who told him," she assumes. "You're the reason we're on a break."

"Give the guy a little credit, Scarlett. He figured it out on his own."

Unconvinced, her expression sparks with fury, making her look like she's two seconds from clawing my eyes out with her two-hundred-dollar manicure. "I'd like to talk to Henry now."

"I'm sure you would, but he's in the shower, so I'll be sure to tell him you stopped by."

Her tongue clicks against the roof of her mouth, her attention drifting to the hallway. "The shower, huh? That's fine. I won't mind the view."

She starts to step around me, but I mirror her movements, preventing her from cornering Henry or walking around his personal space like she owns it.

"Nah, I think you should stay right there. Or leave and never come back." I shrug. "Your choice."

Yup. She definitely looks like she wants to stab me with her sparkly nails. Her focus slides down my body like she doesn't know what to do with me. "Henry hates tattoos," she snarls.

"Funny. He spent the last hour running his tongue all over mine."

"But not in the shower, right?" she challenges. "He's weird about water and sex. Well, unless it's my pussy. He can't get enough of it."

"I'd almost believe you if I didn't know he was the one who forced you to move out of his apartment."

"And I'd almost believe you were more than a puck bunny if he ever claimed you outside his apartment where *no one* can witness him slumming it." She pats my cheek roughly like I'm her little bitch. "Maybe stick with hockey players and leave the real men to the big girls next time."

Her hand drops, and she steps around me again.

"What the *fuck* are you doing here, Scarlett?" a low voice rumbles from the hallway.

36

HENRY

"**W**hat the *fuck* are you doing here, Scarlett?" I growl.

The ugly lines of frustration disappear from my ex's flawless complexion almost instantly as I step out of the hallway into the main living area.

Her eyes fall on the towel wrapped around my waist, trailing along my abs and pecs until finally landing on my face.

Her expression falls even more when she realizes how pissed I really am. I'm *furious.*

"Henry." Her voice is breathy. Apologetic. Hell, almost angelic, if I didn't know any better.

"How did you get up here?" I demand.

"You know David. He knows me. Knows us." She says the word like there is an *us*.

My eyes thin. "Leave."

"I only want to talk, Henry," she pleads. "I want to apologize––"

"I should get going," Mia mutters under her breath. The comment is so quiet, I'm surprised I hear her. She grabs her purse from the counter and heads to the elevator. I haven't seen her in a week. I'm not ready for her to leave. Not yet. Not because of my ex.

"Mia," I growl.

Forcing a smile, she turns to me. "I'll grab my clothes later. Have fun with your"--she motions to me and Scarlett--"chat."

When she starts walking toward the elevator, Scarlett asks, "You think he'll let you walk out of this apartment in nothing but his shirt? What will the neighbors think?"

Mia rolls her eyes, facing us fully. "You know what? You're totally right, Scarlett. What will the neighbors think?" Her fingers find the button between her breasts, and she undoes it, doing the same to the following two buttons. Once my dress shirt is fully open, she slips her arms out. It tumbles to her feet, giving everyone in the apartment a perfect view of her very naked body. My mouth waters at the sight.

"There," she quips. "Now, I'm in nothing at all." She walks toward me and wraps her arms around my neck, kissing me and pressing her front to mine until my dick stands at full attention under my towel.

Fuck, I want her.

The snark. The confidence. The way she isn't afraid to stand up to Scarlett or let her see every inch of her perfect body. It's refreshing, considering how depressed she's been since Pixie died. Confident Mia. Snarky Mia. Bold Mia.

She's incredible.

When she finally pulls away, Mia's attention drops to the front of my towel, and her eyebrows bounce up and down. "See ya later, Professor."

She walks to the elevator, presses the button, and steps inside, naked as the day she was born. Scarlett is left speechless a few feet away.

If I didn't know Mia was only going one floor down, I

would carry her back to my room and fuck the sass right out of her. Scarlett looks like her jaw is unhinged. I have a feeling Mia accomplished whatever she was trying to do.

Good for her.

If only she would take me with her so I don't have to stay with the uninvited guest in my apartment.

As the elevator doors close, Scarlett sets her purse on the kitchen counter like she's planning to stay and plants her fist on her hip. "Really, Henry? *That's* what you do with our break?"

Break?

I would laugh if I wasn't so pissed this conversation is preventing me from being buried inside the woman who just walked out of my apartment.

"We are *not* on a break, Scarlett," I inform her. "We were *never* on a break. You fucked up. I ended things. It's quite simple. Now, pick your purse up and leave." I reach for the strap of her purse and offer it to her. "See? Simple."

"I told you I want to talk," she repeats.

"You lost the opportunity to talk the moment you started sleeping with other men while we were together. Now, get out, or I'll have you escorted out."

With a glare, she snatches her purse from my grasp and stomps toward the elevator, nearly tripping on my discarded dress shirt on the ground.

"Watch your step," I tell her.

With another glare over her shoulder, she spits, "You know, you really are an ass."

"Never said I was anything different."

The intercom buzzes, and I press the answer button. "What is it?"

"Uh, Mia? Mia Rutherford?" a voice returns. "I have your pizza? Is this the right place?"

"Yeah. This is the right place. Give me a second." I push

267

KELSIE RAE

the button allowing the elevator to work and turn back to Scarlett. "Leave. Now."

I don't wait for her response as I head back to the bedroom and find my wallet, retrieving a twenty. Returning to the front of the penthouse, I notice Scarlett is thankfully missing and has been replaced with a seventeen-year-old in a blue and red polo. He's standing right outside the elevator, holding a couple of cardboard boxes balanced in his hands, looking like a lost puppy.

"A-are you Mia?" he asks. "Or was Mia the pissed-off girl who got on the elevator? Sorry, it's my first day, and––"

"Here, I'll take those." I hand the delivery guy his tip and exchange it for the pizza. "Have a good one."

"You too," the kid replies, stepping onto the elevator.

Once I'm alone, I check the rest of the apartment on the off chance Scarlett was crazy enough to hide somewhere. I wouldn't put it past her. Relief spreads after every corner of the place is checked. Looks like I'm home free.

My phone is still on the nightstand. I grab it and text Mia.

ME

Pizza's here. Are you coming back up?

MIA

Meh. Haven't decided yet. Seems I've lost my appetite.

ME

Let the image of your fine ass walking out of my apartment has only elevated mine.

MIA

Ya know, after meeting your ex, I gotta tell you, I trust your taste in women about as much as I trust my taste in men. Which is not very promising. Just sayin'.

ME

I can't decide if that's a diss on you or me.

MIA

Let's just say it's a good thing we have our rules in place.

Also, I thought of another one.

ME

Now look who's making up new rules.

MIA

Like I said, not very promising, but here it is. Are you ready?

I catch myself smiling as I sit on the edge of the bed. I was nervous. Curious if she was mad at me. If she found another reason to run after meeting Scarlett. I'm grateful she didn't.

ME

Hit me with your new rule.

MIA

No. More. Meeting. Exes.

Like seriously. Yikes. I dunno how you pick 'em, but damn. She's a real piece of work.

ME

Like the current girl I'm seeing. Did you really have to walk out of my apartment naked after giving me a hard-on in nothing but a towel?

MIA

I mean, I didn't HAVE to, but I thought it was a nice touch.

ME

Uh-huh. Yeah. Real nice, Brat.

MIA

I told you you have terrible taste in women, remember? Me included.

Also, you said it only increased your appetite, which leads me to believe you liked my little show, so you better get your story straight, Professor.

ME

I like it when you call me Professor.

MIA

Not as much as when I call you Henry.

ME

I like that too.

Are you coming up for pizza or what? I don't know if I'll like it cold.

MIA

You don't know?

ME

I've never tried cold pizza. Even hot pizza has been a while. I already told you this.

MIA

Okay, fine. I'll come up on one condition.

ME

Let's hear it.

MIA

You tell me what your thing with pizza is, and you make me come two more times. Deal?

I find myself grinning as I read her response.
I type my own.

ME

If you insist.

I've never done this. Been this stupid. Let my body call the shots when my mind is screaming at me to tell her I'm different. Let her know I'm interested in more than her body. Despite my own baggage. Despite my ex cheating on me. I'm interested in Mia. Every inch of her. Even her stubborn side.

37

MIA

"So what's the deal with you and pizza?" I ask, then take another bite of pepperoni goodness. A string of cheese stretches from my teeth to the crispy crust, and I pinch it between my fingers and lick the excess grease off.

Chuckling, Henry watches me, taking a bite of his own slice. His strong jaw flexes as he chews and offers a shrug. "Honestly, it's a pretty boring answer. My mom hates pizza, so we grew up eating other foods."

"So, it isn't one of your *things*?" I ask.

His brow arches.

"Ya know, like the showers, and the germs, and the––"

"Thought you said you weren't going to pry," he challenges.

"That was before your ex dropped by and pissed me off."

His amusement falls, and he sets his pizza back onto his plate, wiping the grease from his fingers on a perfectly-squared napkin. "I'm sorry she showed up unannounced."

"Does she do it a lot?" I ask. My eyes drop to my dinner. "Show up unannounced?"

"Only one other time."

"Oh?"

"The morning you were locked out of your apartment," he clarifies. "It's probably why I was a little on edge. I'm sorry if I took it out on you."

"You didn't," I reply.

"You sure?"

"Yeah, of course," I deflect, bunching my napkin up and rolling the edge between my fingers as my curiosity gets the best of me. "Do you miss her at all?"

"Not in the slightest." My gaze snaps up to his, and he adds, "She was simply convenient."

"Don't all guys like convenient?"

"I wouldn't know. I can't speak for all guys."

"Do *you* like convenient?" I push.

A ghost of a smile touches his lips. "I thought I did."

"Thought?"

"I must say, I think I have a thing for brats."

I snort. "Speaking of *things*…if pizza isn't one of them, what are some of your others?"

He looks down at his half-eaten slice and lifts it to his mouth. "Who said I have *things*?"

"Do you really think you're that sneaky?" I volley back at him because, seriously. The guy might hide it well from most people, but anyone who pays attention and is around Henry for more than a day or two would have to notice his quirks.

Wouldn't they?

"I like routines," he offers.

"And?"

"And I like my personal space. I like order. I like cleanliness."

"Kate's boyfriend likes cleanliness too. Macklin," I clarify.

"Yeah, I know. It's one of the reasons why we get along," Henry informs me. He hired Macklin to work with the physical therapists, sports medicine doctor, and emergency crew to make sure the players are well cared for.

"But as far as I know, Macklin doesn't have OCD," I continue.

The bite of pizza he'd been about to eat halts an inch from his mouth. "You caught that, huh?"

I nod. "It was just a hunch."

"My disorder is mild overall."

"But you keep it close to the chest," I conclude.

"I do, yes."

"Have you always had it?" I prod.

"Yes and no."

"What do you mean?"

"I've always obsessed over success and grades and having a clean space, but it didn't alter my day-to-day life until after everything happened with your father and Troy was arrested."

Surprise flickers in my gaze at the mention of Henry's catalyst, the pizza in my mouth turning to sawdust. I force it down my throat and take a sip of the beer I'd stolen from his fridge. "Why not?"

"My therapist thinks it's because it was the first time I felt like something was truly out of my control."

It makes sense. My father's death sent a lot of people spiraling. My aunt. My mom. Me. And, apparently, Henry too.

"You see a therapist for your condition?" I ask.

His brow cocks. "You're surprised?"

I shrug and take another bite of pizza, chewing slowly as I consider his question. Am I surprised? Maybe a little. It's not every day big, bad alpha men see therapists for their mental health. Knowing he does only makes me more attracted to him.

Which is a problem. His pros are slowly adding up, making it harder for me to keep our rules in place.

Sticking a pin in that particular predicament, I swallow my bite of pizza and say, "I guess I always assumed you had the perfect life. Hiring a therapist proves you see your quirks as something worth addressing--worth fixing--instead of ignoring them like most people would."

"When it started affecting other relationships, I decided it was time to find a solution."

"And have you found a solution?"

"There isn't a solution. Or at least nothing concrete. I've been seeing my therapist off and on for over five years. I learned a handful of techniques to battle my triggers with OCD, but there are still certain quirks I adjusted for."

"Like not having your clothes anywhere near the bathroom."

"Yes."

"Why is it a trigger?" I ask.

He shrugs. "It makes me feel like I'm suffocating. Like something bad is going to happen."

"Even when you're naked, and your clothes are sitting on the bathroom counter?"

He hesitates, his body turning rigid. After a few seconds, he lets out a slow breath, and forces the tension in his muscles to soften. "The thought alone is nauseating."

"Why?"

"Triggers aren't always logical, but I'm working on it."

"Like with the whole cleanliness thing?" I motion to his spotless house.

His gaze follows mine, and he chuckles dryly, turning back to his pizza. "This is nothing."

"You're joking, right?"

"After Troy was arrested, I couldn't fall asleep without

vacuuming, wiping down the counter, having the dishwasher running, and my hamper empty. If I even considered going to sleep before my hands were raw from scrubbing the dirt off every surface in my house, I felt like something bad would happen again." A somber haze fills his eyes before he blinks and it disappears. "Now, I only get a little irritated when my house is messy, but I don't act on those compulsions."

"Compulsions?" I question. A sharp pang digs into my sternum at the mention of the *something bad* that happened in his life. He's talking about my dad's murder. I'd always assumed I was the only one affected. I was wrong.

"Compulsions are different for every person," Henry explains. "It can be anything. Like washing your hands over and over or making sure something is the right number or in the right order. It can be a routine and the need to start over if a task is performed out of order. It can be a lot of things."

"So, let me get this straight. You're *not* supposed to act on your compulsions?"

"The more I act on them, the stronger they become, and the more I lose the fight with OCD."

I lean back in my chair, studying the man in front of me. I shouldn't find this attractive. His vulnerability. His honesty. His bravery. Because this is brave. Admitting he isn't invincible. Honestly, I'm jealous. I wish I could do the same.

After taking another swig of my beer, I set it beside the pizza box in the center of his spotless dining table and ask, "So how do you fight it? Your compulsions?"

"Exposure therapy."

"Such as?"

"Such as going to sleep when my house isn't perfect."

I look around his spotless kitchen and family room. "This isn't perfect?"

He laughs but shakes his head. "This is clean, but not as clean as my OCD tells me it should be."

"So, exposing yourself to messes is considered helpful?"

"It's considered exposure therapy," he clarifies. "And the more you're exposed to something triggering without giving into it, the weaker the trigger becomes."

"Got it. So...this." I wipe the crumbs from my fingers onto his table. "This is exposure therapy?"

He smirks, unoffended. I don't miss the way his eyes fall on the crumbs a beat too long before snapping to my gaze. "Yes."

"But if you wipe them up, you're acting on your compulsion. And if you don't wipe them up, you have a dirty table. So...how does it work?"

"Wiping the table off after a meal isn't acting on my compulsion. Obsessively wiping it with multiple cleaning chemicals, then pulling out the vacuum and vacuuming the entire house is acting on my compulsion."

"Got it." I nod, dipping my finger in the marinara. "And this?" I dab the sauce onto the side of my mouth and lick the excess from my finger. "Is this exposure therapy?"

His lips twitch. "Maybe."

"So if you lick it off me, are you acting on your compulsion, or are you helping a dirty girl in need?"

With a mischievous grin, he wraps his hand around the back of my neck, pulls me into him, licks the smudge of marinara off with his tongue, and kisses me greedily.

Man, I love his lips.

How soft yet demanding they are. The way they fit perfectly with mine. Blindly, I reach for the marinara sauce again. It's slightly warm against my thumb, and I cup Henry's face, spreading it along his jaw. It's messy and chaotic, but he doesn't pull away from my kiss. Instead, he reaches for the edge of my chair and drags me closer to him. With our lips still connected, I stand, and he leans back, giving me space as I straddle his waist. Yeah, I've definitely missed him. Way more than I'd like to admit. Even after Scarlett showed up on his doorstep. Even after I went back to my apartment and had to *not* lose myself to my jealousy. Even after he invited me back to his place and told me he isn't perfect. Told me he has his own shit to battle. I still like him. I'm still here. I'm still interested, despite my best efforts. And I still want to do this. To connect with him. To be vulnerable with him. To let him into my body.

But only as friends.

Nothing more.

Because it's all I can offer.

All I can accept.

All I can handle, thanks to my own clusterfuck of a past.

But if I can help with his OCD while I'm at it? Well, I think I can oblige.

Tearing my lips from his, I suck the mess from his cheek, savoring the groan rumbling up his throat. His five-o'clock shadow teases my taste buds, and I trail my tongue along his jawline. He tastes like pizza and bad decisions. Really good bad decisions. His hands find my ass as I suck a patch of his skin into my mouth. He tugs me further up his thighs. The ridge of his dick nudges against my core, and I nearly moan.

Yup. This'll do.

Nibbling on his bottom lip, I undo the shirt buttons, pushing the sides open and running my hands along his tight, tan skin. I memorize every ripple of abs, then find the top button on his slacks.

"Are your suits a *thing* too?" I ask against his lips.

He smirks. "It's a family thing. A business thing."

"Oh?"

"Dress to impress, Brat." He slides his hands under my

shirt, finding my breasts and massaging them. "Are you impressed?"

"I'm a sucker for a man in a suit," I note, tilting my head back and arching into him as he pinches my nipples.

"And a man with scars, right?"

Bending forward, I kiss the healing wound above his eye. "Still bummed I didn't get to use the dinosaur Band-Aid on you after this happened."

"Got a thing for dinosaurs too?" he challenges.

"Maybe."

"What else do you have a thing for?"

His eyes pin me in place, and I pull away slightly, looking down at him and feeling blindsided. It's such a simple question, but I hesitate.

What else do you have a thing for?

A spark of trepidation flashes through me in an instant. Of the things I could say. The words on the tip of my tongue.

I have a thing for dark eyes. Brown hair. Tan skin. Clean apartments. Silly text messages. Navy suits. Buttered popcorn and cheesy movies. The list goes on and on and on, each revolving around the bossy asshole between my thighs.

And it's terrifying.

But what's worse? I think he can see it in my eyes. The truth. The fear. The hesitation. It scares me even more.

He grabs my face and presses his forehead to mine. It's as if he knows the fine line we're walking. How much I don't want to screw it up. How much I want to end it right here. Right now. To save my heart from shattering.

Such a contradiction.

"You got a thing for hard cocks, baby?" he rasps as he shifts his length against me.

I swallow my moan and nod.

I know what he's doing. He's giving me an out. A reason

to stay. An opportunity to *not* second guess my feelings or our arrangement and how stupid it is.

Yes. This is what I need. A distraction. A completion. A way for the itch to be scratched so I can go back to normal. So I can think straight. So I can keep my feelings in check.

"Then I think it's time you let me fill you up," he decides.

I nod again. He picks me up, cradling my thighs with his hands, and takes a step toward the hallway.

"On the couch," I tell him. Because I can't do this in his bed. Not when my feelings––and resolve––are already all over the place.

No. I need this to be physical. I need this to be about getting off and *only* getting off.

"Okay."

Carrying me to the dark leather couch in the family room, he sets me on my feet in front of it, but we both stay standing as I fumble with his pants, releasing his very hard cock and falling to my knees. I rub the head of his dick against my lips, anxiety licking at the base of my spine.

"Mia, wait." His hands find my hair, and he pushes it away from my face. "When I said I wanted to fill you up, I meant––"

"I know what you meant." I peek up at him and tease his tip with my tongue, reveling in the spark in his eyes as I take him deeper into my mouth. I've sucked a lot of dicks in my life, not gonna lie. Call it daddy issues. Call it a need to impress. To be needed. Wanted. Craved. But none of the guys I've sucked have ever looked at me like this.

Like I'm beautiful.

Not hot.

Or sexy.

Or tempting.

But *beautiful*.

And it's all wrong.

Because it's hitting too close to home. The affection in his eyes scares the shit out of me, so I let my eyelids close and suck him deeper, hollowing my cheeks and bobbing my head up and down on his thick length.

I'm desperate to please him, but I'm even more desperate to keep our boundaries intact. They're boundaries I want. Boundaries I need. They remind me this is an arrangement. Remind me we're nothing more than friends who like to get each other off. One of our rules is totally a cliche, but it involves our hearts staying out of the picture, and I hold onto it harder than ever as I swirl my tongue along the head of his dick, refusing to acknowledge the way his groan of appreciation makes my chest swell.

But when he touches my face, rubbing his thumb along my jaw, it isn't rough or derogatory. It's gentle. Sweet. Soft.

I release him from my mouth with a soft pop and squeeze my eyes even tighter. "Henry, stop."

"What's wrong?"

"I need you to use me."

His muscles tense. "Use you?"

"Fuck me. Spank me. Tie me up. Do whatever you want, but don't be gentle."

"Mia--"

I stand, but he grabs my hand, holding me in place.

"We both know what this arrangement is, Professor, and if you can't give me what I need--"

His muscles vibrate with tension as he tugs me into him. My hands slap against his naked chest as I catch myself, my breathing shallow. With deft fingertips, he drags my pants down, twists me around, and presses his hand between my shoulder blades, guiding me toward the wall. It's forceful. Almost rough. And exactly what I need.

"Hands on the wall," he orders.

I do as I'm told.

"Spread your legs."

My feet scoot out.

"Wider," he growls.

I spread them a few more inches, and his hands find my waist, tugging me into him until I'm bent over, displaying every intimate part of me.

He grabs the base of his dick and rubs it against my center, collecting my juices, and fuck me, I'm pretty sure I could come by this alone. Lining himself up with my entrance, he thrusts into me without a word. I jerk forward, nearly hitting my head on the wall as my jaw drops.

"Fuck," I gasp.

He smacks my ass. The delicious burn makes my knees weak. His hard cock slides out of me and he shoves himself back inside with even more force.

Over and over, he thrusts, increasing the pace as he uses my body exactly how I asked him to. My orgasm builds from his bruising grasp on my waist, but he slips out of me, yanking me around until I'm facing him. He picks me up and shoves himself inside me all over again. Chest to chest, the new position is more intimate. My back hits the wall with a loud thump, his pants still hanging around his ankles as I catch my breath.

This angle is different.

It's deeper.

"Play with your nipples," he growls. "Lift your shirt, and let me watch."

I shove my top up and palm my breasts through my bra, savoring the feel of it. Of him. Us. He pounds into me harder and harder until I swear I see stars.

"You wanna be fucked, Brat?" he growls.

I nod. "Yes."

"You wanna be used?"

"God, yes."

"You wanna feel my cum slide down your legs when I'm finished with you?"

I nearly moan, the last of my logic and what a bad idea it is to have sex without protection dissipating into thin air. Besides, he's clean. I'm clean. And what's one more bad decision when they're all I ever make?

"Mia," he growls, repeating, "You wanna feel my cum slide down your legs when I'm finished with you?"

"Fuck, yes."

"Good girl." He smacks my ass again, leans forward, and buries his head in the crook of my neck. The sharp sting of his bite makes me quiver around him, but he doesn't stop pistoning in and out of me.

"Squeeze my cock, baby," he orders. "Let me feel you."

My back arches. "Yes. Yes. Yes."

He carries me to the table, setting me beside the pizza box. Dragging my body to the edge, he tugs me into his hard length with a punishing grip on my thighs.

"Play with yourself. Let me see you."

My hand slides down my body as he enters me at a bruising pace. I rub my fingers against my clit and come within seconds, my muscles turning to mush beneath his expert touch. Euphoria wraps around me like a warm blanket, and he follows seconds later, groaning my name through gritted teeth.

"Fuck," I pant, the room spinning around us. "Fuck, fuck, fuck."

His softening cock slides out of me, followed by his cum. He cups me with his hand and rubs it over my sensitive clit.

"What are you--"

"You told me you needed to come twice," he reminds me, mentioning our earlier conversation.

I shake my head. "Henry--"

"One down. One to go." His fingers dip into my center,

gathering his cum. Finding my clit again, he rubs it in slow circles.

The stimulation feels like I'm being touched with a livewire, and I shove at his hand. "It's too much."

"It's just enough," he argues, continuing his punishing touch while shoving my shirt to my neck. He picks the marinara up from the pizza box with his opposite hand and pours it on my breasts. It's cold now, and my nipples pebble. Then his mouth is on them, sucking and nibbling while his fingers play with me like I'm his own personal toy.

And fuck me, he might be right. Maybe this isn't too much. Maybe it's exactly enough. Because this feels freaking amazing. My breathing turns shallow as I grab his wrist between my thighs, slowly riding his hand, my hips rolling against his fingers.

So good.

So freaking good.

Familiar pleasure builds low in my stomach as his mouth finds the shell of my ear, and he whispers, "You want me to use you? Fine. But only if you understand I'm the *only* one who makes you feel this way. Do you understand?"

"Yes," I breathe out. "It's you. Only you."

"Tell me it's okay. Tell me it's okay to make you feel this way. To make you want me. Crave me. Tell me you aren't going to run simply because you're scared."

His fingers slide out of me and circle my entrance again, leaving me squirming.

"Henry," I beg, but he doesn't finger me.

He leaves me empty, his dark gaze holding me hostage. "Tell me it's okay. Tell me you aren't going to run."

"Henry, I'm close—"

"Tell me you aren't going to run," he repeats, tapping his finger against my clit without giving me enough pressure to push me over the edge. And holy shit, it's the sweetest torture ever.

"I won't run," I whisper.

He pinches me roughly, and I come, my mouth falling wide. His marinara-infused tongue shoves between my lips as he swallows my moans.

Fuck. Me.

38

HENRY

I'm either an idiot or a genius. I can't decide which as I look down at the squirming puppy in my arms.

At first, I debated purchasing a small breed. Something easy to travel with. Something easily accommodating. Then I remembered whom the puppy would belong to and knew I had to go big or go home. With Mia, there's no in-between.

We haven't discussed it.

The possibility of her owning a puppy.

Or the night we shared together with Mia curled against my chest after she found out about Pixie. No sex. No orgasms. Yet more intimate and vulnerable than any moment I've shared with anyone. Ever. We also haven't discussed the way she was spooked the last time we had sex or how I know she was jealous when Scarlett showed up on my doorstep. We haven't discussed a lot of things, knowing it'll only spook Mia into running. But I'm okay with letting my actions speak for themselves, and if a new puppy is what it takes to show her I care, so be it.

I let out a huff of air and shift the German Shepherd into my other arm. Raising my fist, I knock on Mia's door.

Footsteps echo on the other side a few seconds later, and the door opens with a soft squeak.

"Hey, what are you––" Mia gasps and covers her mouth with her hand. "Oh, my–– Who are–– When did you––" She looks up at me and reaches for the ball of fur in my arms. "Come here, beautiful! Or are you Mr. Handsome?" she coos, taking the eight-week-old puppy from me without bothering to ask my permission and snuggling it against her chest.

I smile, taking in Mia's massive grin as she nuzzles her nose against the puppy's face and breathes in deeply.

"It's a girl," I tell her.

"Of course you are," she tells the puppy. "You're far too dainty to be a boy, aren't you, baby girl? Yes, you are." She kisses the top of the puppy's brown and black head, breathing her in all over again. "She still smells like a puppy. Oh my gosh, I'm in love. When did you get her?"

"Just picked her up," I reply. "But she isn't mine."

Mia pauses, her forehead wrinkling. "Who does she belong to?"

"She's yours."

Her pretty pink lips part, but she doesn't say a word. Not right away. She's too stunned. I don't blame her. This is crossing a line. I wouldn't buy a puppy for just anyone, especially not a shedding monster like this one will grow to be. If Mia catches onto the truth, she'll end this. I can't let it happen. Not anymore. I've fallen for this girl. She doesn't know it–– she can't know it––not until she's ready, but it's true. I need to move slowly enough for her insecurities to finally dissipate so she can let me in fully. So she can acknowledge her own feelings and accept this is it for us. She's mine. And I'm hers.

The puppy licks Mia's chin, snapping her out of her daze,

and she pushes the door to her apartment open the rest of the way.

"Come on in."

I follow Mia into her place. It's as bare as the last time I was here.

"Close the door behind you," she adds, giving the puppy her full attention. Once it's closed, she sets the puppy down and folds her arms.

With a pointed look, she asks, "Are you serious?"

I nod. "Yeah."

"You got me a puppy?"

I nod again. "Yeah."

"Why?"

"Because you might not trust your gut, but I do. You've wanted a puppy for years. Ever since you gave Pixie to your uncle."

Her lips are nothing but a slash of pink as she glances at the puppy padding across the floor. "Just because I wanted one doesn't mean it would've been a smart decision."

"I think you'll figure it out."

"Do you have any idea how much work puppies can be?" she challenges.

Again, I nod. "Is it a problem?"

Sitting on the hardwood floor, she stares at the puppy sniffing the ugly floral chair in the family room and bites her bottom lip. I know she's at war with herself. Caught between letting herself be excited and the fear of screwing up. Of not being enough when she's more than capable of excelling at whatever she puts her mind to.

"Does she have a name?" Mia whispers.

"Figured naming her was your job."

Her torn expression shifts from the puppy to me, and she shakes her head. "I can't have a dog."

"Why not?" I ask, stuffing my hands into my front pockets.

"What if I can't take care of her?"

"I think you'll be fine."

"What about when I need to travel with the team?"

"The puppy can come with us. I told you I was going to find a replacement for our mascot, remember?"

"Oh, because I supposedly slept with a guy who likes dressing up as a lion all the time?"

"Can't blame a guy for being jealous," I joke.

She scoffs. "Even if Leo the Lion was a threat, I figured you meant you were looking for another *person* who dressed up in a suit or something, not an actual"--she waves her hand at the puppy--"creature who's almost as big and fluffy as a lion!"

"Don't worry, Leo still has his job," I clarify. "But I think the players will love your puppy, and the fans will too."

"Well yeah, I mean, who wouldn't love her?" she points out while nibbling on the edge of her thumb.

"Do you like her?" I ask.

She peeks at the clumsy fluff ball and back at me. "Of course I like her."

"Then what's the problem?"

Pulling her knees into her chest, she rests her chin against them, her eyes almost glassy.

My tone softens. "Mia, what's wrong?"

"I'm scared," she whispers.

"What are you scared of?"

"I'm scared of screwing her up." She swallows. "Of making a mistake. Of not being enough."

My chest pulls as Mia shoves her hair away from her face. Her vibrant blue eyes are glued to the puppy in front of her, but she doesn't say a word. I know this girl. I know she hates being vulnerable. I know she hates showing weakness. I know she's a walking contradiction. I know she thinks she can take on the world, but she's too afraid to open herself up to anyone who could help her do it. And right now, she's afraid of letting the puppy in front of her down. She's afraid of screwing her up when I know she would never let it happen in the first place. Not when she already cares about her.

"Trust me," I murmur. "You're going to do fine. And when you need help, I'll be here."

Unconvinced, she huffs, "Puppies are a big deal, Henry."

"I know."

"And even if I do love her already, it's still a big responsibility."

"I know," I repeat.

"And how do I even travel with a German Shepherd? It's not like I can put her on my lap during the flight. She's going to grow so big––"

"I have my ways."

Arms folded, she huffs, "Like what?"

"Well, when we aren't traveling with the team, we can buy her a first-class ticket, or if that isn't an option, we can take the private plane. Not a big deal."

Her eyes bulge as she looks up at me from the ground. "You have a private plane?"

I chuckle and sit beside her. Her naivety regarding my net worth never ceases to amaze me. "Yeah, Mia. I have a private plane. I know you hate money, but sometimes it can buy convenience. This is my official invitation. You and the puppy can use it whenever you want."

"Are you serious?"

"Am I much of a jokester?"

Her mouth ticks up before she sucks her bottom lip into it and watches the puppy chew on the edge of her armchair. I reach forward, tugging her away from the monstrosity, and click my fingers against the floor. Taking the bait, she pounces on me like a baby lion and nibbles my hand.

When I finally peek up at Mia, her gaze is on me. It's reserved. Hesitant. But almost hopeful, too, making my lungs stall.

"She's going to shed," she whispers.

"And?"

"And I assume your aversion to messes includes dog fur--"

"Seeing you smile is worth it."

Her lips twitch. "Thank you."

"You're welcome." I pick the puppy up, scoot closer to Mia on the hardwood floor, and plop the beast in her lap. "Now, she needs a name."

Resting her head against my shoulder, she looks down at the puppy in her lap and lets out a soft sigh. I wrap my arm around her shoulders and press a kiss to her temple. "And dog supplies," I add. "Are you ready to go shopping?"

"You know, when you mentioned Nala needed dog supplies, I figured we'd go to PetCo or something, not a furniture store," I quip.

"Where are you going to sit when Nala wants to cuddle?" Henry challenges.

"I dunno? The floor?"

"Nala deserves more than the floor to snuggle on," he informs me, plopping his fine ass on a gray sectional in the middle of the furniture store and patting the cushion next to him.

Grudgingly, I cross my arms but take a seat and rest my feet on the glass coffee table in front of us. "Personally, I think you're trying to convince me to buy furniture for my apartment."

"That's exactly what I'm trying to do." His arm wraps around my shoulders, and he tugs me against him. "I know you have a thing about money, but certain things in life are borderline necessities. Like a place to sit when you're in your own apartment." He drops a kiss on the crown of my head and adds, "Besides, you can afford it now. And if you beg to differ, I'll simply buy it for you."

Glaring at him, I say, "I don't like buying things for myself, and I don't like handouts."

"So don't buy the furniture for you. Buy it for Nala."

My eyes pinch even more, and a knowing grin spreads across his face. "That's my girl."

By the time we're ready to walk out of the store, I'm buying a kitchen table, a coffee table, a massive bean bag bed, and a new couch, all of which Henry convinced me are in some way a necessity for my brand new German Shepherd.

A German. Freaking. Shepherd.

The man's delusional and clearly has more faith in me than I do.

He's also really thoughtful.

And sweeter than anyone gives him credit for.

After handing my credit card to the sales associate, she casts a quick glance at Henry and gives it back to me. "It seems the bill has already been paid, and the items you purchased will be delivered to your apartment next week."

I glower at Henry beside me. "Excuse me?"

He hooks his arm around my shoulders, whispering, "Strange, isn't it?"

"Very strange," I agree. "Especially when you already bought me a freaking puppy. One currently sitting in a brand new kennel with a brand new cushy bed at my apartment."

"Humor me, Mia," Henry replies. "I like taking care of my..." he hesitates, the same cocky smirk wreaking havoc on my insides, *"friends."*

"Friends," I repeat. "Mm-hmm. Sure." I elbow his ribs, but the bastard doesn't even flinch as we walk outside and head to his car at the edge of the parking lot. "You were sneaky. I don't like sneaky."

"I wouldn't have to be sneaky if you would let me take

care of you without throwing a fit every step of the way."
He opens the passenger door, motioning for me to climb
inside.

Arms crossed, I give in and sit but hold his gaze through
the still-opened passenger door. "I like being independent."

"I like you being independent," he replies. "And you're
right. I overstepped my bounds. I'll be more forward with my
intentions from now on."

Shifting in my seat, I make myself comfortable and say,
"Thank you."

"You're welcome." He closes the door, rounds the front of
the car, and slides behind the steering wheel. As the engine
roars to life, he adds, "And to help make up for me overstep-
ping my bounds, I'll let you buy me dinner."

"Let me?" I quip.

Turning in his seat, he grasps my hand and brings it to his
lips. "Mia. Friend. *Brat*," he teases. "Will you please buy me
dinner tonight?"

My teeth dig into the inside of my cheek as I try to maintain my amusement. Then, my expression falls.

His brows dip. "What's wrong?"

"I actually have to go home."

"Why?"

"I have plans tonight."

"What kind of plans?" he prods.

My nose scrunches, and I shove my guilt aside. "Blake and
Theo invited me to their place for a small housewarming
party."

"Oh." He lets my hand go but doesn't shift his car into
drive. He simply stares at me. Waiting. When I stay quiet, he
nods slowly. "I assume you are not going to extend me an
invitation."

My guilt flares, and I open my mouth, but nothing
comes out.

The light in his eyes dims, and he puts his car into drive. "Don't worry about it."

"Henry--"

"I understand our arrangement, Mia. It's not a problem." He pulls out of the parking lot.

The drive back to our building is torture. The silence makes me sick to my stomach as I pick at my cuticles. But I don't know what to say. I don't know how to fix this. I don't know how to make him feel better while maintaining our arrangement and not muddying the waters further.

He waits on the edge of the grass while I let Nala pee. Once she finishes, he guides us inside the building, nodding at David without uttering a word. He's still quiet. Still disappointed.

My keys jingle in my hand as we ride the elevator and stride down the hallway toward my apartment with Nala in Henry's arms. When we reach my door, I crumble under the silence and peek up at him.

"Listen," I start.

"Seriously, Mia. It's okay."

"It's not okay," I argue. "I feel guilty--"

"Don't." He smiles, but it doesn't reach his eyes. "Like I said, I understand our arrangement."

Yeah, but I don't, I want to argue. Instead, I bite my tongue. My mind is a mess. Especially after today. After the last few weeks. It's made our arrangement confusing and convoluted and messy and--

"Hey," he murmurs. The softness in his voice cuts through my obsessive thoughts like a knife. He lifts his hand and taps his finger against my temple while balancing Nala in his other arm. "I can see you overthinking things. Don't. I'm a patient guy."

A patient guy? What does he even mean? Does he expect an invitation next time? Should I give him one? What's he waiting for? Our arrangement to change? To shift into something else? It can't. I won't let it. I *can't* let it.

"Mia," he soothes, grasping my chin and tilting my head until our eyes lock.

"I'm not worth your patience," I whisper.

"I disagree." He smiles again, and this time, it's almost real as he lets my chin go. "Have fun with your friends, okay?"

"Henry––"

"Do you want me to watch Nala for you?"

I take the puppy from his arms and hug her against my chest. "I was thinking about bringing her."

"Good idea," he agrees. "They'll be excited to meet her."

"I think so too." My chest swells under the silence until the steady *thump-thump* of my heart is almost painful. It's like I miss him already. But he's one foot in front of me. How can I miss someone when they haven't even left yet?

"You should call me after," he adds.

I smile. "I think that can be arranged."

"Good." Bending forward, he brushes his lips against my cheek. "Thanks for hanging out with me today."

"Thanks for Nala and for…" I lick my lips. "Everything else."

"Always." He waits for me to open my apartment door and heads back to the elevator.

40
MIA

"Hey!" I greet Blake when her front door opens.

"Mia!" she cheers, gasping when she sees Nala in my arms. "Shut up! Is it yours?"

I laugh. "Yup. This is Nala. Also known as Baby Lion and Monster Baby." I shift the bundle of fur, waiting to be invited in. "Can I come in?"

"Of course. Sorry. You caught me off guard with this precious girl." Blake pushes the door the rest of the way open, and I step inside as more gasps ensue.

"A puppy!"

"Oh my goodness, I need it."

"You got a dog?"

"Aww, what's its name?"

I wave at my friends mingling in the front room of Blakely and Theo's new house. Blake swipes Nala from my arms.

"She just peed," I tell her.

"Dude, I don't even care," Blake informs me. "We have hardwood floors. Nala is fine."

"You named her Nala?" Ashlyn asks from the kitchen

while balancing a baby boy on her hip. "Jaxon loves *The Lion King*."

"Yeah, it's a classic," Colt adds beside her. He brushes his lips against Ashlyn's temple and steals Jaxon from her. With the baby propped on his hip, he heads toward me in the foyer. "What are you gonna do with her when we travel?"

"Henry said I could bring her along," I answer.

"Cool. What kind of dog is she?" he asks.

"A, uh, a German Shepherd, actually."

"Sick," Theo compliments from the couch as Blake sits next to him. Colt and Jaxon join them in the family room, leaving me alone with Ashlyn, who's busy staring a hole in the side of my head.

My lips pull to one side as I tear my attention from Nala and give Ashlyn a pointed look. "Yes? Something you want to say?"

"So, Henry knows about Nala?" she prods.

I fold my arms, rubbing my hands up and down my bare arms. "Yup. He does."

"Interesting," she notes. "Did you ask permission or something before getting her?"

Damn, this girl and her detective skills. She knows. She doesn't even have to ask, and she already knows. She simply wants to hear it from the source.

"Actually," I mutter, "he's the one who bought her for me."

Ashlyn's eyes pop, and her mouth spreads into a grin. "I knew it!"

Tugging on her arm, I peek at our distracted friends a few feet away. "Can you keep your voice down, please?" I grit out.

"Why?" She glances at Nala in Blakely's lap and turns back to me. "Because you're afraid our friends will find out your *boss* bought you a dog?"

"Don't be a smartass. You know why," I hedge.

"Yeah. I do," she returns. She's nice enough to keep her

voice quiet. "Which is awesome and all, but I'm really curious when you're going to stop playing around and finally admit you like the guy."

My lips press together, and I fold my arms. "I admit nothing."

"What doesn't she admit?" Kate asks, coming back from the bathroom.

"Theo, hold Nala," Blakely says from the couch. "I think I'm missing out on girl talk."

I groan and drop my head back. "You guys are the worst."

"No, we're the best, and you know it. Now, what did I miss?" Blake asks.

With a pointed stare at the boys hanging around the couch, I mutter, "Can we talk about this later? Or maybe... somewhere more private?"

Ashlyn hooks her arms through Blake's and Kate's. "Let's have Blake show us the guest room. Come on, Mia."

Grudgingly, I follow the girls into a bedroom at the end of the hall and collapse onto the plush mattress, crossing my legs and leaning back onto my hands as everyone stares at me like I've grown a second head.

"*Whaaaat?*" I groan under their scrutiny.

"Nala was a gift," Ashlyn informs the room. "From Professor Buchanan."

"Ooooh, so you're still tapping that, I assume?" Blakely asks.

"He was around when I found out Pixie died, and I think he could tell how much it crushed me, so he bought me a dog," I explain. "Not a big deal."

"Pretty sure for ninety-nine percent of people, buying a living thing for someone else is considered a big deal," Ash states.

"He's my friend. I'd do the same for you if you wanted one," I point out.

"Yeah, but you and Buchanan are bumping uglies," Blake reminds me. "And he bought you a gift. One that eats and pees and poops and snuggles and––"

I raise my hand into the air. "I get your point. But even so, it's not a big deal."

The lie sounds forced, even to my own ears, but I don't back down. And I sure as shit don't acknowledge the sharp twinge following it, either.

Kate sits beside me, and the slight jostle from the mattress scatters my thoughts. "No offense, but I think Blake is onto something. You might be adamant it isn't a big deal, but Buchanan might be thinking differently, and you need to keep that in mind."

Frustration simmers in my veins, leaving me speechless as I pull my hands into my lap. The problem is, I don't know who I'm mad at. My friends? For calling it like it is? Am I mad at myself for not acknowledging my feelings for Henry, let alone the fact I miss him way more than I should? Am I mad at Henry for hinting he wants more earlier in the hallway and how it's turned me into an emotional wreck? Honestly, I don't even know anymore. But I hate it. I hate it a lot.

Because it shouldn't matter.

He shouldn't matter.

Sensing my annoyance, Ash sits beside me on my opposite side and murmurs, "Can I ask you something?"

I grab the nearest pillow from the head of the bed and tuck it against my chest. "What?"

"Do you like him?"

I roll my eyes. "Ash––"

"Answer the question from your gut, Mia," Blake interrupts. "Do you like him? Inside of bed. Outside of bed. Do you like talking to him? Do you get butterflies when he texts? How does he make you feel?"

"I dunno?" I shrug. "Happy, I guess."

"Macklin makes me happy too," Kate chimes in.

"So does Colt," Ash adds.

"And Theo," Blakely informs me.

"Yeah, well, just because he makes me happy doesn't mean I'm looking for anything else, and if Henry thinks a puppy changes things…" My voice trails off, and dread blazes in the pit of my stomach.

"If that's the case, you might want to have a heart-to-heart with him," Ashlyn suggests. "Because he deserves to know if he's wasting time on a girl who won't let herself fall in love."

Well, shit.

My mouth opens with a rebuttal, but I close it almost instantly, digging my teeth into the inside of my cheek.

I feel like I've been slapped by my best friend. It doesn't feel good. Actually, it feels pretty shitty. Because love? Falling in love? Being in love? It's not possible. It can't be possible. Not for me. Not when it'll only bite me in the ass. Bite us *both* in the ass. But the idea of him wasting his time on me when I know I won't let it go anywhere significant doesn't exactly make me feel better, either. Is it selfish? Am I selfish? To want to steal his time when I know it can't go anywhere? When I don't *want* it to go anywhere?

Touching my fingertips to my parted lips, I try to maintain my composure, but it's hard. Really hard. And the worst part is the little voice inside my head wishing I could call Henry. Wishing I could tell him I miss him. Tell him I regret not inviting him to come with me tonight.

But what's worse? I'm afraid he's the only one who could make me feel better in this moment, and how messed up is that?

He's my friend. And we have our rules. Rules we put in place to keep us out of this exact situation. Yet here I am, feeling overwhelmed and confused and anxious and frustrated and sad. Sad because I don't want to let this go. And I'm not stupid. I know I don't have to. I know Ash and Blake and Kate might be onto something. I know Henry might be willing to cross the line into relationship territory if I suggest it. But I also know losing him would hurt. It would hurt more than I want to admit. And we haven't even crossed the line into relationship territory. What happens if I fall in love? If I open up to him, rely on him, and he leaves? Or cheats on me, falls out of love with me? What happens if his family doesn't accept me or he gets bored? There are a million different scenarios, and only one winds up with us together, allowing us to live happily ever after. One. One in a million. Fate doesn't like me enough to let those odds be in my favor.

So where does it leave me? Where does it leave us?

"Enough sad talk," Blakely decides. "Come on. Let's go play with your new puppy while we turn on *The Lion King*."

"Excellent idea," Kate agrees. She takes my hand and tugs me to my feet. Ashlyn hooks her arm through mine and guides me back to the family room. It's probably a good thing. With all the conflicting thoughts swirling in my brain, I wouldn't be surprised if I ran into a wall or something without her guidance.

But they're right. Now isn't the time to dissect my arrangement or feelings with Henry, so I decide to stick my head in the sand and deal with that particular shitshow later tonight when I'm alone and can think clearly.

When we reach the family room, the coffee table has been pushed against the south wall, and *The Lion King* is already on the screen. Theo, Colt, and Macklin are sitting in a circle, passing a ball back and forth between each other. Nala is in the center chasing it while Jaxon squeals and chases her. Within seconds, the klutzy puppy trips over her own feet and face-plants onto the floor, pulling laughs from all of us and loosening the noose wrapped around my chest. When the guys hear our amusement, they scoot further apart, and we join the circle, passing the ball while catching up on life.

And I'm grateful for it. The reprieve from *my* reality. From the idea of having a conversation I really don't want to have with a man I'm really starting to like, no matter how terrifying––or stupid––it is.

And it is stupid.

Liking Henry.

Falling for Henry.

Wanting to be around Henry.

Wanting to snuggle with him. And kiss him. And ask about his day.

We didn't even have sex today. We spent it together. Shopping. Laughing. Flirting. But no sex.

Fuck.

It's too late. I broke one of our rules. I like Henry.

And I have no idea what to do about it.

"Ya know, if you don't want to take Nala with you to Ohio this weekend, I'd be happy to watch her," Kate says.

"Ohio?" I ask. The blood drains from my face, leaving me light-headed as I register her words.

Colt passes me the ball, but I'm too stunned to catch it. It bounces off my shoe and rolls toward Kate.

"Yeah, it's where the next game is, right?" Holding the ball in her hand, Kate turns to Macklin, and he nods. "Yeah, Kate. We're headed to Ohio this week."

Theo confirms, "We play the Tumblers. Didn't you look at the schedule?"

I shake my head and swallow hard, fighting the adrenaline in my veins. "Must've spaced on it."

"You gonna be okay?" Ashlyn prods, exchanging a concerned look with Colt.

"Shit," he mutters. "I forgot Shorty plays––"

"It'll be fine," I announce. "I'll keep a wide berth from him. Not a big deal."

Him.

I can't even say his name.

The realization only makes my anxiety skyrocket further, turning my blood to ice. I find a knot in the wood floor a few feet in front of me and stare at it, attempting to keep my expression blank. I'm going to Shorty's stomping ground. I'm going to be in his arena. I'm going to see him again. I'm going to look him in the eye. I'm going to feel his gaze.

I'm going to be sick.

"Stick close to us," Colt tells me. "We'll make sure Shorty doesn't come near you."

"Thanks," I reply, tearing my attention from the knot of wood and pasting the same facade of confidence I'm used to wearing. "But seriously, I'll be fine."

"What if Jaxon and I come too?" Ashlyn suggests. "Eleanor asked me to watch him this weekend, and Colt's been begging us to tag along for a few away games. What do you think? We can all hang out."

Eleanor is Jaxon's birth mom. She hooked up with Colt and became pregnant before Colt transferred to LAU and met Ashlyn. It was quite the surprise when she popped up with a baby a few months ago. Despite being a bumpy ride for a while, Ashlyn has latched onto her role as Mama Number Two like a champ, and Colt is the best daddy on the planet.

"Great idea," Blakely adds, but Kate frowns.

"I have to stay back for a doctor's appointment, but it's totally fine. Like I said, I can watch Nala while you're away. You guys should go. Have fun."

"I don't need any babysitters," I argue.

"You're right. You don't. But we'd love to come and hang

out, anyway. What do you say?" Ashlyn asks. "It could be fun."

"Fiiiine," I mutter.

"Yay!" She pulls me into a hug, squealing when Nala pounces on her foot out of nowhere, scaring the crap out of her. Another laugh escapes me, but even it can't erase the impending doom I feel from the reminder I'll be seeing Shorty soon, and there's nothing I can do about it.

Nothing.

And the reminder of Shorty only confirms what I'd been dreading all along. Whatever's going on with Henry is a bad idea. And I need to fix it. But only after I get through this next week.

41

HENRY

Tuesday

Hey, how was the house party at Theo's? You didn't call me on Sunday.

MIA

It was good. Thanks for being understanding about not attending. And I'm sorry I didn't call. Nala's been a handful.

ME

No problem. Glad you had fun. If you need help with Nala, I'm happy to help.

MIA

I'm okay. Thanks, though.

ME

I missed you at today's game. Where were you?

MIA

I had to leave a few minutes early to let Nala out. Sorry. Next time, I'll let you know.

ME

Not a problem. I just noticed you left.

MIA

Yeah, sorry. Being a dog mom is quite the adjustment.

ME

Like I said, I'm happy to help. Especially since I kind of threw the title on you.

MIA

I'm a big girl. I can handle it.

Wednesday

ME

Hey. The furniture is supposed to be delivered today around 4. Does that work for you?

MIA

I'll be home.

ME

Okay. Do you want me to come over and help set things up?

MIA

I'm okay.

Thanks, though.

Thursday

ME

How's Nala doing?

MIA

Good, thanks. We're working on kennel training.

ME

Sounds exciting. How are you?

MIA

I'm okay. Trying to make sure I have everything packed for tomorrow.

ME

Want me to come help?

MIA

Pretty sure you'd only distract me. Thanks, though. I'll see you tomorrow.

I reread the cold messages again and slide my phone into my pocket. I replayed our day shopping a hundred times, but nothing stood out to me regarding her aloofness. It doesn't make sense. None of it does. I want to ask if she's upset with my disappointment over not being invited to the party, but I felt like we ended on good terms, even if I did hint about wanting more from her. I want to ask if she's upset I bought Nala in the first place, but I saw the way her face lit up. I want to ask if she's upset with me for taking her shopping, but I saw the way she gushed while buying dog treats and a fluffy bed for the beast. Besides, I've seen the way she walks Nala in the grass outside our building. The way she beams and coos Nala's name.

It can't be the dog.

And I swear it wasn't the shopping.

Meaning her distance must have been triggered at the house party. Asking Mia is out of the question since she's avoiding me. Asking any of her friends feels like it's out of the question, too, since Mia seems hell-bent on keeping us apart.

I don't want to break Mia's trust. I don't want to mess with what we have before she gives me a chance to prove I'm the real deal. But doing nothing feels like shit, and her silence is eating me alive.

My eyes zero in on Mia as she steps into Ohio's arena. She's chatting with Ashlyn and Blakely and hasn't spotted me yet. She looks distracted. Uncomfortable almost. Her eyes keep bouncing around the arena as if she's scared something might pop out and grab her at any second.

"Mia," I call out.

Her attention darts to me. She gives me a fake-ass smile but rushes into the women's restroom with her friends, avoiding me entirely.

Fuck it.

I stride down to the visitor's locker room and search the space for Colt or Theo. When I find them in their pads and jerseys, I growl, "Follow me."

Their heads snap in my direction.

"Buchanan?" Theo questions.

"*Now.*"

They follow me into a corner of the locker room where we have an ounce of privacy. I cross my arms. "What happened at the house party?"

Confused, Colt asks, "What do you mean?"

"Mia's acting...strange," I hedge. "I want to know why."

They exchange a tense look. Colt lifts his shoulders, and Theo says, "It probably has something to do with Shorty."

"What about Shorty?" I demand.

"Shorty plays for the Tumblers," Colt explains. "When Mia found out we were flying to Ohio to play them this week, she looked spooked. If something's up with her, I bet it has something to do with him."

My chest deflates.

Of course, it does. I should have known. Should have

considered how being here would affect Mia. Should have given her another week off if it would have made her feel better. She still hasn't told me what happened with her ex. But it doesn't take a genius to figure out their breakup was far from amicable, and after the hint of abuse the morning she lost her keys? It must be killing her to be here, and I was too self-centered to recognize it.

"Thanks." I nod and turn on my heel, anxious to find her, but Colt stops me. "Hey, Buchanan?"

I face him again, my expression unreadable.

Scratching his jaw, he looks around the crowded locker room and steps closer. "If you hurt her…"

My chin dips in understanding. I walk away and head back to the main floor of the arena in search of Mia.

The game is supposed to start in twenty minutes. She should be in the locker room filming the team. Instead, she's missing, and I have no idea where she is.

Reeling in my frustration, I head to the box seats Erika reserved and wait, promising to talk to Mia after the game because I can't give her the support she needs if she continues to keep me in the dark like this. It's time she stopped running. From her past. From me.

Buckle up, Brat.

My patience has run out, and I'm ready for some fucking answers.

42
MIA

I wait for the whistle to sound and head down the tunnel. I shouldn't. I should've caught the start of the game on camera, but I couldn't help it. Not when the idea of seeing Shorty again leaves me wanting to puke my guts out. At least Jeffry's gone, and I don't have to worry about being yelled at for acting like a coward. Then again, I'm avoiding his replacement, too, so...

Slowly, I push the oxygen from my lungs and lift my camera, ready to start filming when the ice comes into view. The Lions have the puck in the neutral zone, and Theo snaps it off the board and over to Colt, but Shorty crashes into him, slamming him into the glass before Colt has a chance to make another pass. One of Shorty's teammates slaps the puck to the opposite end of the rink, and the Tumblers' fans scream from the stands. Our defensemen battle with the Tumblers' left wing a moment later, but I miss the epic steal from Greer, too caught up in the feel of Shorty's eyes on me.

Against my better judgment, I glance his way to find him watching me from the ice. He isn't even paying attention to the game. Nope. He's solely focused on me. And I don't like it

311

one bit. When our gazes connect, he lifts his chin and smiles, the look alone leaving an oily film across my skin.

I do my best to ignore it. To focus on the game. To focus on my job. But I swear he uses every opportunity to skate close to the Lions' bench. When the referee blows his whistle a minute later, I find Shorty a few feet away, his attention rolling over me from head to toe. It makes me feel exposed. Bare.

The knowing look in his eyes makes my stomach curdle. It's as if he's picturing me naked. And what's even worse? He doesn't need to use his imagination. No. He knows exactly what I look like. Every curve. Every tattoo. Every freckle.

"Shorty!" one of his teammates warns, closing in on him. "You can focus on pussy later!"

His gaze darkens. "I look forward to it." He skates past me with a cocky grin, and I drop my camera to my side.

Why is he such an asshole?

Why does he still get under my skin?

He doesn't matter.

We aren't together anymore.

He can't hurt me.

He. Can't. Hurt. Me.

Ignoring the way my hands shake, I force my limbs to move, hitting the record button as Greer smashes into the Tumblers' center, and the rest of the period passes in a blur. I don't know how much time elapses before the whistle blows, and the Lions skate off the ice, preparing for their twenty-minute intermission in the locker room. Instead of Shorty heading to his own tunnel, he stays near the Lions' bench.

His stare pins me in place as he calls, "Hey, Mia!"

I keep my eyes glued to the camera screen, pretending I'm busy checking footage, when Beck hooks his thumb over his shoulder toward Shorty.

"You know him?" Beck asks.

"Uh, yeah," I mumble through the cotton in my mouth. "He's my ex."

Beck's eyes widen with understanding. "Oh, shit." He lifts his hands in surrender and steps around me. "Good luck."

"Yeah," I mutter under my breath.

"Mia, c'mon. Give me a second." Shorty calls. "I only wanna say hi."

The bastard's full of shit, and we both know it, but I don't want to cause a scene. Not here. Not now. Not when it could potentially make the Lions look bad.

Squaring my shoulders, I force myself to look up at him. "Hey, Shorty."

"How've you been?"

"Great, grand, and wonderful," I lie. "But I should probably get back…"

I start to turn around when he stops me in my tracks.

"Did my buddy Darryl come say hi?"

Mother. Fucker.

Facing him again, I march closer to the edge of the ice and grit out, "What do you think?"

Shorty's mouth lifts. "I'll take it as a yes."

"Fuck you, Shorty."

"Ah, come on," he pleads as I give him my back. "It was funny."

"Oh, it was?" Twisting around again, I step even closer, grateful for the barrier separating us because I honestly might strangle him. "Was it funny when you Tweeted about my OF account too?"

His amusement dissipates. "Shouldn't have had an OF account in the first place."

"I'm sorry, are you my daddy?"

"I used to be," he growls. "You need me to slap your ass again, baby?"

"Not necessary." I turn around again and smack into a

very hard chest. Warm hands grip my biceps, holding me in place as I lift my head and realize it's Henry. But he isn't looking at me. He's staring over my head at Shorty.

"Everything okay?" he demands. Cold. Calculating. Downright lethal.

Hello, business shark Henry.

"Yeah, it's great," Shorty returns. "Just catching up with an old *friend.*"

My nose wrinkles, but I bite my tongue to keep from causing a scene. I hate the word. I hated it when I slapped the term on my relationship with Henry. And I hate it as soon as it slips past Shorty's lips in an attempt to describe what we were to each other.

Because we were never friends. We were toxic. We were poison. We were deadly.

Fucking asshole.

I want to rip him a new one. I want to slap him so hard his teeth clatter. I want to kick him in the balls and make him fall to his knees. I want to hurt him the same way he hurt me. I want to show him I'm not the same girl he once knew. And I won't cower. I won't let him push me around. Not anymore.

But I can't.

Because there are cameras everywhere. And since Shorty's loitering around the opposing team's bench area, they're poised and ready for any drama that might occur, and dammit to hell, it's feeling particularly precarious right now.

"Come on, Boss." I press against his chest, but he doesn't budge. He simply keeps holding Shorty's gaze from a few feet away.

"*Friend.*" Henry says the word like he's a damn robot, and his expression is just as lifeless. Just as monotone.

"Yeah," Shorty repeats. "Friend." He pauses, and the warning bells in my head start clanging.

Go away, Shorty, I silently plead. *Please go away.*

"Who I used to *fuck*," Shorty finishes. I know he's smiling. I know he's goading Henry. I know he's trying to piss him off and cause a scene for all the cameras to capture. Because Shorty's known for having a short fuse. Hell, it's expected. He's a hockey player. But the owner of a team? He's supposed to have better control.

My eyes close as Shorty's comment hangs in the air. A moment later, I force them open to find Henry as unreadable as before. Maybe even more so. He looks like a freaking statue.

"Henry," I whisper. Hell, it's not even a whisper. It's a breath. A plea.

He bends down, closing the distance between us, but he doesn't look at me. No, he's too busy staring at my ex behind me as his hands find my waist, and he tugs me into him.

"Henry, wai--"

His mouth is on mine, swallowing my plea. And the kiss? It's predatory. Dominating. And wreaks of alpha pheromones so potent, my core clenches, and I grasp onto his suit to keep from crumbling.

I haven't kissed him since we went shopping for furniture. I've barely spoken to him. I've been avoiding him at all costs because it felt easier. Instead of admitting I'm falling for him and, therefore, need to end our arrangement, I've kept my distance, praying for some freaking clarity. I almost wavered. Almost gave in and admitted I want to give a real relationship with Henry a shot. And I might've if the impending doom of facing Shorty this week hadn't paralyzed me. When I saw him on the ice tonight, the memories of what it's like to be in a relationship came flooding back, hitting like a Mack truck.

Realizing I've been holding my breath, I press my hands

to Henry's chest and tear my mouth from his, sucking in oxygen as my mind continues to spin.

What the fuck?

Did he really kiss me?

In front of everyone?

Shorty? The cameras?

Shit.

I glance over my shoulder, attempting to count witnesses, but only the back of Shorty's jersey comes into view as he skates away. It taunts me, mingling with the flashing cameras. The combination makes my pupils burn.

Cameras.

The kiss.

They had to have captured it.

Facing Henry again, I seethe, "What the hell was that?"

A soft scoff escapes him, but he doesn't let me go. "That was me staking a claim long past due."

"I didn't need you to stake a claim," I argue. My hands are fisted at my sides, and it takes everything inside of me to keep from shoving at his chest. To keep from yelling and screaming in his face. "We had a rule, Henry," I continue, keeping my voice quiet. "We had a rule, and you blatantly broke it in front of who knows how many people."

"Fuck the rules." He lets go of my waist and reaches for my arm, but I tug it from his grasp.

"We are at *work*," I remind him. "Kissing me here was the last thing you should've done, especially after this week."

"What happened this week?" he growls as the rest of the team ambles back to the rink. Both of us shift to the side, leaving room for the players to slip past us while searching for a bit of privacy, though it's not like we're going to find any. Not right now. Not here. Henry watches the team over the top of my head, the same indifferent persona taking over his expression as he nods at someone behind me.

I'm gonna freaking kill him.

"I need to work," I mutter.

His hand encases my wrist, and he keeps me in place, bending down and whispering against the shell of my ear. "I'm finished being patient. We will continue this discussion after the game."

"No," I breathe out. "We won't."

"Yes, we will. No more running, Mia."

"Whatever you say, Professor." I yank my wrist out of his grasp and march toward the benches with my camera poised.

43

HENRY

The Tumblers lost. Shorty played for shit, and our offense took full advantage, scoring four goals to their one. It should have felt good. Winning. Instead, I feel like a storm could break any second as I search the massive room during post-game interviews. I probably shouldn't have kissed her in public. Not until we had a chance to talk. I couldn't help myself. My need to claim her. To prove to Shorty and anyone else who was watching she's mine. There's nothing he can do about it.

Still. The kiss wasn't for Mia, and that's where I fucked up. Now, Mia has disappeared, despite my promise we would discuss this later. The cameras stop flashing a few minutes later, and I find Theo at the edge of the room beside Colt, who's bouncing a baby in his arms.

"Where is she?" I demand when I'm within hearing distance.

Their heads turn, and they find me stalking toward them. The last of my restraint is barely hanging on by a thread.

"Mia?" Theo clarifies.

I give him a jerky nod.

318

"She left with the girls. Needed a stiff drink after putting up with Shorty's dick comments."

"Before or after the first period?" I growl.

Confusion creases the corners of Colt's eyes, then he clarifies, "The dick comments?"

"Yeah."

"They didn't come until after the first period. Why?"

They were still in the locker room when I kissed Mia in front of Shorty, but even so, I don't bother to fill them in. I'm too frustrated. Too pissed off by my lack of restraint and Shorty's bullshit ribbing. But I can't find it in myself to regret the decision. Shorty needed to understand Mia is mine. I don't care if she's delusional enough to believe I only care about the sex between us. I'm done being patient. After her cold shoulder this week, I've made myself clear. I'm not letting her go. Now, he knows it too.

And so does Mia.

Which is probably why she left in search of a stiff drink.

But if she honestly believes I will let her off the hook this easily, she is sorely mistaken.

"Good game tonight," I compliment them as I pull my phone out and dial Gordy.

"Hello, sir," he greets me.

"Two things. First, I need you to contact every reporter at tonight's game and convince them to keep any photos of me out of the press."

"I'll get right on it."

"Second, I need you to add me to Miss Rutherford's room."

"Why?"

"Because I need her room key."

"Give me two minutes," Gordy replies. *Tap-tap-tap.* "Make it one."

"Perfect."

I hang up the phone and head to the hotel. She has to come back to her room at some point. When she does, I'll be waiting.

No more running, Mia.

Not from me.

44
MIA

The lights are flashing in the middle of the bar as Ash and I take our drinks from the black lacquered counter. "Thank you," I yell to the bartender above the music. She nods at me and turns to the next customer, dismissing us.

"And thank you for making this a girls' night," I add to Ashlyn and Blake. "I really didn't feel like being the fifth wheel tonight."

"You know we love you," Ash starts.

"And we get it," Blake adds, "But you didn't *have* to be the fifth wheel."

Ash grins. "You could've always invited Henry––"

"Henry and I are over," I snap, tossing back half my beer in hopes of it numbing my regret.

"Oh, you are?" Blake pulls out a metal stool from an empty table. "No offense, but it didn't look like it during the first-period break."

"You saw?" I grab the chair next to hers and sit down.

Ashlyn takes one across from me and admits, "Maybe?" Chewing on the edge of her straw, Ashlyn has the decency to look sheepish as she explains, "But only because we could see how much Shorty was making you uncomfortable, so we were keeping a close eye on you."

Blake shakes her head. "I still can't believe the asshole had the audacity to talk to you like that."

"Me neither," I mutter into my cup.

"Seriously. He's an ass," Ash agrees. "But at least he played like shit during the rest of the game."

I nearly snort into my cup at the memory of Shorty slamming his stick against the ice and screaming at the top of his lungs. Yeah, he was definitely fuming by the end of the night. He could barely see straight, let alone play his role correctly, even though he took every opportunity to call me a bitch anytime he was close. Too bad for him, it was nothing I haven't heard many times over. But it definitely didn't hurt to watch Theo and Colt making him look like an absolute ass on the ice.

It was refreshing.

And a little vindicating.

Fuck you, Shorty.

"Not gonna lie. Watching Theo and Colt play well against him was hot as hell," Ash agrees.

"Hey, that's my brother, remember?" Blake quips.

"And he looked hot as hell during tonight's game," Ash repeats with a grin.

Blake chuckles into her glass but drops it before taking a sip of her drink as the bass thumps in the background.

"Don't worry, ladies. I got the whole thing on camera," I tell them. "I'll be sure to send you copies of the game when I get back to the hotel."

"Oooo, thank you," Ash says when my phone buzzes with a text.

UNKNOWN NUMBER

Say you need to use the restroom.

My eyebrows draw together as I read the message a second time. Scanning the bar, I see Shorty near the back with his arms folded and a phone clutched in his hand. But the look in his eyes? The absolute rage?

This is bad.

"Everything okay?" Ashlyn asks.

I end my staring contest with Shorty and force a smile. "Yeah, it's fine. So, what's it like playing mom nowadays?"

The bar lights bounce off Ashlyn's face as she grins even wider. "It's actually really fun."

My phone buzzes again, and against my better judgment, I read the message.

UNKNOWN NUMBER

We can talk in private, or I can make a scene in front of your friends. Your decision.

You have fifteen seconds.

"Mia?" Ash questions.

"Sorry." I clear my throat and shift on the stool, slipping my phone back into my pocket. "Shorty texted me and wants to talk for a second."

"You told him to go to hell, right?" Blakely demands.

"Not yet."

"Mia," Ashlyn warns.

I roll my eyes. "Let me finish."

"No," Ash pushes. "Shorty doesn't deserve another second of your time."

"Ashlyn's right," Blake agrees.

"I know," I reply with a laugh. "Don't get me wrong. I love how overprotective you both are, but I also know

Shorty, and he isn't going to leave us alone until I let him call me a whore so he can go screw a random puck bunny." I toss the rest of my drink back and set the empty glass on the table. "So we have two choices. Either I let him yell at me for five minutes, and when he's done, we can go about our night. Or we leave now and hang out at the hotel, letting him kind of ruin our girls' night out. Thoughts?"

Without hesitation, Ashlyn grabs her purse from the table and stands up. "Hotel. Definitely."

"Are you sure?" I ask. "Like I said, I don't want to ruin our night."

"Times up, Mia," Shorty growls from behind me.

The hair along the back of my neck raises as I turn in my seat to face him.

"Come on, Mia. Let's go," Ashlyn prods.

I glance at her and turn back to the massive hockey player. "Sorry, Shorty. We were just leaving."

He grabs my arm roughly, tugging me out of my chair and closer to him. "You think I'm afraid to make a scene in front of your friends, Mia?"

"I think you're drunk and have no idea exactly how much this is going to bite you in the ass if you keep touching me like this." My eyes fall to his punishing grasp and snap back to his surly face. "We are in *public*, Shorty. You're not gonna hurt me in public."

"You're right," he agrees, but he doesn't let me go. "I won't hurt you. I only want to talk."

"There's nothing to talk about."

He leans even closer. The stench of beer lingers on his breath and makes my nose wrinkle. "Follow me outside right now, and I'll leave your friends alone. Or don't. See what happens. Your choice."

"Are you threatening my friends?" I ask.

Keeping his voice low, he grumbles, "Just calling it like it is."

"You're lucky I'm not interested in causing a scene, or I'd knee you in the balls right here."

"I'm not either, or you'd already be over my shoulder." His grip tightens. "I only want to talk."

My eyes fall on Ashlyn. Her phone is out, and she's texting someone. Relief floods my veins.

Good. We'll have backup soon.

"You coming, Mia?" Shorty prods.

It's a busy street. People are outside. A lot of people. It's not like I'll be alone with him. But even that thought doesn't give me any warm fuzzies.

"Colt and Theo are on their way," I lie. Well, it's sort of a lie. If my assumption's correct, Ashlyn's already alerted them.

"I guess we'd better make this quick, huh?" he counters.

I suck my lips between my teeth and turn to the girls. "If I'm not back in five, call the police."

"Mia," Ash snaps.

"She's being dramatic," Shorty muses. "I'm not gonna do anything. I only want to talk––"

Blake steps in front of him like she isn't going toe-to-toe with a freaking giant. "You can talk with us around," she challenges. I'd be impressed if I didn't know Shorty would backhand her for it if there wasn't a room full of witnesses.

Ass.

"This is between me and her. I don't need either of you sticking your nose in our relationship when you don't know shit about it."

"Oh, trust me," Blake quips. "We're well aware of what you are."

Shorty's fingers dig harder into my bicep, but I don't flinch. It's a warning. One I read loud and clear.

"You guys, it's fine," I tell them. "You really think

Shorty will try anything when at least a handful of paparazzi are camped outside this place? This is the closest bar to the arena, and it's packed full of players and fans. Shorty might be an asshole, but he would never do anything to ruin his precious career, right?" I glare up at Shorty, hating how small and inconsequential he makes me feel.

"Exactly." He tugs me a little more roughly toward the exit. "Five minutes."

"And if you're a second longer, they'll call the cops," I remind him.

"Always the dramatic one, baby." He shoves me through the doorway and into the cool air.

I let it wash over me, praying it'll bring clarity, but I'm as overwhelmed as before.

I was right.

It *is* busy out here.

Good.

Without a word, he begins dragging me toward the edge of the parking lot and as far away from the street as he can manage, which is saying something. The guy's definitely drunk and can barely walk a straight line.

Classy, Shorty. Really classy.

He tugs me a little harder, and I almost stumble over my own feet. "Shorty, you're making a fool out of yourself," I mutter, but I follow his lead. The sooner he finds some semblance of privacy—but not too much because I don't have a death wish—the sooner we can end this stupid confrontation, and I can go back inside with the girls.

When we reach the edge of the parking lot, I dig my heels into the ground, but he tugs me between a few cars, causing a wave of fear to push through me.

"This is far enough." I jerk my arm from his grasp and tumble to the ground as he lets me go. My tailbone lands on the hard asphalt, and I curse under my breath, rolling to my knees.

"Asshole," I seethe. Pain radiates from my spine and down my legs.

"Why the fuck did you do it?" he growls.

I glare up at him. "Do what?"

"Why'd you have to kiss him, Mia? Why'd you have to fuck with my head?"

With a dry laugh, I shake my head. "Do you have any idea how insane you sound, Shorty?" I start to stand, but he wraps his hand around my throat and yanks me to my feet.

"You were right." He squeezes my neck and presses his forehead to mine with such bruising force I swear I can feel my skull pulsing. "In the bar. When you said I wouldn't do anything to jeopardize my career. You were right." He squeezes tighter, and my fear catapults into full-blown panic. It wasn't supposed to go like this. We're over. We've *been* over. I've been called names and taken a few hits from him when we were dating. And I've survived emotional abuse bad enough to haunt some people's nightmares. But this? I've never actually feared for my life before.

My fingers claw at his wrist, leaving red ribbons of torn flesh, but he doesn't let go.

Bringing us nose to nose, his upper lip curls, and he seethes, "You just *had* to get in my head, didn't you?"

What the hell is happening?

Is the man completely unhinged?

We're under a lamp post. There are people outside. Someone has to be seeing this.

Black spots dance in my vision, and my lids flutter as I stand on my tiptoes, willing him to let me go.

"Can't. Breathe," I mouth.

I'm going to pass out.

I'm going to die.

Right here. In the middle of a fucking parking lot, surrounded by unsuspecting people.

His grip tightens even more, and my vision tunnels. "If you ever fuck with my career again, I'll kill you."

He shoves me back to the ground, and my body slams against the pavement with such a bruising force, I feel like I've been tackled by a linebacker. My shoulder and back take the brunt of the hit as the air whooshes from my lungs, and I choke on oxygen, attempting to catch my breath. The back of my head hurts. I must've hit it against the pavement when he threw me to the ground like I was a freaking ragdoll. But there's no blood. Only a goose egg the size of my fist.

"See?" Shorty adds. "Our chat didn't even take two minutes." He steps over my body, adjusts the sleeves of his leather jacket, and leaves me nothing but a helpless heap on the pavement as he heads back inside the bar.

My hands shake, and my vision is still blurry from the hit to the head as I push myself up and let out a few unsteady breaths.

Fuck.

Shoving my hair away from my face, I scan the crowded parking lot, but no one notices me. No one sees my fear or how I'm clutching the back of my head as the goose egg takes up residence on my skull.

Shorty's smart. We were between cars. No one saw a fucking thing. The music from the club must've drowned out my grunts, and he was sure to keep his voice low so only I could hear it. I guess he wasn't as drunk as I thought.

Good one, Mia.

I blink back tears as I take in the starry sky shining down on me.

I hate him.

I hate him more than anything.

Wiping beneath my eyes, I let out a slow breath and head

back inside, avoiding the curious gazes as I find a very concerned Ash and Blake at the bar.

"What the hell—" Ash starts, but I cut her off.

"I'm fine."

"Did he hurt you?" Blake demands. "Why is your face red?"

"My PTSD is making me a mess, but I promise I'm fine. He made his point and got his asshole-ish behavior out of his system. I promised to keep a wide berth from him *and* his career from now on." I glance at the door. "Are the guys still coming?"

"Yeah, they're on their way," Ash replies. "Erika was nice enough to watch Jax so Colt could come."

With a ruthless grin, Blake glances at Shorty at the back of the bar. "When they find out what happened, they're gonna kick the shit out of—"

"Can we..." I bite the inside of my cheek and tear my attention from the entrance. "Can we not discuss this with the guys?"

Ashlyn's eyes bulge. "You want us to *lie* to them?"

"I want you to enjoy your evening, celebrate tonight's win, and *not* worry about me or my shitty decisions regarding the opposite sex. One, I'm not their problem, and two, think of how this could potentially distract them when they play the Tumblers in the future. It isn't worth it. Shorty made his point. It's done."

"Mia," Ash starts, but I cut her off again.

"I promise I'm fine," I repeat, praying they can't see the bruises along my throat. "I'm...drained, I guess."

"What can we do?" Blake asks.

"You can stay and enjoy your night with your amazing men and *not* bring up the confrontation with Shorty. See? Simple."

"Mia," Ash repeats with the same dose of concern I both

love and hate. She really is the best friend a girl could ask for, but right now, my throat feels shredded, my body feels drained, and all I want to do is end this night as quickly as possible.

"Please, Ash?" I beg.

Ashlyn's frown deepens. She exchanges a look with Blake, and they both nod, albeit grudgingly. "Fine."

"Thank you," I murmur. "Now, I'm going back to the hotel, taking a nice hot shower, scrubbing tonight from my brain entirely, and starting fresh tomorrow, okay?" I pull each of them into a hug. "Thanks again for standing up for me. You guys really are the best friends a girl could ask for."

"We love you, Mia," Ash says.

"Love you too. I'll see you on the flight home."

"Sounds good." Blake gives me one more squeeze, and it takes everything inside of me to keep from flinching as her hands graze the bruises along my back.

"And be safe," Ashlyn adds.

Hiking my purse further onto my shoulder, I wiggle my fingers back and forth. "Always."

I leave and head back to the hotel.

45

HENRY

It's dark. Quiet. Almost peaceful if I wasn't drowning in my fury.

She's running. Hiding. Like I'm the one who fucked up by kissing her in front of Shorty. Like I'm her dirty little secret. Like I'm her side piece, and Shorty's the one she can't get out of her head.

My grip tightens on the leather arms of the chair as I stare at Mia's hotel room door, willing her to come home. To come back to me.

Maybe I was wrong. Maybe I assumed Shorty had hurt her while they were dating, but it was someone else who hit her. Her past is shitty enough to have more than one contender for asshole of the year. Maybe she wants Shorty. Maybe she misses him. Maybe I've been wrong all along. Maybe she isn't mine.

It's been an hour. She won't be home anytime soon if she's having a girls' night, but I can't focus. Not on work. Not on emails. Not even a fucking show is enough to distract me from her absence.

Where are you, Brat?

~

THE HEAVY HOTEL DOOR OPENS WITH A QUIET SQUEAK. LIGHT spills into the dark room from the hallway, painting Mia's silhouette in the doorframe. She hasn't noticed me yet. But she looks distracted. Worried. Anxious. I watch from the darkness as she reaches for the light switch, but before she has a chance to flick it on, she gasps and clutches at her chest.

"Dammit, Henry!"

"I told you I wanted to talk."

She releases a shuddered breath and sets her purse on the credenza, letting the hotel door close behind her with a loud thunk. The room is dark. The light from the window is the only glow available. I wait for her to turn the lights on like she was ready to do before she spotted me, but she doesn't. She simply stands there, staring at me like I'm a ghost.

"Let's talk, Brat," I order.

"I'm not in the mood. So, if you could let yourself out, I'd appreciate it." Her voice is hollow, and her movements are almost unnatural and forced as she makes her way to the bathroom without a backward glance. It's like she's hit the gym too hard and is sore when earlier today, she was walking fine.

My lips tug down, and anxiety lines my stomach. Without waiting for an invitation, I push myself up from the armchair and follow her into the bathroom.

Something's wrong.

Something happened.

Sensing my presence behind her, Mia hesitates and closes her eyes. Defeated. Exhausted. Almost shameful. The lights are off in here, too, and I reach for the switch, but she covers it with her hand.

"Please go, Henry," she whispers.

"We need to talk."

"There's nothing to talk about."

I shake my head and step closer, pressing my back to her front. "Bullshit."

Turning her head, she leans into me slightly but doesn't move her hand from the switch. "You shouldn't have kissed me in front of anyone."

"I shouldn't have waited so long to kiss you in front of anyone," I argue.

"It wasn't your decision. We had rules——"

"Fuck the rules," I spit. "I saw you from the box seats, Mia. Saw the way you clammed up as soon as you locked eyes with him."

Her body sags a little more against me as if the weight she's carrying is too much. Too heavy.

"He's my ex," she whispers. "Of course, I clammed up."

"I didn't like seeing what he was doing to you."

Spine straightening, she seethes, "Fuck Shorty."

"Yeah. Fuck Shorty," I repeat. "Why did you care that he saw me kiss you? Do you still want him? Is that why you're mad at me? Why you wouldn't date me when I asked? Why all you want to give me is your body and your fucked-up frenemies with benefits compromise?"

She doesn't answer, choosing to gnaw on the inside of her cheek as if it will get her out of this conversation, but I'm too tired to drop it. Too frustrated to give in again. To be patient. To let her push me away when we both know it's a mistake.

Our reflections gaze back at us in the darkness as I wait for her to say something. To tell me the truth. She looks so fragile right now. Wounded almost. I hate it. Her hand is still resting on the light switch. Still withholding the light when we've been trapped in a murky darkness for far too long. Both literally and metaphorically.

I lean closer, breathing in her shampoo's scent, letting it

calm the storm raging inside me. "Tell me why you refuse to give me anything but your body, Mia."

"I didn't make you say yes to my compromise," she whispers. "And I sure as shit don't want Shorty." A tear seeps from the corner of her eye. She closes them and sucks in a shaky breath, but she doesn't wipe it away.

I hesitate, zeroing in on her reflection and hoping my eyes are playing tricks on me. I gently touch her chin and lift her head up. It's too dark. Too fucking dark to see much. But I see them. Bruises. Along her throat. Carefully, I twist her to face me and examine the damage more closely. Yeah. Those are definitely bruises. One on the right side of her neck. Four on the left. Rage explodes in my chest, and I drop my hand from her chin, flexing it at my side as I try to control the violence barreling through me and licking at my soul.

"Who did this to you?" I growl, desperate for confirmation before I put his body in the ground.

The dark mascara is smudged around her eyes as she stares blankly in front of her. "No one."

I wrench her hand from the switch, flick it on, and inspect the damage again. The fingerprints are purple and blue against her ivory flesh, fanning my fury until all I see is red.

"Who did this to you, Mia?" I repeat.

She shakes her head but doesn't look at me. "No one."

I grab her chin again, more gently this time, and force her to look at me. "We both know I always get what I want. Tell me."

Her numb gaze locks on me, but her bottom lip trembles. "I need to shower his touch off of me."

"What else did he do?" I seethe. My teeth gnash together. The last of my restraint slowly slips away as all the possibilities of what might have happened while I was sitting on my ass in her hotel room filter through me. "If he––"

"He didn't rape me. He might've if he had enough time," she mutters. The distance between us grows as she steps into the glass shower and flips the faucet on. "But he didn't. He only wanted to prove a point."

"What point?" I demand.

Waiting for the water to heat up, she steps back onto the tile floor beside me and closes her eyes. It's as if the weight of the situation is more than she can bear. "I want to shower. You should go."

"I'm not leaving you, Mia."

And I'm not.

Not ever again.

Carefully, I lift the hem of her shirt and pull it off. A lacy black bra covers her breasts, but I don't remove it. Instead, I reach for her pants and slide them down her long, lean legs.

When I catch a glimpse of her back in the mirror, my molars grind. Her smooth, flawless skin is covered in differing shades of black, blue, and purple. Slowly, I spin her around, examining the damage along her back and ass. More bruises. The one above her tailbone is the size of my palm. Another angry mark runs along her shoulder blade. Shifting her hair to the side, I lean forward and brush my lips against the closest bruise.

"Tell me it wasn't Shorty," I murmur against her heated skin. I already know the truth, but I need confirmation. And I need it now.

"It doesn't matter."

"Tell me it wasn't Shorty," I repeat.

She glares up at me. The same familiar shame swirls in her gorgeous eyes. "It. Doesn't. Matter."

With a dark laugh, I growl, "You're mine, Mia. You might not want to admit it to yourself, but it doesn't change the truth." I wrap my arms around her middle and hold her gaze

335

in the mirror's foggy reflection. "No one touches what's mine."

"What if I don't want to be yours?" she whispers. Her eyes are full of fear. But she isn't scared of me. She's scared of submitting to me. Of giving up her control willingly when we both know it has been ripped away from her more times than she can count.

Resting my chin on her shoulder, I slowly sway us back and forth. "I'm never gonna hurt you, Mia."

Her watery smile greets me, and she shakes her head. "If only you knew how many times I've heard that statement, Professor."

"Not from me."

Her hesitation is louder than a siren, and she sniffs quietly.

"I'm sorry I broke our rules." I place another kiss on her bare shoulder. "I'm sorry I made our rules in the first place when I've wanted you from the beginning." My lips brush against where her shoulder and neck meet. "I'm sorry I didn't step in when you were dating Shorty the first time. I'm sorry I didn't claim you the way I wanted to in the beginning." I place another kiss on the bruises marring her throat. "But I'm not sorry for claiming you. For pursuing you." I kiss her jaw. "For showing Shorty, and the rest of the world, you're mine. Because you *are* mine, Mia. For as long as you'll have me."

"You don't want a girl like me, Professor."

"You're right," I agree, "I don't want a girl *like* you." My arms squeeze her softly, careful not to hurt her or aggravate her sore body. "I want *you*. Mia Rutherford. The sassy brat who crawled her way under my skin whom I refuse to let go."

She sniffs again. Her eyes are cloudy as she looks down at my arms wrapped around her torso, avoiding our reflection.

"Did you hear me?" I press. "There's only one you, Brat. I'm not letting you go."

"Promise you won't let me down," she whispers.

I twist her around and clutch her cheeks, rubbing my thumbs along the moisture and smudged makeup making her look beautiful and broken and *mine*. All mine.

"Not a fucking chance."

46

MIA

My mind reels as Henry's words wash over me.

"I want *you*. Mia Rutherford. The sassy brat who crawled her way under my skin whom I refuse to let go."

I've never been wanted. Or maybe I have, and I never recognized it. But this? His words? His determination? His sweet kisses and strong hands? It's like I'm being torn in two. No, it's like I'm being sewn back together again. And it hurts. The needle pushing through raw flesh, promising to make me whole. But it's a good hurt. A cleansing hurt. One I want to grab hold of. One I never want to let go.

"Did you hear me?" he pushes. "There's only one you, Brat. I'm not letting you go."

"Promise you won't let me down," I beg.

Henry turns me around and runs his calloused thumbs along my cheeks. They're wet. I've been crying. I hate crying. But it feels good to stop fighting it. To stop shoving my emotions down until they're choking me.

"Not a fucking chance," he rasps.

Then, his lips are on mine, devouring me whole as he

338

blindly opens the glass door and pushes us into the shower. Water floods from the showerhead in hot rivulets, making me shiver as I wrap my arms around his neck and press my front to his. He's so warm. So hot.

But the crazy part?

He's still in his clothes. Fully dressed from head to toe while I'm in nothing but my bra and underwear. I wouldn't think anything of it if I hadn't witnessed his quirk the first night we shared a hotel room. But instead of calling him out on it, my fingers fumble with the buttons on his white dress shirt as I kiss Henry back, undressing him as quickly as I can. Because I need him. I need him to hold me. To love me. To accept me. The water warms even more, heating my skin. Our clothes hit the marble floor beneath our feet with a wet plop, soaking up even more water. He presses my back against the glass wall, carefully keeping the pressure off my bruises. He tangles his fingers in my hair. I wince when he grazes the goose egg along the back of my skull, and he tears his mouth from mine.

"You hit your head too?" he seethes.

I shrug one shoulder. "I'm fine."

"I'm gonna kill him." His lips are on mine again in an instant, but he's careful not to touch my injury as he shoves his tongue into my mouth. I moan. The steam billows around us as one of his hands trails down to my breast, tweaking my nipple into a bud and traveling lower. Cupping my sex, he rubs the heel of his hand against me, and I gasp at the pressure.

It isn't fair.

How good he makes me feel.

How much I want him inside me. How quickly I've fallen for him and how confusing it is to admit it, even to myself.

"You have no idea how much I want you," he rasps. "But I don't want to push you. Let's go at your pace, okay?"

Droplets of water cling to the tips of his hair before leaving trails of moisture down the side of his face as he waits for me to take the lead. To give me back my power after Shorty stripped it from me earlier tonight. He looks so sexy like this. Almost unhinged, he's so desperate. Desperate for me.

Giving in, I slip to my knees and reach for his erection, running my tongue against the bottom of his mushroom head, then teasing the slit. Salt falls on my taste buds, and I take him in my mouth, hollowing my cheeks and sucking him hard.

"Fuck, Mia," he groans. His fingers find the back of my head again. He keeps his touch surprisingly gentle despite the way his muscles are coiled against me. I peek up at him and find his other arm pressed against the glass wall, his frame protecting me from the water, and his head hanging like I'm torturing him. It only turns me on more. Up and down, I bob my head. Saliva drips from the edge of my lips, mingling with his precum and the water slipping past Henry's protective stance.

"You have no idea how much I want to come down your pretty little throat," he grunts. "But not today." He tugs softly on my hair and pulls me off of him. As if I weigh nothing, he hoists me up, twists me around to face the wall, and knocks my legs open with his feet. Once I'm spread wide, he thrusts inside me, and I moan.

God, he feels good. Stretching me. Claiming me. Branding me.

Without giving me a chance to catch my breath, he pounds into me over and over again. His arm wraps around my waist, and he finds my clit, pressing on the sensitive spot in rhythm with his thrusting until I see stars.

I come with a scream. My fingers dig into the glass until the tips of them are white, but he doesn't give me a chance to come down. Instead, he slips out of me, turns me around, and grabs the back of my thighs. The cold glass presses against my spine but feels surprisingly good on my sore back as he picks me up and shoves himself inside me again. I grab his shoulders for balance, letting him use my body while watching his expression twist with pleasure.

"Need you to come again, Mia."

My head falls gently against the glass, and I shake it back and forth. "Henry--"

Leaning forward, he bites my neck beneath my bruises. The slight sting of pain mixes with pleasure, and I squeeze my thighs tighter around his waist, shifting my hips against him as he pistons in and out of me frantically.

"Feel good, Brat?" he asks, his fingers digging into my ass.

"Yes," I moan. "So good."

"Rub yourself for me. Rub your clit."

I do as I'm told, slipping my hand between us as he continues his punishing thrusts. I spiral a second time.

My orgasm hits like a sledgehammer, and I come around him, savoring the slap of skin and wet muscles beneath my fingertips. Burrowing his head in the nape of my neck, he follows right after. His cock throbs inside me. And it feels so good. Really good. Not only the orgasm. But all of it. The connection. The skin on skin. The steam wafting around us.

When he's finished, he carefully sets me back on the ground, his softening erection slipping out of me. His cum follows suit and slides down my inner thighs, so I press them together. Desperate to keep the connection. The moment. The look in his eyes and the feel of his hands. All of it.

"Turn around," he orders.

I face the glass and close my eyes. Exhaustion creeps into my muscles as the familiar squirt of shampoo hits my ears, followed by magic fingers running in slow circles along my scalp.

"Oh," I moan.

I drop my head forward, leaning my forehead against the glass, and close my eyes as Henry washes my hair, helping me rinse it a minute later. Once the shampoo is gone, he adds conditioner to his hands and carefully runs his fingers through my thick strands, being sure not to aggravate the knot on my scalp. When he pays extra attention to my ends, I smile, relishing the moment.

Relishing him. And his thoughtfulness. And his masterful hands.

"I should take you to the hospital," he grumbles.

I laugh dryly. "I'm good, thanks."

"Mia——"

"Professor," I quip, mimicking his tone while drawing a smiley face on the steamy glass. "Seriously, I'll pop a few painkillers, go to sleep, and wake up tomorrow morning feeling right as rain."

"We should file a report."

"Again, no thank you," I repeat. "Besides, we're in different states, and as long as I keep a wide berth from the asshole from now on, I'll be fine."

"You don't look fine, Mia."

I peek over my shoulder. "Are you saying guys don't dig scars the same way chicks do?"

"Those are a hell of a lot more than scars." His eyes darken as they roll over my body, taking in every inch of exposed skin while reexamining the bruises. "They make me want to kill him."

"Don't," I murmur. "Trust me. He isn't worth your time, and it'll only piss him off more."

Henry doesn't comment, choosing to continue conditioning my hair instead. I'm grateful he gives in to my request.

I've always been a strong, independent woman, even when it's detrimental. But right now? I'm okay with relinquishing my control. I'm okay with letting him take care of me. Letting him make me feel better. Because after the shit night I've had? The shit *life* I've had? I'm starting to think I've earned it.

But I wasn't kidding when I begged him not to let me down. Because the idea of losing this? Losing Henry?

The thought alone nearly brings me to my knees.

And it's scary. Giving so much power to a man.

A man I thought I hated.

A man who could ruin me in an instant.

And if this goes south...he just might.

But for once in my life, I think it's worth the risk.

I think *he's* worth the risk.

47

MIA

We flew home this morning, and I headed straight to SeaBird for a staff meeting. Henry insisted on babysitting Nala while I was gone, and by some miracle, I let him.

I'm not used to trusting people. Relying on them. Even Ashlyn has wanted to smack me upside the head a time or two--or a dozen--whenever my instincts scream for me to push her away. Thankfully, she's too stubborn to let me go through with it, and I have a feeling Henry might be the same way.

Keys in hand, I open my apartment door after the meeting at SeaBird. An adorable furball gets in the way of me opening it fully and slips through the crack.

"Ah!" I kneel on the ground and catch Nala's collar, letting her attack me with kisses as soon as she recognizes me. "Hey, baby girl. You almost snuck away from me." She continues her assault and laps at my face while her entire body wiggles back and forth. With a laugh, I push her away so I can scratch behind her fluffy ears. "I think you missed me."

"We were about to go outside for a potty break," Henry tells me from the doorway.

"Care if I join you?" I ask.

Offering me the leash, he sways it back and forth a few inches from my nose. "Only if you're not too exhausted."

I kiss Nala's forehead one more time, clip the leash onto her collar, and stand. "Nope. I'm good to go. Let's get you outside, Li'l Miss."

Before I have a chance to head toward the elevator, Henry's hands wrap around my waist, and he tugs me into him.

"Whoa." I loop the leash onto my wrist and slide my hands along his chest. "Hey, there."

"Tell me you're okay if I kiss you."

"I'm okay if you kiss--"

His lips are on mine in an instant, and I laugh against his mouth, kissing him back. My endorphins spike from the intimacy, but it feels nice. Natural. Easy almost. And relationships have never been easy for me.

When he finally pulls away, I'm sporting a dopey grin as I ask, "What was that for?"

"Missed you," he murmurs.

"I was gone for what? Two hours?"

"Still missed you."

Caught between surprise and a strange sense of ease, I stare back at the man in front of me, unsure what to think.

We haven't had a chance to talk about our encounter in Ohio yet. After our shower sex, he carried me to bed, and we spooned all night. The next morning was a blur thanks to our early flight, and I rushed to my meeting after we landed.

Which leaves us...where exactly?

I'm not sure.

And it's weird. Being openly intimate without the guise of friends with benefits. It's weird listening to someone express

345

their feelings or even expressing my own when I'm used to bottling them up. But the truth is, even if it is weird, I like how he missed me. How he can tell me he missed me. How, apparently, we aren't hiding behind said bullshit guise of friendship anymore. Not after my encounter with Shorty. Not after Henry promised he wouldn't let me down if I dared to open up to him.

I like this. Having him at my apartment when I get home. Watching him interact with Nala without making me feel like a burden. Having his lips pressed against mine in the middle of a hallway where anyone can see us.

"Is it bad I missed you?" he asks carefully after pulling away.

I shake my head. "Not at all. I was thinking how much I missed you too."

With a soft, satisfied smile, he closes my apartment door behind him. "Good."

"How was your meeting?" he asks as we step into the elevator.

I shrug. "Fine. I have a shift tonight, which kind of sucks."

"You know you don't *have* to work at SeaBird anymore, right?"

"Yes, Professor. I'm well aware."

"All right. Just making sure."

"Mm-hmm," I hum. When we reach the main floor, the doors slide open, and I ask, "Any chance you'd wanna babysit Nala tonight?"

"Does it mean I get to see you after your shift?" He grabs my hand and laces our fingers together like it's the most natural thing in the world. Like he's been wanting to do it for weeks and is taking full advantage since I'm not pushing him away. I stare at our entwined hands, unsure what to make of the gesture and how perfectly they fit together.

When he catches me studying them, he asks, "Are you okay?"

My eyes snap to his. "Never pegged you for a hand-holding kind of guy."

"Only with you." He lifts our hands and kisses the back of mine. "Do you have a *thing* against hand-holding?"

"Honestly, I'm not sure," I admit. "But I don't think so."

"You don't think?"

Ignoring the way my cheeks heat, I mutter, "It's kind of a first."

His chin dips in understanding. "Well, if you change your mind and decide you're not a hand-holder, let me know. For now, I'm going to enjoy it." He kisses the back of my hand again, guiding us toward the exit and continuing our conversation like I didn't have a minor—and very random—existential crisis in the middle of the elevator.

"I'll order pizza, so you have food by the time you finish your shift," he continues.

"You don't have to—"

"Humor me, Mia."

I hesitate near the entrance to keep from tripping over myself as Nala tugs at her leash. But seriously. Who is this guy? I mean, Henry's always thoughtful and has a way of putting me first. But *this* Henry is even more swoony than *friends-with-benefits* Henry, and I'm not sure how to handle it. Honestly, I didn't even think it was possible.

"Are you craving something other than pizza?" he asks when I've been quiet for too long.

"No, pizza's fine. It's…"

"It's what?"

"It's really thoughtful of you."

"I'm a very thoughtful guy," he agrees, and I laugh.

"I've noticed. And I'm sorry if I'm acting weird. I'm trying to connect *friend* Henry and"--I wave my hand at him--"this one."

"I'm still the same Henry, Mia. Only, I'm not holding back anymore. If I want to kiss you, I'm going to kiss you. If I want to hold your hand, I'm going to hold your hand. If I want to buy you dinner, I'm going to buy you dinner. Is that a problem for you?"

I shake my head. "No problem."

"Good."

Nala leads the way as Henry opens the door for me, bypassing David at the main entrance, and I step over the threshold with the same dopey grin making my cheeks hurt. It happens a lot when I'm around him.

So. Damn. Thoughtful.

The air is turning cooler now. Summer is long gone, and autumn is upon us. But I've always liked autumn. The boots. The sweaters. The scarves. The fallen leaves crunching beneath said boots. And pumpkin spice everything.

My mouth lifts as we walk down the sidewalk. Henry asks, "What are you thinking about?"

I glance at him and smile wider. "Pumpkin spice."

His brow lifts. "You like the stuff?"

"You don't?"

"Never pegged you for being trendy."

"Pumpkin spice is trendy?" I question.

The guy looks at me like I must be an idiot for even asking and replies, "Very."

"Is there something wrong with being trendy?"

He shakes his head and takes the leash from me, allowing Nala to walk on the grass as we continue moseying down the pathway side by side. "Not at all. You continue to surprise me, Mia Rutherford."

"To be fair, Ash is the one who got me hooked on the stuff," I inform him.

"Ah, that makes more sense." He nods knowingly. "She seems like someone who would be a big fan of pumpkin spice and everything nice."

I laugh under my breath and give him a nod. "Sounds about right."

"How did you two meet?"

"Both of us saw an advertisement for a townhome near campus our freshman year and jumped on it. When we first met, I was sure we couldn't be more different if we tried. I thought she was a Goody Two-shoes, and she thought I was going to throw parties and get shitfaced every weekend, which would prevent her from keeping up with her scholarships. However, we took the time to get to know each other, and what do you know? We wound up being two peas in a pod."

"I'm glad you found her freshman year," he returns.

"Me too." I bump his shoulder with mine. "Even if she did get me addicted to pumpkin spice."

He snorts. "Are you going to let me meet them one of these days?"

"You already know my friends," I remind him.

"I mean on a more personal level," he clarifies. "And it doesn't have to be today or tomorrow or even a month from now, but I want to be sure we're on the same page."

"We are," I reply. "I'm in this." I swing our interconnected hands to prove my point. "But...making this public and admitting it to others versus keeping it to ourselves is a little...daunting."

He hesitates, his expression bunching as he brings us to a halt on the sidewalk. "They're going to find out about us, Mia. I know you don't like acknowledging it, but I'm a Buchanan. For some reason I can't fathom, articles are posted with my name and face all the time. It's not something you can run from. It's not something I can protect you from. I asked Gordy to hold them off for as long as he can, but it's only a matter of time before a picture of us together is posted somewh--"

"I'm not ashamed to be seen with you," I interrupt.

"Then what is it?" he prods. "Why don't you want to make this public?"

My thumbnail digs into my middle finger's cuticle as I consider his question. If I make it official to the outside world, it becomes real. It becomes tangible. It becomes something able to be lost. To be ruined. And I don't want to ruin this. I don't want to lose this.

"Tell me." He angles my head up. "Tell me what's holding you back."

"It makes me nervous," I whisper, hating how stupid and vulnerable I sound without any ability to change it.

"Why?"

"Like it'll jinx it. Jinx this." I slide my hands along his chest and tangle my fingers in the short, silky hair along the nape of his neck. He's warm. So warm I want to wrap myself up in him and never let him go.

"I'm not going anywhere, remember?" he murmurs.

"I know."

"Do you?"

"I do," I reiterate. "It's...well, what goes up must come down, right?" I step away from him, hoping he'll let me drop this conversation if we continue our walk. Hoping he'll pick a different topic. One that doesn't make me feel like a deer caught in the headlights.

Catching up to me, he prods, "What do you mean when you say *what goes up must come down?*"

I bump his shoulder, thread my arm through his, and rest my head against him. "How did I know you wouldn't let me dodge your question?"

He drops a kiss on my head and pushes, "Answer it, Brat."

With a pathetic laugh, I explain, "I mean, I'm happy. Really happy, Henry. Happier than I've ever been, and it terrifies me."

His steps falter. "Why?"

Sucking my bottom lip into my mouth, I sigh. "Because anytime I've even felt a semblance of happiness, something always comes around and knocks me on my ass, bringing me back to reality."

"*Reality?*"

"Yeah."

"Because you're not allowed to be happy in your reality?"

"You know what I mean," I hedge, hating how close this hits to home. Because he doesn't get it. He doesn't understand how dangerous it is for me to feel hope. To feel peace. To feel love without knowing if or when it'll be ripped away, leaving me even more hopeless and lonely than before.

And fuck, it hurts. The idea of losing Henry. It doesn't matter if we've barely admitted our feelings run a hell of a lot deeper than sex. I've been falling for him for months. The idea of screwing this up? Of losing him? It's almost more than I can bear.

"You deserve to be happy, Mia. You deserve to have money. To have conveniences. To have a dog you love and a man who takes care of you."

My eyes burn, and I shy away from him, shoving my hair away from my face as the wind whips around us. "Now you're being all mushy."

"Don't tell my business partners." He wraps his arms around my waist again, denying me any space when he knows what I need is the opposite. I need him. His hands. His smile. His suits. The leash tangles around us, but it only makes me feel lighter. Like maybe I can tie him to me. Like maybe I can keep him forever.

"You can tell Gordy to stop scouring the internet for

photos of us," I murmur. "When I'm all in, I'm all in, and..." I swallow, take a deep breath, and look up at Henry. "I'm all in."

"That's my girl." He leans in for another kiss, brushing his lips across mine with a tenderness I've come to crave. It's sweet and innocent and sends tingles racing down my spine. He pulls away and adds, "Come on. Let's find you some pumpkin spice."

My cheeks pinch with amusement as I reach for his hand. "Sounds like a solid plan to me."

48

HENRY

After Mia's shift, we took Nala out for another walk, then came back to my apartment to watch a show and unwind. Giving Mia free reign over the remote, I change into basketball shorts and a T-shirt and return to the living room.

When I round the corner, Mia whistles, shamelessly checking me out as her eyebrows bounce up and down.

"Day-um, Professor."

"You like what you see?" I ask.

Biting her bottom lip while grinning from ear to ear, she nods. "Don't get me wrong. I'm a slut for the suit, but this?" She waves her hand as if to showcase my outfit. "My libido's quite the fan."

"Oh, she is?"

"Mm-hmm." She pats the couch cushion on her right side since Nala is snuggled up on her left. "Now, get over here, Professor. I wanna snuggle."

I stride toward her and take the empty seat, propping my legs on the coffee table in front of us, recognizing the show set to play on the television.

"*The Bachelor?*" I ask.

"Is that a problem?"

Hooking my arm around her shoulders, I pull her into me and press play. "Did you know the producers asked if I wanted to be on it?"

Her jaw drops, and she pushes herself away from me. "Are you serious?"

I nod.

"No freaking way. You're really serious?"

I nod again, and she laughs. "Okay, that's the coolest thing ever."

"Glad I can impress you."

"Yeah, it's gonna impress the shit out of my friends too. Just a heads up, I'll most definitely be bragging about this when we hang out with them this weekend."

The way she slips our plans into the conversation makes me smile. I reach out and squeeze her knee. "We're going to hang out with them?"

"Technically, they're coming here," she announces. "Is that a problem?"

I shake my head. "No problem."

"Good. Figured I'd rip the whole thing off like a Band-Aid, right?"

"Whole *thing?*"

"Ya know, the fancy building, the sexy boyfriend, the happy Mia."

With another smile, I pull her into me again and drop a kiss on the crown of her head. "I think it's a great idea."

"Me too."

"And for the record, I like the *happy Mia* part," I add.

Tilting her head toward me, she skates her lips against my chin and repeats, "Me too."

My phone rings, pulling me from sleep as I shift on the couch. Mia is snuggled into my side, and a notification is centered on the television screen, asking if we're still watching *The Bachelor*. Nala snores softly on Mia's opposite side. The familiar buzz sounds again, and I shift, taking my phone out of my pocket.

It's my father.

Careful not to wake Mia, I slip away from her and answer the call, keeping my voice low. "Hello?"

"Did you see the article?" my father asks.

I scrub my hand over my face, attempting to wipe away my exhaustion, but it doesn't do shit. "What article?"

"With the photos of you and Mia outside your building."

That quick, huh?

After my conversation with Mia, I called Gordy and told him to stop screening any articles of me, but I figured we at least had another day or two before someone found out about us and deemed my relationship worthy of an article or photograph.

Apparently, I underestimated them.

My laptop is on the table, so I open it, search my name, and almost instantly find the article my father is referring to.

"Henry," he starts.

"One second," I mutter as I scan the article.

Billionaire off the market. OnlyFans extraordinaire. Official couple. The words blur together, and I snap the laptop closed.

"What about it?" I ask.

"You have nothing to say?"

"No."

"So, it's true?" he prods.

I glance at Mia on the couch, curled in the fetal position with Nala tucked behind her legs. Warmth spreads in my chest, and my mouth tugs up on the sides. "Yeah. It's true."

"I told you to stay away——"

"Did you *not* learn anything after meddling with Evie's love life?" I challenge, mentioning my younger sister. Our father pushed Evie to date Troy for years, basically creating an arranged marriage for her since my father was business partners and best friends with Troy's dad, Dick McAdams. But it blew up in his face.

"Was she really a sex worker?" my father demands.

I let out a slow breath and pinch the bridge of my nose. "Yes and no."

"Explain."

"Not sure it's any of your business."

"The Buchanans——"

"Toe the line," I finish for him. "And, yes. I understand falling for a girl who used to have an OnlyFans account might reflect badly on the Buchanan name. I understand Mia being connected to Troy in *any* way might reflect badly on the Buchanan name. I understand you prefer I end up with someone who comes from money so you don't have to question your future daughter-in-law's motives." I glance out the window, taking in the skyline and stars shining in the sky. Its beauty reminds me of the girl asleep on my couch and gives me strength. "But I need you to understand I love her. I love Mia Rutherford. And you have no control over who I love. Who I marry. Or who I choose to protect with our family name."

His silence is deafening, but I don't break it. Instead, I wait. For his opinion. His assumptions. His declaration of war or the gauntlet I have no doubt he's considering throwing down if I don't handle this conversation with care.

I stare out the large windows at all this world has to offer those willing to take it and simply wait.

"So you noticed?" my father prods. "The article mentioned potential stalkers——"

"I'm aware," I grit out, giving the window my back. "And, yes. I noticed. I've been aware of her situation for a long time, but it doesn't change anything." I hesitate and scratch my jaw. "Or maybe it does. I'm not afraid to give her my last name. Not afraid to make a formal statement warning anyone foolish enough to come within a hundred feet of her without her consent, repercussions will be handed out by the Buchanan name."

"And you think it's wise?" my father asks. "To put your name, your status, your *family's* status, on the line for her? For someone with her background?"

"Didn't even need to think twice," I return. "Is it a problem for you?"

He hesitates, and I know we're at a crossroads. I know this conversation could go either way. I know this could make or break our relationship. Straining or strengthening it with a single word. Because if he says yes. If he says my relationship with Mia is a problem, I'm done. *We're* done. I'm not going to let Mia go. I'm not going to let her down. Not even for all the money in the world or the connections my father can offer.

"Is. That. A. Problem?" I grind out, the silence leaving me impatient.

A voice on the other end of the call sounds, but I don't register who it belongs to or what's said. "We'll discuss this later," my father breathes out. "Goodnight, son."

Annoyance burrows under my skin, and I end the call, dropping my arm to my side when I catch movement from the couch. It's subtle, but it's enough. Mia isn't sleeping anymore. She's staring at me, her expression unreadable.

"Hey," I rasp, unsure how much she heard or how much damage control I need to perform to keep her from hating my father.

She swallows, and her lips part as if she wants to say something, but she's simply unsure if she should.

"Say it, Mia," I push.

"Did you stand up for me?"

My eyes fall to my phone as I set it on the kitchen table and nod.

"To your father?" she clarifies.

My chin dips a second time.

"How did he––"

"There was an article," I explain.

"What did it say?"

"It said I'm the luckiest man alive."

Her mouth lifts, and she shakes her head. "Liar."

I don't deny it.

"Did you really say you want to give me your last name?" she asks.

Of course, she would overhear that little nugget.

"One day," I tell her.

Chewing on one of her cuticles, she gives into her anxiety, watching me through her dark lashes. Letting her hand fall to her lap, she asks, "Are you serious?"

With a smirk, I round the edge of the couch and sit beside her. "Is that a problem, Brat?"

"We just started dating."

"Dating, yes. Falling for each other?" I wrap my arm around her shoulders and tug her into my side. She instantly melts against me. "Hardly," I continue. "Don't worry. I'm not afraid of the long game. One day can be as soon or as far away as you want it to be."

Snuggling against my chest, she releases a sigh and plays with the hem of my T-shirt. "Thank you, Henry. For standing up for me. For being patient. For everything."

"I wouldn't have it any other way." I kiss the top of her

head. "It's late. Get some rest. I'm going to let Nala outside one more time. I'll join you in bed after."

Peeking up at me, she whispers, "You want me to sleep over?"

I laugh, leaning down and kissing the tip of her nose. "Haven't you figured it out yet, Brat? I don't want you to leave. Ever." Without waiting for her reply, I stand. "Wait here."

I jog into the bedroom, finding the rectangular black box I've been storing for weeks, and head back to the family room. Mia is still perched on the sofa, but her ass is closer to the edge as she watches me carefully.

Curious. Cautious. Nervous.

"What is it?" she asks.

"Here." I hand her the box.

With a soft frown, she lifts the black lid and laughs. "Are you serious right now?"

"Do you like it?"

She picks up the black and pink sleep mask, examining the silk and shaking her head. "I already have a sleep mask."

"You have a sleep mask for your place. Now you have one for mine too." I kiss her forehead and grab Nala's leash from the hook beside the elevator, leading her to the main floor so she can pee. Once she finishes, I head back to my apartment and put her in her kennel. When I reach the bedroom, Mia is naked on the bed, her new sleep mask pushed up as she smiles coyly.

"Do you think we can reenact our first time in Creekside, Professor?"

As I stalk closer to her, I realize I'll never understand how I became such a lucky asshole to claim her.

"Fuck yes, Brat."

49
MIA

As I pull into the arena's parking lot, I find it busier than usual. The entrance is packed with people, and cameras are set up along the perimeter. I have no idea what they're hoping to film since the game doesn't start for another hour or so. Parking beneath a light post, I turn my ignition off and reach for the door handle when my phone rings.

"Hello?" I answer.

"Hey, it's me," Henry returns. "Listen, when you get here--"

"I just pulled in."

"Don't get out of the car."

"What?" I ask.

"I'm going to escort you inside."

"Why?" I peek out the windshield again, taking in the paparazzi outside the entrance. "What's going on?"

I swear I can hear his annoyance as he grumbles, "The article of us walking the dog seems to have sparked people's curiosity."

"Curiosity about what? Us?"

The tightness in his voice grates on me, turning my amusement into an annoyance matching his own as he confirms, "Yeah."

"What's there to be curious about?"

"Not sure. Erika thinks it's because I never announced my breakup with Scarlett."

I grimace. "Oh."

"Yeah," he mutters. "We'll clear it up later, but for now, I want you by my side so I don't have to worry about you being alone in the stampede."

"Henry, I'm fine."

"Humor me, okay? You've never dated someone like...me."

"You mean someone who's kinda, sorta famous?" I offer, finding his shyness way more adorable than I should, considering the circumstances, but he doesn't answer me.

"Are you parked in your usual spot?" he asks.

I glance up at the light post nearly touching my bumper. "Yup."

"Don't move. I'll be there in a minute."

"Okay, Professor."

"Not your professor anymore," he grumbles, and the call goes dead.

Puffing out my cheeks, I wait for Henry to escort me inside. I find him stalking toward me a few minutes later with a dude in a black suit beside him.

Whoa. He's bringing security with him?

As Henry opens the door, I try not to gawk at the stranger, but I can't help it. The guy's built like a bear. A big, burly bear with sunglasses and a bald head. He clearly has a thing for black since he's covered in it from head to toe.

"Is he a bodyguard?" I ask him quietly.

The tightness surrounding Henry's eyes fades into amusement as he offers me his hand, helping me out of the car. "Don't say anything to the reporters. We'll make an official statement together after the game once we've decided exactly what to say."

"You didn't answer," I argue, glancing at the behemoth again.

"Yes, he's a bodyguard," he concedes. "His name is Paul."

"Hi, Paul," I greet him.

"Hello, Ms. Rutherford," he returns.

Henry grabs my hand. "Come on."

Hand in hand, we begin our trek to the large building as Paul flanks our backs. His presence makes me feel like I'm sleeping with the President or something.

It's surreal. And weird. Being in the spotlight like this. Thankfully, I know Henry well enough to have seen this isn't exactly the norm, and I hold onto the reminder like it's a lifeline.

When we get closer to the door, cameras begin flashing around us. I tighten my fingers around Henry's hand, anxious to get the hell out of here.

"Henry!" a reporter calls. "Henry! Can we ask you a few questions?"

"Keep your head down," Henry mutters to me.

"Henry! The single ladies around the world want to know if you're really off the market!"

He winds me through the crowd, and I keep my eyes glued to the sidewalk, ignoring the flashes from the cameras as they burn my irises like a branding iron.

"Mia?" another reporter calls. "Rumors are circulating stating you dated Bradley Ackerman before he played for the Tumblers. Is this true? Do you have anything to say about your connection to him?"

"Mia!" someone else yells. She's closer than most of the others, and I flinch, my ears ringing as I register her shrill tone. "Are you only dating your boss to make Ackerman jealous, or is it for Buchanan's family money?"

"Don't acknowledge them," Henry orders, quickening his pace.

The distance from us to the door feels like a mile. And it might as well be. There are so many people. So many faces. So many cameras and recorders and flashes.

"Keep your head down," Paul reminds me from behind.

I drop my chin to my chest and hold on to Henry's hand for dear life, blindly weaving between throngs of people.

"Henry!" another reporter yells. I glance their way to find a recording device a few inches from my face.

Dude. Chill.

I stare at the back of Henry's suit and trudge on. A different stranger calls out, "Mr. Buchanan! Mr. Buchanan! Do you have anything to say about your girlfriend being a sex worker?"

I close my eyes as Henry's shoulders stiffen. He halts on the pavement, and I almost run into him but stop myself from face-planting into his broad backside.

Shit.

Apparently, we found Henry's breaking point.

And it involves two words: sex worker.

Bile rises up my throat, and my free fingers brush against the back of his suit, urging him forward, but he doesn't move.

"Henry," I whisper. I don't even know what I'm pleading for at this point. Part of me wants to grab the stupid recorder from the guy's hand and chuck it into the crowd. The other part of me wants to disappear entirely.

Not because I'm ashamed.

Honestly, I'm not. The money has helped more children than I can count, and I wouldn't go back to change my actions even if I could. But bringing Henry shame? His family? His work? His team? It hits on an entirely new level, leaving me raw and vulnerable in front of a sea of cameras. They're outside his arena, for chrissake. And they're talking about *me*.

Guilt wraps around my chest, squeezing tighter and tighter until it's almost impossible to breathe.

This man has done everything. Earned his Ph.D. Built a successful professional hockey team from the ground up. Wormed his way into my heart, which I was pretty freaking positive was impossible.

And this is what the media is choosing to focus on? That he's dating a sex worker? *Ex*-sex worker?

Fuck them.

I want to shout it from the rooftops. I want to spit in their faces and tell them to find a freaking hobby. Instead, I stay quiet. Because whatever I say, however I act, can influence Henry's business. Everything he's worked for. Everything he's sacrificed. And here I am, potentially screwing it all up simply by being here. By holding his hand. By walking outside with him on a cool autumn day.

What is wrong with people?

Henry's grip tightens on our entwined hands. He turns around to face the cameras, keeping me at his side.

"Do you care to repeat your last question?" he demands.

A beat of silence passes, and the same reporter calls out, "We're curious if you have anything to say about your girlfriend being a sex worker."

"That's what I thought I heard." A vein in Henry's forehead pulses, though I doubt anyone else notices. No. He looks as peachy as can be. Actually, no. He looks downright lethal. Like the shark I've come to love who's currently circling his prey.

My heart skips.

Love? Do I love him?

I glance at Henry beside me. Strong and proud and impenetrable. Putting himself between me and the rest of the world. Like a shield. A protector. My protector.

"I'm aware of my girlfriend's connection to OnlyFans," he announces, addressing every single reporter in the parking lot. "I know plenty of photos and videos of her are still floating around if you dig hard enough. However, let me make one thing clear."

The same strange but heavy silence falls over the crowd.

"Mia Rutherford is not a sex worker," Henry booms. "She is a social media manager for the Lions. She is smart. She is kind. She is resourceful. And she is *mine*. Every inch of her body. Every hair on the top of her perfect little head. Every polished nail covering her dainty little toes. She. Is. Mine."

"Are you afraid of others feeling differently based on the photos and videos she's sold in the past?" the reporter asks.

"Not at all," he returns without a single ounce of hesitation. "Because if anyone tries to hurt her, if anyone tries to disrespect her or belittle her, they'll have to deal with me. And trust me. You can ask any of my business partners or associates––past and present––you do not want to piss off me or the Buchanan name. Because the consequences?" His chuckle is dark and threatening, causing goosebumps to break out along my skin. "Well, I'm sure you can imagine the lengths I'll go to keep this woman safe." He brings my hand to his lips and kisses it in front of everyone, staking his claim. "Now, if you'll excuse us, the Lions have a game to win."

The cameras begin clicking even faster, and the flashes are damn near blinding me as Henry pulls me inside the arena.

"Whoa." My eyes close, yet it doesn't block the bright lights from being imprinted on my eyelids as the door closes behind us.

Once we're alone, Henry's hands are on my cheeks, his threatening persona yet to release him as he examines every freckle on my face. "Are you all right?"

"It's fine," I rush out. "I'm fine. Seriously."

But he doesn't let me go. If anything, he tugs me closer until I'm surrounded by all things Henry. His scent. His heat. His dark, penetrating gaze.

"Let me make something clear to you too," he growls.

"Seriously, Henry, let's not––"

Lifting my chin, he forces me to look at him. "The shame I know you're feeling—"

"I'm not––"

"Don't lie," he interrupts. "You're perfect. Okay? I might not fully understand the reason behind some of your decisions, but they make you, *you*. I wouldn't change a single thing about you or the experiences you went through to make you who you are today. I know it's selfish. To think it and to say it out loud, especially considering the shit I know you've been through, but I mean it. I wouldn't change a thing." He teases my bottom lip with his thumb. "Not the makeup. The tattoos. The piercings. The OF account. Nothing. Are we clear?"

I grab his wrist still holding my face in place and slowly encourage him to lower it. To let go of his anger. His fury. Not at me but at the people who cornered us. Because even though I love how he stood up for me, how he doesn't resent me or my decisions, seeing him like this? So frustrated and amped up?

I hate it.

Slowly, I watch the furrow in his brow smooth and the frown marring his lips lose its rigidity. When he lets go of my face, I rise onto my tiptoes and kiss him gently.

"Thank you," I whisper. "For standing up for me. For not being ashamed of me. For claiming me despite my past."

His eyes soften, and he presses his forehead to mine. "Never gonna let you down, Brat." I smile. "Never gonna let you go."

With another quick peck against his lips, I let my heels touch the ground and smooth the lapel of his suit with my hand. "You better not."

"Never."

50

HENRY

The Lions are up two to one as we head into the third period.

With a tumbler of Pappy hanging from my fingertips, I sit in the box seats and watch Colt slap the puck into the top right corner of the net. The crowd goes wild.

"They're good," a familiar voice calls from behind me.

I turn around. My hackles rise, but I keep my expression blank as I calmly ask, "What are you doing here?"

Ice clinks against glass, and my father splashes some whiskey into a tumbler, making himself at home. In *my* arena. The arena he's never deemed worthy of his time until today. The question is, why?

"I saw your remarks about Mia before the game," he mentions, but he's only half-paying attention to me. Instead, he's slowly walking around the private room, examining every inch of the space like he's in a museum.

I swallow the rest of my drink and watch him carefully from the corner of my eye. I want to know why he's here. The real reason. Whether or not he's decided to be a good father or make an enemy out of his oldest child. But I know him. I know him well. So I wait.

"They shouldn't have cornered you like that," he continues.

"It was to be expected."

"Yes." He nods once and takes a sip of his drink. "Doesn't make it any easier."

Jaw locked, I let my empty glass hang from my fingertips. "I guess not."

His strides are slow but confident as he comes closer and sits beside me.

Unwilling to play his game and confront him, I keep my eyes glued on the rink beneath us. Theo has the puck and passes it to Colt, but I'm too distracted to follow the rest of the play.

Why is he here? What does he want to talk about?

"Yesterday, you asked me if it's a problem," my father adds. "Your relationship with Mia."

I stay quiet and run my fingers along the edge of the glass, refusing to look at him.

Leather squeaks as he shifts in his chair. Like he's uncomfortable. Anxious. Unsure. "Buchanans toe the line, son," he continues. "We're willing to toe it for you."

My heart rate spikes, but I don't let him see my surprise as my gaze finds his. "What are you saying?"

"You have your parents' support, Henry. No matter what."

"Did Mom put you up to this?"

"She may have nudged me in the right direction," he mutters. "But after hearing your statement, I realize it was the right choice."

Relief spreads behind my ribcage, and I take a deep breath. "Thank you."

"I was wrong. You'll understand when you're a parent, but it's fascinating. How often we get things wrong. How often we make mistakes." He lifts the glass to his lips again and takes a short sip. His expression tightens as he swallows. "How long it takes us to see the truth and to let our kids go. I know you're not a child anymore, Henry. You haven't been for a long time. But I'm proud of you. For standing up for Mia. For chasing your dreams, even when they didn't align with your father's." His mouth lifts, and he leans forward in his seat, taking in the fully-packed arena beneath us. "This is quite the life you've built, and you've done it on your own."

"Don't be humble now, Christopher," I quip. "You've given your kids everything, remember?"

"And my kids have chosen not to squander it," he points out. "I'm proud of you."

Pride.

It's the foundation on which the Buchanan name is built, though I don't hear my father doling out compliments often. I clear my throat and tear my attention from the game, giving him a smirk. "Thank you."

"You're welcome." He glances through the glass again and stares down at the rink. "I still prefer golf."

With a laugh, I pat his shoulder and stand. "I wouldn't expect anything different."

I pour myself another glass.

Puttering around Henry's massive kitchen, I rearrange the takeout containers for the hundredth time and shove my hair away from my face.

"Stop touching everything. It looks fine," Henry calls from the hallway as Nala licks my toes.

"Yeah, yeah, I know," I mumble, bending down and scratching Nala's ears. He's right. Everything's fine. Except my anxiety levels. But hey, what's new?

The intercom buzzes, and I stand, wiping my hands against my jeans and activating the elevator when Henry's head pops through the doorway to his bedroom. With his phone to his ear, he covers the mouthpiece. "I'll be out in five. I need to take this phone call."

"Okay."

I rock back on my heels, and within a minute, the elevator doors slide open, revealing the whole gang. Ashlyn, Colt, Blakely, Theo, Kate, and Macklin.

Nala's heavy footsteps echo off the hardwood floor as she races toward them, and Blake bends down with her arms open wide. Like a missile, Nala lands in Blake's lap, and I give Theo a pointed look.

"You know you're gonna have to buy her a German Shepherd one of these days, right?"

"Or knock me up!" Blake quips from the floor.

"Don't tempt me," Theo grumbles, and Colt decks him on the shoulder.

Rubbing at the sore spot, Theo asks, "What was that for?"

"That was for talking about knocking up my little sister while I'm in the room. I thought we agreed to not bring that shit up," Colt tells him.

"Oh, come on," Ash interrupts. "It's not like you don't know they have sex. They're living together *and* engaged, remember?"

Colt's expression sours. "Doesn't mean I need the reminder."

"We brought cookies!" Kate interrupts.

She lifts a Tupperware filled to the brim with Mama Taylor's famous chocolate chip recipe, making my mouth water instantly.

"Oh, thank you." I take it from her and set it beside the fried chicken platter and French fries Henry picked up a few minutes ago.

Theo pops a cookie into his mouth and heads into the family room, sitting on one of the leather couches like he owns the place. "Not bad, Mia."

"Yeah, not bad at all," Macklin agrees, pressing a kiss to my cheek. "Thanks for inviting us."

"No problem," I reply.

"So, where's the man of the hour?" Blake asks. "Is he hiding in hopes of dodging Ashlyn's interrogation tonight?"

"I'm not going to interrogate him," Ashlyn starts, but Colt wraps his arm around her shoulder and tugs her into his side. "It's okay, Ash. None of us would expect anything less from you."

"You guys are the worst," I grumble. "You know it, right?"

"Yup." Blake grabs a piece of fried chicken, takes a bite, and rips off a small chunk, handing it to Nala. "Seriously, though. Where is he? I want to thank him for the insane donations he's been giving to Boost."

"What donations?" I ask.

She shrugs. "I dunno? For the last few months, he's been sending Fender's foundation a shit-ton of cash, and we're working on leasing a building near campus. Hopefully, we'll be able to start watching kids whose parents want to attend LAU. Isn't it a cool idea?"

"Actually, it's a really great idea."

"Buchanan thought of it," Theo explains.

"Or at least it's what his assistant said when she dropped off the first check a month ago," Blakely adds. "Which was massive, by the way, but my NDA says I'm not supposed to say how many zeros were involved." She pretends to zip her lips with her fingers when the floor creaks from the hallway.

I glance toward the sound, finding Henry's gaze locked on mine. I'm not sure how much of our conversation he caught, but I have a hunch it was enough. Enough to know I know his dirty little secret, and he's waiting to see how I'll respond.

"Have you been donating to my uncle's foundation?" I murmur.

"Is that a problem?"

I swallow and shake my head. "No problem."

The same soft gaze I swear is only reserved for me fills his dark eyes as he strides toward me and kisses my temple. I lean into his touch, practically brimming with awe at how sweet this man really is when I realize how quiet the room has become. Everyone's staring at us. Even Nala's fascinated with our interaction. I'd laugh if I wasn't so uncomfortable.

Waving a head at the man beside me, I mutter, "Guys, as you all know, this is Henry."

"Her boyfriend," Henry clarifies.

I glare at him and continue, "My *boyfriend*. Henry, this is everyone else. Whom you already know."

"Hey," he greets them. "Anyone want a drink?"

Blakley nods. "Yes, please!" Ash adds, "Sure. I'd love one."

"Got any more Pappy's?" Theo jests. "Or do you only save it for special occasions when you're not trying to impress your girlfriend's friends?"

Henry chuckles as he heads to his liquor cabinet. And just like that, he's in. I can see it in my friends' expressions. Their smiles. Their laughs. The way they kick their feet up and fill him in on my quirks, most of which he's already familiar with.

But it's nice.

Really nice.

I kind of love it, actually.

MIA

As I take my makeup off in Henry's bathroom, he lets Nala out one more time and puts her in her kennel. Humming a Broken Vows song under my breath, I reach for one of the fluffy gray towels on the rack and wipe the water from my eyes when I catch Henry leaning against the bathroom doorjamb. His white button-up is pushed to his elbows, showcasing his muscular forearms dappled in dark hair as he stares at me.

The guy's so gorgeous it's almost scary. Yet here he is. Checking me out. Me. The girl who couldn't be more of his opposite if I tried.

Suddenly shy, I murmur, "Hi."

"Hey."

I peek at my reflection, confirming I don't have raccoon eyes or anything. Giving him my attention again, I practically squirm under his gaze. "What?"

"What, what?" he returns.

"Why are you looking at me like this?"

"Like what?"

"I dunno? Like...*this.*" I motion to his soft expression.

375

"Appreciating the view."

I snort and go back to wiping my face while ignoring the pitter-patter of butterfly wings in my stomach and chest cavity.

"You're gorgeous, you know," he muses.

I set the towel down and motion to the oversized T-shirt I stole from his closet. "I'm in a massive T-shirt that swallows me whole, and I have my hair pulled into a messy bun on top of my head, *and* I'm not wearing any makeup." My hand flaps around my face as if to prove my point. "You call this gorgeous?"

He nods and pushes himself upright. "Yeah. I really do." Prowling toward me, he slips his arms around my waist, swaying us back and forth. "You know what else is gorgeous?"

"What?"

"This." His hand slides down to my thigh tattoo peeking beneath the hem of the T-shirt.

"Oh, you think so?"

"Yeah. I don't think I've ever told you, but I like your tattoos."

"Good, because they're not going anywhere," I quip.

He smirks, trails kisses along my cheek, and sucks my earlobe into his mouth. When he lets me go, he whispers, "I like these too."

"My piercings?"

He nibbles softly on the shell of my ear, and I push him away with a laugh. "Hey, that tickles."

Cupping the side of my face, he doesn't let me get too far. He presses his forehead to mine. "Do you want to know what else I like?"

"What?"

"You being here. In my space. My clothes." He tugs at the

hem of my shirt, lifting it a few inches until the cool air hits the back of my thighs. "My bed."

"Oh, you do, do you?"

"Mm-hmm." His hands slide up beneath the shirt, and he cups my ass. "I like it a lot."

"Well, I guess it's a good thing we're on the same page, huh?"

"Mm-hmm," he repeats, swaying us back and forth, though there isn't any music. Only us and the sound of our breathing. "I'm proud of you."

I roll my eyes, but he doesn't let me pull away. "I'm serious. You killed it today."

"Only because you made me," I mutter.

"You really think I can make you--the infamous Mia Rutherford--do *anything* you don't want to do?" he returns.

"Well, since you've convinced my own friends to turn against me and all..."

He laughs and tugs me even closer, bringing us chest to chest. "You think I passed?"

"The friend test?" I clarify while attempting to *not* rub myself against him like a cat in heat. "Yes, I definitely think you passed. They love you."

"Good."

"Probably a little too much," I muse. "Especially after they saw your penthouse and you let them drink all your alcohol. They might insist we spend every weekend here."

"I wouldn't complain," Henry returns. "You'll have to invite the girls over next weekend."

"Why?"

"I'm giving you Saturday off."

I stop swaying, even more confused. "Why?" I repeat.

His nonchalance morphs into hesitation, and he lets me go, scratching his jaw as he avoids my eyes.

"Henry--"

"We're playing Ohio at home," he admits.

Blindsided, my shoulders hunch. "Oh."

"Yeah."

"So, Shorty will be in town," I murmur, staring blankly in front of me.

"Yes."

My eyes lock with his as I snap myself out of the familiar funk accompanying my ex's name. "And you think I'd be smart to stay home instead of attending the game?"

"After the shit that went down last game?" He scoffs. "Yes."

"I'm not staying home, Henry."

"Mia––"

"You really think he deserves that kind of power?"

"I don't want you to be uncomfortable," he argues.

"I'll be uncomfortable either way," I point out. "But I'm not going to let him interfere with my life anymore, including letting him influence whether or not I go to work."

Frustrated, Henry scrubs his hands through his hair and shakes his head. "He doesn't deserve to be in the same room with you after all the shit he's done."

"Henry, I'm going."

His jaw ticks as he shakes his head again. Like I'm being irrational. Stubborn. *Stupid.*

The last thought stings. I probably am being irrational. He has every right to be concerned about my well-being when it comes to Shorty. The guy's an ass. But it's still my decision. My choice. And if Henry can't support me in it, we have an entirely different conversation ahead of us. One I really don't want to have.

Folding my arms, I wait him out, curious––and terrified––to hear what he has to say and whether or not I have his support.

However, when he stays quiet, my impatience gets the best of me, and I repeat, "Henry, I'm serious. I'm going."

With a sigh, his head drops back, and he looks toward the ceiling. I swear the bastard's counting to ten. "Promise you won't hate me after," he demands.

"Why would I hate you?"

"Promise me."

I try to step back, but he holds me in place. "Henry, you're freaking me out."

"Mia," he warns.

"Okay, I promise."

"Promise me you'll never be alone, either." His eyes meet mine. "Not inside the arena. Not outside of the arena. Not when taking Nala on walks. Nowhere. Not until he's back on a plane headed home."

"Okay," I concede as relief and trepidation spread through me. Relief that I have Henry's support. Trepidation over Shorty being in my stomping grounds this weekend. But I can face it. I can face *him*. As long as Henry's by my side. "I promise."

His strong hands engulf my biceps, rubbing up and down my arms. He kisses my forehead and pulls me into a hug. His own relief practically emanates from every cell in his body as he sags against me. "Thank you."

53

MIA

"Where are you taking us?" I ask Henry as we pull into the parking lot.

LAU's soccer field is laid out in front of us. Blakely's here, too, her red curly hair piled on top of her head and a pair of gray earmuffs covering her ears as she cups her hands around her mouth, yelling something. It's getting colder now, and her breath turns to mist almost instantly. A dozen kids are huddled around her. Each of them wears a hand-me-down jacket and worn sneakers as they line up in a single row. Thankfully, it isn't snowing yet, and once the kids get moving, I'm sure they'll warm up in no time. Give it another couple of weeks, and they'll probably have to move their activities indoors.

Part of me wonders if the foundation was able to lease the building yet, like Blakely mentioned, but I've been too hesitant to ask, afraid I'll be roped into helping somehow if I do.

"Henry?" His name hangs in the air as it slips out of me. I tear my attention from the soccer field to the man behind the steering wheel.

"They want to meet Nala," he explains.

I glance at the backseat where Nala is sprawled out as she snores peacefully. "And how do they even know about Nala?"

Henry shrugs, cutting the engine off. Nala perks up and peeks out the passenger window. Her tail starts wagging as soon as she spots the kids.

"Everyone knows about the Lions' newest mascot," he reminds me.

He's right. A few days ago, she was even spotlighted on ESPN after Colt and Theo insisted she hang out on their bench during warm-ups.

"Okay," I concede, "but how did they find out there was a possibility of meeting her?"

"One of the kids found out Blake was engaged to Theo, so they asked if they could meet her, and you know socialization is good for a puppy."

My lips bunch. I know what he's doing. He's attempting to help me face my past and all the dirty laundry hidden in my very-cluttered closet.

Clever, Henry.

The man's smooth. And convincing. I'll give him that much.

Crossing my arms in the passenger seat, I challenge, "Are you using my dog mama instincts against me?"

"Maybe."

"Why didn't Blakely ask me if the kids could meet Nala?"

"Because she knows you would have said no." He grins.

"Ah, so she reached out to you instead."

"Thornes know how to get what they want."

"Sure they do," I mutter. Waving my hand at the field, I tell him, "Go on. Have fun. I'll wait here."

With a laugh, he snatches the front of my shirt and drags me toward him, placing a kiss on my lips. "Come on, Brat. You know Nala would love to meet everyone."

"Then go introduce them."

"I want you to introduce Nala to everyone *with* me."

"Why?"

"Because it will be good for you."

Glowering at him, I fold my arms. "Henry."

"Mia," he volleys back as sternly.

"I already tried, remember? Fen roped me into kid duty, and I did the whole thing with a fake smile before wrangling Blakely to take the job."

"You really don't think you've changed at all in the last year or so?" he challenges.

"Okay, maybe I've changed a little," I mumble, "but I don't want to be triggered--"

"You won't be. And if you are, I'll be by your side. Besides, they're only kids."

"Kids who have a shitty upbringing--"

"Kids who need hope that their shitty upbringing won't last forever," he argues. "You're living proof of it."

"Yeah, but they don't *know* I'm living proof--"

"Tell me something," he urges. "Have you asked for any of their backstories?"

My mouth goes dry, but I force out, "No?"

"Yet, you already know them," he assumes. "Don't you?"

I wipe my sweaty palms against my jeans, my stomach twisting into knots. "What's your point?"

"My point is, maybe they don't need to know your backstory either to know you're a kindred spirit with them. And if meeting a furball mascot in the middle of a soccer field surrounded by friends while sipping hot chocolate is the only sense of normalcy they get, don't you think they deserve the opportunity?"

"Dammit, Henry," I grumble. "Why do you have to always make such good points?"

"It's what I do." He kisses me again, then lets me go. Once Nala's leash is in place, we walk to the soccer field. Blake announces, "Kids, this is Henry Buchanan, Mia Rutherford, and the famous Nala."

"Nala!" an adorable eight-year-old squeals. "Can I pet her? Can I pet her?"

With a laugh, I answer, "Sure. Go wild."

Thankfully, Henry and I have been working with Nala on her training since day one. The little monster is more obedient than I could've ever imagined as the kids circle her like a bunch of vultures, giving her hugs, tugging on her ears, and scratching her belly. Nala takes it in stride, basking in the attention while Henry pulls me into his side.

"See?" he murmurs. "Is this really so bad?"

"No," I mutter. "I guess not."

"Good. Because we're going to bring her back once a month and keep exposing you to this until you decide you're ready to tell them your story."

My eyes well with tears at the thought alone, and my legs itch to run in the opposite direction, but I keep them planted and shake my head. "Henry."

"It's a good story, Mia," he murmurs, snaking his arms around my waist and bringing us chest to chest. "One ending with a roof over your head and a stable job and a full belly and a cute dog and a hot boyfriend--"

"*Someone's* flattering themself."

He grins and grabs hold of my sides, digging his fingers into my ribs until I squeal with laughter.

"Okay, okay," I concede. "I see your point."

"Good. Because I think it's time they have a chance to see it too."

Lips pursed, I mutter, "I'll think about it."

"That's my girl."

5 4

HENRY

Despite hoping Mia would cave and take the weekend off, she was too stubborn to skip tonight's game. I have to admit, her strength is sexy as hell. After everything Shorty put her through--all the lies, abuse, and manipulation--and she's still here?

Fuck. I'm hard thinking about it.

However, I wasn't exaggerating when I told Mia I'm a patient man. I've been waiting for today's game since I saw the bruises on Mia's perfect skin in Ohio. I also wasn't kidding when I told her she's mine. No one touches what's mine. Tonight, I'm going to prove it once and for all.

Striding into the locker room before the game against the Tumblers begins, I find Colt and Theo in their pads, talking to each other by their lockers.

"Follow me," I order.

Without hesitation, they follow me into Coach Dawson's office, and I kick him out. Once the door is closed, I sit behind the desk and give Colt and Theo a pointed stare.

"Is there a problem?" Colt asks.

"I need each of you to beat the shit out of Shorty during tonight's game."

Theo cocks his head. "What?"

"Every time you wind up in the penalty box because of Shorty, I'll give you a ten thousand dollar bonus."

Silent, Colt takes a seat across from Dawson's desk. Theo follows suit, both of them sensing the shift in the air and what it means for us to even discuss something like this, let alone actually contemplating it.

Keeping his voice low despite our privacy, Colt asks, "What happens when we get thrown out of the game?"

"You get an extra fifty grand."

"And if we get suspended for multiple games?" Theo starts.

"I'll give you another fifty grand for every game you miss."

Resting his elbows on his knees, Colt counters, "You said we need *good* publicity, Buchanan. Getting two of your best players thrown out of the game for brutality against a single player isn't exactly good publicity."

"I'll handle it."

"Why?" Theo challenges. "We already made Shorty look like a dumbass the last time we played."

"I want him to hurt," I clarify. "If he looks like a dumbass while he's hurting, more power to you, but I don't want him walking off the ice tonight. I want him limping. Or leaving on a stretcher."

Again, they exchange looks. "Why?" Colt pushes. "I mean, yeah, he's an ass, but his shit with Mia's in the past."

"And no offense, Buchanan, but we have plenty of money," Theo adds. "We're gonna need a better reason than a couple bonuses to fuck with someone on the level you're suggesting, especially when it could affect our careers."

"Shorty hurt Mia—badly—after the last game when we

were in Ohio," I snap. "Mia told the girls to keep you in the dark so it wouldn't distract you from any upcoming games. After seeing the bruises, I decided to be patient and take matters into my own hands when the opportunity arose. Tonight is that opportunity."

"You mean you decided to recruit *us* to take matters into our own hands," Colt clarifies.

"Unfortunately, I can't be on the ice like the rest of you." I steeple my fingers in front of me. "However, tonight will be Shorty's last game in the NHL."

Theo's eyes thin. "How do you figure?"

"No one touches what's mine," I seethe. "After tonight's game, Shorty will understand, but I'm hoping you can help make it count by taking advantage of your last opportunity to hand him his ass."

"Just to be clear," Colt says. "You're giving us full autonomy from our actions tonight. Correct?"

"Yes."

He glances at Theo again. "*Full.* Autonomy?"

"Do we have a problem?" I demand. "Can I count on you both to do as I ask or do I need to--"

"We'll take care of it," Colt interrupts.

"Yeah," Theo agrees. "No one touches Mia."

"Good." I tilt my head toward the door. "Make it count. Now, get out of here."

"Yes, sir."

They stand, leaving me in peace as I rub my hand over my face. Their voices echo off the lockers a few seconds later.

"Listen up!" Theo yells.

My head snaps up, and I look through the glass separating the office from the main locker area. Theo's standing on one of the metal benches, making him two feet taller than the rest of his teammates as he turns in slow circles, waiting until he has everyone's full attention.

The room quiets almost instantly, and he shares a look with Colt. "Since the start of the season, you've all gotten to know Mia."

"And for most of us," Colt continues, "she's become something of a little sister over the past few months." He moves up beside Theo on the bench, his frustration nearly matching my own. "You also know she doesn't date hockey players."

"Which fucking sucks," Beck adds dryly while the rest of the room chuckles.

Everyone except for Theo and Colt.

"What you don't know," Theo growls, "is the reason behind her decision."

The locker room is so quiet you can hear the sound of fans growing restless from the tunnel, but no one says a word. They simply stare at their leaders, Colt and Theo. The dynamic duo rookies.

"And it isn't because one cheated on her or broke her heart or some shit," Colt explains.

"Okay, it's true, the asshole cheated on her," Theo grumbles.

"But he also liked to use her as a punching bag," Colt says.

Greer pushes to his feet. His hands fisted at his sides. "Who is he?"

Mortinson joins him. "And how do we get our hands on him?"

With a grin, Theo lifts his hands from his sides. "It's our lucky day, gentlemen. He's gonna be on the ice tonight."

"Let's fuck him up," Beck spits, and the rest of the team rumbles their agreement.

"Yeah." Theo nods. "That's exactly what we're gonna do because when we played the Tumblers in Ohio, Mia's ex cornered her--again--and hurt her right under our noses."

Colt looks around the silent locker room as they each understand the severity of Mia's past and all she's been through. His gaze is filled with determination, and his upper lip curls. His deep voice is thunderous as he booms, "Win or lose, we're gonna show him how we protect our own. The only number we care about tonight is the one on the back of Ackerman's jersey. Twenty-one. Let's make him bleed."

The team slams their sticks against the closed lockers. It drums up so much noise, I have no doubt the arena can hear them, but so can the Tumblers. So can Shorty.

He might not know his world is about to be rocked. But he will. And afterward? He'll wish he'd never heard of Mia Rutherford, let alone laid a hand on her.

That, I can guarantee.

An intense energy permeates the locker room as the announcer drums up the crowd. I can't put my finger on whether it's good or bad, but the strange charge is there, nonetheless. Positioning myself outside the locker room, I lower onto one knee and begin snapping photos and videos as our lineup waits for their names to be called.

Colt and Theo are hanging out near the side, looking ready to kill someone. Their hands practically throttle their sticks as they talk to each other in low voices, and I grab a few photos of the two of them. When Colt catches me staring, I ignore the shiver down my spine and lower the camera.

Oops.

Without a word, they both head toward me and squat next to me as Beck's name is announced over the speakers. The guys are big. To be fair, they've always been big. But in their skates, pads, and helmets, they look like gladiators about to enter the Colosseum.

Pissed-off gladiators with their gazes directed at me.

"Is there a problem, gentlemen?" I ask.

Colt tilts my chin up with his gloved hand, forcing me to look at him.

Shying away from him, I swat at his hand, but he doesn't let me go.

"Dude, what are you--"

"Don't *ever* ask our fiancées to lie for you again," Theo warns me from beside his best friend.

I freeze.

They know.

The question is, *how?*

Licking my lips, I shove my guilt at being caught aside. "I didn't--"

Colt drops his hand. "I've lost family, Mia. And so help me, if I ever lose you--if Ash, Blake, or Kate ever loses you--we'll never forgive ourselves. And I'll never forgive *you* for being too stubborn to ask for our help when you needed it most."

My bottom lip trembles as I register the sadness in his voice, but I'm too stubborn to acknowledge it. To open up the door. To even consider the possibility of hurting them. "I didn't--"

"Stop lying to yourself," Theo scolds. "You're not invincible."

My gaze snaps to his. "I never said I was invincible."

"No, just suicidal if you honestly think you can handle a guy like Shorty on your own," Colt counters.

Theo rises to his feet, offers his gloved hand, and helps me stand, not even giving me a chance to argue or defend myself.

I'm not sure I want to. Not anymore. I'm so tired of brushing everything under the table. Of pretending I'm invincible when I'm not. Clearly, I'm not. No, I'm exhausted. So exhausted it makes my head spin some days when I really look at everything I've been through, but I'm getting better. They have to see it. Don't they?

"You're right," I whisper. "I'm sorry."

"Apology accepted," Theo replies.

"But listen," Colt adds, casting him a quick glance, then turning his full attention on me while the announcer continues calling names. "I know you have Buchanan now, and I know he loves you."

"He doesn't--"

"He does," Theo argues with a smirk. "But let Colt finish."

"What I'm trying to say is, you had us before you had him, Mia," Colt explains. "You've always had us. And honestly? With us marrying two of your best friends, you're kind of stuck with us."

Damn them and their sweet promise.

I swallow the lump in my throat and nod, whispering, "I know."

"Good. Enjoy the game. It's gonna be a hell of a ride." With a wink, Theo heads onto the ice with a hockey stick in one hand, his expression unreadable, and his best friend by his side.

They're right.

It doesn't matter what the reasoning behind my actions is. I should've asked for help. In the beginning. After the first time Shorty hit me. In Michigan, when one of the fans hit on me and made me uncomfortable. The list goes on and on. I should've asked for help. I shouldn't have pretended I'm invincible. I should've taken their own views into account and how much my distance has hurt them in the past. All of them. Probably more times than I can count, and it doesn't exactly give me any warm fuzzies.

But things are different now. I'm changing. I'm opening up. Dating Henry is proof of it. And I hope they recognize the baby steps I'm making. Because I *am* making them. One tiny shuffle at a time.

Raising the camera back to my face, I look through the lens and snap a few more pictures before turning on the camera's video mode, capturing the team as they make their way to their positions while the referee heads to the center of the ice.

When the whistle blows, Colt slaps the puck to Theo, beelines it to Shorty, and slams into him. The loud crack of Shorty's helmet hitting the glass reverberates throughout the arena. Colt pushes himself away from the asshole and races to the goal. Theo chips the puck off the board, reading his best friend perfectly, and Colt catches it with his stick, slapping it into the corner of the net. The red siren wails, indicating the first goal for the Lions, and my lips part in surprise.

Holy shit, that was fast.

Dawson screams at the players, complimenting the play, then yells at Greer to get his ass back to his side.

In a flash, the puck is back in play, and I focus the camera on the black disc as it slides between players and across the blue line when another crack distracts me. I flinch, turning to the opposite side of the rink where Theo has Shorty pinned against the glass. He's snarling something at the defenseman, and the referee blows his whistle.

"Fuck you!" Shorty yells, shoving Theo away from him.

What the hell is going on?

I glance at Coach Dawson, expecting him to be pissed at Theo for the dirty play, but he isn't. A smirk tugs at the corner of his lips while he watches the heated exchange with his arms folded and his clipboard pressed into his chest like everything's great, grand, and wonderful.

Theo backs away, his eyes never leaving Shorty as they spark with an unspoken challenge. A few uneventful minutes later, I'm finally focusing on Greer in the faceoff circle. He steals the puck from between one of the offensive players and slaps it back to Wells, the right wing for the Lions. Shorty rushes toward him, but Theo and Colt body slam the dude again from opposite sides. Only this time, Theo hits high, and Colt stays low, causing Shorty to nearly flip over Colt's back. Theo throws his gloves off and starts punching Shorty near the blue line. Within seconds, the rest of the Lions join them despite the shrill whistles blown by the referees. Together, they create a barrier around the fight, preventing any of Shorty's teammates from jumping in and defending him. Whistles continue blaring as the referees attempt to break the mess up, but by the time they squeeze past the outer perimeter of Lions players, the damage has been done.

Shorty, Colt, and Theo are all missing their helmets and gloves. Their sticks are lying on the ice, and blood soaks the front of Shorty's jersey as it flows down his face from his nose.

The crowd bellows behind me as the entire Lions line is shoved into the penalty box across from me, leaving my jaw nearly unhinged.

Did that really just happen?

I mean, yeah. It was completely uncalled for, but it was also kind of vindicating.

He deserved it.

He'll always deserve it.

To be ridiculed. And punched. And fucking raked over the coals. It might make me a bad person for enjoying the show, but I'm too busy soaking it all in to care.

The really crazy part, though? After Colt and Theo are escorted from the game, their replacements are sent to the penalty box to pay for Colt's and Theo's punishment, but as soon as their skates hit the ice again, they're charging. Cross-checking. Clipping. Slashing. Beating the shit out of Shorty until he looks ready to piss himself anytime someone skates close to him. Halfway through the second period, the Tumblers' coach pulls Shorty from the game and sends him back to the locker room with a pack of ice pressed against his bloodied face and likely broken nose. The crowd boos as another Lions player is hauled to the penalty box, but me? I'm feeling lighter than ever.

Fuck you, Shorty.

I look up at the box seats, finding Henry on his throne. He's overlooking the game and Shorty's abuse with a blank expression. Cold. Detached. Lethal. And downright sexy as hell.

This is why he didn't want me here.

Because he had retribution plans and was nervous the violence would scare me. In a way, it probably should. But Henry wouldn't hurt me. No, he's protecting me. He's making a statement. Making it clear I belong to him.

And dammit, I do.

He owns me. Body. Heart. Soul. *Everything.*

I really want to kiss him for it. Well, *that* and screw his brains out.

Now they know. My stalkers. Shorty. They'll never be able to touch me again without reaping the consequences. Consequences like tonight. Like this. I'm not alone. Not anymore. And if he messes with me? If any of them mess with me? Well, I think they now understand the full picture.

And man, does it feel good.

56

HENRY

I love doing business with a willing partner.

I spoke with Chris Tormund before we left Ohio. He owns the Tumblers and is as averse to bad publicity as I am. When I told him what's been going on with one of his players, he was more than happy for us to come to an agreement.

After another short phone call with Tormand, he assured me Coach Navarre was waiting with Shorty in the guest coach's locker room, so I hung up and headed there.

The hinges are as smooth as butter when I open the door to the spare office, reveling in the moment and how long I've been waiting to do this.

Shorty's back is to me. He doesn't know I'm here. I shouldn't find it amusing, but I do. The asshole has no idea who he's dealing with.

An ice pack is pressed to Shorty's cheek as he rests his elbow on the arm of a metal chair across from an indifferent Coach Navarre, who looks bored and tired.

"You gonna tell me why I'm here?" Shorty finally asks his coach, slouching further into his seat.

KELSIE RAE

"If you'll excuse me," Coach Navarre stands and nods at me as he slips out of the office.

Confused, Shorty turns around, his attention catching on me for the first time.

"What are you doing here?" He tries to stand, but I squeeze his trapezius muscles with my hand and shove his ass back into the chair.

"Sit down," I order.

He relaxes into his seat but doesn't stop glaring at me.

Good.

Give me your anger, Shorty. It won't protect you.

Rounding the edge of the desk, I sit in Coach Navarre's recently-vacated chair. Shorty is still in his jersey. The collar looks stretched, and it's stained with his blood. His hair is damp with sweat, sticking up in every direction. There's a split in his lip and another above his brow.

He looks like a fucking train wreck, and I bask in it.

"You gonna tell me why I'm here?" Shorty seethes. His impatience is getting the best of him.

He's even weaker than I thought.

"You made a mistake when we were in Ohio," I tell him.

He scoffs, and I raise my finger, warning him to stay quiet. Rage sparks in his eyes, but he presses his split lips together and waits.

"Actually, you've made a lot of mistakes," I continue. "And most of them were *before* our trip to Ohio, so I think we should start there. Tell me, Shorty. How many times have you hit her?"

Another scoff escapes him, and he kicks his feet out. "Can't believe she bitched to you about our history."

My eye twitches, and I stand again, rounding the edge of the desk. My rage blurs my vision, but the need to throttle the asshole in front of me spurs me on, clearing my head.

"That's it?" I question. "You're not even going to try to defend yourself? To defend your career?"

His eyes narrow to slits, and his spine straightens in his chair. He drops the ice pack to his lap, giving me a front-row seat to the damage Colt and Theo caused during the game. The sight makes me want to wire them another fifty grand.

"Fuck. You," Shorty barks. He reminds me of a disgruntled Chihuahua.

"I gotta be honest with you. You were good. Hiding what you did to Mia while you were dating her at LAU. I saw a few red flags, but not enough to make me feel the need to intervene." I rest my ass against the edge of the desk and grip it until my knuckles are white. "Unfortunately for you, that wasn't the case when we were in Ohio, was it?" Letting the desk go, I rub my hands together. Slowly. Memorizing the worry in his eyes. The tension in his shoulders. "You touched my woman. Probably more times than I can count. Now, you'll be lucky if I let you touch anything ever again."

His attention flicks from my hands to my eyes. "Are you threatening me?"

"I'm ensuring you understand we aren't playing by your rules any longer. You may have been one of the big boys at LAU. You might have even shown promise here on the Tumblers. But guess what?" I smile ruthlessly. "You mean nothing. You hold zero power in this industry. Tormund doesn't want an abuser on his roster, and I don't blame him. So, to save any potential hockey career you're clinging to, you will take a leave of absence for the rest of the season."

Blood rushes to his face. "Bullshit!"

I lift my hand to silence him. "And you will announce your decision at the press conference today."

"You think you can make me play by your rules, Buchanan?" he challenges.

"I do," I reply as blandly as before. "Because if you don't

play by my rules, not only will your career in the NHL, AHL, and CHL be over for the season, it will be over indefinitely."

His eyes bulge with fury. "I'm not gonna let that happen!"

"You have no idea who you're dealing with, Shorty. Fucking with any girl is a mistake, but fucking with *mine*?" A smirk tugs at me. "It's suicidal. You will take the rest of the season to enroll in anger management courses. You will also see a therapist for whatever mommy issues you have bottled up inside of you. If you fulfill your commitment, there's a team in Manitoba willing to give you a spot on their roster next season. If you don't?" I shrug. "Well, I don't give a shit." I push myself away from the edge of the desk.

The metal chair Shorty had been sitting in clatters onto its side as he stands, his expression twisting with fury. "You're banishing me?" His tired body shakes from adrenaline and rage like he might snap at any second.

Tugging at the cuffs of my sleeves, I reply, "I'm protecting what's mine."

Like a rabid dog, he lunges for me, but I dodge his flimsy attack and cock my arm back, my muscles coiling with anticipation. My knuckles land along the bridge of his nose. He screams as I register the crunch of his nose breaking, and blood pours from it once again. Colt and Theo already put him through the wringer during tonight's game. This is simply the icing on the cake.

He stumbles back, nearly tripping on the discarded chair, and clutches at his bloodied face while expletives fall from his mouth like rain during a storm.

Good.

I have wanted to kick the shit out of Bradley Ackerman for years. While I would love for him to wind up in a body bag, I don't want to go to prison unless it's absolutely necessary, so I reel in my rage. Fisting and unfisting my hand, I shake off the ache from the hit. Satisfaction swells in my chest.

Bending down, I pick the fallen chair up and snap, "Sit."

Grudgingly, he does.

"One more thing." My gaze narrows as I stare down at him and rest my ass against the edge of the desk again. "Follow her on social media again?" I grab both sides of the chair he's sitting in, caging him. "I'll end your entire career. Look at her again? I'll take everything you've ever cared about. Touch her again?" Grabbing the fabric of his jersey, I yank him to his feet, bringing us nose to bloodied nose. "I'll fucking kill you. That's a promise, Shorty." When I let him go, he collapses back into his chair, and I slap my hand against his shoulder to prove my point. "Better wash up. Post-game interviews are starting soon."

I walk out the door.

57

MIA

The room is buzzing as everyone waits for the players from both teams to make their way onto the stage and answer questions about the game.

I don't blame them.

I have a few questions too.

Like, what the hell the entire Lions roster was thinking by beating the shit out of Shorty on live television. Colt and Theo were ejected from the game after their little stunt and will likely be suspended for at least one more. The NHL hasn't come out with their official ruling yet. They're also going to be fined. I have no idea how much money they'll be paying. We also lost the game. Five to one.

It makes sense, considering the penalty box being chocked full of Lions players for almost the entire game.

My emotions have been all over the place. Vindicated. Proud. Almost giddy. With a side of guilt, thanks to the loss, fines, and suspensions.

Yeah, I'm kind of a mess, and all I want is to go home and sleep for a week.

"Hey," Ashlyn greets me, toying with the VIP lanyard

around her neck. She bumps her shoulder against mine. "How you doin'?"

"Fine, I guess. Confused," I clarify. "But fine."

"Dude, did you see our fiancés out there?" Blake gives her fingertips a chef's kiss as she sidles up next to us. "Perfection."

"Yeah, it was definitely something else," Kate quips. "Macklin was a little worried he'd have to set a couple of broken bones or something after the last fight, but man." She whistles. "I think Shorty finally got what was coming to him."

"Amen." Blakely raises her hand for a high five, and Ashlyn suppresses a laugh as she returns it.

"Amen," Kate repeats. "Did you guys have any idea they were going to beat the crap out of Shorty tonight?"

They shake their heads. "Nope. We had no idea."

"Which is probably a good thing," Ashlyn adds. "Because I would've been a mess."

"Dude, same," Blakely agrees.

"Listen." I tug us off to a corner of the room, doing my best to ignore the cameras and recorders scattered throughout the large rectangular space.

"You sure you're okay?" Ash prods.

"I want to apologize," I rush out.

Blakely frowns. "For...?"

"Well, for starters, I want to apologize for your fiancés feeling like they needed to make a statement on the ice toni--"

"They would do anything for you, Mia," Ashlyn interrupts.

"I know," I reply. "And I know you guys would do anything for me."

"Duh," Blakely chirps. "We're your best friends."

"I know," I repeat with a laugh, then sober. Reaching for Ash and Blakely's hands, I give them a squeeze. "Which is another reason why I want to apologize. I know it isn't easy being friends with someone who always seems like they're hell-bent on making it impossible to get close to them."

Blakely chuckles. "Kate, you better grab Macklin. It seems like Mia bonked her head."

"I'm serious," I reply. "I know I push people away. I know I hate letting people in or relying on them. I know I should've told you guys about Shorty and fake dating Colt and my OF account and having stalkers and the list goes on and on and on, and I want to say I'm sorry. I'm done putting you all through hell simply because I don't like admitting I care about each of you."

"Aww, honey, we know you love us," Ashlyn says as she tugs me into a hug.

"I do," I mumble into her shoulder. "I really do." Two more pairs of arms wrap around me, and I soak it up. "You're the best friends a girl could ever have. I literally don't know what I'd do without all of you, and I know I'm not always great at showing my gratitude, but I'm going to work on it."

Knowing I'm not a huge fan of hugs, Ashlyn lets me go and shoos our other friends away.

Once I have a bit of breathing room, I continue. "Without you guys, I don't know where I'd be."

"You'd be screwed," Blakely agrees. "But without you guys, I'd be screwed too."

"So would I," Ash says.

"And so would I," Kate repeats. "But the great thing about best friends is, for better or worse, we know each other inside and out."

"Yup," Blakely says. "We know you. We know your past. We know how you tick. We know when you need space. We know when you're struggling."

"We know when you're hiding something," Ash quips.

"And we know when you're happy." Her tone softens, and she smiles. "Like how you are with Henry."

My cheeks pinch at his name, and I let out a dry laugh. "I *am* happy with Henry."

"Speak of the devil." Kate's head tilts toward the entrance to the press room. "He's walking this way."

My eyes fall on Henry striding toward us while my heart rate turns feverish. Long stride. Dark gray suit. Perfectly tousled hair. Sexy smirk.

Goodbye, dry panties.

"Ladies," he announces once he reaches us. He places his hand on my hip and pulls me against his side. "Do you mind if I steal Mia for a few minutes?"

"Of course," Ashlyn returns. "Besides, Colt's coming on stage as we speak, and I want to hear how he answers everyone's questions."

"Yeah, it's gonna be a real hoot," Blakely jokes as Henry laces our fingers together and guides me into the hallway.

"Is everything okay?" I rub my thumb along the back of his hand. My brows cave. Lifting his arm, I examine his swollen, angry knuckles, my lips parting in surprise.

"Henry——"

"I'm fine," he grunts.

My eyes snap to his. "What happened?"

"You should see the other guy."

"Henry," I warn.

"I needed to make something clear."

"To whom?" I ask.

His jaw flexes. "You know who."

My lungs stall, and I lick my lips, the potential repercussions swirling in my head one after the other until I'm practically dizzy.

"You were behind this," I murmur. "Weren't you?"

"I told you I'm a patient man."

I laugh. It sounds forced even to my own ears. "Patient?"

"He needed to know there are consequences to the shit he put you through."

Grabbing his bicep, I tug him further down the hall, searching for eavesdroppers before demanding, "Did you tell Colt and Theo to hurt him?"

"It didn't take much prodding."

"And what happens the next time they play against each other? Will there be more fighting? More penalties? What if Colt or Theo get hurt?"

"It won't be a problem."

"Oh, it won't?"

"No," he confirms. "It won't."

"Why not?"

"Because Shorty is taking the rest of the season off."

A crease forms between my brows. "Since when?"

"Since I told him to."

"No offense, but I'm pretty sure you'll have to pry Shorty's hockey stick from his cold, dead fingers before he gives into something like that."

"You don't believe me?" he questions.

"I do," I murmur, glancing over my shoulder again as if my ex could pop out at any second like Beetlejuice if I say his name too many times. "But...I know Shorty. And I know it would take a lot to convince him to--"

"You still don't have any faith in me?" he asks.

I hesitate a moment, but unable to help myself, I reach for his bruised hand. I need to feel him. His warmth. His skin. His unyielding confidence and determination.

Peeking up at him, I whisper, "You know I do."

"Then you know I'd do anything for you. Anything, Mia Rutherford. Even if I have to get my hands dirty to do it."

I lift his bruised knuckles to my lips and kiss them gently. These hands. They wield so much power. So much control. If they belonged to anyone else, I'd be terrified. But they're Henry's. And I trust him. With my life. My heart. My soul. My future. And my past, no matter how heartwrenching it is.

He cups the side of my face, slipping his fingers into my hair as he urges me to look at him. When my eyes meet his, he murmurs, "Shorty will never bother you again, Mia."

"Promise?" I whisper.

"You really think I'd let you down?"

My mouth quirks up. "No. I don't think you'll let me down."

"Good. Because I won't."

"Never?"

"Never ever." He pulls me into him and kisses me as his fingers slide down my body, finding my hips and digging into them as if the idea of letting me go is unbearable.

Sinking into his affection, I close my eyes and breathe him in, committing the moment to memory. The feel of him. The taste of him. The sound of his voice. The steady thrum of his heart against my palm. All of it.

"I love you, Professor," I whisper.

He tilts my head up again and waits until my eyes open. When they do, a playful grin tugs at his lips. "Not your professor anymore."

"I love you, *Henry*," I emphasize.

His chuckle warms my insides, and he pecks the tip of my nose with his lips. "Love you too, Brat."

"So, I guess we're both rule-breakers?" I quip. "Ya know, since we promised not to fall in love and all."

With a cocky smirk tugging at my insides, he shakes his head. "I never promised I wouldn't fall in love with you."

"You didn't?"

"No." He kisses me again. "I always knew you'd be the one to bring me to my knees, Mia Rutherford." He nuzzles his head into the crook of my neck and squeezes me tightly. "I figured if I was patient enough, I might convince you to give me a real shot."

"So, this was your plan all along?"

"I told you I was patient," he reminds me.

I snort and smack his back, but he only uses his anaconda grip to squeeze me tighter, pulling a laugh from me. "Whatever, Professor. You're lucky your plan worked."

"Mm-hmm." His throat vibrates against my shoulder, making me squirm, but he doesn't let me go. "I knew you wouldn't let me down."

Under different circumstances, I wouldn't believe him. I'd warn him to stay away. Remind him I'm not worth it, and any kind of love between us would only wind up hurting us both. But after everything we've been through, I can't help but appreciate his faith in me, even when I didn't have any in myself.

Resting my head against his, I whisper, "Not a chance."

EPILOGUE

MIA

"I still can't believe you convinced me to do this," I mumble, smoothing out my worn Broken Vows T-shirt as I stand outside the building.

"You look perfect." Henry kisses my cheek. "You're going to kill it."

"We'll see," I mutter under my breath.

The door in front of us opens, and Blakely appears. "All right, we're ready for you."

"Mm-hmm," I hum, my nose scrunching.

Blakely laughs. "Seriously, you're going to do fine. Come on." Pushing the door open the rest of the way, she waits for us to step through, then announces, "Hey, guys! I want you to give my best friend, Mia Rutherford, a big round of applause."

The kids clap their hands, causing Nala's ears to perk up beside my thigh. Henry guides her away from my side and nudges me toward the podium at the center of the stage where Blakely's standing. There's a set of steps along the side. Henry leads Nala down them and toward the anxious kids. They look like they're about to have a meltdown if they don't get their hands on Nala's fluffy black and brown fur within the next three seconds. We decided it was a good idea to let them pet Nala while I told them my life story. I'm grateful for the distraction as well as the sweet smiles each of the kids have anytime Nala comes within arm's reach.

As Henry starts winding Nala between the rows, Blakely reaches for the microphone behind the podium and continues, "I know some of you are familiar with my best friend since she's brought her dog to hang out with us a few times, but today, we're lucky enough to hear something she'd like to share. Mia?" Blakely steps away from the podium, and I inhale softly, taking her place in front of it.

"Uh, hi," I offer. "Like my friend said, I'm Mia. Can any of you tell me your names?"

A little boy in the front raises his hand. He can't be more than eight and has shaggy brown hair in need of a trim. My heart clenches. I point to him, and he says, "I'm John."

"Hi, John," I return.

A little girl with a messy blonde ponytail waves from the front. "Hi! I'm Tabatha."

"Hi, Tabatha!"

A few more join in, telling me their names, and I say hello to each of them, my heart squeezing tighter and tighter with every introduction.

"It's so nice to meet all of you," I announce. "Once upon a time, I was a little girl like you, Tabatha. And you, Maria. And just like you, Navie." I smile. "I grew up in a home where it was hard to find food sometimes. Do any of you know what it's like?" Nearly half their hands raise into the air, and I nod. "Yeah. Sometimes, it was hard to make friends, too, because I didn't want them to come to my house and see how tiny it was. My mom couldn't take me to their houses since she was working all the time, so I decided to keep to myself. Does anyone know what that's like?"

A few more hands raise. "Yeah. I get it. I really do. I had a daddy who loved me so much, but he also had an addiction to drugs and alcohol." A few heads fall. "I bet a lot of you know what that's like too." A lump forms in my throat, but I force it down. "I know some of you are afraid you're going to wind up like them. Whether it's your mom or dad, or your brother or sister. But I want to tell you something. I've been there. I've looked at myself in the mirror and wondered if life would ever get easier. If I'd make the same mistakes my family did. If I was going to graduate high school. Or college. Or if I could find a job or someone who loves me." Henry looks up at me, the warmth in his eyes spreading across the space between us, hitting me square in the chest. "I want you to know you *can* do this. You can play the cards you've been dealt and still come out ahead. And if you ever question it, think of me. Think of Nala. Think of the you you want to be, and don't be afraid of fighting for him or her. Because trust me. You deserve every single happiness. Every single one. You deserve someone who loves you and treats you right. You deserve ice cream and puppies and television shows and friends and laughter and happiness. You deserve it all." My voice cracks, and my eyes burn with unshed tears.

As I blink the moisture away, Tabatha stands from her chair. Slowly, she walks up the steps onto the podium and wraps her arms around me.

"Hey, honey," I start, but the words are lost when I realize she's crying.

Her tiny body wracks with sobs as her little fists find the back of my shirt, and she holds on with all her might. My legs give out, and I lower her to the ground with me, pulling her into my lap. Tears streak her freckled complexion, and I swear I'm looking into a mirror as her watery gaze meets mine.

"You promise, Mia?" she cries.

With a nod, I peek at Henry again. Looking down at the girl in my lap, I tell her, "Yeah, Tabatha. I promise."

Another stuttered breath makes her back heave, and she nods against my chest. The rest of the group is silent as they watch us. Blakely helps Tabatha back to the group a few minutes later. Once I'm completely finished with my speech, Blake passes cookies out while I sit on my ass, way more emotionally drained than I'd like to admit. Henry approaches and squats beside me while Nala stays with the kids, lapping up their love without missing a beat.

His hand is warm as he squeezes my thigh. "You did good."

"You think?" I ask.

His smile makes me melt. "Yeah, Brat. I do."

"Thanks. And thanks for pushing me," I add. "And for being here for me despite everything."

"I'm not going anywhere."

"I know. Thanks for loving me. Even when I make it hard."

"Not going anywhere," he repeats. "And you don't make it hard. Honestly, it's pretty easy."

"Even when I'm acting like a brat?" I challenge.

"Especially then," he whispers. "Gets me all hard and shit."

I snort. "You're an ass."

"An ass who loves you."

Practically beaming, I lean closer, giving him a quick, innocent kiss. "Love you too, Professor."

"Not your professor anymore," he notes.

"I dunno. I think *Professor* has a nice ring to it, don't you?"

"You know what has a better ring to it?" he asks.

"What?"

"Husband."

My eyes pop. "Husband?"

"Yeah. It's a lot better than *Professor*, don't you think?"

"Henry––"

"And speaking of rings…" He digs into the front pocket of his slacks. "I was going to ask you to marry me at dinner tonight, but seeing you up here?" He glances at the empty podium. "I don't want to waste another second without making it official. Without you calling me husband." He slides the ring on my finger without asking for my permission, pulling another laugh from me as I take in the gorgeous, slightly over-the-top, salt-and-pepper diamond. The swirls of black in the sparkly gem are mesmerizing, and my lips part as I study it. It's perfect.

"Do you like it?" he asks.

My attention shifts to Henry. "I've never seen a ring like this."

"Never took you for a traditional girl." He brings my hand to his lips and kisses it. "It looks good on you."

"Mm-hmm," I hum, lifting my hand to let the light shine on the unique kite-shaped diamond in the center. "So are you gonna *ask* me if I'll marry you, or are you assuming I'm going to say yes?"

Henry forces himself into my line of sight and orders, "Say yes."

With a laugh, I give in way more quickly than the old Mia would ever approve of.

"Yes."

"That's my girl."

EPILOGUE

HENRY

"**O**uch," I grunt.

I squirm in the chair as the needle digs into my skin, but Mia laughs. "Oh, come on, ya big baby. It's only a tattoo."

Tearing my attention from the tiny bee stings, I glower at Mia. "You're not going to kiss me and tell me everything will be all right?"

"Oh, my sweet baby," she gushes, wrapping her arms around my neck and smacking loud, wet kisses against my cheeks. "You're so big and brave and––"

"You're making me regret this decision already," I grumble, but she laughs harder.

"Careful, Mia, You're gonna make me fuck it up. And don't give him too much shit. Finger tattoos can be a bitch," Milo scolds. He's Mia's favorite tattoo artist, and if he keeps defending me like this, he'll be mine too.

"Well, I wouldn't know since I can't get my tattoo until the babies are born. Which I'm pretty sure was Henry's plan so I couldn't show him up during his first tattoo appoint-

412

ment by not whining the whole time," Mia teases. Kissing my cheek once more, she plops back into the extra rolling chair Milo brought in for her.

Mia found out she was pregnant a couple of months ago. Pretty sure she pulled the goalie as soon as Ashlyn announced she was pregnant so they could go through everything together.

I'm not complaining, though. I've wanted to tie the girl down for far too long. Having twins, however, threw us both for a loop. But I shouldn't have expected anything less. Mia has never been one to take the easy route, so why stop now?

"When's the big day?" Milo asks, motioning to the half-done wedding band tattoo on my left hand.

"Already had it," Mia announces. "It was yesterday, and it was awesome."

"I didn't get an invite?" Milo's brows raise, and Mia grimaces.

"Oops."

With a grin, Milo adds, "I'm kidding. Congratulations, by the way." He helps me rotate my left hand so he can continue the band around my ring finger. The bottom side isn't half as tender as the top, and I relax a little more into the seat.

It was my idea to have it tattooed on me.

My idea to wear my commitment to the love of my life on my body where anyone can see it. I still can't believe she's mine. That she said yes.

She looked so beautiful walking down the aisle yesterday in a black lace gown. The slit reached her upper thigh and showcased the gorgeous floral tattoo I love to skate my tongue along. Of course, she chose to wear something other than white for our wedding. I assumed my parents would have a heart attack when they saw her, but they welcomed Mia and all of her quirks with open arms. So much so, she somehow managed to convince my mom to get a second piercing in her ears. It's nothing crazy, but for Georgia Buchanan? It's a fucking miracle.

I was almost sad she isn't far enough along in her pregnancy for her baby bump to show in her dress. The idea of everyone knowing she's growing two tiny humans inside of her is enough to make my heart erupt inside of me. We made those. I can't wait to meet them. To hold them. To see if they have Mia's sass or my stoicism.

I glance at my wife again. Awe fills me, practically spilling out as I watch her. I should be used to it by now. The familiar awe I feel anytime I think about how far we've come. Everything we've endured.

When she catches me staring, she gives me a shy smile. "What is it?"

"Love you."

Her cheeks pinch. "Love you too."

The rest of the appointment goes by in a blur, and we head to the airport, where our private plane is waiting. We're going to New York as she's never been. I figured the food, the plays, the museums, and the view of Central Park from our hotel will be an excellent precursor to the rest of our honeymoon in Costa Rica.

It's taken her some time to wrap her head around the money she now has access to, but once she realized she could hand as much of it as she wanted to homeless people, animal shelters, and rehabilitation programs, she welcomed it with both hands.

Shorty has left us alone. He lives in Manitoba and continues seeing his therapist once a week when he isn't playing hockey.

Nala is still the face of the Lions and loves coming to all the games. When she isn't with the team, she's hanging out with me in the suites and has even helped me close a few business deals with a wag of her tail and a lopsided grin. She also convinced Fender and Hadley to adopt another dog. His name is Simba, and he's almost as cute as my own little lion.

As for the rest of the group, they're all doing well. Kate and Macklin had their baby about six months ago. His name is Everett. He was born healthy and strong, despite their concern about Kate taking her epilepsy medication during her pregnancy. Mia thinks they'll probably have one more baby. I agree.

Ashlyn and Colt tied the knot six months ago. It was a small wedding. Only a handful of people were invited. The intimate setting fit them perfectly. Jaxon is too young to understand he's going to be a big brother, but Ashlyn and Colt couldn't be more excited to see how he handles it. I'm sure they'll have a dozen kids, and Ashlyn will love every second of it.

Blakely and Theo are still engaged and are waiting to have children until Blakely graduates college. When she isn't elbow-deep in classes, she's busy volunteering at Boost Youth Foundation. They also have a revolving door of foster kids they look after, and Theo has taken to it like a toddler to cookies.

Life is good. For all of us. Really good. So much so, I sometimes forget the shit we had to endure to get here, but damn. I wouldn't change any of it. Not a single thing.

Whoever may or may not be in control of our lives didn't let us down. And I'm not going to take it for granted.

Not for anything.

The End

A Little Complicated
(A Don't Let Me Next Generation Novel)
Copyright Kelsie Rae - Subject to Change

Prologue
Ophelia

"You know the only reason I'm going to prom tonight is so I can meet Mystery Man and make sure he isn't a dick, right?" Dylan asks. She's my cousin as well as my best friend, and it's been killing her that she's yet to meet the infamous Mystery Man I've been dating. It's the only reason she's standing in front of my floor-length mirror in my bedroom, examining her outfit and fiddling with the skirt. Her dusty blue dress makes her eyes pop even brighter, and the sweetheart neckline and tulle fabric make her look straight out of a Cinderella movie despite the skirt not being too full or fluffy. But even the fairytale-esque dress does shit to hide the anxious energy radiating off her.

"Dylan, you look gorgeous," I tell her for the hundredth time. She forces herself to stop fidgeting with her skirt, turns to me, and shamelessly checks me out. "Ditto. We almost look like we know how to dress up for these things."

"Almost," I repeat with a grin before smoothing down the black satin fabric along my stomach in front of the bathroom mirror. My bedroom is connected to a private bathroom, leaving us plenty of room to chat while getting ready without feeling squished or running into each other.

"Are you nervous?" she asks. "To introduce the family to Mystery Man?"

Mystery Man.

I roll my eyes, but the butterflies in my stomach continue flapping away despite my laid-back facade. Nervous doesn't even begin to cover everything I'm feeling. Anxious. Excited. Terrified. The list goes on and on.

I've never had a boyfriend before. Even the title gives me anxiety. But I've been dating Mystery Man for a couple months, and it's been…kind of awesome.

Okay, the term *dating* is sort of a stretch. It's more like stolen kisses and late-night phone calls, but I think those still count. After all, he's taking me to prom tonight, which is insane on so many levels, especially considering the fact that he's going to be a senior in college in the fall. It was his idea-- not mine--which, in my opinion, gives it even more weight.

So yeah. We're dating…I *think*.

"Yeah, you're totally nervous to introduce him to me," Dylan decides. A wry grin plays on her full lips.

I give her the side-eye in the mirror. "It depends. Are you going to be a brat when you meet him?"

"Hey, I'm the nice one," she argues, lifting her hands in defense. "If you want to worry about anyone being a brat when meeting the man who stole your heart, it's Finley."

With a laugh, I pull the mascara wand from its pink tube and lacquer my lashes. "It's a good thing she's across the country, isn't it?"

"Yup. Pretty sure you dodged a bullet until Mystery Man's forced to face her at LAU in a few months."

LAU is the university we're all attending in the fall, but Dylan's right. Mystery Man is in for a rude awakening once we all move in, that's for sure.

"But for tonight," Dylan continues, "he'll only have to deal with your parents and me. As long as he isn't a dick, we should be good to go."

"Mm-hmm," I hum. "And you're most likely going to be too busy attempting to make conversation with your own date to interrogate mine, so I call it a win-win."

She groans and collapses onto my bed. "Don't remind me. Why are boys the worst?"

"Boys aren't the worst."

"Uh, yes, they are," she argues. "Every time I'm in the same room with one, I get all tongue-tied and awkward."

"Technically, you only get tongue tied around the hot ones."

Her nose wrinkles, and she tosses a pillow at me. As I dodge the lump of feathers, she adds, "You're not helping!"

I laugh a little harder. "No offense, but with two older brothers who both play hockey, and have hot friends who *also* play hockey, you'd think you'd be used to hanging out around hot guys by now."

"Well, yeah, but--"

My phone rings, cutting her off.

Seeing Mystery Man's name flash across the screen, I grin.

"Let me guess," Dylan mutters. "Mystery Man?"

My smile widens as I answer the call. "Hello?"

"Hey," his low voice rumbles.

"Hey," I repeat.

Silence.

My brows pinch. "Everything okay?"

"I'm, uh, I'm not going to make it tonight."

I turn away from Dylan's concerned stare and face the empty shower instead. "What's going on? We talked an hour ago, and you told me you'd be coming right after your physical."

"I know what I said," he murmurs, but his concession is laced with defeat. "Look." He hesitates. "This is a bad idea."

"What? *Prom?*"

Silence.

"Okay, so we won't go," I offer. "It was your idea anyway--"

"You know what I mean, Goose." The stupid pet name doesn't give me any warm fuzzies, and I close my eyes.

Is this really happening?

My bedroom door closes with a quiet click that rings louder than a siren, pulling me back to our conversation. With a quick look over my shoulder, I find the room empty. Dylan must've slipped out, sensing my need for privacy.

The girl's a saint.

Who would've thought I'd need it right now.

Shifting my cell to my other ear, I let out a slow breath and walk into my now-empty bedroom, a chill falling over my skin. My body is on full alert, my muscles poised for fight or flight despite not being in any danger. I don't like it, though. The quiet. The heaviness. The way my skin feels tight and cold, then hot and uncomfortable.

"Seriously, what's going on?" I ask. "Where are you? Are you close yet? Maybe we can talk about this in person––"

"Ophelia…"

The silence following my full name sears me, and I collapse onto the edge of my bed. "Are you breaking up with me?"

Another beat of silence passes, and nausea churns in my stomach.

"Are you breaking up with me?" I repeat. My voice is stronger this time, but even I can hear the twinge of desperation. It makes me sound so immature. So stupid. Of course, it does. I might be a senior in high school, but Mystery Man? He's in college. He's used to dating mature girls. Girls who wouldn't cry over a dumb school dance. It's so stupid. This whole thing is.

My nerves get the best of me, and I push, "Just answer the question."

"We were never together," he rasps. "Not officially."

"Because that makes this better." I scoff. "You're ending

things over the phone and bailing on me an hour before my senior prom after twisting my arm into letting you take me in the first place. Gee, thanks. You're a real peach."

"You don't think I already feel like shit?" he asks.

"Then don't bail on me," I beg. "My parents, and my sister, and Dylan? They're all dying to officially––"

"Don't make this harder than it has to be," he interrupts.

"Harder than it has to be?" I look down at my dress. "I'm literally sitting on my bed in my prom dress. My makeup is done. I curled my hair. None of which would've happened if you hadn't asked me in the first place."

"I'm sure you can find someone else to take you."

"You're right," I say with a laugh. "A whole slew of seniors are waiting at my door, praying my date will fall through. And what do you know? That's exactly what happened." Another scoff slips out of me. "Ya know, you were the one who wanted to take this to the next level––"

"Yeah, and I was wrong," he mutters. "Like I said, I'm sorry, but it is what it is."

"It is what it is?" I repeat, convinced I'm hallucinating because this guy? He's cold and indifferent and...a fucking asshole.

"I don't know what else you want me to say, Lia. I'm sorry."

"Mav–"

"I gotta go."

He hangs up the phone, and I touch my lips with my fingers, willing the burn behind my eyes to go away, when a light knock echoes from the opposite side of my bedroom door.

Dropping my phone onto the mattress, I blink away my unfallen tears. "Come in."

The door opens with a soft squeak, and my mom, Blakely,

rests her shoulder against the doorjamb, her expression pinched. "Hey. Everything okay?"

"Dylan already told you?" I ask.

She grimaces. "She may have voiced her concern."

"Of course she did," I mutter as my mom walks into my room and sits beside me on the edge of the bed.

"What can I do?" she asks.

"Nothing. Actually, scratch that. I want ice cream. Lots and lots of ice cream."

"Your Aunt Ashlyn would be so proud," she muses, mentioning Dylan's mom. "She's a big believer that ice cream fixes everything, but I have another idea for this particular situation."

I frown. "What is it?"

"Well, Mia mentioned the twins are coming back from LAU tonight. They're staying for the weekend. What if Archer takes you?"

Archer.

He's my best friend. Well, other than Dylan and Finley. We text daily and talk about everything with each other. Everything except dating. The idea of actually *going* on a date with him? It feels like I'm crossing a line, one we've both drawn without ever discussing it. And after everything with Mystery Man? I'm pretty sure the timing couldn't be worse.

"That's a bad idea," I murmur.

"Why? He's your best friend."

"It just is," I snap before seeing the hurt in her eyes. I love my mom. She's seriously the best mother on the planet and isn't used to me lashing out. Then again, neither am I. But after the phone call, I'm feeling on edge. Like a shaken-up can of soda that could explode at any second. It's a real possibility if I can't get my emotions under control.

Reaching for my mom's hand, I tangle our fingers together and close my eyes. "He's probably busy tonight, anyway. Dylan's date is picking her up in less than an hour. It's not like he can be ready that fast."

"Pretty sure Archer can steal one of his dad's tuxedos. Actually, I'm pretty sure he already owns one. Those boys have been attending events fancier than this since they were babies."

My lips press together, knowing she's right. Their parents are freaking billionaires. Literally.

"What if I just mention it to his mom?" she suggests. "Let her feel him out and see if he'd be okay taking you?"

"And make me the pity-party prom girl who can't keep a date?" I stick out my bottom lip. "No, thank you."

"Too late!" Dylan chimes in from the doorway. "I already texted Archer."

My shoulders fall, and my eyes cut to hers. "You did?"

"Yup."

Shit.

"What did he say?" I ask.

"He said he'll be here in thirty, and there's nothing you can do about it."

Swallowing the lump in my throat, I will away the stupid burn in my eyes—again—and nod. "Okay."

It'll be fine. Everything. Will. Be. Fine.

I sniffle and stand up, pulling on my proverbial big girl panties and letting out a slow breath.

"Let's do this."

Chapter One
Ophelia

"YOU REALLY THINK THIS IS A GOOD IDEA, BLAKE?" MY DAD asks as he sets the final cardboard box down in the center of the cluttered family room of my new home for the next four years.

"Come on, Theo," my mom urges. "When the girls decided to attend LAU, we agreed it was best to have the boys stay close and keep an eye on them."

"That was before my oldest daughter started dating one of them." My dad gives me a pointed look from beneath the brim of his worn baseball hat. Placing his hands on his lower back, he arches it, probably hoping it'll ease the ache he's been complaining about ever since he tweaked it while playing hockey a few years ago, though I doubt it helps much.

"Just because Lia's dating one of the twins doesn't mean all of our plans should implode," my mom scolds from across the family room.

"Yeah," I pipe in. "It wasn't my idea for you and your friends to build a massive house for all of your kids to stay in. Pretty sure if you wanna blame anyone, you should look in the mirror, old man."

"Har, har," he grumbles. "That decision was made before I remembered what it was like to attend LAU while living at the Taylor House when I was your age. You can't blame an old man for wanting to keep his baby safe."

Ah, the Taylor House.

I've heard stories. Lots of them. I was wondering when he was going to bring up his college shenanigans with his friends. The original Taylor House was owned by my grandparents, and my dad took full advantage by offering housing to the entire LAU hockey team under the guise of building camaraderie. I'm pretty sure it was more along the lines of making things easier for puck bunnies to warm the players' beds, but what do I know?

The Taylor House must not have been all bad since my parents and their friends agreed to invest in a massive duplex near LAU's campus as soon as their kids started reaching college age. One side is for the girls, the other for the boys. It was either a clever decision or a ludicrous one, though it's too early to tell.

Jaxon, my oldest cousin, was the first to enroll at LAU after he received a full-ride hockey scholarship. A year later, his little brother and the twins were also accepted onto the roster. Now, two years later, here I am, attending LAU like the rest of them.

One. After. Another.

Dylan and Finley will be moving in with me at the end of the summer, but since I was recruited to play for the new girl's hockey team this year, I was asked to come early to train with the rest of my teammates in preparation for the new season.

It's crazy. That LAU is kicking off an all-girls hockey team. Then again, I guess it makes sense, considering the men's team's fanbase. Who knows? Maybe the concept will even spread.

It's a well known fact that girls' sports are rarely taken as seriously as men's. Things are slowly changing, though. My parents have been nothing but supportive since I was a little girl and chose to play hockey with the rest of the boys despite the odds stacked against me in terms of it becoming a career.

That being said, I'm not completely delusional. The chance of actually making a living while playing hockey professionally are slim to none, which means I need to pick a major at some point. But that's a problem for future Ophelia. And I have no issue passing the puck to her and enjoying today's moments while I have them.

Like right now. In the middle of a family room right down the hall from a bedroom I get to call home for the next four years. I could leap for joy right here, right now.

"Look at the bright side," my mom offers. "At least there's a wall separating the girls from the boys."

"Like that makes it any better," my dad mutters under his breath. "You sure you're going to be okay here by yourself, Lia?"

Stealing my dad's hat from his head, I slap the worn black material on top of my curls and smile at him. "I'm a big girl," I remind him. "Trust me, I'll be fine. Besides, it's like you said. The guys are only a wall away."

He scrubs his hand over his face. "Knowing your boyfriend's one of them doesn't exactly make me feel better."

"And now this conversation is going in circles." I laugh and kiss his cheek. "Have a little faith in me, Dad."

"What about the motorcycle out front?" he questions.

My forehead wrinkles. "What about it?"

"Well, who does it belong to?"

"How would I know?"

His bushy brows dip, and he peeks out the front window, taking in the sleek, black motorcycle parked in the driveway.

"It probably belongs to Reeves," my mom suggests. "'Cause it's not like any of our friends would let their kids buy a motorcycle."

"No offense, but all the guys are over twenty-one, which means they're officially adults," I remind them. "I doubt they need their parents' permission to buy a motorcycle."

"Are you saying you're gonna do whatever you want now that you're a big girl living all alone at college?" Dad demands.

I pat his chest. "I'm saying it doesn't matter who owns the bike because it's none of our business. And it sure as hell doesn't mean I'm going to be riding on it, so what's the problem?"

"You don't own a car," he points out.

"And who's fault is that?" I volley back at him without bothering to hide my amusement.

My parents might be awesome, but they're also the anti hand-your-daughter-free-stuff types, so I'm saving up to buy a car with my own money. And since I've been focusing on graduating high school and preparing for the upcoming hockey season, I've been a bit preoccupied. Thankfully, the duplex is right next to campus, so it's not like I need a car to get to and from my classes or anything. If I do need a ride anywhere, I have three cousins and a boyfriend who would be happy to drive me somewhere. I'll be fine.

"Don't remind me," Dad mutters, glancing at my mom. "You know I wanted to--"

"Don't you dare throw me under the bus, Teddy." Mom points her finger at him and steps closer, jabbing it into his chest. "We both agreed raising strong, independent girls included being the bad guys every once in a while."

"But does she have to figure out how to be strong and independent while living next to her boyfriend without a car?" he whines.

"Give her a break, will you?" my mom interjects. "She'll be fine. And it's not like you don't love Archer and the way he treats your baby girl anyway."

She's not wrong.

Our relationship might still be relatively new, but Archer and I have been best friends since puberty. Before then, he had a stick up his ass like his twin brother. But as soon as Archer's balls dropped, he decided the opposite sex wasn't so bad, and we became really close. Then, when my prom date bailed on me a few weeks ago, he stepped up and took me instead. Despite my reservations, we danced all night, he kissed me on my front porch, and the rest, as they say, is history. The guy's never let me down and is basically a saint with a side of Greek god. Then again, both of the Buchanan twins are droolworthy. But other than their looks and their interest in hockey, the two couldn't be more opposite if they tried.

Which reminds me... I kind of want to go see my boyfriend before he leaves for his internship.

My mom scans the boxes littering the family room before ordering, "Theo, why don't you go pick up some breakfast for us while I help Lia—"

"Nope," I interrupt. "I love you guys, but I think it's time you got out of here." I push my parents toward the door, adding, "I can unpack on my own like the strong, independent woman you raised me to be, and if you don't leave now, you'll be late for Tatum's piano recital."

"Your little sister would kill us if we missed it," my mom agrees. "Although, we were hoping to stop by to say hello to the boys."

"You really think the boys want to be woken up before 9 am on a Saturday?" I question.

"Good point." Mom follows my lead and pushes my dad toward the door, but he barely budges before giving in like a great, big teddy bear.

"Fine." He kisses me goodbye, and my mom does the same, giving me one final squeeze.

We all head outside. The sun is shining bright in the sky despite it still being relatively early, and I lift my head, basking in its warmth as my parents head back to the cherry-colored truck in the driveway.

"See you guys on Sunday!" I call.

"Love you!" My mom waves as they climb into the truck, pull onto the street, and leave me in blissful silence.

Well, other than the birds.

Yup. They're chirping in the trees lining the sidewalk and acting like the final cherry on top of a pretty picturesque morning. It makes me feel like I'm Snow White or some shit, and if I didn't have neighbors, I just might start whistling. Biting back my grin, I stretch out my arms and lift my head toward the sky again.

Hello, freedom.
Hello, future.
Hello, college life.

ALSO BY KELSIE RAE

Kelsie Rae tries to keep her books formatted with an updated list of her releases, but every once in a while she falls behind.

If you'd like to check out a complete list of her up-to-date published books, visit her website at www.authorkelsierae.com/books

Or you can join her newsletter to hear about her latest releases, get exclusive content, and participate in fun giveaways.

Interested in reading more by Kelsie Rae?

Don't Let Me Series

(Steamy Contemporary Romance Standalone Series)

Don't Let Me Fall - Colt and Ashlyn's Story

Don't Let Me Go - Blakely and Theo's Story

Don't Let Me Break - Kate and Macklin's Story

Let Me Love You - A Don't Let Me Sequel

Don't Let Me Down - Mia and Henry's Story

The Little Things Series

(Steamy Don't Let Me Next Generation Series)

(Steamy Contemporary Romance Standalone Series)

A Little Complicated

Wrecked Roommates Series

(Steamy Contemporary Romance Standalone Series)

Model Behavior - River and Reese's Story

Forbidden Lyrics - Gibson and Dove's Story

Messy Strokes - Milo and Maddie's Story

Black Jack

Royal Flush - Download now for FREE

Stand Alones

Fifty-Fifty

Sign up for Kelsie's newsletter to receive exclusive content, including the first two chapters of every new book two weeks before its release date!

Dear Reader,

I want to thank you guys from the bottom of my heart for taking a chance on Don't Let Me Down, and for giving me the opportunity to share this story with you. I couldn't do this without you!

I would also be very grateful if you could take the time to leave a review. It's amazing how such a little thing like a review can be such a huge help to an author!

Thank you so much!!!

-Kelsie

ABOUT THE AUTHOR

Kelsie is a sucker for a love story with all the feels. When she's not chasing words for her next book, you will probably find her reading or, more likely, hanging out with her husband and playing with her three kiddos who love to drive her crazy.

She adores photography, baking, her two pups, and her cat who thinks she's a dog. Now that she's actively pursuing her writing dreams, she's set her sights on someday finding the self-discipline to not binge-watch an entire series on Netflix in one sitting.

If you'd like to connect with Kelsie, subscribe to her Patreon. Patrons receive a wide range of goodies including:

- Exclusive sneak peeks of works-in-progress
- ebook releases one week early
- Special edition signed paperbacks on all new releases
- So much more

You can also sign up for her newsletter, or join Kelsie Rae's Reader Group to stay up to date on new releases and her crazy publishing journey.